A Promise Not Kept

by

Jim Turner

ISBN: 978-1-4251-3237-8

We at Trafford believe that it is the responsibility of us all, as both individuals and corporations, to make choices that are environmentally and socially sound. You, in turn, are supporting this responsible conduct each time you purchase a Trafford book, or make use of our publishing services. To find out how you are helping, please visit www.trafford.com/responsiblepublishing.html

Our mission is to efficiently provide the world's finest, most comprehensive book publishing service, enabling every author to experience success. To find out how to publish your book, your way, and have it available worldwide, visit us online at www.trafford.com/10510

www.trafford.com

North America & international
toll-free: 1 888 232 4444 (USA & Canada)
phone: 250 383 6864 ✦ fax: 250 383 6804
email: info@trafford.com

The United Kingdom & Europe
phone: +44 (0)1865 722 113 ✦ local rate: 0845 230 9601
facsimile: +44 (0)1865 722 868 ✦ email: info.uk@trafford.com

10 9 8 7 6 5 4 3

DEDICATION

For

Joyce Gammell Turner

Whose love and extraordinary patience made this book possible

ACKNOWLEDGMENTS

I pay homage to the persons who assisted me in my nine-year journey to complete my first novel, *A Promise Not Kept* (APNK).

I thank Jack Remick, Bob Ray and Scott Driscoll, my first fiction-writing instructors; Stewart Stern, Randy Sue Coburn and Geof Miller, who assisted mightily in the completion of my full feature screenplay, having nothing to do with APNK; Katherine Bond, my writing coach; Dr. Peter Knoepfler, retired psychiatrist, who advised on many, many medical matters; the incomparable Ask-a-Librarian researchers of the King County Library System; Steve Ehmry of StarKomPC, who offered impeccable computer support and prepared the manuscript for submission; artist Gary Gumble, creator of the breathtaking cover design; Michael Dilley of the American Red Cross, who generously explained details of CPR (cardiopulmonary resuscitation) and AED (automated external defibrillator) for the river rescue episode; Mitzi Simmons, also a CPR/AED resource, who expanded my understanding of how the machines are used; Greg Grannis, Bellevue Police Department public information officer, for help with police procedures; John Urhardt, medical relations officer of the King County Sheriff's Office, who responded promptly to my questions and advised on many aspects of that office; acclaimed criminal defense attorney Tony Savage (a law school classmate), who provided insight into criminal law procedures and jury instructions in capital cases; Dave Sweeney, former law partner and first reader of APNK; Dena Barker and Erika Wilder, honor UW Literary Arts majors and my first two editors, later editors Karalynn Ott and Michelle Whitehead and, later still, developmental and line editor Kathy Bradley; Marsha Weese, who trumped at least 30 much younger applicants to complete the final line edit; Takeshi Matsui, who gave me valuable insight into how U.S. business people operated in Japan, likewise advice on Japanese-U.S. commerce from Seattle attorney, Doug Palmer; Peter Langmaid, who met with me on many occasions to review the progress of the story; Gordon Gammell of Sun Valley, adviser on river-rafting; the American Medical Association, provider of a copy of Physician's Ethics (which clearly allows a medical relationship among the four principal characters); the University of Washington Willed Body Program, which allowed me to include a Donor Registration form; Lt. Bruce Kroon of the Bellevue Fire Department, who demonstrated the AED and offered written comments on the river scene; my granddaughter Lydia Palmer, who researched Washington State law; the National Brain Tumor Foundation, which allowed use of an excerpt about tumors; Boston photographer Lydia May, whose photos refreshed my memory of the Wellesley campus; Italy tour friends Ron and Colleen DeVincenzi, Robert and Shannon Gammon, James and Donna Roberts, Ken and Janet Ramsey and Arnold and Debbie Schouten, who took time to read the early chapters; short-story writer Jean Majury, who read my many drafts; Gary Marshall, Seattle intellectual properties attorney, who gave excellent counsel on copyright matters; Dr. Bob Fouty, adviser on forensic medicine; and, praiseworthy Trafford Publishing and Support Representative Elizabeth Bennett.

Finally, my mother, Ann Kinsella Turner, devoted a great deal of time to community service, which served as my inspiration during my lifetime. It is fitting that my wife and I intend to contribute a portion of the profits or a percentage on the sale of each copy of the book, *A Promise Not Kept*, to the King County Library System Foundation as set forth in its Mission Statement.

CONTENTS

And Port said: "Death is always on the way, but the fact that you don't know when it will arrive seems to take away from the finiteness of life. It's that terrible precision that we hate so much. But because we don't know, we get to think of life as an inexhaustible well. Yet everything happens only a certain number of times, and a very small number, really."

- Paul Bowles
The Sheltering Sky

PART I

HARRY ENROLLS IN THE $H^2 L^2$ STUDY

Every morning you are handed 24 golden hours. They are one of the few things in this world that you get free of charge. If you had all the money in the world, you couldn't buy an extra hour. What will you do with the priceless treasure? Remember you must use it, as it is given only once. Once wasted you cannot get it back.

- Author unknown

ONE

"Alex, why do you have to always stick your fuckin' finger up my asshole? I just hate this," whined Harry Adkins, a tall, overweight man.

He stood, shaking a bit, in a small, sterile examining room, bathed in fluorescent white.

He wore an institutional gown, made darker in spots by his sweat, ties in back untied. A thin sheet of paper lay atop the examining table's Naugahyde cover.

Harry bent over and grasped the table's sides with white-knuckled hands, his legs spread, his eyelids shut. Sweat dripped off his brow, as it had years before when he'd run like a cheetah in one of his many marathons.

Alex wore a white smock and hovered over his rotund buttocks. A black stethoscope dangled from her neck.

He dreaded the pending invasion of his rectum as it penetrated to the core of his being. His toes clutched at the floor like an eagle's talons. He feared he would lose control of his very essence to his doctor and friend, Alex. He could feel her forefinger stealthily move up his anus, and desperately gasped, "Holy shit."

Alex chuckled. "You're such a wimp. It's just once a year. It's medical malpractice if I don't check for a possibly enlarged prostate. You've heard about prostatic cancer. Wouldn't want my dearest friends, Carol and Harry, suing Tom and me. Otherwise, I wouldn't poke my very small finger up your very fat ass every year. Suppose your doc were a former football lineman with huge, crooked fingers? Don't be a crybaby."

Harry continued to moan, groan, huff, puff, and whine.

"Ah-ha! Good news, Mr. Adkins -- your prostate seems only modestly enlarged."

"I guess that's good news. But you laugh all the way to the bank, you rich little bitch," he shot back.

"I deny I'm rich." Alex withdrew her finger, removed her latex glove, dumped it in the medical trash, and washed her hands.

Harry's central being returned to him, abetted by the smell of the antiseptic soap, by Alex's act, by the glove, and by the cleanliness of it all.

"Okay. Stand up, boy." Alex pinched his left side just above his hip and pushed aside the mint-green gown. "Very generous gluteus medius."

"What in hell is a gluteus meaty-us?"

"You might call them 'love handles.' Carol's lucky to have such big ones to grasp. Unfortunately for me, Tom's pretty skinny there."

"Very funny, Doctor." Harry stood up, moved away from the table, and stuck out his tongue at Alex. Had to retaliate somehow.

"Naughty, naughty boy," she laughed with her mischievous coal-black eyes on high sparkle. He returned a winsome smile.

She handed Harry a clean tissue with her left hand and looked away. He wiped his rear end with it and plunked it in the same trash container.

Alex smirked and said, "Wash your hands, my wimpy friend."

Finally, he moved to the sink, pumped the wall-mounted soap into his hands, scrubbed like a maniac, and dried his hands with a paper towel. He muttered to himself, *"Bitch."* She took Harry's hands with urgency, looked into Harry's sky-blue eyes, and said in an Eliza Doolittle-like pace and menace, "Listen, my dear Harry, someday I may refer you to a urologist to study your urinary tract, and then -- ha, ha -- you'll be given a cystoscopy." Her tone was teasing.

"And what the hell is that?" Harry quivered.

"You don't want to know."

"I do," he demanded.

"All right, if you say so. Listen up then -- you lie supine. Your urologist places a small catheter in your penis gland and punches it down through your penis and into your bladder."

Harry felt a rip tide of terror surge throughout his body. He was almost in tears when he gasped, "Stop right there. I'll never submit."

"It could save your life. God, Harry, I announce you the first winner of my lowest award." She took his arm and extended it vertically. "The Biggest Coward in My Clinic."

He pulled his hand away and glared at her. "This amounts to patient abuse. God, I wish I had a flamethrower."

"What about scalpels at six paces? Get dressed and I'll come back in a few ticks with the results of today's exam, last week's blood work, and all that jazz." She started toward the door, then paused and turned around.

"In all seriousness," she said, "I want to tell you about a new medical study I'm involved with at the Seattle Research Institute -- SRI. Starts in January. I think you might want to participate. It's free. They claim they can estimate -- approximately -- the date of a person's death. You've heard of SWAG?"

"Yeah, Scientific Wild Ass Guess," he said, with the tone of *I told you, smart-ass.*

"It's called 'Predictive Medicine,' which is in its infancy. Dr. Jonathan Dunne, the study's director at SRI, told me there will be growth in medicine associated with the predictability of medical conditions. You're eligible for the study because of your family heart health history and your present rotten physical condition. The Seattle study's called $H^2 L^2$."

"What the hell does $H^2 L^2$ mean?"

"Healthy Hearts Live Longer. Think about it. I'll be back in a few ticks, fatty. Take off your sweaty green gown."

Ah-ha. I got her. He grinned from ear to ear, brought both hands to his neck as if he would drop his gown and said, laughing, "Oh, boy! Now?"

Chortling, Alex said, "Oh, shit! *Touché!* Harry, stop!"

He stopped fooling around with his gown, but advanced toward her.

He provoked a playful fight by raising both his fists. Alex flashed her usual saucy smile and poked her right forefinger (the same forefinger!) on his chest, pushing him away. "No, Harry," she said.

"Hey, you know something?"

Alex lowered her tone pitch, jutted out her jaw and said, "I know everything."

"From now on, I'm gonna call you *Dr. Cool.* I want to apologize, as I usually do, for what I say when your finger's up my rectum, but I just can't handle it. I'll work on tempering my reaction."

"Well, thank you for your apology and your accolade about being cool," she laughed. Alex gently spanked his left buttock, winked, and left the room, nearly closing the door on his nose.

He started to say, "Up yours, kid," but Alex had disappeared.

Slowly, he began to like her again, just as he always did.

Harry dressed, sans his tie, seated himself in a chair by the side of a small desk. Through the little window he saw a large, sun-struck maple that had shed most of its leaves. *Yes, a fair fall day.*

The medical study intrigued him. *Yeah.* Something dawned on him: he needed a new challenge. The business thrived, his golf game got better, the kids were doing well in school, sex was still great with Carol -- although she'd been something of a nymphomaniac lately -- the study might fill his need for another challenge.

A few minutes later, he heard two hard knocks and Alex strode directly to him. She carried a clipboard and sat at the head of the small desk, with Harry on her left.

She rested her eyes on his. Harry nodded and said, "So how's your fat friend's health, Dr. Cool?"

Harry noticed the glint in Alex's dark eyes, which had always cast a spell on him. He was not unaware that their custom of sitting rather close had been observed today. He relished the thought...

"Your lab work was normal, except your cholesterol needs to be much lower. Remember your BMI. I remind you you're obese. Stand up. Look down at your feet."

Harry rose. "I can't see my feet. My stomach's in the way." He remembered when, years ago, his awful, harsh, father-in-law, O.W. Madden, couldn't see his shoes because of his own big belly. *Oh, God, I've let that happen to me.* He backed slowly into his chair.

"You need to head for a gym and start an exercise program. I'm writing a prescription for the Exercise Training Center. It's free if you join the $H^2 L^2$ Study." She paused to scribble on a notepad. "With your parents and grandparents all dead at early ages from cardiovascular problems you're nine times more likely to suffer sudden cardiac death than the rest of the population."

"You know, I think you're trying to scare the shit out of me."

"You got it."

"There you go again being a smart-ass. Dr. Cool, with you, it's a chronic condition."

Alex ignored him. "SRI wants to study forty-something males who are at risk for heart disease and scientifically determine if altering their lifestyle will prolong their lives. After one year of examination and treatment, we intend to *estimate* the date of death of a patient based on medical tests and the patient's adherence to suggested lifestyle changes."

"Wait just a damn minute." Harry got up. "Time out. Are you telling me some committee's going to predict the date I'll die?"

"Yes."

"The exact date?" Harry asked incredulously.

"Well, the date, given as a prediction, expressed as a possibility."

"Will they tell me what that date is?"

"It's up to you."

"So, I'd have the option to know the date or not…"

"Yes. But I ask you, my friend, is this something you'd really want to know? Is it something you should carry with you every day of your life? Until your last day? What about Carol and the twins?"

He sat back in his chair, reached over, and held her wrist. He saw that she remained steadfast.

"You know, I don't know if I'd want to carry it with me all my life. I'll have to think about it. I sure wouldn't like Carol and the kids to hear about it. But, if I choose to learn the date, regardless of whether it's a possibility or a probability, I'd consider the date as being a reasonable certainty, but I believe by living a healthy lifestyle I'd have the opportunity to extend the date. Now, what else should I know about this study?"

"How it works is that you'll be medically monitored each month for the first twelve months. Also, in January on the second, fourth, and fifth anniversaries of the study you'll be examined by a physician at SRI. Read the fine print. We're loaning hand-held, state-of-the-art medical scanners, EKGs, and up-to-date blood pressure kits, all of which the study group patients will be able to plug into their home computers so they can send their data to the research people's computers weekly, assuming the computer technology is in place. And all of the clinical cardiac examinations, exercise training, and scanning would be free. When you sign up for $H^2 L^2$, an addendum will list all medical devices that will be on hand."

"I already get exercise," he said defiantly.

"Riding in a golf cart is not exercise. And lifting those drinks to your mouth is not exercise. Those sorts of things can cut your life short. Slow down on those iceless Rob Roys."

"How's my blood pressure?" Harry wanted to change the subject.

"That's a tough one to call. Your blood pressure is somewhat elevated, but it's just short of needing prescription medication for hypertension."

"Hey, Doctor, what about letting me have one juicy porterhouse steak?"

"If that makes you feel better, eat a steak. The predicted date of death would remain confidential under state law, except for you, your family, and the researchers. The program begins just after the first of the year, so you have a little while to think about it. If you want to join the study, please let me know by…let's see, it's November 15th, so…December 15th. And speaking of steaks, your blood draw indicates it would be prudent for you to begin taking one of the statins. Here, I'm writing a prescription for a low dose anti-cholesterol tablet."

Before leaving the examining room, Alex turned her eyes on him and said, "Two things. First, you're terrible about missing our medical dates, but please don't miss any appointments in this $H^2 L^2$ program. If you don't keep them, the flow of the program will be stalled, and, frankly, we have too many blame-games in medicine."

"Ah, you know, I've been screwing up dates all my life. Tom must've told you about the time I forgot about the big business deal in Tokyo?"

"He did. You got to the JAL gate as they were shutting the airplane doors. That irresponsible behavior shouldn't happen during the study; they'll be on your ass to keep stress out of your life."

"What's the other thing?"

She placed her hands on her hips as if to raise holy Hell. "You and my Tom have an office in Tokyo and you travel around Asia a lot. And I know you're one of those guys who has to have it with other women. This isn't about morality, Harry. Asia's a hotbed for AIDS. Enough said. Lecture over."

At first, Harry was stunned.

An image of Naomi's breasts, her face, her eyes closed in rapture as she sat on him slowly crept into his mind. His face flamed. *Did Tom know or suspect that Harry and Naomi were lovers? Had he said something to Alex?* For the first time, he asked himself, *Should I shed myself of Naomi?* He had no answer to his question, and was in no mood to respond to Alex's accusations. She was his doctor, not his confessor.

"You're never one to mince words." He patted his belly. It draped over his belt line like a Sumo wrestler's. "This little fella's gonna disappear."

Alex smiled and moved to the door, " 'Bout time." Her eyes lit up. "Oh! Cheers to you, Harry, for something else."

"Why, what did I do?"

"I ran into one of the docs out at the Eastside Children's Hospital at a Halloween party, and he remarked what a great job you do with those really sick kids out there."

"Well, the Bereavement Program does some good. But, personally I'll tell you, friend, when we lose one of those kids, after the memorial, I sneak out to some bar, go in a dark corner, turn my back to the action, and dampen a lot of napkins."

"From now on, try to bury the sorrow without the booze."

"You got that right, Dr. Cool."

"Are you still seeing Dr. Nick Nelson?"

"Not professionally. When he's ready to retire from teaching school, he'll go back to clinical psychology. Before I got fat, I helped him coach track part-time."

"Two recommendations."

"Yes?"

"First, you've got to tell Carol if you learn the date the study predicts."

"Frankly, I'm not leaning that way."

"To be brash, would you lie to Carol?"

"I'm taking the Fifth."

Alex looked disconcerted.

"What's the other recommendation?"

"You're one of Izzy Cantor's golf partners…"

"I think I know where you're headed. Izzy's a shrink and I

ought to see him professionally if I'm going to choose to know the date of my death?"

"Izzy's a well-respected shrink. Best in this state and region. There are lots of psychological land mines out there if you choose to learn what most folks shouldn't know."

"Do you happen to have his office phone number?"

Alex reached for a rotating file index, pulled out a card, and handed it to Harry.

He looked at his pocket calendar and saw he had no appointments today. He dialed Alex's phone to reach his office.

"Yes, this is Harry. Any messages? Anybody call me? Very important: Please call Dr. Isidor Cantor's office and make a three-hour appointment in his office ASAP...Yeah, the same guy I play golf with. I'm not coming back today. Bye."

"Anybody in the psychological advice picture besides Izzy and Nick Nelson?"

"No."

"I think it's a wrap." Alex headed for the door. She held the clipboard to her chest and waved goodbye to Harry.

Alex wheeled around, faced him and said, "What's your greatest fear?"

"Where did that one come from?" Harry was not prepared for Alex's question.

"Maybe it was our conversation about psychological experts."

Two knocks were heard, followed by the appearance of Alex's medical assistant. "June called and said she'd like to cancel today's appointment. We made another one. So no more patients here today. Good night, Doctor."

"Good night."

Alex seated herself and looked eagerly for an answer. "Your greatest fear?"

"My greatest fear? Johnnie Allegro."

Alex wrinkled her brows. "You've never really talked much about him."

"Of course you remember Judge Standish."

"Sure, he married Carol and you."

"Well, a couple years after Carol and I were married, I was on jury duty. I ended up as the jury foreman in the prosecution of Johnnie Allegro who'd been charged with six counts of first-degree murder. I ended up with two full-time jobs -- the jury and *Nippon/USA*. Tom worked his ass off during that time. We didn't talk much about the trial, of course, while it was going on, and actually, when it finished, we still spoke very little about it. Even after the trial, Carol had never wished to discuss it; then a letter came in the mail..."

"A letter came in the mail? Sounds kind of ominous."

"It was. The letter was sent before Allegro went to prison. He threatened to kill my family and Judge Standish's family."

Alex's eyebrows went up. "I'm surprised that Carol never talked about it with me. Did you guys see a counselor about all of this?"

"Carol didn't want to see one."

"Do you mind if I broach this with Carol?"

"That's okay. We bought a Beretta 9mm pistol through Steve Rindal, who gave her lessons. She's become a pretty good shot. I still have my Colt."

The State, in a three-week trial that had concluded two days before, had persuaded the jury to convict Allegro of six counts of aggravated murder. The jury elected Harry as Presiding Juror in the first trial dealing with Allegro's guilt or innocence, and had re-elected him for the penalty phase.

The twelve-person jury had not yet decided whether the defendant would be sentenced to death or life in prison. Harry and ten others had been working for a day and a half on Juror Harmony Smith to get her to vote for the death penalty. She was middle-aged, slim, and attractive, with thick, curly blonde hair, and was a tad too deferential to the defense in the first part of the trial.

The other ten men and women had moved to the opposite end of the jury conference table, enabling Harry and Harmony a kind of privacy.

"Harmony, I can tell you're a religious person."

"Yes, Harry, I am. How did you know?"

"At first, I just guessed from your demeanor. But then I noticed you made the sign of the cross just before and after we heard evidence in the courtroom. Does that mean you pray to God a lot?"

"Well, yes, I do."

Since the jury began to debate the penalty phase, her forehead had been locked in a frown. But, he noticed the scowl had begun to diminish just after his question about prayer. Soon, her face brightened. She seemed as if she might be open to another approach.

Ah-ha, Harry had thought. *It may be kind of risky, but…*

He focused on her eyes -- friendly, gray, and framed by long lashes. "Have you prayed to God for guidance on whether to vote yes or no on the death penalty?"

He saw her glance heavenward. "Gosh, let me think for a moment or two."

She folded her hands in her lap. "You know, I felt I shouldn't pray to God. You know, church and state. Mr. Adkins, do you think I should consider prayer?"

He felt he was on the cusp of resolution. Lowering his voice, he said, "I'm no lawyer, but I can't see how the separation of church and state interferes with you praying to God about this."

"Sir." She said in an almost challenging tone. "Are you a religious person?"

"You know, honestly, no. But I consider myself a spiritual person."

"You're honest. I've noticed the other jurors trust you and so do I. My friend here, Catherine, is a Catholic, too."

"Catherine Clement, juror five?"

"Yes. We've become pretty close…Catherine and I think you're charismatic," she said shyly. Harry paused. He had never considered himself charismatic, and although he'd thank people who had praised him, he'd never quite believed them.

"Well, thank you. I appreciate it."

She took Harry's hands and said softly, "If you say it's not a problem, then, I will pray to God for guidance. But, I couldn't pray in this room with all these folks." Still holding his hands, her eyes came alive. "I know what I can do! I can go in the ladies' room and shut the door."

He was ecstatic. "Good thinking!" She released her hold on his hands, held her purse over her shoulder, marched with a *glory, glory, hallelujah* persona toward the restroom, and walked straight in without looking back. The other jurors watched as the lock clicked behind her.

Another juror, scooting his chair back to its usual place at the table, addressed Harry. "What's going on?"

Harry said, *sotto voce*, "You know, I think Harmony's going to resolve, one way or the other, her concerns about the verdict. I can't give you any details. Harmony may." Harry picked up his *Wall Street Journal* and leaned back in his chair.

Thirty-five minutes later, when Harry heard the unbolting of the restroom lock he turned toward the door. Harmony walked to her chair, carrying her rosary, and grinned. All jurors took their cues from her, moving back to their stations. Harry said, "Have you reached a decision?"

She changed her focus from Harry and looked at each juror, beamed and said, "I considered the enormity of the crimes by Mr. Allegro, and I thought of Exodus 21: 'life for life, eye for eye, tooth for tooth.' I thought of that verse, and those six young boys, their terrible pain, and all the other evidence. So, I will vote to impose the death penalty."

"Harmony, thank you." Harry moved his hand across his chest, squeezed the musculature of his shoulder on the other side, and felt the tightness that had gripped his shoulders disappear.

Someone said, "I applaud Harry Adkins. He brought us to consensus in the guilty phase and the penalty phase." Each juror came to Harry to shake his hand. After a few minutes, Harry said, "You're too generous," though he secretly enjoyed the approbation of the others. "But, thank you, thank you."

Harry held up a single sheet of white paper. "We've got to finish our business. I'll pass down the Sentencing Verdict that I've completed, except for my signature. You'll see I've placed a check mark in the brackets next to the word 'YES.' Harmony, I ask you and the other members of the jury to read it and then to pass it on back to me." *Sure hope it'll pass the Harmony test.* She passed it on. Harry silently said, *whew!*

Once again, Harry held the verdict. "Ladies and gentlemen of the

Jury, I'm signing the verdict." All twelve jurors shook one another's hands. As Presiding Juror, Harry knocked on the inside door of their room, signaling they had something important to report to Judge Standish.

Mike, the bailiff, unlocked the door of the jury room. He stood in the doorway, a strapping, black-haired, Irish-looking fellow, looking hopeful but cautious.

"Mr. Adkins, we sure hope you have a verdict."

"Yes, we do."

The bailiff replied, "Thanks, but I can't let you out until all the attorneys and everybody gets back here."

"How long will that be?"

"About an hour."

"An hour? How come? Hope it doesn't have anything to do with the attorneys. They all work close to the courthouse."

Mike shrugged dismissively.

Harry turned back to the other jurors, sent a wink, and said, "It looks like we can finish the poker game, folks."

Mike appeared surprised and worried. "Gosh, you folks playing poker? Don't know if the judge would like that."

"Just kidding, Mike."

"He ain't kiddin', buddy," piped up one of the jurors.

Mike, looking a little bit distraught, nonetheless stepped out into the courtroom, shut the door, and locked it. Harry heard the drooping chain re-strapped across the door, and he sighed.

Just over an hour later, Harry stood in the front row of the jury box holding a letter-sized piece of white paper -- The Verdict. His fellow jurors solemnly sat around him: seven women, five men. Allegro, his attorneys, his family and friends, and the media people, some holding video and still-camera equipment, glanced expectantly at the two rows of them. The family and friends of the six dead boys also were in attendance, dabbing tears from their eyes. Allegro sat with his two attorneys at a large oak table, with the two deputy prosecuting attorneys at the end of the counsel table.

Harry thought Allegro seemed to be the most menacing person

he'd ever seen -- a big, muscular dude, with at least a week's growth of black facial hair. The trial evidence revealed that before he was arrested as a pedophile, he had played rugby and was known to carry three or so members of the other team for ten yards when he got the ball. *You wouldn't want to ever meet him in an alley, even at noon on a sunny day.* When the attorneys and Allegro had arrived, the bailiff announced that all those in the courtroom should rise, and the judge took the few steps from his chambers and climbed two steps to his desk.

Gathering his robes, he calmly seated himself, invited the audience to sit, and surveyed the crowd. Johnnie Allegro and his two attorneys, a man and a woman, sat at a table facing the judge, with the jury box at right angles to the defense team's niche. The deputy prosecutors sat at right angles to the defense and faced the jurors. Judge Standish pounded his gavel, and a hush fell over the anxious courtroom.

The judge turned his gaze to Harry. "Have you reached a verdict in the penalty phase of the matter of State v. Allegro?"

"Yes, Your Honor."

"Is the verdict unanimous?"

"Yes, sir."

"Please hand the jury's written verdict to the bailiff."

The bailiff took the verdict from him. Harry exhaled heavily and slowly sank into his chair.

Had a single sheet of paper landed on the floor, the sound would have been heard in the courtroom.

Judge Standish ordered, "Will the bailiff please read the verdict of the jury?"

The bailiff complied: "Having in mind the crimes of which the defendant has been found guilty, are you convinced beyond a reasonable doubt there are not sufficient mitigating circumstances to merit leniency?"

"The jury has answered, 'Yes.' "

The boys' family and friends rose with applause and shouts of support while some spectators simply remained still in their seats, letting the verdict echo around them.

Jubilance and shock and screams of agony and disbelief erupted from Allegro's family and friends, mixed with silent tears and dropped jaws. An elderly woman siding with the defense suddenly passed out and fell to the floor, causing a deputy sheriff to rush to her assistance.

Judge Standish stood up and banged his gavel on the dais, shouting, "The courtroom will be in order. Please be seated. Those who wish to stay in the courtroom must take their seats immediately or they will be expelled from these proceedings."

He pounded his gavel several more times.

Harry saw Allegro rise from the defense table, his legs in a wide stance, and physically struggle with his attorneys. He stood between them and swung his bulky left and right arms forward and then back again; he struck both attorneys in the upper body and knocked them to the floor.

Allegro pointed his right forefinger at Judge Standish and the other finger at Harry, shaking his fist and roaring, "You bastards, this isn't over! I'm gonna get every fuckin' one of you, and your fuckin' families."

Allegro's black eyes fixed on Harry and frightened him as he never had experienced before. The now-convicted killer towered over the two potbellied deputy sheriffs, one of whom was extending handcuffs toward him. Allegro held out his wrists as if he would submit to the cuffs, then quickly brought up one arm and caught the first deputy under the chin; with his other hand he grabbed the second deputy's revolver from his bullet-laden belt. Without thinking, Harry leaped over the rail of the jury box and made a beeline for the defendant. Allegro, his back to Harry, maintained his wide stance and aimed the gun at Judge Standish. From behind, Harry kicked between Allegro's legs with all his might. The felon screamed, dropped the deputy's weapon, and fell writhing in pain to the floor. Harry quickly picked up the deputy's handgun, held it with both hands, and pointed it at Allegro.

Another deputy whipped his revolver from his holster and swung his gun arm in an arc, hitting the back of Allegro's head. Allegro slumped to the tiled courtroom floor. The deputies pinned the unconscious criminal and secured handcuffs and footcuffs.

Blood dripped from Johnnie Allegro's head and snaked on the tiled courtroom floor.

When order was restored at least forty-five minutes later, Allegro, still unconscious, had been hauled away on a gurney, and the crowd had departed, Judge Standish struck his gavel and addressed the jurors. "Before I dismiss you, I want to ask Mr. Adkins to stand." Harry complied, wondering what was going on.

The judge continued, "Mr. Adkins, if you hadn't kicked Mr. Allegro…I shudder to think what could have happened. Thank you."

Harry bent his head to acknowledge the judge's words and softly said, "Thank you, Judge."

"It's getting awfully late. Ladies and gentlemen of the jury, you are dismissed from jury duty for the balance of your current term."

Alex said, "We were visiting my family in Boston the week the trial ended and never saw the write-up about you. You could have saved the story in the papers for us!" Alex hugged him with her left arm. "I'm so proud of you."

"I'm pleased that you're pleased."

Picking up her clipboard, Alex said, "I guess I didn't realize Johnnie Allegro was such a big thing in your lives. Carol and you've both got to get a shrink to deal with Allegro. I'll call Izzy. Maybe both of you could be treated by him."

"We'll do just that. One more thing."

"Okay."

Harry reached in his briefcase and pulled out several color photographs and handed them to Alex.

"Oh my gosh. It's our gang at that glorious Fourth of July party at the U.S. Embassy in Tokyo."

Harry handed them to Alex. "Oh, Thank you. Are these for Tom and me?"

"Of course. So let's sing, *Those Were the Days…*"

They both sang, holding hands, *"Those were the days, my friend…We thought they would never end."*

"Oh, thank you. You're so thoughtful." She gave him a kiss.

Harry realized that everybody had done a good job of retaining their looks and bodies except him.

He thought about his life. About changing his life. Maybe he needed the discipline of the study as much as the study needed him.

Harry wondered what were the pivotal events in his short life? While Dr. Nick Nelson's counseling in high school following the deaths of Harry's mom and dad had helped in getting some relief from his deep depression back then, a lot more needed to be done.

He remembered the way Tom had stuck with him in their college days and their discussions about starting their own business.

Didn't his past and present aberrant behavior, like his drinking, and yes, his relationship with Naomi, have to be changed? And now the Johnnie Allegro thing had to be faced. He looked back in time to get answers.

TWO

When Harry Adkins was a high school junior, he'd lost his father to a heart attack mid-spring, and his mother was killed by a stroke the same year on Christmas Eve. He had lettered in track in his sophomore and junior years. He thought it was a good idea to really get into long-distance running because of the exercise -- and a long run gave him great blocks of time to think.

A big problem: his aunts and uncles wanted him to live with one of them and tried to be his parents, but it didn't work. Stubbornly, he needed to live in the house where he had grown up. Besides, he cried a lot -- his spells lasted for sometimes an hour. Not good to subject his relatives to his crying. For some time Harry had been hoping for a guy friend. Oh, sure, he had lots of friends -- boys and girls -- but not a real close friend.

Harry awakened one Saturday morning and recalled a dream from the previous night. He was at the bottom of a well. When he looked up he saw a black starless night, and he searched for handholds so he could climb out of the well, but there were none. He saw his parents at the top of the well. He screamed, "Mom, Dad! Get me out, Get me out!" He saw them smiling and waving. Harry screamed again.

His cry brought him out of his bed as he awakened. He swung his legs out of the bed and quivered. *Oh my gosh. I've slept in.* He found himself angry with his parents for dying so soon, and felt guilty about his thoughts. Harry thought that he must clean himself in the shower. The shower got him wet, but not clean.

He dressed, sat down at the breakfast table and tried to eat a bowl of cornflakes with milk, but when he took a bite he felt sick to his stomach. He had to get out of his house, and he ran several miles to the high school track. He had come to run a series of sprints. He glanced upward at a cloudy and cool November day. Harry had just finished his fifth sprint and took a break to jog before going for the sixth round when he heard footsteps behind him.

A deep, friendly, and familiar voice said, "Slow down so I can keep up with you. How's my track star?"

Harry looked around, startled, and then smiled. "Hi, Dr. Nelson. How's my favorite teacher?"

"Simply grand. And you?"

"Haven't decided," he lied.

Dr. Nelson also wore track clothes, running shoes, and a sweatshirt in deference to the cold south wind. Harry's high school track coach and counselor, who had obtained his degrees in psychology, stood about five inches shorter than Harry's six-foot-three. Dr. Nelson's critics said he allowed his thick, wiry, red hair to grow too long -- and that he looked like a hippie. Dr. Nelson always showed a smile.

They jogged.

"Out here you can call me Nick.

"What's your evaluation of your grades since your parents died?"

"Pardon me…Shitty. Yeah, I know I have to ratchet them up." Harry teared up and wiped the moisture away with a sweatshirt sleeve. "I know I've got to get them up. But, umm…Nick…Hard to call you Nick. Yeah. I've been pretty depressed."

"How depressed?"

"Depressed enough to think of ways to kill myself." Harry detected that Dr. Nelson's eyes flashed alarm. Nick placed his arm around Harry's shoulders. "I have an idea I cooked up yesterday," said Nick.

"What's your idea?"

"I'm a licensed psychologist…"

A frown formed on Harry's face. "Sorry to cut you off, uh…but, well, my parents didn't leave me enough money for that."

"I wouldn't charge you. You're a doggoned good runner and have the gift of gab. You could be a student coach. It'll keep you busy, also. I've been watching you and you seem to be substantially depressed. Then the idea kicked in. Looked up bartering in the American Psychological Association Ethics and it's allowed."

Harry listened intently. He neither heard nor thought of anything else but Nick's words.

Nick said, "Let's do it! We'll start talking about a schedule, what you would do as a coach, how much time, and a whole bunch else."

The weather warmed about noon. They ran for about an hour

more on their way to Dr. Nelson's house.

Harry saw the Nelsons' home and picked up the pace. Dr. Nelson revved up his speed, and for a moment he was a chest ahead of Harry. Harry responded and turned up his pace -- he knew his legs looked like the wheel spokes of a bicycle crossing a finish line.

"God, what a burst, Harry," said a clapping Ruby Nelson who hugged both men.

Harry said, not breathless, "Thanks. Are little Nick and Ruby Junior home?"

"They're at dry land training. Snoqualmie Summit's going to open the lifts next weekend," Ruby said.

"Still head ski coach?"

"Sure am. Competing in Master's, too." Harry stood a good head above Ruby's prematurely gray hair. Her ponytail ended about ten inches down her back. Ruby presented no other hippie characteristics, in contrast to Nick; in fact, Harry had heard she had been raised in an upper-class family. Like Harry's mother, Ruby was stocky.

"She won a Master's National Women's downhill last year," said Nick.

"Come, you guys. I've prepared a huge lunch, let's eat."

Harry talked about his nightmare and about his depression. By the end of the meal, they had agreed on an outline for Harry's coaching responsibilities and a tentative counseling schedule. Also, Harry agreed to call Nick when he became depressed.

After a couple of hours of eating and talking, Harry remembered he had not finished his household and yard chores, took leave of the Nelsons, and ran home.

As he neared his house, the sun began to set and he went west into the gold of the expiring sun, which had always thrilled him. He was sweating and stretching his legs on the front porch of his family's home when he saw a young male, about his age, walking briskly down the sidewalk.

Harry saw the sun paint the stranger's face. The boy wore clothes that were similar to Harry's; he also looked as if he'd been running. The new young fellow was skinny and tall, and he caught Harry's stare.

Smiling, he said, "Hi, I'm Tom Campbell." Nodding toward the house just west of Harry's, he added, "Tomorrow, my parents and I are moving into that house right there."

"I'm Harry Adkins. I live here. You just get through with a run, too?"

"You bet."

"You want to come up and stretch together?"

Tom nodded and approached him and held out his hand. Harry noticed his dark hair, deep black eyes, and square chin. He was a good-looking guy, that's for sure. Their right hands met. Harry prided himself on his vise-grip handshake and noted that Tom held his own when put to it.

The two stretched, sweated, and spoke in the arcane code of upper-division high school guys.

Harry said, "Hey, do you guys have a moving company to help you?"

"No, we'll do it pretty much without movers -- too expensive."

"You know, I have a lot of time on my hands these days."

"I'll ask my parents. But don't your parents keep you busy around the house? Mine sure as hell do."

Harry looked at Tom; his unstoppable tears lightly flowed down his cheeks. He knew Tom had seen his eyes and must have realized what he was about to say.

"No. I live mostly alone. I lost both my parents last year, one to a heart attack and the other to a stroke."

"Oh, God." Tom placed his arm over Harry's shoulders "Shit. I didn't know. I'm really sorry. Damn, losing both parents in one year! Is there anything I can do?"

Tom's arm still rested on Harry's shoulders. Harry looked up at Tom, now not trying to hide his sorrow. "There is something you can do."

"What's that?"

Wiping his eyes, Harry responded, "Let me help you move."

"You bet. And, we'll pick you up in our driveway at eight a.m. and drive to the Pancake Place?"

"Wouldn't miss it. Good night."

"Good night."

The next morning he picked up the phone and dialed Nick's number.

He heard Ruby's voice on the answering machine and said, "Dr. ...Er, Nick. This is Harry. I'm a little less rocky today. A guy named Tom Campbell is moving in next door. He's going into his senior year and wants to be on our track team. I'm gonna help his family to move in today. Ya know, I bet we're gonna be good friends. I'll be moving most of the day. I'll call you in the early evening. By the way, okay to call you Dr. Nick? See ya."

As he shaved, he saw a different face in the mirror. His hazel eyes now seemed more vibrant. A face of despair had been transformed into a face of hope...faint maybe, but with expectations of a better life. He dressed quickly and sprinted to the Campbells' front door. Tom had been waiting for him on their front porch and said, "Hi. Mom and Dad, come meet Harry."

From the first day they met, Harry and Tom were conjoined. They attended the same college and each obtained a U.S. Army ROTC scholarship. Harry and Tom double-majored in Business and Computer Science, taking as many classes as their college offered in computers, and in the Japanese language, too. Harry remembered that in 1977 they bought and assembled a Heathkit H-8 Computer. It was then they planted seeds that led them to the computer industry.

Although Tom and he were roommates in their college dorm, on weekend nights Harry drank booze, smoked pot, and slept with one or two of his girlfriends. When he bought his usual large supply of condoms, the clerks winked at him. Depression remained with him, and once in a while he'd see a college counselor or call Dr. Nick as he tried to manage his anger against his parents.

After receiving their college degrees and U.S. Army Commissions, the young men found a local library where they religiously read the *Wall Street Journal* and observed that the *Journal* gave good coverage of computer news. Also, they visited the local office of the Small Business Administration.

After Vietnam, in 1981, Harry and Tom were stationed at Camp Zama, twenty-five miles south of Tokyo, as officers attached to United

States Army Intelligence.

Early in July, they obtained ten days leave from their Army duties to form their new company.

Harry sat in a small Japanese café in Tokyo in the late afternoon of July Fourth waiting for Tom to join him for their meeting about their start-up computer translation company. Harry hoped Tom would get there soon. Across the street was the U.S. Embassy, and he stared at the many red, white, and blue flags dancing in the wind.

The embossed invitations to the U.S. Embassy's Fourth of July party were lying on the table in front of him. Harry noted with pleasure that supply trucks had been hauling copious amounts of food and liquor into the Embassy.

Finally, Tom burst through the doorway still wearing his sunglasses.

Harry waved his hand and called, "Over here, Tom."

Tom waved back and flashed a sizeable smile, which showed off his gleaming white teeth and his photographic face. He could have been mistaken for a film star with his classic, gentlemanly good looks and mischievous grin. Between the two of them, Harry would have been surprised if they didn't meet some girls tonight at the Embassy party.

Harry clicked his heels together, and saluted Tom with, "Hut. Second Lieutenant Campbell."

Mocking Harry, Tom copied his movements, and said, "Hut. Second Lieutenant Adkins."

Tom removed his hat and jacket and laid them on the chairs flanking the tables; they embraced as always. Harry reflected that they had done so every time they saw each other for about a decade now, sometimes to the apparent consternation of some strangers.

Harry asked, "How did it go with Light Colonel Collins?"

"For you and me, just great. The Colonel had just talked with a CIA guy who said we're -- " Tom stopped all of a sudden and glanced around the café. He reached in his shirt pocket and pulled out a pen and a pad of paper and furiously wrote, *"Our duty assignment will be cancelled. Good news!"*

"You know, that is good news," Harry said, as he glanced up

from the paper. The two men grinned, careful not to let their secret leak to anyone around them.

Harry paused and stared into the street as Tom ripped up the piece of paper and placed it in his briefcase. "Look! Our dates for the evening -- preview of coming attractions."

Tom also peered at the twosome. "Lovely."

The women wore full tennis garb, carried tennis bags and pulled small, wheeled suitcases on the sidewalk across the street from them. *USA* was written invisibly all over them. They turned left and entered the main entrance to the U.S. Embassy. Harry immediately favored the shorter of the two who had curly black hair and an undeniably large bust.

He checked his watch and commented, "It's about 1600 hours. Let me see the invitation…the party starts at 1800 hours, which I bet is when the talent will walk into the ballroom. Lieutenant, what time do we want to march into Uncle's party?"

"Lieutenant, gosh, I'd say about 1750 hours, sir. We'll fire the first volley before anyone else gets a chance."

"Good call. Now, it's time to talk again about our new company."

Harry reached into his weathered leather briefcase, rich with worn brass accoutrements, pulled out sundry pieces of paper and laid them in front of Tom.

Tom said, "What do we have here? Ah-ha. A company application for the Tokyo American Club. Great idea for business entertainment and maybe finding new clients." He paused. "Squash courts, even! I move we join. Sounds like a reasonable expense for *Nippon/USA.*"

Harry said, "I found out they're having a squash tournament tomorrow evening."

"Let's sign up."

"Yeah, I did. Let's get on with the agenda."

Tom placed his arm around Harry's shoulder, smiled, and said, "You're something else."

Harry opened his fully stuffed briefcase and covered the table with stacks of paper.

At 1755 hours, July 4, 1981, Harry and Tom, now in full regalia in their Army dress uniforms, gawked at the opulence of Tokyo's U.S. Embassy Grand Ballroom. The Great Seal of the States, the American eagle, and flags and bunting were draped on the ballroom wall over the raised bandstand. The U.S. Army orchestra interspersed patriotic music with ballroom tunes. Hundreds of guests crowded the ballroom, milled about, snacked on *hors d'oeuvres* and swilled alcoholic beverages while they laughed, listened, and eyed persons of the other sex. Most of the invitees came from the embassies and consulates, military bases, or from the Japanese government, while a few were lucky civilians.

The room also was awash with diverse clothes, faces, accents, and languages. Corks popped, glasses tinkled, dishes rattled, and music played inciting flirting and dancing.

Harry grabbed Tom's arm. "Smell the soy, boy." Harry held his nose up and sniffed, "Get a load of that shrimp."

In the midst of his excitement, Harry spotted the two attractive women they had seen walking toward the Embassy, now in party clothes with smiles on their faces and drinks in their hands.

"Our dates to be. Time to move out smartly, soldier." Tom saluted with his right hand, held his wine glass with his left, clicked his heels together, and said with enthusiasm, "Yes, sir." Harry and Tom exchanged snappy salutes.

The two strode quickly and decisively and approached the talent.

Harry assumed that they were college girls. One stood tall and willowy with shimmering, shoulder-length blonde hair, intense blue eyes, and eyelashes to die for. She wore a powder-blue silk dress that was form fitting and off one shoulder with a light silk wrap around her shapely shoulders.

The other young lady's complexion was darker, and she was about four inches shorter than her friend. She was endowed with wiry black hair and jet black eyes. She presented a figure curvier than her friend's, and her long, black, sequined gown evinced a most enticing cleavage.

Harry liked the shorter woman even more up close than he had when he had spotted her from far away. She wore a delightfully mischievous and saucy expression that made him want to know more about her. He extended his right hand, first to her, and then to the taller blonde woman.

"I'm Harry Adkins; call me Harry. And this soldier is Tom Campbell." Tom offered his right hand to each woman.

The shorter woman said, "I'm Alexandria Quick. Alex is my nickname. I graduated from Wellesley and this fall will be in my last year at Harvard Med School. Your turn, Carol." Alex sipped her white wine.

"Let me see…Madden is my last name. I'll be starting my fourth year at Wellesley. We're here because the two of us decided to study Japanese at the University of Tokyo this summer."

Harry brightened and responded, *"Watakushitachiwa nihongoga yoku wakarimasu,"* which translates to *we are fluent in Japanese.*

Carol replied in Japanese: *"Jaa nihongowo oshietekudasaimasenka?"* meaning "What about some lessons, guys?" Tom winked at Harry.

"I'm Tom Campbell. Harry and I were neighbors in Seattle and attended the same college. Here we're in the United States Army Intelligence, and we can't tell you what we do."

Harry thought the girls exuded awe.

But Carol piped up in a credible English accent, "Miss Moneypenny wishes to know who in our immediate circle is M and who is James Bond."

All laughed, and Harry said to Carol, "An acting bent, too." Carol nodded matter-of-factly.

Alex stood on her toes and peered through the crowd, said, "Hey, look, there's open space at the bar. Let's get another drink."

Harry took Alex's arm and Tom took Carol's; they assembled at the bar, and ordered white wine, except for Carol who asked for red.

Harry was pleased that he got to Alex first. He thought he felt her rub her breast on his arm. *All right!* She glanced up at him and winked at him. Of the two, Alex was absolutely sexier.

Harry ran with the first conversation starter that came to mind, just to hold Alex's attention. "Alex, I have a question -- we celebrate July 4, I guess, in U.S. embassies all over the world. I wonder if the French have their foreign embassies celebrating Bastille Day on July 13?" Harry paused and wondered if he should correct himself about the exact date.

But Tom interrupted Harry's thoughts, gently taking Alex's wrist.

"Oh, that's a pretty tennis bracelet. Does it hint at an interest in tennis?" He winked playfully at Harry, showing an indication of competitiveness.

Harry burned with anger.

"You could say that. It's *Tom*, isn't it?" she responded coyly. Tom's face brightened, while Harry grew increasingly anxious -- in fact, his nose tickled.

"Carol and I are doubles partners at our tennis club back in Cambridge, Mass."

Harry looked for an opening to break in and resume his flirtation with Alex. But watching her and Tom and hearing their banter he thought he had better temporarily entertain Carol; he could make another move on Alex when the time was right. Carol seemed to be interested in the conversation between the other two, so Harry waited for an appropriate break to talk with her.

"Do you play mixed doubles?" Tom asked.

"If my guy's good enough," Alex said.

"Did you bring your racket to Japan?"

"Of course."

Harry continued to listen to the conversation of the other couple.

"It's *Alex*, isn't it?" Tom asked, touching her arm. She batted her eyes and brushed Tom's sleeve.

"It is," she said with a grin. Harry frowned.

"May I show you the Embassy tennis courts? Ever play on grass?" Tom said.

"Yes, to both questions," she giggled. Her eyes were fixed on him.

Tom bowed in front of her, pointing with his arm toward the spacious, windowed balcony doors and held out his other arm, which Alex accepted.

As Tom walked arm in arm with Alex, he turned back toward Harry and grinned at him. *Damn,* Harry said inwardly.

Carol stared at him, clearly hopeful. Once he made eye contact with her, thoughts of Alex temporarily left him.

Carol held her wine high to Harry's and they clinked glasses.

"Here's to the Fourth of July," she offered cheerfully. Smiling, they both took a sip from their glasses.

"You know, I thought I was watching a mental tennis match between Alex and Tom...she's competitive. Is Tom?" she asked.

Harry said, "Yes, he is, but he can be quiet about it. I noticed Alex is pretty quick with words."

"And *Quick* is her last name. Quite fitting, if you ask me."

"You know, I could see that." Right away, Harry knew that Carol was a smart woman.

He noticed two Marine Corps second lieutenants, who wore brass wings with their medals, moving quickly toward Carol; their eyes were locked on her like radar.

At that moment, the band struck up Glenn Miller's *In the Mood*. Carol and Harry held both hands and stuck out a foot, tapping to the beat. They rose from their chairs and bowed to one another. Each sweeping an arm toward the bandstand, they said, as one voice, "Let's dance." They took each other in their arms and moved to the dance floor.

"May I cut in, ma'am?" drawled one of the Marines. Harry stiffened.

"No, he's my date for the night, Lieutenant. But thanks for the offer."

"*I am?*" Harry said. Though he wished he could be with Alex, he was pleased that a pretty lady wanted to be on his arm.

Carol and Harry laughed together. She leaned toward her date and softly bumped his nose with hers.

"Were you stationed in Alaska, Lieutenant Adkins?"

"Call me Harry. No, but, why do you ask?"

"You give a practiced Eskimo kiss," she said with a grin.

Harry laughed, "You know, I didn't see that one coming."

Soon, they glided to the music, fell silent, and held each other a little tighter. *She's wearing pretty sexy perfume,* he thought.

About a minute or two passed before Carol moved her head back. "Were you a tennis player?"

"I lettered in high school, but didn't play in college. My games were track, gymnastics, platform diving, and second team football in high school. I was the team's punter when I was a junior and a senior," he said proudly.

"I have a feeling you did some dance, too; you've been leading me well."

"You know, my mom and dad had me in ballet and ballroom dance for a few years. I got into some fights with the guys over the ballet bit. What did you do in high school?"

"I took art classes in and out of school, was on the debate team, and was into a lot of acting. I took my first lead when I was a freshman in *Diary of Anne Frank* and acted through high school and into college. It came pretty naturally," she said modestly. "I think the Pasadena Playhouse would accept me.

"I also swam competitively in high school and college and life-guarded when I had time. And lots of dance lessons."

"Ever think of acting as a career?"

"Oh, sure. That's one of the things I'm thinking about."

"So what's your major?"

"Double major -- Drama and English Lit, with a minor in French. In fact, I studied abroad for a year when I was a sophomore in Aix-en-Provence."

Toward the end of *In the Mood*, they began to dance faster. Harry spun Carol masterfully around and around. They hopped and bounced together, and he even dipped her. He gave her body a fast scan, and he thought, *not bad, not bad.*

Carol, with her flaxen hair and fair skin carried a delicate air about her. Her smile, gestures, movements, and voice -- even her very being -- seemed celestial. She carried a kind of quiet determination about her.

"You're a pretty tall girl," Harry noted. She chuckled. He only stood about one inch taller than she, and he discovered she was in excellent physical shape. After several fast jitterbug numbers she didn't breathe hard, and in a couple of dances he'd held her muscular triceps.

Carol, Harry, Alex, and Tom dined together that night at a table for four. The Embassy buffet offered a few Japanese dishes, such as sushi, but featured roast beef and all the trimmings, as well. Before the dinner was over, the four of them drank three large bottles of sake.

Harry poured for everyone and raised his glass. "Let's toast King George III. If it hadn't been for him we wouldn't be here celebrating July the Fourth."

They all stood, cheered, rang each other's melodic glasses, and gulped their sake.

Alex raised her goblet. "Here's to Adam's rib, and what happened thereafter!" More sips, more smiles, more *hurrahs* for the evening.

Carol and Harry laughed together. "My turn," Tom declared. "And here's to all of us and to our future lives."

Carol held her glass in the air. "I'm getting a little tipsy. Maybe that's why I raise my glass to Margaret Sanger." *You know,* Harry said to himself, *I really like Carol.*

Alex, holding her glass aloft with one hand, hugged Carol with the other. "Let's give three big *hip, hip, hoorays* to Carol!" As they bellowed for her, Harry thought, *Wow, we make an awful lot of noise.* He noticed that, about twenty feet away, some guy who had been sleeping off his drinks suddenly awakened just after their first round of ruckus.

All sat down looking pleased with one another. Even in his cloudy mind, Harry reckoned that they all were at least a bit drunk.

Alex reached for her purse. "It's time for Carol and me -- or is it I? -- to leave for the ladies room," she said, speaking with a slight slur.

"I presume Tom and I are heading for the men's room. Meet you ladies back here."

Alex intoned, "Yesh. I mean, *Yes.* Oh, my, Carol. A hand please, dearie." Each girl leaned to the guy she had been with and puckered up to him and he to her.

At the end of the night, the guests *oohed* and *ahhed* over the fireworks display. Carol and Harry sipped golden champagne in a relatively quiet corner of the moon-struck balcony, and chose to ignore the colorful Independence Day explosions.

About midnight, the band played *Goodnight Sweetheart.* The lights dimmed so low that the dancers around them became shadows of fuzzy black.

"Lieutenant, did you save this dance for me?" Gazing earnestly at him, Carol reached for both of his hands.

"Yes, ma'am."

They rose and slipped into each other's arms. Slowly, they danced, cheek to cheek. Harry caught a glimpse of Tom and Alex dancing together with their eyes closed, transfixed.

Harry felt Carol's lips on his ear. She whispered, "No matter what the future brings, I'll never forget this moonlit night in Tokyo, especially dancing close to you, hearing *Goodnight Sweetheart.*"

"I feel exactly the same way." He smiled at her.

They moved slowly, eventually gliding to nonexistent music. Harry moved his pelvis forward to meet hers and swayed with her, side to side; their lips still touched. A yardstick could not have slid between their bodies.

An alto voice penetrated Harry's head. "Lovers, come back to us. The music's over." Harry opened his eyes. Carol and he were still locked in an embrace.

"Carol, gosh. We're the only ones on the dance floor. How long have we been here?" They broke the embrace but continued to hold each other's hand.

"Isn't that Alex's voice?" Harry said.

Just below the bandstand, a dozen or two party-goers were forming a snaky line, holding the waist or shoulders of the person ahead following the directions of a tall, well-tanned cowboy type who was addressing the participants as 'mate.' Harry heard it pronounced 'might.'

The cowboy came up to Carol and Harry and said, "Mates, I'm Aussie Layton. Care to join our conga line?"

Carol replied, "Sure…uh…mate!" and held the waist of the person next in line. Harry jumped in and held Carol's buttocks, giving a squeeze to each side.

Carol looked around. "Aye, keep it up, mate." Harry said, "It's a treat to see you go crazy."

"Hey, boy, you got to go crazy sometimes to keep sane." She shouted to Tom and Alex, "Get in our conga line, mates!"

Layton said, "Okay, mates, let's shake it," and launched the line.

About ten minutes into the conga, Carol, followed by Harry, left the line and purloined a bottle of champagne, returned, and drank a snootful or two. They passed the bottle up the line, with others upending it.

The band, also flavored with champagne, sped up the pace of the music, to the yells and screeches of the dancers.

As they were drinking and dancing, Carol grabbed his hand, and said, "Harry, come with me to the bandstand." At the bandstand, Carol asked the director, "Let's change to *When the Saints Come Marching In*. And what's your name?"

"Andy, Ma'am."

"Harry, go tell Layton what we're up to." Harry found himself awed with Carol's verve.

She said, "Andy, get your guys to the head of the line and start playing. I'll stay at the microphone."

Harry came running back. "Layton thinks it's a great idea."

"Harry, stay with me up here."

Harry smiled yes. He was bursting with pride and felt the happiest he'd been in years. When she saw Andy's men at the head of the line, Carol spoke into the mike. "Hit it, Andy!"

The first notes of *The Saints* were played. Cheers and brass horns bounced loudly on the ceiling, reverberating in the room.

She began:

> *Oh, when the saints go marching in,*
> *Lord, how I want to be in that number…*

The band circled round, and still playing they stopped in front of the bandstand and closed out the number. They moved to the stage, picking up their instruments and belongings while emptying the last dregs of champagne.

Tom, Alex, Harry, and Carol, holding hands, slowly left the dance floor for the street, hired a taxi, and loaded themselves like bags of rice into the back seat, first Carol, Harry, Tom, and then Alex. The cabbie closed the passenger doors and sped off into the night of an octillion stars or more. Alex said, as she faced Tom, "Let me take your hand. And place it right here. Ohhhhhh, that feels too good…First thing, Tom, I really like you and I'm excited to get to know you better. How do you feel? Pardon the hiccup."

"Oh, likewise," Tom said.

Harry found himself thinking he may have to accept Alex wanted Tom and not him. "Alex, do you have a steady?" Tom asked.

Alex inverted her thumbs, pointing to the cab's floor.

Harry saw Tom and Alex cuddle for a moment or two and fall asleep. The cab cruised over the darkened Tokyo streets.

Carol whispered into Harry's ear. "I wanted you to know, except when I'm performing on a stage, I'm kind of inhibited about certain things. Like your tongue on my lips. French kisses. I know I didn't respond. Before tonight, I had never pressed myself forward so hard against a guy's zipper."

Harry whispered back, "How do you feel about what you did."

"My lips are parted."

Harry softly and slowly passed his tongue on hers.

She sighed, "More, please."

Suddenly, the driver over-steered on a hard turn that propelled the others to collide into Alex, waking her. Alex announced, "We're here." The cab parked in front of a two-story building. Carol and Harry left the cab holding hands.

Alex and Tom sprawled all over each other, squeezing hard with their arms. Harry thought a crowbar might be needed.

Carol slurred, holding onto Harry, "Sorry, guys, we've got to get in before they lock us out." Carol walked around the car to Alex and took her hand to pull her out of the cab. Tom assisted Carol in managing Alex.

Harry grasped Carol's hand and said, "Ladies, let's do the town two days from now; can we meet you both here at five? Tom and I have a big meeting tomorrow afternoon…might last late."

Carol said, "But you're in the service."

"We're on leave this week. Actually, we're getting out in a few months." Harry wondered if he was making sense.

Carol held both of Harry's hands and said, "Encore!"

Carol released his arms and showed two thumbs up.

Alex placed her arm on Carol and Tom to hold herself on her feet. "Carol, I think I need to go in the dorm, okay, honey? I'm tipsy…feel like I'm going to throw up."

Slurring her words, Alex managed to say, "Shee you guys here day after tomorrow. About five."

In a moment, the two disappeared behind the door. The taxi driver drove Tom and Harry to their hotel.

When Harry returned to his room he knew that he cared about Carol. Yet, he felt a strong sexual attraction to Alex. As he crashed onto his bunk, he remembered the modest embraces, the kisses, and the tongue touches, some of which Carol had not responded to. He drifted into a heavy sleep and dreamed of a *ménage a trois* involving Alex, Carol, and him.

THREE

Harry smiled to himself, still seated in Alex's exam room. In his mind, he focused on the morning after the Fourth of July Embassy party.

Harry sighed, as he buttered his dark toast. "I'm a little hung over this morning, but feel better than I should, with the wine, the champagne, and the sake."

The sun streamed through the large windows reflecting on the men's blue and white striped seersucker mufti on this, their second day of leave, as they ate breakfast in the dining room of a Japanese-U.S. chain hotel. The tables in the dining area featured shiny aluminum legs and red tops.

"How's your bod after all that booze last night?" asked Harry. "And, more important, what did Alex say this morning when she called you?"

"Take that 'I gotcha' face off. How in the hell do you know she called me?"

"Our Japanese receptionist mistakenly called me. I gave your extension number to Alex. Alex loved that I called her beautiful."

"Lieutenant Adkins. You're a scoundrel."

"Been called worse. But, what did you and she talk about?"

"I'm taking the Fifth. But, I admit I really fell in love with her last night. We talked on the phone when we were in our own beds. Have you spoken with Carol?"

"Sure. She's the first woman I've ever met that I want to be a companion of -- not somebody that I just want to screw up front...uh, so to speak."

"Yeah, you and your women were the talk of the campus," Tom winked.

"I know. I owe you more than one on that. To change the subject, do you have our corporate papers with you?"

Tom lifted his battered briefcase from the empty chair.

Had the well-dressed Japanese businessman sitting across the aisle from them understood American English, he would have seen the two Americans pour over the proffered agenda and heard comments from them about it; he watched each of them scribble notes for nearly thirty minutes. The balance of the two hours was devoted to non-stop discussion about the possible charges for their translations of documentation of English to Japanese and Japanese to English.

"Phew." Tom said, and then he consulted his watch. "It's 12:30." I'm a little tired, and it's time to think about lunch.

"I have a great idea. Let's move the whole corporate kit and caboodle over to the Tokyo American Club, sign up for the membership, take the mandatory tour, sign up for the squash match, and have a late working lunch there."

"Partner, you've got more energy than Saudi Arabia," said Tom.

As their waitress approached their table, Harry did a sitting bow and said in Japanese, "Please bring our bill, and get us a cab to take us to the Tokyo American Club in about fifteen minutes. Thank you."

They arrived at the club, and the new membership tasks were completed shortly before they sat down to their working lunch on the Vineyard Patio, outdoors and under an umbrella. They agreed to wrap it up at 6:15. A pitcher of lemonade and two large glasses stood ready to quench last night's thirst.

They discussed their business plan that dealt with Instruction in Foreign Business Practices. Promptly at six, they organized their documents and completed the work before their deadline.

Tom and Harry changed clothes and walked to the squash courts. The courts looked like those at home but, here, clear glass provided the framework for the court door and the entire back wall.

A tall, slim, twenty-something Japanese man, who carried a squash bag filled with racquets, bowed and said in reasonably good English, "Are you gentlemen Mr. Harry Adkins and Mr. Tom Campbell who signed for matches tonight? My name is Ki Shoyo. I am the squash and tennis pro."

Harry noted that three smiling Japanese men stood in the background, attired in white shirts and shorts, with squash racquets in their hands.

Tom responded, bowing, in Japanese, "Yes, I'm Tom Campbell and this is Harry Adkins, my long-time friend, fellow soldier, and business partner."

Harry also bowed and spoke in Japanese, "Yes, we're in the process of opening an office in Seattle and a branch in Tokyo."

One of the three Japanese men, somewhat graying, heavyset, but with grace and authority, stepped forward, bowed, and said in English, "I am Masura Takano, an executive in the Computer Division of Kurosawa International and could not help but overhear your conversation. You are both fluent in Japanese." He bowed toward Ki and said, "One interruption, please. Gentlemen, what is the nature of your business?"

"Quickly," Harry said, "we offer translation in computer documentation."

Takano flashed a hearty grin of approval and winked at Harry.

Shuji Muramoto and Ry Hayami shook hands with Tom and Harry.

Ki said, handing racquets to Tom and Harry, "I have drawn a ladder with all of your names. Isn't the English term 'Sudden Death'? Except in the final, there will be no overtimes. It is the best two out of three games. Let you begin."

After two or three hours, two of the men had not lost a game. Harry and Takano triumphed in their matches and met in the final.

Each had won one game. The third game score: 14-14. Word had gotten around the club about the match, and now thirty-one club members watched. One point would determine the outcome. Harry launched a lofty serve that bounced off the back wall. Takano railed the ball close to the right wall. Harry matched him with another rail shot. Both hit tight and hard to the right front wall about seven times.

Harry knew how to win. He struck a ball low off the floor barely over the tin in front. Takano returned it a few inches off the floor, apparently trying for a cross-court winner, but the spheroid flew too low and struck the nineteen-inch high tin baseboard, making a loud and metallic bang, which confirmed that Harry had won.

Takano bowed to Harry, who bowed back, and heartily shook Harry's hand. The crowd exploded with applause for both men's prowess as the two left the court, their clothing dripping sweat.

Takano smiled and said, offering his hand, "I want a rematch."

Harry gripped Takano's hand. "You deserve one. You're terrific."

After they showered and changed into their business suits, the three Kurosawa men and Tom and Harry sat with drinks in hand in the club's Trader's Bar.

Takano turned to his immediate right during a lull in the conversation and said to Harry, "Mr. Adkins, I first saw your honesty in playing squash. As you know, a business relationship in Japan is a close personal relationship. Also, I was very interested when you mentioned that you and Mr. Campbell were forming a company that would offer computer documentation translation services."

Harry felt warmth in his cheeks. Strangely, when things seemed as if he were on the brink of success he noticed a sudden rush of blood to his face.

"Excuse me, Mr. Takano. Tom, please give our business cards to Mr. Takano."

"Here, Mr. Takano," said Tom as he handed him three cards. "We picked these up from the printer yesterday."

Takano stared intently at the cards. "Very nice. One side English and other side Japanese. Let us see...the name of your company is *Nippon/USA*. It is very good." He spoke in Japanese and said *"Dai Nippon."* And translated in English, "Great Japan. Most appropriate. Now, what services other than computers do you offer?"

Tom said, "We also offer seminars on business practices in Japan, in the U.S. and in other countries."

"Mr. Adkins and Mr. Campbell, are you interested in explaining your company's possible services to Kurosawa, Limited?"

Tom signaled *yes* to Harry.

"Yes, Mr. Takano. When do you suggest?"

Takano glanced at his watch. "Tomorrow, July six, 0900 hours at Kurosawa."

"Mr. Takano, we look forward to seeing you."

The five men bowed to one another.

July 6, 1981, 0900

Harry and Tom wore three-piece civilian khaki suits and regimental ties with stripes running diagonally from the heart. They checked into the reception lobby of Kurosawa International, Ltd.

They were escorted to an office where they were given the option of drinking tea or coffee served in a ceremonial fashion.

Finally, they were moved to a conference room, with a large window on the fiftieth floor of the headquarters office of Kurosawa in Tokyo, the world's third-most-populated city. This sprawling capital stretched before them on a perfect-weather day. Next to them, a large, oblong, dark oak conference table and leather rolling chairs occupied a fair amount of space. Harry couldn't help but notice that they did not go cheap on the furniture or the tan, deep-pile carpeting.

They heard business-like knocks on the conference room door and Takano, Shuji Muramoto, and Hayami entered.

Takano, with his graying hair, appeared to be at least one generation older than Muramoto and Hayami.

Takano was about six feet tall, and despite his portly appearance he moved gracefully. Rarely did he lose his continuing smile. He presented confidence and quick intelligence.

The three Kurosawa men were attired in dark clothing, conservative ties, and white shirts. Muramoto seemed to be the shortest of all the men and had his hair cut militarily short. He didn't say much, but appeared to comprehend the mostly English conversation. His spectacles magnified his dark eyes.

Hayami presented a thick neck and broad muscular sloping shoulders. He, too, wore thick spectacles and exuded athleticism. It seemed to Harry that he'd like to get to know this guy better.

The men bowed to each other and chit-chatted in Japanese while selecting their chairs. Takano quickly seized the spot at the head of the table.

Takano asked in Japanese, "Is it Japanese or English?"

Tom replied in Japanese that Harry and he would like to honor their hosts by speaking Japanese. Hayami suggested English; although they thanked Mr. Campbell and Mr. Adkins for their suggestion, they needed to practice their English.

Takano said, "Mr. Adkins, we very much want to learn more about you two men and the company you are forming, in English."

"Yes, Mr. Takano. I'll talk about that, and Tom will fill in the details. First, we have some written information about us and our company. Tom will now distribute copies of our individual Curriculum Vitae. Please take a moment to look them over."

Tom passed the papers around the conference table. Harry heard many mutterings, mostly, *Ah, I see.*

Muramoto raised his hand. "Mr. Adkins, good of you to include versions in Japanese and English."

Harry nodded at Muramoto. "Thank you." He watched the men silently sitting in their large chairs; after a few moments he noticed that most had stopped reading but were smiling as if they were attracted to *Nippon/USA.*

"Our lawyer in Seattle," Harry continued, "has filed our corporation papers in Washington State. Mr. Takano, we understand we would register in Japan as a branch of the Washington State corporation."

Tom added, "Would you be so kind as to have your lawyers recommend a Japanese law firm to help us out?"

"Of course, as you Americans say, I think, 'in the fullness of time.' "

Harry opened his mouth to speak again, but Takano pressed on. "Mr. Adkins, tell me more about your business."

Harry nodded. "I was just getting ready to tell you. I'll give you a little background first, and you'll see how we decided on this specific industry. In college we both double-majored in Business and Computer Science and thinking Japan's business scene was taking off we managed to take some courses in Japanese, as well as other Far Eastern languages."

"When Tom and I were juniors in college, we studied Japanese in Tokyo for the summer term and got jobs here, and later we enrolled in Japanese language courses in college. Also, as you know from our C.V.'s, we joined the R.O.T.C., U.S. Army Training Corps, and we graduated from college and went into the Army."

Harry, silently assessing Hayami, continued, "We have two main purposes. First, it's my understanding that, if your company manufactures computers and sells them in the USA, you must get a private translation service to help customers understand the text documentation that comes with them. We would translate your computers' documentation from Japanese to English.

"Conversely, if you buy computer hardware and software from a U.S. company, documentation would be written in English, and we would translate it into Japanese. We recently met with a computer company in the USA that was thinking of moving to the Far Eastern market, and they determined we could be a useful service to them and we entered into a contract with them."

Takano waved his hand, chuckled, and asked, "What is your other face?"

"In our studies of business customs and practices we've found they differ greatly from country to country. We plan to hold seminars in the Far East and in the Western world, teaching the differences to companies who work with multiple cultures."

Hayami raised his hand, addressing both Takano and Harry. "A question, please?"

"Sure," they both nodded to him.

"How do you charge for the translation part?"

Tom answered confidently, "We review the documentation and quote an hourly fee based on its length and complexity."

Takano spoke up, "What about the seminars?"

Tom replied, "We need to have a guaranteed minimum number of attendees, and upon agreement, we will look at our costs and charge a competitive fee per person."

Harry heard a soft knock on the door. Muramoto walked to the door and opened it to reveal a twenty-something Asian woman in the doorway, followed by an Asian male, who was pushing a two-tier metal rolling rack filled with multi-page documents.

Takano approached the young woman. They bowed. She wore a chic black jacket over a white lace blouse. Harry thought that her bust thrust exceeded that of the average Japanese woman. The hem of her black skirt lined up with her knees and impeded any kind of a decent stride. Her leather shoes and sheer hose matched the rest of her outfit. Her short hair had been coiffed recently, and she wore large, loopy silver earrings.

She had a bit of an aquiline nose, which, Harry concluded, may mean her ancestry was not entirely Japanese.

She remained next to Takano, who addressed the rest of the group. "This is my niece, Naomi Takano." Even from where he was sitting, Harry could smell her heavy-duty perfume.

"Naomi, this is Mr. Adkins and Mr. Campbell." They bowed to Ms. Takano.

"These gentlemen are contemplating opening a branch office of their U.S. company in Tokyo, and we are discussing doing business with them."

Harry and Tom rose and approached her, with all three bowing to one another.

Harry observed that she was simply one of the sexiest women he'd ever seen. The eyes, hair, her clothes, her come-on, her hip swing, and more.

Takano gestured that all sit and that the worker who brought in the cart leave. Harry was also quick to note that Naomi took the chair next to him, dispossessing Tom. Harry was lazily inhaling Naomi's perfume when Takano spoke again.

"Naomi, please explain what's on the cart."

"Thank you, Uncle Masaru. Gentlemen," she began, looking at Harry and Tom, and speaking in British English. "I'm a trained bean counter," she joked. "My accounting degree was attained at Oxford University in Great Britain. I'm a Chartered Accountant in Britain and belong to the Japanese Institute of Certified Public Accountants, the Japanese equivalent to a CPA. Uncle hired me as an independent contractor, not an employee, to supervise the collection of the documentation of computers, software, and peripherals that Kurosawa has in production in its companies. Uncle said that he needed to show the documentation, in Japanese, to an outside technical translator so a bid on the translation could be made."

As Naomi was talking, Harry watched Takano hold his hands to form a tent, rooting for his niece.

"I imagine that you'll be hiring a Japanese attorney to assist you in registering your company. Good idea. The attorney will tell you that you must appoint an official representative who is a legal resident of Japan.

"I would be glad to talk with you, but must go now to meet Al, my fiancé. Last-minute wedding preparations, you know. My wedding will take place in two days. I'll be absent for two weeks." All three bowed. Harry watched her hips swinging on her way to the door.

Takano then addressed Tom and Harry. "Gentlemen, I have another appointment in the next few moments. If you are interested, I would like to meet again one week from today in this room at nine o'clock in the morning. I observed you are good gentlemen and we might do business together."

"Tom, do you think we can get leave next week?" queried Harry.

"Yes, I do."

"Good," Takano smiled. "First, please read the computer documentation for the operating system. I ask if you would translate Part One from Japanese to English. It looks to me the papers on the cart are well organized."

Harry and Tom strode to the cart and picked up a notebook. "We'll take a look." Harry and he took chairs next to a small conference table. They thumbed through the notebook.

Tom, after about fifteen minutes, spoke in measured tones to say, "Mr. Takano, we first need to go through all, yes, I repeat, *all* the documentation relating to the operating system; it would take us about two to three hours to give an estimate of the cost of translating Part One of the operating system. We also would like access to one of your computer engineers."

Takano consulted his watch. "Hayami is your consultant. He will ask you to sign a confidentiality agreement. Sorry. Must leave." Muramoto accompanied Takano. All bowed.

Tucking the signed confidentiality agreement into his briefcase, Hayami said, "My business card carries my extension number. Give me a call when you have your work ready."

Harry gave Hayami a puzzled stare.

"Mr. Adkins…"

"Hey, please call me Harry." *I know. This guy's been exposed to American English for a long time, I bet.*

"I will, but maybe not when Takano's around. My nickname's Ry. I saw your perplexed look, probably because you heard me speaking with an American accent. I'm able to turn my accent on and off."

"How'd that come about?"

"I was born in Tokyo. My father was a diplomat and he was assigned to D.C. when I was about five. An only child. I attended a private school."

Harry and Tom rose to bid him goodbye and Tom said, "Your phone will ring in a couple of hours."

For two and a half hours, they read, commented, and translated. When they had finished, Tom breathed a big sigh. "I bet Ry wrote the instructions. Go ahead and call Ry, and I'll find the little boys' room."

Ry arrived just a moment before Tom did.

"Ry, we took turns writing our separate comments on the various instructions. I suggest you read them," Tom advised.

Ry took about a half hour to read the comments. "Except for page 23 where I messed up a little bit...see here, guys...I should have been more careful.

"How much time did you spend?"

"Little less than three hours," said Tom.

"It could take our lawyer back home at least twenty pages to say the same thing as the Kurosawa legal beagle did in one page," offered Harry.

Ry placed a sheet of paper on the table. "Here's a duplicate copy of the Agreement. I'm authorized to sign for my company.

"For your effort in writing your comments, translating, et cetera. I'm authorized to pay you 500 U.S. dollars as a token retainer -- it's been earned. I will recommend using your company as our technical translators for our computers and, when they come out, for our communication devices. You should know that before we employ you your analysis and your translation will be scrutinized by outside experts and scholars trained in the English language. But don't tell anybody I told you that."

"We're proud to have been selected to work with you and your company," Harry said. "What I'd be concerned about is if we don't have you personally writing the instructions, but someone less fluent in English, we might have to spend a lot more time, which might not be fair for you."

"Whoa. You have the cart way ahead of the horse. I said I will recommend you. I think Takano has to agree with me and then take it upstairs to his superiors. I can promise you the process is deliberate.

"You're aware the Japanese contract is not necessarily as detailed as a U.S. contract, but insists the contract must be fair to both sides."

Both Tom and Harry said in one voice, "Absolutely."

They bowed to each other and agreed they'd meet here on July 15 at 0900 hours.

Harry and Tom caught a down elevator, and after leaving the building, found a bar and tinkled their glasses that held a couple shots of sake.

"Tommy, my boy, I predict we've got our first Japanese customer."

"Yes. Here's to us!" Both men took down their sake shot in one swallow.

Tom clinked his glass on Harry's. "I've been thinking. We have another small arms competition at the post in a couple of days, and I think we ought to resign from the competition since we'll be out of the service pretty soon and swamped with our business."

"You're right. I've had a lot of fun, and, we got our share of prizes, but we won't have the time." Harry poured sake in both glasses and said, "Here's to our Colt pistols." Their glasses clattered again.

Promptly at 0900 hours, on July 15, soon-to-be-retired Second Lieutenants Adkins and Campbell, wearing the same clothing they had before, showed up at the Kurosawa International Limited Headquarters. Immediately, the lieutenants were led by a young woman to the same place as last Wednesday, where they were served, as before, with coffee or tea in the same ceremonial fashion. No sooner had the two Americans been served, than their filled cups were carried on a tray to the large conference room by the same young woman.

The tray was placed on the table and the young woman bowed and left the room.

Harry glanced at the city and the sky and found himself nostalgic for Seattle; he began to sing to himself:

> *The bluest skies you've ever seen are in Seattle*
> *And the hills the greenest green, in Seattle*
> *Like a beautiful child, growing up, free an' wild…*

Three firm knocks came from the door, followed by the reappearance of Muramoto, Hayami, and Masura. Harry murmured, "Get ready to rock and roll."

Takano took his same seat at the end of the table. On his right were Hayami and Muramoto, and on his left were Harry and Tom. Takano spoke softly. "We may enter into a contract with you, including retainers. Unlike U.S. contracts, here they are a loose agreement. We are interested in signing short agreements, and leaving details for later.

"Here, all personal commitments have a far greater meaning than in the U.S.

"Kurosawa may have you do technical translations for our computer products, software, peripherals, and other products -- like telephones."

Muramoto jumped in, "Also, our contract might include you giving seminars on Western business customs for us. Yes, I will recommend the prospective contracts to my seniors in Kurosawa."

Takano said, "Is there any more to discuss right now? I suggest we meet Wednesday, July twenty-second, same time, same place, like you Americans say."

"Yes, we'll be happy to."

All came to their feet, bowed, and left the conference room.

Tom and Harry pushed the down button in the elevator and plunged nonstop to the building lobby.

After they reached the sun-stricken sidewalk, Tom said, "What do you think, Harry?"

"I'm thinking about how well we did today as *Nippon/USA,* worrying whether our girl friends will beat our asses in tennis, six-zip, six-zip, and as a result, we buy dinner."

"Could be worse, much worse. But, a banner business day for us."

July 22, 0900

The precise protocol, which had been observed the two previous Wednesdays, was followed on this, the third Wednesday.

Again, after Harry and Tom were shown into the conference room, Harry took in the view and, in his mind, dropped Seattle's skyline over Tokyo's. No time for reverie because the usual three suspects, as Harry had come to nickname them, had entered the room. Harry felt excitement because Takano had brought a briefcase.

Harry moved toward his usual chair, and then bowed; the usual suspects also bent over.

Each man took his regular and accustomed chair.

"Good morning. How are you gentlemen today?" Takano asked.

Harry answered by saying, "Never been better."

"I think you may be even better because Kurosawa has approved the technical and seminar contracts. In fact, I will present you with two signed originals of each. You will notice there are very few pages, unlike the usual USA contracts," Takano proclaimed.

Harry hoped his poker face was in full operation, but deep down, he wanted to lead a conga line around the conference table with joy. He did notice Ry was sitting on Takano's right, who winked his right eye.

"As an aside," Harry said, "you know, our lawyer told us the reason why U.S. and U.K. contracts are so long is because hundreds of years ago in Great Britain the English scriveners were paid by the word." All chuckled.

Takano said, "Here are both originals for your reading. Take your time."

Tom examined the papers, as did Harry. Harry cast his eyes to the ceiling and silently said, *Mom and Dad, nothing will bring you back, but thank you for all the good raisin' you gave me.*

About fifteen minutes later, Tom and Harry glanced at each other. "Do you have anything, Tom?"

"I'm ready to sign."

Harry faced Takano, "So am I, but our U.S. banker wants our lawyer to review important contracts. If we can use your fax, we'll send copies to our lawyer. We should be able to sign and deliver a set of both contracts to you within twenty-four hours."

Takano, again making a tent with his fingers, asked, "Would you gentlemen be available tomorrow morning at nine o'clock here to, as Americans say, 'seal the deal?' Our computer experts want to start selling our computers in the USA, Canada, and in England."

Harry could no longer hold off his broad smile, and, well, his glee. "Yes. We can do that. Tom?"

"I extended our leave until Monday."

Harry turned to Takano, "Until we get an office, could we use some space here in this building?"

Takano said, "Hayami, I would be pleased if you would take charge of finding our friends some room in our building while they are shopping for space."

Hayami, first looking at Harry, said, "I would be pleased to help."

Takano continued, "One more item, Mr. Adkins and Mr. Campbell. My niece is back from her honeymoon and is available tomorrow to interview with you here at nine o'clock, and she has been looking for office space for you."

"Nine o'clock tomorrow morning is fine for us."

"I will meet you in the Kurosawa reception area. Then, I shall escort you to your temporary quarters for *Nippon/USA*. I will be sure to have the metal cart and its contents over there," pointing to the cart in the conference room, "delivered to your temporary space."

All bowed to one another and took elevators to various floors, including the first. Harry turned to Tom, "I think we deserve at least a double shot of sake."

"At the risk of being zapped on the tennis court again by the girls?"

"Yes."

"Cheers," proposed Harry, and Tom followed.

July 23 0900

By sheer coincidence, Naomi Takano, Ry Hayami, Harry Adkins, and Tom Campbell arrived in the Kurosawa Headquarters Office reception area at the same time. All bowed to one another. Hayami said, "Please follow me." His guests followed him into the elevator lobby; Hayami pressed the button for the thirtieth floor.

Naomi stood close to Harry; yeah, he sniffed the same perfume he had inhaled several days before. Naomi grinned at him and flashed her black eyes, accompanied by lashes that were so long she sometimes must have had trouble seeing. Her clothes were black and white, her jewelry extravagant silver. Dark hose ran into her spiked heels. Her skin was darker than that of most Japanese, and her complexion perfect, without signs of aging.

Her husband either was wealthy or had bought her white gold engagement ring and wedding band on a long-term contract.

Their elevator arrived on floor thirty and Ry led them to a good-sized room with empty file cabinets, the steel cart that had arrived with Naomi when she first met Tom and Harry, and a large rectangular table corralled by six or seven chairs. Harry spotted a generous supply of office equipment, from reams of paper to paper clips.

"Ry, you set up a great work space for us," insisted Harry.

Ry held up his hand. "Time for me to go." He bowed and closed the door behind him.

Naomi reached into her briefcase, ready to take charge of the interview. Harry observed, *the doll's got balls.* Naomi gave a copy of her CV to both Harry and Tom. "Here's is my business card should you consider me for the position."

"Naomi. Okay to call you Naomi? I'm Harry and Tom's Tom."

"Of course."

"Your CV's pretty impressive. You're fluent in Mandarin, Cantonese, Japanese, of course, Thai, Vietnamese, *and* Korean?" *We have to work on Korean.*

"Yes. I also know five computer languages."

"I'm awed," praised Tom.

Naomi walked to her purse and pulled out a lighter and a cigarette. "I'm trying to quit, but I have this craving. Excuse me. I'll go to the ladies' room and will be back shortly."

Harry focused on Tom's eyes. "Well, what's your take on Naomi?"

"As a person, or as a potential employee? As a person, I'd say she's smart, scrappy, and -- let's face it -- gorgeous."

Harry nodded.

"Earlier today, Takano told me his sister. Naomi's mother, Marta, a receptionist at the Great Britain's Tokyo Embassy, worked as an undercover agent for Japan. While there, she had an affair over twenty years ago with a Brit who served as a military attaché in the same embassy. They didn't marry because the attaché had a wife and young kids.

He was independently wealthy. He agreed to pay Naomi's living expenses through five years of higher education in any school. Takano also said Marta took maternity leave and went back to work at the British embassy as a receptionist for the Brits and to continue to spy on them. Apparently, Marta's still at the embassy."

"Well, I'll be dammed." Harry declared. "Further comment?"

"Naomi could help us meet the legal matter of having a resident director and agent for *Nippon/USA*. And with her accountant's training and grasp of languages, what could we lose? Plus, we need office space here, and she knows the area. Shall we hire her?"

Harry winked at Tom. "Well, partner, you didn't say anything about who her uncle is." A wide smile erupted on Tom's face as if he hadn't thought of that advantage. Harry also thought of the lingering look Naomi had cast on him.

"Your question was, shall we hire her?" Harry repeated. "My answer is, let's do it. But, you're still going to direct our foreign operations, aren't you?"

"Nope, it's got to be you," Tom said, shaking his head.

"Why do you say that, partner?"

Tom said, "It wouldn't work with Alex. I don't want to commit to travel, especially when there's a beautiful woman."

"Why not?"

"Alex and I started talking about getting married. I don't know if you've picked this up, but although she is the most terrific woman I've ever met, she has a jealous streak. Listen to what happened a few days ago. While Alex and I were eating lunch on post, a colleague, Lieutenant. Emily Harris, sat at our table to meet Alex and talk. Emily's a cute little blonde. In a few minutes, Emily got up to leave, and with a smirk on her face said to Alex, 'If I were you, I'd keep him' -- meaning me -- 'under lock and key.' Well, Alex became upset. I tried to talk her out of it, but she made it clear that she just couldn't share me with any other woman."

"So you're going to let Alex influence your decisions?" Harry said straightforwardly.

"You bet your ass I am," Tom said in a whisper, staring his friend right in the eye.

Harry sensed his chest twitch at his friend's revelations. He said dryly, "Well, I guess I have to take that job. I have no history with Carol about jealousy."

Naomi breezed in from her smoke break. Harry suggested they all sit down at the table.

As he sat, Harry said, "Tom and I have arrived at two decisions. Naomi, we'll reach an agreement on your pay. We want to employ you as the official representative responsible for our local operations in Japan and as a director in the corporation."

"I accept your offer. I'm sure we can agree on the terms. You fellows need an office. I was a broker for a real estate firm before I was married. So, since my husband flies for JAL we took some time off to go around the world." Harry noted she focused on him intently, or at least he thought she did, with the phrase at the end of the last sentence.

She went on in her clipped British-speak: "I have about four possibilities for good office space. I think we could get around faster by hiring a cab. You'd want to be not too far away from Kurosawa, and there are other computer and communications companies to consider, also."

About four hours later, they sat in the last rental property, fatigued by the heat and the Tokyo traffic.

Harry said, "It's time to make a decision. I love this possibility; it's like our other office near Sea-Tac at home. Expansion possibilities, lots of daylight coming in, reasonable rent. Long-term lease. Close to Kurosawa and other electronic companies. In fact, we might be able to buy the Tokyo property we're now renting. So, let's lease this place. I rest my case."

"Harry, you're right. Naomi, get the lease papers."

"You fellows have made a jolly good decision. Actually, I thought you would prefer this space so the paperwork has been started. I have some lease papers you two can look at."

Harry glanced at his watch. "Naomi, do you have any dinner plans?"

"No. My husband's sitting in the cockpit of a 747 somewhere over the Pacific."

"Tom, let's call Alex and Carol and ask them to meet us here and then the five of us can make it a night on the town."

Tom reached for a nearby phone. "I'm dialing their number right now."

Naomi reached for a file folder. "Here are the lease papers I want you to read. Please excuse me, I need a little more nicotine. Be back soon."

For the first time, Harry caught a wink from her. He wondered.

Harry watched those hips, and since he would be the point man in the Far East, he knew he'd see those hips, and those other delightful sights, not infrequently. With the speed of a bullet, he discarded the notion that he might become involved with Naomi -- after all, Naomi was taken and he may be on his way to marrying Carol.

Harry and Tom read the lease.

Tom asked, "What do you think?"

"Looks fine to me, but let's fax it on to our lawyer in Seattle."

Naomi came back, with a smile on her face and smelled of cigarette smoke and perfume.

"Is the lease satisfactory?" Naomi asked.

"Yes. Subject to our Seattle lawyer's approval, as well as the Tokyo lawyer referral we were supposed to get…Naomi, will you bird-dog that?"

"I will," replied Naomi.

The conference room phone rang. Tom punched the speakerphone function.

Naomi spoke in Japanese and then turned to Tom and Harry and said, "Carol and Alex are at the front desk."

Looking at the two men, she said, "Are you ready, gentlemen?"

The men nodded their affirmation.

Naomi spoke in Japanese to the speakerphone and Harry said in Japanese, "We'll be there soon."

Naomi let both men take an arm to escort her out of the room and down the hall. Harry felt a little squeeze on his arm and caught a quick smile from her as she winked.

Naomi, Carol, Harry, Alex and Tom sat at a circular table in a sushi restaurant on the top of a Tokyo high-rise near the Kurosawa company headquarters. Harry sat with Carol on his right and Naomi on his left. Their table nestled near a window and looked west. The sun had set to the point where its rays still bathed the panorama before them but not as copiously as a few minutes before.

"This restaurant is a five star on a scale of five. Don't panic Harry, my uncle is much taken with you guys. He's the skeptic in the organization, so when he embraces you, it's meaningful. He gave me enough yen to order what we want. So, as the Americans say, the sky's the limit."

The champagne flowed. Most of the party had taken a few sips when Naomi signaled that her glass should be refilled.

"And how did you meet your husband?" Carol asked.

"Al flew the Tokyo-London flight. You know I was raised in Japan, but schooled in England. I was on Al's plane so often we finally met. He's about a decade older. We fell in love. The problem was he was married -- to a Brit. I won't get into details, but they fought it out in the British courts. I got dragged in. It was a bloody nasty divorce."

Naomi signaled again for champagne. Harry deduced Naomi had consumed three glasses to his two and noted that the ashtray nearest her kept on being emptied.

Suddenly, their waiter stood on Naomi's left with a phone, which he handed to her. She held the phone to her left ear. She said, "Yes" in Korean. Harry spoke very little Korean, but enough to pick up Naomi's yeses and noes. He felt she was being intimidated. After about five minutes, still speaking in Korean, which Harry couldn't follow, Naomi quickly cradled the earpiece as if she were angry with the caller.

As the others continued to discuss the topic raised before Naomi's phone call, Harry whispered in her ear, "What's going on?"

As Naomi's right hand lightly stroked his thigh, she said, "I'll tell you at an opportune time."

Throughout the next two-plus hours, lots of banter accompanied the food.

Following her phone call, Naomi drank water, ignored the champagne, and continued smoking cigarettes. Shortly after the dinner ended, they all, including Naomi, ordered brandy "neat," which none of them needed. Naomi ordered a taxi to take her home alone.

They called a cab to take the girls to their dorm and the guys to their hotel.

FOUR

Still seated in Alex's office, Harry continued to reminisce. He let his thoughts take him to one bright day with Tom.

Tom and Harry were on their way from their Seattle office near Sea-Tac to go to lunch, traveling in Tom's convertible with its top down, which allowed the spring sun to bridge the transition from the waning winter. After they left their air-conditioned office and stepped into the sunlight, Harry said, "It's strange, I guess, but I've always loved the first spring day when my armpits sweat in a car."

As Tom started his car, the local classic FM radio station broadcast a segment from *The Four Seasons*. Harry's parents reveled in that melody each spring; his mom played it after his father died and seemed to gather strength from Vivaldi's masterpiece.

Harry reflected, as a passenger in Tom's car, that nearly two years had passed since they had opened *Nippon/USA*. A staff of eight served them -- five in the company's Seattle headquarters and three in its Tokyo office, including Naomi. Harry traveled to Tokyo from Seattle every six weeks. He departed on a U.S. Monday and returned to Seattle on a Japanese Friday.

While business burgeoned beyond his expectations, he worried about Naomi's sexual overtures, which were getting difficult to ward off. He resolved not to have more than one drink when they visited a Tokyo bar after work. He knew his weaknesses. And she seemed to be drinking more.

Harry skimmed their company financials on the way to their weekly executive meeting, which they held every Friday noon at a restaurant overlooking Puget Sound called Des Moines Crossings.

He glanced at Douglas firs, other evergreens, and the deciduous trees as they showed off their new growth, inviting busy, tweeting birds that carried nest-building materials in their beaks, with the goal of establishing homes for their developing progeny.

Harry followed Tom as they walked to the restaurant's outdoor decks. Like Tom, he held his jacket over his arm and wore sunglasses. Light breezes rustled the budding branches, and out on the sun-bussed Sound the sailboats nudged forward setting their sails a-flapping.

They sauntered slowly and wound through the assembly of chairs flanking tables with white linen and sparkling utensils dazzled by the April sun, and Harry noticed the restaurant was well occupied by diners.

"Well, if it isn't the nascent computer nerds from *Nippon/USA*. Cheers," greeted Ned Mason, an architect, as he airlifted his half-filled glass of white wine.

"Ned, thanks. I see you didn't try to commandeer our table today," said Tom as he patted Ned's professional partners, Pat Wiseman and Bill Rorick, on their shoulders. "Fat chance, with Henri here today," acknowledged Ned.

"Hey, Harry," shouted Ray Olsen, a car salesmen, who sat at still another table, waiting for his usual Friday date, Ann Hopkins. "How was your flight back from Tokyo?"

"You know…boring…but wouldn't want it any other way, huh?" Harry shouted back as catcalls, whistles, smiles, and waves came from other friends on the deck.

Ray Olsen said, "This is my brother-in-law Wade Wayne. Meet Tom Campbell and Harry Adkins." Wade rose and shook hands with them. "Tom and Harry buy cars for their company and their families from me."

Ray Olsen turned quickly to meet Ann Hopkins's outstretched arms. All the guys around Ray's table extended greetings to Ann.

Henri Eiffel, proprietor, beckoned Harry and Tom to come with him, escorted the men to their table, bowed to them after they were seated, and said, *"Bon Jour, mes amis,"* as he filled each man's glass with white Bordeaux.

Harry touched Henri's shoulder and said, "Henri, *merci* for reserving Henri's Hideaway table for us on these spring and summer Fridays, allowing us a little privacy out here on the deck." Feeling fortunate to be alive on this five-star day, he held his yet untouched glass of wine above his shoulder, and Tom followed with his uplifted glass. "Tom, here's to the first day on the deck this season." Both men sipped their wine. Harry always had admired Henri for his wine selection.

"I'll drink to that. And to *Nippon/USA.*" He again raised his glass, as did Harry.

"One more toast, Tom. Here's to your Alex and my Carol." Harry and Tom once more hoisted their glasses and sampled the vintner's product.

Harry noted that at other tables women with their men looked longingly into each other's eyes, held hands, and neglected their menus, instead ordering another glass of wine. They repeatedly ignored the eager waitpersons, and occasionally bussed each other's lips.

Harry reminded himself of Tennyson's words found in *Locksley Hall* and turned to Tom. Paraphrasing the author, he said, "In the spring a young man and woman's fancy lightly turns to thoughts of love."

"I've heard that before," offered Tom, with a lilt in his voice.

Harry often pondered whether some of the amorous goings-on in these spring scenes didn't in fact cause spring. There were enough signs of the year's second season this day to cause Henri to open his deck for the summer and maybe, for a golden autumn.

"How's your love life, Tom?"

Tom lowered his voice and leaned in to Harry. "As you know, I went back to see Alex during the Harvard Med School spring break. And frankly, man, the lovemaking got hot and heavy. One time we got careless…you know how that can go…"

Harry raised his eyebrows with high interest and pressed Tom to follow through.

"Well, when I got back here, Alex called and said she thought she was PG."

So Harry had figured correctly when he'd first thought Alex was a good roll in the hay. He experienced some lingering regret, trying to accept that she would just have to be a close friend, not a lover. *And who would be his lover? At this point, Carol, absolutely.*

"Well, of course we talked about getting engaged and setting a wedding date. So get this, Harry boy, your favorite business partner got himself engaged and we shopped for a ring. Even asked her dad for her hand…You know, that old-fashioned stuff…and now she wears my ring."

Harry raised his glass, followed by Tom lifting his, and both men shook hands and clinked glasses. Harry said, "Here's to many years of a happy marriage." He hoped he had come off sincerely.

"Both Alex and I have been living on pins and needles since she told me she might be PG. Having a kid would delay her graduation from med school, to say the least."

Harry saw Henri, who carried a phone set with a long connection line, wave to him. He seemed a little out of breath, *"Monsieur* Campbell, *Mademoiselle* Quick is on the telephone for you." He passed the phone to Tom who put the receiver to his ear. "Thanks, Henri. Alex? I love you, too. Harry, Alex threw a kiss to you."

Harry said, "Tell Alex hello and tell her I just tossed a kiss and a hug clear to Cambridge."

"Did you hear that, lover?" Tom turned to Harry and said, "Alex heard you." Tom cradled the phone to rest on his shoulder. Harry's gut had told him their engagement was going to happen and he secretly harbored some jealousy.

"What's new, my dear?" Harry saw Tom's face brightening.

"You're not? Whew. There's lots of time for that…" Both men took generous sips from their glasses. Tom appeared much relieved. "Hey, lady…brilliant idea. Let me check with my business partner." Turning to Harry, he said, "Carol and Alex have been talking. Their program is, we get married just after Alex graduates from Harvard Med in June."

"Tell her it sounds pretty good to me," said Harry.

"Harry approves." He paused to listen, adding, "Alex said she knew you would.

"Alex. Say that again. I must be dreaming."

Harry noticed the pal he'd secretly nicknamed old Taciturn Tom beamed brighter than he ever had before.

"Yes. Uh-huh. Yippee! Pardon me, Alex -- and Harry -- but I'm putting down the phone and giving the loudest two-fingered whistle either of you have ever heard."

Tom laid the phone on the table and did just that. Harry swore he had drowned out even the noisy four-engine jet that had just taken off from Sea-Tac. Every diner at the Crossings came to attention. He had never heard anybody whistle as loud as Tom did when he puckered and blew at the American Embassy at the Fourth of July party, but, man, this one was close.

Tom grabbed the phone and stood up. "You're going to do your internship and residency in Seattle in family medicine? That's unbelievable!"

Harry put on his best smile. So Alex was spoken for. But she was coming to town. *Hmmm.*

Tom then turned to his many friends on the deck, and shouted, just like he was on a microphone hooked to a loudspeaker. "Hey, everybody! I see a few unfamiliar faces here today. Hi, friends. Guys and dolls. I'm Tom Campbell. My fiancée Alexandria -- call her Alex -- is coming to Seattle after we get married. She's got an internship at Harborview Hospital. Henri, pour everybody on the deck a drink of champagne. It's on me."

Faster than one could have said "ambrosia of the gods," Henri and four servers popped champagne corks and poured the bubbly amber drink into the deck patrons' glasses.

Harry stood up next to Tom. "Let's everybody drink a toast. Here's to Tom and Alex for a long, sexy, and happy life." Cheers erupted from the deck, and the din was so loud Harry thought they had drowned out the sound of yet another jet.

Tom spoke into the phone again and said, "Hear that, Alex? Quite a show of support, my dear." After the excitement dropped off to a restrained hum on the deck, he added, "Lots of fun, huh? Then we'd get married in late August somewhere near Boston…Let me ask Harry."

"Carol's agreed to be Alex's maid of honor." Tom turned to Harry. "Will you be my best man? Alex, Harry's leaning into the mouthpiece on my phone."

"I'd be honored to be in your wedding." Harry thought he couldn't be more satisfied; he would be around Alex, not only in the context of Tom and Alex's engagement and wedding, but also she'd be living out here, conceivably for the rest of their lives. *Damn, why wasn't I swifter at the Embassy party?*

"Okay. Talk with you later then."

Tom lowered his voice so Harry could barely hear him.

He said, "How's nine this evening Pacific Time for a cozy talk with pillows and sheets around each of us? I can't wait either. Good-bye. I love you, too."

Harry smiled. Indeed, on this spring day, Tom's fancy had lightly turned to thoughts of love.

Harry reached over and shook Tom's hand and with his other hand slightly squeezed Tom's left forearm. "Partner, congratulations. Tell me, I'm sitting here and really thinking about getting engaged to Carol. What do you think?"

"What do I think? I think you'll never find any girl who's anywhere near as great as Carol. Just in the first few minutes I spent with Carol when we all met, I formed an opinion. They don't come better than that. Alex has always said Carol is one of the very best people she's ever met. Last week, when I was in Boston, Alex introduced me to mutual friends of theirs. They went out of their way to praise Carol." Tom's voice dropped to a slightly more serious tone. "Look, old buddy, I'd go after Carol before she finds somebody else...and I *know* Carol dates other guys."

Harry was startled by a hot sensation on his face that must have come from jealousy. Carol hadn't mentioned dating other guys. He pulled out his reminder calendar and wrote, boldly, *Call Carol!*

"For God's sake," Tom added, "don't lose her to another guy." Tom read his watch. "Oh, oh, let's get our asses in gear and head for the office."

FIVE

Harry lingered in Alex's exam room and considered Carol's Wellesley graduation weekend -- one of his most vivid memories.

Maya Angelou, a U.S. Poet Laureate, served as the college's commencement speaker that day. Also, he met Carol's family in Massachusetts for the first time. After the commencement program, they enjoyed time on the campus before they headed to the Madden home.

Harry had carried his double-breasted navy blue linen blazer, complete with brass buttons, over his shoulder with his right hand; his left hand grasped his well-worn briefcase. Carol clung to his upper arm on a hot, windless, and cloudless June day in Massachusetts.

"Do I ever wish I could wear your linen dress instead of my blazer and wool pants." Harry pulled his tie to half-mast and felt his damp collar.

He saw a mischievous cast on Carol's face and in her eyes. She stopped and turned to him. Little daylight separated them. Harry hugged her and she him. He pressed his hips forward into hers. She took her right forefinger and probed between the buttons of his shirt, lightly touching his skin and hair. He was enlarging and he could tell she knew.

Another couple paused and nodded as Harry and Carol passed by a wooden bench. Harry thought Carol and he could rest a spell, and he led her to the bench. He saw pure pleasure in her eyes.

Still concentrating, he pointed with his forefinger. "What's the name of that lake?"

"Lake Waban," she said. "We just passed the Boat House and the Lake House. The treed area bordering the lake is called Green Beach."

Not listening, his eyes drifted to the ample cleavage presented by the cut of her dress. Carol drew her eyes into his and took his forefinger in her hand. Harry thought provocative thoughts as she slowly ran his finger on her chest and traced the outline of the front cut of her sundress. She released his finger, but it remained touching her chest and, ever so slightly, moving up and down, up and down. She winked. He winked. Harry had never had a woman take his finger as Carol had just done. He felt supercharged and aroused. He'd simply never met anybody like her.

"Let's rest for a moment and get out of the sun, sweetheart." He spotted a thin veil of moisture on her forehead.

"Great minds run in the same channel." Carol studied him. "I love your straw boater. You look great in a hat. Why are you carrying that little briefcase?"

Before he could answer, she pulled his hand down, "Let's sit down on this bench." He then placed his hand on the inner side of her thigh, just above the knee.

Harry felt her hand stiffen against his. "A little inhibition?"

"Yes, but just a little," she said.

Why did she come up with inhibitions about things sexual?

Harry shifted in his seat as he distracted himself with, "I brought along this." He reached into his briefcase and handed her *Ethan Frome*. "I haven't read it since high school."

She glanced at the cover and handed the book back to Harry.

She commented, "Well, it's a pretty dark and dreary story for such a nice day."

As he returned the book to his briefcase, he fished for the small box that contained Carol's engagement ring. *Ah, it's still there*, he thought and smiled to himself.

Carol started to stand up, and she pointed to love notes, which were carved in the slats of the bench. "Look at these."

Harry half-stood to follow her eyes. "Just think, I wonder how many couples spoke of their love for each other here. What happened to them? Where are they now?"

They continued to hold hands as they sat on the bench. His left hand on her cheek brought her lips to his. "Pardon my irresistible impulse, my dear Carol."

"Sweetheart, thanks for your kiss," she whispered.

This is nothing but good, really good, he thought, wanting to play a bit.

Carol wrapped her arms around Harry and kissed him so hard that his boater fell to the ground and rolled on its side a few feet away. He nearly was knocked off the bench and secured himself by grabbing the bench to keep his balance.

Carol got up to retrieve his hat and faced Harry as she bent down toward the hat. Her dress drooped, and he saw her braless breasts. His mind drifted; he couldn't help but wonder when they would go to bed together.

She twirled his boater on her forefinger and placed it on his head, then adjusted it so the hat was perched at a jaunty angle.

"I loved being attacked like that, and I enjoyed the full view as you bent down," he said coyly.

She said, insincerely, "Oh-oh. No bra." She pointed one forefinger to Harry while she stroked the top of his other forefinger. "Shame on you, Harry Adkins, you looked. In fact stared, you stared. You naughty boy. Gee, Harry, what do you think of that?"

"More important, what did you think about what you did to me, like push me off the bench?"

She moved her hands to her lap and said, "Oh my! I just went and did it without thinking about it. It was spontaneous. Most of the time I over deliberate."

Carol took his hand and laid it on her lap.

Both were silent for a minute or two.

"Carol, I need to ask you a really personal question: I'm not, but are you still a virgin?"

"A good question. I'm still a virgin."

Harry ventured. "Why did you hold out so long?"

"Because early on I made a deal with myself that I would wait for the man of my dreams. Without a sister, you probably don't know that most girls have dreams about different men as they grow up." She paused. "Do you know what I'm thinking about our relationship?"

"I think so," Harry responded, "But go ahead."

"Compare our conversations today on intimate matters to the night we first met. I think we're much more open now," she commented.

"Right on," Harry declared.

"And, on another subject," offered Carol, "We're much more secure with each other, e.g., now we don't have to feel we should continue yapping when there is really nothing more to say."

"All right!" he exclaimed.

With a Cockney accent, "To paraphrase Rita, as she said in *Educating Rita*: 'very good, ten out of ten, we go to the top of the class an' collect a gold star.' "

"Absolutely. You know, you're so literate. Frankly, few people I know say 'e.g.' "

"That's not a bad foible to have."

Several minutes of shared silence passed between them as they grasped hands as if they would be forever holding hands, resting on the bench.

When first they met, as Carol had just intimated, Harry would have felt awkward not finding appropriate words to exchange with her. *Maybe I'm a dyed-in-the-wool Motor Mouth.* But, now he felt at peace with himself and at peace with the woman he was with...and what could be better than that? *By gosh, I gotta relate that to Carol.*

"Hey, I thought you ought to know that Motor Mouth here," pointing to himself, "has kept quiet."

Standing up, she pulled Harry's hand. "I thought you were quiet. Right now, I'd like to go to my stone bench and sit and dream there. Are you with me?"

They left the wooden bench and walked wordlessly along the path next to the lake.

"We've had another silent period. Are you okay with that?" Carol squeezed Harry's hand.

He replied, "I'm relaxed. We don't...don't really need to *talk* to communicate. I think we can relate without having to speak."

Carol took his head lightly in her hands so their faces nearly touched. She almost whispered, "I'm thinking of a proverb."

"Let me guess...Is it, *speech is silver, but silence is golden?*"

"Yes. See? That proves it."

"We communicated, but needed not a spoken word. That was big Carol, really big. Maybe it's trite, but we moved to a higher place on the mountain."

Carol wrapped an arm around Harry. Again, several silent minutes passed with them looking into each other's eyes.

Harry paused and allowed himself to go back to the night of the Fourth of July party. He flashed back to the many feminine faces he had seen since that affair.

"I have dated, you know. A fair number of girls."

"Yes. I was aware of that. And I dated guys."

"You know what? You're smarter, warmer, and prettier than any other woman I've ever met. Where's that stone bench?"

"We're close. Not too many feet away."

He could see the end of the trail merging with the lake.

Suddenly, the stone bench appeared, almost from nowhere.

"Please sit down with me. Sometimes when I'm here I come under a spell.

"Have you been enjoying the campus scenery?"

He looked at her hungrily.

"My dear, I'm thinking of other things…they do not include the Wellesley landscape," he quipped.

Her face reddened. She sang, *"And when you touch me…and there's fire in every finger, I get ideas, yes, I get ideas."*

"I get ideas too," he sang into her ear.

Carol giggled, in manufactured innocence, "Oh, what would that be? Pray tell, sir?"

His hand was at her mid thigh over her clothing, and he moved it slowly up. She took his hand and lay it on her dress on her crotch.

"Are you okay with that?" he gasped.

"I'm a little nervous -- never got this far with a guy."

She took a deep breath and rested her hand on his fly, and then caressed an immodest hardness against his wool pants. She panted and held him hard with her cupped hand. She began breathing in short bursts.

In between her panting, she said, "I…don't…know…how to say this, but I want you so badly I couldn't possibly express it." She shuddered. "Right now! I mean now!" She shouted her words. "You got to take me now. Please, please. I gotta have it." She was shaking.

Harry grabbed her hand. "Look Carol. Over there…trees and shrubs…about thirty yards."

They joined hands, sprinted, and breathed hard. He said, his words staggered, "You…said…you…wanted…to wait…you're on the pill?"

"I'm not on the pill…I have this wild urge to fuck you…God. I never said fuck before. You have condoms?"

He agonized. "I don't."

"I'll take my chances. I can't stop…It's that exigent."

As they entered the secluded area, they both looked around to see if they were visible to others.

Harry flung his blue blazer aside and dumped his briefcase on the ground. They began grabbing at each other as if there were no tomorrow, no yesterday, no day before, only now! Both continued to deeply pant, and they sat on the ground.

She rose to her knees and used both hands to knock him on his back. His boater flew off is head, but neither noticed.

Carol mounted him quickly and placed her legs outside his thighs.

Suddenly, she slowed down everything and deliberately unbuttoned his front suspender buttons, pulled up his shirt, slid the zipper down his fly, slowly pulled down his trousers and shorts to his knees, and fondled him with both hands.

She pulled up her dress, shed her panties for him to see, trophy like, and said, "I got these off before I mounted you."

She took him with both hands, and she must have felt he was stiff as warm stainless steel.

He looked at her eyes and saw the desire of a wild animal in her now yellow, glinting eyes. Harry felt Carol take him in one hand now and ever so slowly sink toward to him. He perceived she struggled for breath with her eyes closed and her neck tightened. There was physical contact, and in a delicious moment, he would be deeply within her. She paused in her descent, her eyes still closed and said, "Oh, my, this is rapturous…never before…thank you. Now, I'll finish you off."

He hadn't quite penetrated her.

He closed his eyes and waited for the moment they would be joined. He was ready…close, close to the brink.

Harry realized that she had completely stopped her descent.

He heard her sobbing and looked up at her. Tears rolled down her cheeks. Her hand left him and she rolled off him.

"What's wrong?" he pleaded.

She cried, "Sweetheart, just couldn't do it…I'm sorry, sorry…You must hate me…Again, like pushing you off the bench, I didn't make a choice, I couldn't stop myself...until I thought -- I would be breaking a promise to myself...not until marriage. I disappointed you...please forgive me. Also, my sexual inhibitions..."

"My dear Carol, think of it this way: I love you. I was looking at satisfying my sexual needs, without considering your promise not to have sex until marriage. Please forgive *me.*"

Carol was smiling at him, wiping away her tears. "Look at the two of us. It's kind of funny, us sitting on the grass on our bare asses in this thicket." Hastily, they re-dressed.

Fully clothed, they sought a way out of their foiled tryst.

"Harry, hold it just a second, we forgot something." Carol ducked under some brush and emerged with Harry's briefcase and boater. She placed the hat in a rakish position on his head.

"Give me a crunchy hug, Harry." They embraced and exchanged enticing French kisses. They held hands and gently strolled toward the Clapp Library.

Without warning, the sky darkened. A Massachusetts monsoon more than emptied its rain. Thunder sounded like the bass beats of thousands of giant kettle drums all around them. They ran a hundred yards pell-mell to the Clapp Library, crashed through the door and found dozens of other refugees soaked from the sudden storm.

Carol tugged on Harry's forearm. "Sweetheart, I'm going to the ladies' room to try to put myself back together. I'd better make a phone call to my mother, as well."

"I could use a restroom, too. Let's meet in the hall outside the women's john."

They saw each other fifteen minutes later. The trees and the bushes still dripped water from the storm, though the sun had come back, hot.

Harry said, "Let's walk up Washington Avenue to Wellesley and get dinner."

"First though, let's go back to our walk. I want to take you back to the stone bench. Lord, sweetheart, look at my pretty pink linen dress, it's soaked. Good thing I didn't wear a bra today."

As Carol and Harry walked by their thicket, Harry pointed to the rainbow.

"Harry, my needs right now are simple. I just need to walk with you to the stone bench. And go from there."

"I see the two-story brick building, so aren't we just about there?"

"Yes, my lover." They smiled, knowingly, at each other.

"I remember you had…" she sang, *"fire in your fingers when you touched me."*

Harry saw an assemblage of rectangular quarried stones, some ochre. There was a shaped mortared wall, four feet by three feet and one foot thick, retaining about ten to fourteen inches of soil on the back side, another set of rectangular stones, about eighteen by eighteen inches deep by eighteen inches tall, stacked against the inside perimeter to form a corner bench, seating at least four to six adults.

"Harry dear, the bench is a sacred place."

"You know, when we're married and live in the countryside…I don't want to live in the city…"

"Neither do I," she affirmed.

"When school starts, would you get a photo of the bench; I think it's a work of art. And we should build a bench like it with a gazebo around it."

"Yes, and every anniversary we'll spend some time on it."

A stand of trees framed the view from the bench of a large two-story brick residence that had been sited about seventy feet behind the wall.

Well, okay, he told himself. *Do it. Ask her now.* After all, his plan to get an engagement ring and present it to Carol today was on track.

"Carol, I want you to know, I love you, as they say, 'truly, madly, deeply.' " He clicked off, overcome with emotion in the moment.

"I feel the same way about you. I've been thinking about living together, having babies, and all that stuff."

"You've been thinking that, too?" Ardor engulfed him like a large wave on a tropical beach.

"Yes." She gripped his hands.

He reached in his briefcase and slipped a small box into her hand, saw her blue eyes, and asked, "Will you marry me?"

She paused for several moments, as she seemed to have choked a little. She took a deep breath. "Absolutely, Harry. Yes."

They again hugged each other tightly, and after a few moments, ever so slowly withdrew.

Carol carefully untied the satin ribbon over the green box, opened the latched cover, and pulled out a gold band with a solitary diamond. The sun suddenly peeked out from a cloud; the sunlight, reflected from the prisms of the diamond and sparkled on her face.

"Sweetheart, please take the ring and place it where it belongs."

Harry took the ring and placed it on her finger. "This is the best day of my life."

"Of mine, too."

"I have an idea," offered Carol.

"You get more ideas than there's sand on the beach at Atlantic City. What is it?"

"You know how important it is to me to not have sex before marriage, right?"

"Right."

"Yes. But," she excitedly grabbed his fists and said, "I think I climaxed when I was on top of you. I never did that before."

"Hmmm. Dumb question to ask, but how are your inhibitions going?"

"Okay, but they're still there. We've not had real sexual intercourse yet and I'm a little nervous, you know. Now, here's my idea: I propose we get secretly married in Seattle, not tell anybody about it -- except my mother and of course Alex and Tom -- and set up a formal wedding date in a couple of months. And, I'm going to see a doctor post haste and get on the pill."

After a while, clocks not consulted, each placed an arm around the other's shoulder and glimpsed at the blue sky, the trees, and Lake Waban. The sun, sky, buildings, and trees were mirrored on its surface.

She took her arm and brought his face to her face. "Are you up to a short, well-known, but apt poem by Elizabeth Barrett Browning?"

"I am." *Actually, I know what she's going to quote.*

Carol recited:

"How do I love thee? Let me count the ways.
I love thee to the depth and breadth and height
My soul can reach, when feeling out of sight
For the ends of Being and Ideal Grace.
I love thee with the breath,
Smiles, tears, of all my life! - and if God choose,
I shall but love thee better after death."

He pulled her closer to him. "Exquisite. You're a talent!"

Soon, they left the Wellesley College campus and walked until she suggested that they stop and dine at a small café. The sky had returned to blue. A large street clock proclaimed the hour was five forty five. They sat in the sunlight at a round table and held hands, and from time to time smooched.

"Harry, I'm already asking for money...for a phone call to my mother." He handed Carol some quarters. She rose from the table. Harry noticed that a former diner had left today's *New York Times*, which he had snatched off the table.

She came back in about five minutes.

"What did your mother have to say?"

"I think she's excited for us."

"I've been kind of dreading asking your father if I could marry you," he teased.

"Don't worry, my mom's a good actress. She'll make it sound like it was a surprise to her when you ask Father." She reached across the table and squeezed Harry's hand, saying, "You know, I'm still a little unsettled, frankly." *This woman keeps coming up with surprises.* Actually, it was one of the things that attracted Harry to her.

"Would you two like to hear the dinner specials?" interrupted the waddling waitress, holding her order pad.

"Carol, you order first."

"I'll have the fresh lobster."

"And I'll have lobster, too," asserted Harry.

"Drinks?" Carol and Harry shook their heads. The waitress disappeared.

Harry finally got the waitress' attention. "We need the bill."

"Yes, sir. Right away."

Harry read the chit and covered it with fifty dollars, making the tip about seventeen percent.

He looked at her and began to chuckle. "Remember, earlier when things were getting passionate, and you used the shorthand, 'e.g.'?"

"Aaah, yes."

"Also, I was tickled when I heard you say 'exigent' while you were talking about making mad passionate love."

"Did I really say exigent? Tell me I didn't," she laughed.

SIX

Carol and Harry entered the family library, holding hands. She wore a choker pearl necklace, a light-pink long-sleeved silk blouse and a pleated light-blue silk skirt. Harry's right thumb and forefinger playfully touched her left hand. She turned to the left and brushed his lips. She said, "Nice."

"This is my father's library. Mother has a degree in architecture, which she didn't use much outside the home because of raising us kids. But Father pretty much deferred to Mother when it came to exterior and interior building design."

"You know, this is some library," Harry said as he walked slowly with Carol and glanced at the high ceilings and dark oak shelves filled with hundreds and hundreds of law books, some from England -- some hundreds of years old.

"Frankly, I think Mother did a great job on the design. Yikes, but the hanging art that Father ordered is...well, stodgy. Father's a trial lawyer and the only art in here is about his profession and from the nineteenth century." She touched his sleeve. "By the way, your double-breasted blue blazer, with those gold buttons and the regimental tie and blue shirt will go over very well with him." Carol brought her face close to Harry.

"When will your family show up?"

Carol glanced at the grandfather clock. "In about ten minutes. Let's go over and look at my family photo albums. See the one on the coffee table?" She grabbed his hand and led him to the large purple velveteen couch. They were about to sit down when the library door opened. And, simultaneously, the grandfather clock came to life.

Harry heard Alex's peppy voice saying loudly, "Surprise, surprise. Tom and I are here to chaperon you two and all that jazz." She and Tom walked in, hand in hand. Alex wore a breezy, low-cut, summer white linen dress that revealed ample cleavage. Despite how much Harry enjoyed spending time with Carol, he yearned to know how it would feel to be in Alex's arms.

Carol hustled to Alex. They embraced and kissed each other's lips.

"Tom and you had such a beautiful wedding. How was your honeymoon week on the Maine coast?"

"We wished we could have stayed longer than five days, but the weather cooperated. Outside, I don't think we ever took off our sunglasses."

Tom and Harry shook hands and held each other. *What a great guy Tom is*, Harry thought. He was a terrific business partner and a fantastic friend. Yet, Harry still held a tiny glimmer of resentment over the night Tom had moved in on Alex at the Embassy party.

Alex and Carol still held each other in their arms, looking at each other with affection. Carol finally spoke: "Harry and I have lots of news for Tom and you. Don't we, Harry?"

"We sure do," agreed Harry.

Carol then moved to hug Tom, and Alex kissed Harry on his mouth.

Alex gestured to the couch and suggested, "Why don't we sit and hear this news? I'm curious." As they sat down, Carol said, "Well, Harry took the diamond from his mother's wedding ring and had a jeweler reset it."

Alex crossed her legs. "So this news, let me guess." She grinned devilishly and shouted, "You're *engaged!*"

At the mention of his mother, Harry remembered her beautiful face moments before she suffered the fatal stroke. For a moment, his parents and he were the only people in the room. Yet, he couldn't still his anger from his parents' demise.

Carol placed her forefinger on her lips and said to Alex, "My father doesn't know yet. In a few minutes my family will be here, and only Mom knows so far. She's the one who said Harry must ask my dad for my hand." As Carol continued, turning to Harry, her voice fell softer. "Alex and Father are not exactly friends. He's made a number of passes at her."

Alex rolled her eyes.

Harry thought he saw Alex looking at him when Carol mentioned her father's passes. It almost seemed as if she wanted his help. "Now, Alex and Tom, Harry and I need you." Carol paused, ready to ask them a huge favor. "Harry and I want to go back to Seattle with you and get married surreptitiously," she began.

"Why?" Alex challenged.

"You and I will do some detailed girl talk later. But, yesterday Harry and I were innocently strolling on campus when we began to realize we were seriously ready to be together, in every possible way. He asked me to marry him, and I said yes..."

She was interrupted by several almost violent knocks on the door.

The library door opened and two men and two women, all sharply attired, walked into the room. The older man smoked a cigar.

Carol stood up formally and announced to Harry and Tom, "This is my family."

Harry detected a chill in her as the apparent patriarch, Mr. Madden, reached his hand to Harry and said, "I'm Oliver Wendell Madden. You can call me O.W. You must be Harry. Nice to meet you, boy."

He guffawed heartily and slapped Harry on the back. Harry had a feeling that O.W. and he would never be friends. "I don't know your last name, Harry," he stated.

"It's Adkins, sir."

Finally, O.W. offered his hand. Harry made a point to vigorously grip the offered hand of anyone he met. He detected a wince on O.W.'s part as he crushed the older man's hand. O.W. wore glasses and despite his apparent age -- mid-sixties probably -- no gray was seen in his hair. It may very well have been a toupee, but Harry couldn't be sure although he towered over O.W. by about five inches. Regardless of his height, the older man had a presence of his own. O.W. wore a black three-piece suit, made gloomier by the darkest tie Harry had ever seen. And finally, Harry couldn't help noticing the man's generous stomach. He hid a smile as he noted surely O.W. had not seen his feet in years. "Son, you have quite a grip," he boomed. Harry detected a slight Northeastern accent.

"Yes, sir. I learned that from my Dad."

"Carol tells me you lost both your parents when they were in their early fifties...Stroke and heart attack? Sorry to hear that."

"That's correct, sir. Thank you, sir." Harry made a point to try to keep eye contact although Mr. Madden seemed to avoid Harry's gaze.

Harry assumed the tall and slender middle-aged woman standing behind O.W. was Carol's mother. Her hair was as white as a polar bear's, and she was nearly as tall as her husband. Despite years of marriage, she still seemed wary of him.

Harry instinctively liked her.

"Harry, of course, this beautiful woman is my wife. Meet Joan Madden." She was an impressive woman: lithe, attractive, and in fine shape.

"Hello, Harry," she welcomed him warmly and offered him a handshake. "Both Carol and Alex have said nothing but good things about you."

"Hello, Harry, I'm Claire, Carol's big sister by about nine months," she said with a smile. Claire grabbed Harry's hand firmly and looked him right in the eye. He noticed how much the two sisters looked alike.

"And I'm Chad, Carol's younger brother -- by about a minute." Chad offered his hand to Harry, and they shook heartily, maintaining their respective grips for some time.

Harry looked puzzled for a moment and said, "Are you and Carol twins?"

"I thought you'd never ask!" Harry was willing to bet Chad was a lawyer. He seemed to be an affable guy and was undeniably good-looking.

"Chad, I'm guessing you're a lawyer?"

"I'm doing law school now."

Harry liked Chad a lot better than he did O.W.

O.W. returned and waved everybody to sit down on the velveteen sofa with an expensive and extended coffee table before them.

"Joan is bringing up the coffee and goodies to us. So, Harry, you've noticed all these family photo albums here on the table."

"Yes, sir." Harry began to turn pages. He humored O.W. and engaged in the general banter about who's who in the pictures.

"And this album is full of photos taken several years ago," the old man said after flipping through some pages. He handed the book to Harry.

"O.W., why did you give all your children names that start with the letter C?" Harry interrupted.

"Harry you ask the damnedest questions," he said obnoxiously.

"If you must know, my parents named all their children with the letter O: Owen, Olive, Oliver. I just took a page from their book." Harry detected a leer in O.W.'s eyes as the old guy glanced at Alex.

"Tell us about your business that you operate with Alex's husband. It's Tom, isn't it?"

Tom seemed uncomfortable. He replied, "Yes, sir." Harry winked at Tom, who rolled his eyes, out of O.W.'s view.

"Yes. Basically, our company does translations between English and Asian languages in computer instructions and documentation."

"Oh." O.W. looked unimpressed. "Sorry, I don't have a computer at home or in the office. I don't think I need to know anything about computers to practice law. After all, I don't want to be a secretary, I want to be a lawyer."

Joan served the coffee and goodies. Everyone was silent as they ate for a few moments. It felt so awkward and uncomfortable in the Maddens' living room that Harry would have preferred to be in his dentist's chair or, perish the thought, at a doctor's annual physical exam.

"I understand, Harry, you wish to make a request of me," O.W. finally bellowed.

Harry resented the fact he had to ask O.W.'s permission to marry his daughter.

"Yes, sir. I ask your permission to marry your daughter."

All in the room wore smiles, except O.W.

Harry, speaking from where he was seated, said, "Mr. Madden --"

"Sorry to interrupt, Harry. But please call me O.W."

"Yes, sir." Harry thought it better if he smiled at O.W. "Carol and I request that you and Joan give your blessing to our marriage."

Joan spoke first, not at all tremulously. "Welcome to our family. When is the wedding? Here, of course."

Harry glanced at Carol, who responded, "In about a year from now. Here."

O.W., looking a tad chastised, said, "Yes, of course."

In a moment, Harry stood and walked to Carol, reaching in his pocket for the ring, placed it on the appropriate finger, and spoke as he slid the ring down her finger.

"Forever."

Carol replied, "Yes, forever."

As all applauded, Chad got up, opened a door, rolled in a cart with champagne bottles and cut-glass goblets, popped off the corks, and poured.

Chad raised his glass and spoke, "It may be trite, but heck. Here's to the bride, here's to the groom, may their life be one long honeymoon!"

Carol and Harry crossed arms, facing each other, and sipped the bubbly.

SEVEN

Carol and Harry had flown back early Monday morning to Seattle with Alex and Tom and stayed in their two-bedroom condo. On the way from the airport, they stopped at the courthouse and obtained a marriage license that required a three-day waiting period, which meant they had to wait Tuesday, Wednesday, Thursday and could get married Friday.

Harry smiled to himself as they all sat in Tom and Alex's condo, looking at Seattle's downtown from the bay windows after getting the license. The late afternoon sun poured into the room. Harry noted that Tom kept looking at his watch. "We have twenty minutes to claim our reservations at this great restaurant perched on the south end of the Aurora Bridge. Jackets are encouraged; jeans and other casual attire discouraged for all."

Alex, Harry, and Carol looked at themselves in the mirror, which resulted in hastened clothing changes.

The view from the restaurant was of Lake Union boat and float plane traffic, Seattle, and the not so distant Cascade Mountains, Lake Union, and the I-5 Freeway. A scene that was not likely to be diminished by other buildings.

The restaurant was faced with congregated rocks outside and inside that were interspersed with branches that pierced the building's wall. Well-attired husky young men sprang into action to take the car keys and escort the guests inside. Harry thought the atrium was drop dead gorgeous. The Asian staff led them to what turned out to be a private room.

Carol and Harry were followed by Alex and Tom.

The door to the room was opened by a greeting person.

Seven *Nippon/USA* people, held a five-by-eight-foot white banner with two-foot-high purple letters that read, "Marriage License Celebration for Carol and Harry."

Andy, *Nippon/USA's* computer guru, held a large drum that he beat rapidly and continuously.

Amid the din, Harry raised his voice and explained to Carol: "I think Tom and the staff put the party on for us." Alex and Tom seemed gleeful.

Eileen, *Nippon/USA's* office manager, with live-in-boyfriend Matt, placed Carol and Harry in a sort of reception line. First, a wait staff person brought a glass of merlot to Carol and a martini to Harry.

With the arrival of the guests of honor, Andy subdued and then stopped the drum roll.

Harry introduced Carol to Eileen and Matt, then to Amelia and Mike, Megan, Bonnie, and, of course, Andy.

The last person in the line was Naomi, who had come over from Tokyo to discuss expansion plans. Carol walked ahead.

Naomi stepped closer to Harry; her right hand held a glass of Chardonnay and her left hand grasped a twelve-inch silver cigarette holder. She inhaled, blew the smoke out of her nose and lowered her voice. "Remember, when the five of us ate our first dinner together?"

God, she's sexy. And that perfume!

"Sure. Whoever called must have known Korean pretty well."

"He did. My uncle, for control purposes…I'm his only niece…he's my self-appointed chaperon. He paid off some waiter to monitor my drinking. It really, pardon me, pissed me off."

"I noticed that night, except for the after-dinner drink, you pretty much stopped drinking booze."

"I did. I think we should walk over to Carol. She looks uncomfortable. You don't need to tell Carol what I just told you." Naomi took his hand and led him to Carol's group, and let loose of it as they both greeted Carol.

All celebrants chatted for about forty minutes, when Andy once again rolled the drums as a signal to sit down to dinner.

Another hour passed while they ate their steaks, dinner salads, and seafood, washed down with a not inexpensive red or white wine. Quite a number of toasts brought fresh drinks to the party-goers.

Soon, the dirty dinner dishes moved into the dish washers and orders were taken for dessert and Five Star Hennessey Brandy.

Eileen spoke a word of welcome to Carol and then asked that the diners pass their gifts to Carol and Harry for opening.

"The first gift is from Matt and me," she said. "Carol, why don't you open it and read what it is?" Carol stood by her chair and carefully unwrapped the package and held up the item.

"It's called the 'Ultimate Couples Enhancer'…I've never seen a vibrator. Oh my, what do we have here? Potential passion? Reading along, 'Batteries included.' Thank God," she quipped.

Carol flicked the switch and placed it in his hand. By this time, Carol was turning red-faced while she was reading "…sensuous," as it hummed, "vibrations for her!" She twittered. "Discrete and comfortable phthalate free…"

"Ya know what gang, I'm so excited it's free from toxins, unlike many sex toys."

"Carol, Andy here. How in the hell did you learn that?"

Carol looked at Harry and said, "I took a couple of years as a college wanna-be chemical engineer and learned about phthalate in classes."

"Carol, you never told me that," pleaded Harry.

"Yuh never asked, dude." *Harry was hurt. She was making fun of him.*

"Pardon the hiccups. Let me continue." As she held the vibrator, she read that it is a "stretcher enhancer with raised pleasure dots." Carol looked at Harry, bestowed a lingering kiss and said, "Ooh la. Hey dude, I can hardly wait."

"Also, it comes with a 'resizable super-speed wireless micro stimulator," which she turned on and handed to Harry. Harry held both humming simulators, but he couldn't find the on/off switches. At this, his audience was roaring with laugher.

For some reason, he'd never heard Carol being so jocular.

Carol opened other packages that night, like hooch flavored warming massage lotion; a mistress kit with cuffs, feather and mask; playgirl massage oil; Couples Double Delight Straw; Cupids Confetti soap; Adam and Eve Love Restraints; *Deep Throat* video, etc.

Alex whispered to Harry not to open the wrapped *The Joy of Sex* book.

The party adjourned at about midnight.

That night, after he donned his pajamas and she her negligee, and before they parted to separate beds, they sat on a couch in the dark. A song, *As Time Goes By* from a local Public Radio FM station, played lightly in the background.

Harry said, "I'm sorry, but I have feelings. It seemed you were making fun of me."

"I was just kidding you. In fact, I didn't hear that come out...all of a sudden I kind of had to do it. Understand?"

Carol was forced to do something she didn't want to do. Very strange.

"Harry, here's a make-up kiss. Hey, let's open the *Joy of Sex.*"

Alex and Tom had written their names in the book and a greeting, *With Love: Tender Is the Night and the Day.* She pulled her negligee up to her shoulders and lay on his front side while they kissed.

Harry responded in kind for several minutes. His hands were all over her, but she rolled off him and said, "I want to keep going, but we have a couple days before we can get married. Damn! But, time will pass fast. Abstinence makes the heart or whatever grow fonder or longer."

They parted in the darkness with a simple kiss.

The next morning, they awakened to a view of the Seattle Center and Mount Rainier. Rainier, at one time, a tumultuous fiery volcano that spewed rivers of molten lava from its core long before the ascent of man, dominates Seattle's southerly view as kind of a high vast sprawling white sentinel.

Harry had always wanted to get Carol to attend a Tuesday noon staff luncheon. When either Tom or Harry was traveling, they attended the Tuesday event by long-distance phone. Today, in honor of Carol and Harry, Eileen persuaded Henri Eiffel to personally manage the meal.

Harry was pleased that Henri spoke in French, and Carol translated what the *Nippon/USA* crew said into French. Occasionally, Andy would join in the French part of the conversations.

Harry noticed that Eileen had engaged Carol in a short discussion before the luncheon began.

Eileen announced that all should be seated, with Carol's empty chair to her immediate left in the neatly set conference room, which was decorated with last night's banner.

Eileen remained standing.

"I have an important matter to be attended to. As a preface, what did you think about Carol's handling of the Marriage Certificate Celebration last night?"

All stood up cheering, whistling, clapping, and then chanting, "We want Carol. We want Carol. We want Carol."

Eileen pointed to Tom. "Whistle."

At Tom's vibrant piercing whistle, Carol walked to the table next to Eileen.

"Please be seated, except for Carol. I recognize Andy. Do you have a motion?"

"Yes, I move that Carol be installed as the Mistress of Ceremonies at the end of this meeting and that Eileen be installed as Assistant Mistress of Ceremonies."

Eileen said, "Is there a second?"

Amelia said, "I second the motion."

Eileen said, "All those in favor of the motion, say Aye."

A burst of ayes erupted in the room.

Eileen ruled, "The ayes voted for the motion unanimously and it is passed."

Eileen asked all to be seated and Henri and his meal minions rushed in to satiate the hunger of *Nippon/USA's* Seattle office workers.

After lunch, Tom remained at the office, but Alex, Carol, and Harry sped to Queen Anne Hill in the Cabriolet, leaving Tom's Porsche at the office while Alex drove the Cabrio to stock up on food and sundries. Alex dropped off Carol and Harry, with the admonition, "Go crazy, and close the door to the guest bedroom."

Carol gripped *The Joy of Sex* and said, "You know there are other ways. Let's read *The Joy of Sex,* and come up with some...substitutions?"

With a sublime smile, Carol walked over to Harry, nestled in his lap, and spoke, "You're as disappointed as I am. Oh, Gawd, I want you more than any person or anything in my life."

Her frame shuddered as if an Arctic blast had hit her. "We'll wait 'til Friday. Why? In *Hamlet*, it is said:

"This above all:
to thine own self be true,
And it must follow, as the night the day,
Thou canst not then be false to any man."

Still in Harry's lap, she said, "Okay, here's the plan. I'll call Judge

Standish now and ask him to perform the ceremony in his court chambers, first thing in the morning on Friday. Good for Tom, he left the judge's court phone number. I'll make the call from our hosts' bedroom."

Carol planted a lingering kiss on Harry's lips and went to Alex's bedroom.

Carol emerged with a bright smile on her face. "I talked with Mike the bailiff, and he has the judge's permission to conduct the marriage ceremony in his courtroom at 8:30 a.m. on Friday."

Harry placed his arms around Carol and said, "You're a take charge girl." *He could not possibly express the pride, love, and joy he felt for Carol; her virgin decision was the right thing to do --- damn it.*

"I put some book marks on some pages. Let's go to the guest bedroom and close the door. I put *The Joy of Sex* and our sex toys in this nice little bag. We...or at least I, need some hands-on training." They entered the room and closed the door.

As they sat, on the bed clothed, Carol said, "Harry, know I feel...maybe...my inhibitions are relaxing...I'm vulnerable..."

"I promise to honor your promises to yourself."

Both Carol and Harry had fallen asleep. Carol put her mouth to his ear and said, "Alex's back. How are you?"

"Horny as hell. Let's get dressed and help Alex."

"You're a man of your word. Thank you."

They opened the bedroom door and walked to the kitchen.

Harry, Carol, and Alex had sorted and placed the various foodstuffs where they belonged, when Tom walked in from work.

"Yippee, we got the judge's okay to an 8:30 wedding ceremony Friday morning!"

Harry reached his arms on high. "Great job!" And hugged Carol fiercely.

Carol had begun writing a diary last Monday, as the commercial jet left the ground at Logan International and headed for Seattle. Much space was filled on Monday and Tuesday. But, writer's block prevented her from making any entries for Wednesday and Thursday. Friday, on the way to Judge Standish's courtroom, she wrote: *Today marks the last time I am Carol Madden. Soon, I will become Carol Adkins. In a few hours, I will lose my virginity. So what! Voltaire wrote: "It is one of the superstitions of the human mind to have imagined that virginity could be a virtue." But I kept a promise to myself, which I will keep on my mental shelf.*

Standing in Judge Standish's courtroom on the seventh floor of the King County Courthouse with Alex and Tom as their witnesses, Harry heard the judge, ending the ceremony, say, "Mr. Adkins and Ms. Adkins, you are man and wife."

After the wedding party embraced all around, he shook hands with the bride, the groom, Alex, and Tom and said, "Please, will you come with me into my chambers? Mike's made coffee, and my wife baked her famous cinnamon rolls for us. I thought you might want to visit for a few minutes -- in fact we only have fifteen minutes because the presiding judge is sending a jury case down for trial."

All walked into Judge Standish's chambers and sat down. "You know, my wife graduated from Wellesley, as I understand you ladies did, and she would probably proselytize both of you as alumnae."

They talked incessantly until a couple of knocks sounded on the door, Bailiff Mike stepped in and said, "Judge, the jury and the lawyers are just walking in."

Judge Standish picked up a brown paper bag and handed it to Harry and Carol, "Here's your first wedding present -- the remainder of my wife's cinnamon rolls.

"Mike, tell them I'd like to talk with the attorneys before anything else."

Hearty handshakes, good wishes, and goodbyes were exchanged in the judge's chambers, and the wedding party made good time getting out of the courtroom, while dodging numerous litigants, hanger-ons, lawyers, and prospective jurors.

"What do you think of Judge Standish's wedding ceremony?" asked Harry.

Carol said, "He did some research, like he knew what my father did. He also cared about us and let us know how our ceremony was important to him."

Soon, the foursome found themselves in the courthouse parking garage next to their vehicles and hurried hugs and kisses ensued. "Hey kids. Champagne's in the fridge with two Waterford glasses," Alex announced.

Harry started Alex's red Cabriolet convertible and with the top down, the newlyweds were nearly on their way to a horizontal surface. Suddenly, Tom and Alex, holding large bags, surrounded the Cabrio and dumped birdseed on the neophyte married couple as Harry and Carol sped off toward Queen Anne Hill.

They began to go down a ramp. "Oh my gosh," said Harry as he slowed the car, "Do you hear what I hear?"

"I'm afraid I do hear tin cans, but you know what, we're only a few miles away, so let's keep 'em on and let Alex and Tom take 'em off."

"I agree." He took her hand and plopped it down on his fly.

As they drove back, lots of car horns honked at them from the rear, accompanied by shouted happy catcalls by drivers and by pedestrians. Harry and Carol shouted replies.

Carol said, "You know what? I bet Tom and Alex wrote *Just Married* all over the trunk.

"You must know, my new husband, I've had zero sex experience, except what I learned on the Wellesley campus from you. Did you notice if *The Joy of Sex* was on our marriage bed?"

"It was." Harry began to fret; he was pretty aroused, but he was reassured when he saw the briefcase to cover up things if they encountered condo owners in the garage or in the elevator.

As she was brushing off the birdseed, Carol said, "Sweetheart, I think I can manage my emotions. No promises. We could we read our book together before anything else? Oh, man! You blew the red light. Lucky."

Harry breathed a sigh of relief. "We're close. No cop in my rear-vision mirrors. It's just a couple of blocks."

He wheeled into the garage. The convertible top was lowered into place. They garaged, locked and parked the car, and held hands, ready to go upstairs.

"Do I look as desperate as I feel?"

"More desperate, my husband," she tittered.

Carol walked around the back of the car. "Harry, come take a look." Harry complied and said, "You were right about the Just Married writings on the trunk. No wonder we got so much attention."

Harry was annoyed at himself; it took a long time to unlock the door to the condo, but he finally broke through. Still holding hands, they pulled each other up the stairs, and both were out of breath.

"I had better go to the bathroom," she said, as she grabbed *The Joy of Sex*. "Let's undress each other very slowly, not like we did in Wellesley."

"I just found some interesting positions," he heard, as her words wafted from the bathroom.

She bolted back through the door, carrying the book in her hand, with her finger between two pages, and jumped in the bed fully dressed.

He said, moving to the bathroom, "My turn."

Moments later, he left the bathroom and got into the bed.

"Ladies first," she said, "start with my shoes."

They removed each other's shoes, stockings and hose with stumbling deliberation.

They sat on the bed looking hungrily at the other.

"Take my shirt and tie off," he requested.

Carol untied his tie and dropped it on the floor. Then, she unbuttoned each button slowly and dumped his dress shirt on the floor. Harry helped undress her. Except for her bra, she wore no clothes.

Carol, for God's sake, it's not the time to take a rain check.

"My turn," he said, and he sat on the bed in back of her and slowly placed his palms on her breasts and gently squeezed them. "Lie on your back." Carol complied.

She lay before him with his hands on her bra. He removed one of his hands and held a small container that he passed to her and said, "Put some lubricant on me with both hands." Harry reached around her back and removed her bra, which also found its way to the floor.

Carol glanced up. Her words became staccato. "I, uh, never saw a…naked man before…"

"Are you ready now? No reservations or inhibitions?"

"No. But, it's just my first time you know."

"Carol, place me in you."

"Yes. I can't wait."

"Go. I can go, too. Same time. Oh, boy!"

They gasped, oohed and aahed, groaned, writhed, and moved in ecstasy for some time. Finally, they stirred no more and cuddled side-to-side. Carol pulled a sheet over them and they slept.

Harry awakened to Carol's front side against his backside. "Hi, sweetheart," she said coyly. "Look at the two pages in *The Joy of Sex* I've opened. Let's try that position."

She held the book near his face. He looked at the pages and said, "Sure."

"Oh, thank you sweetheart."

He had a feeling that Carol had been restrained in giving when they were making love. He'd better find out.

"How're your inhibitions doing?"

Carol fondled him. "Can't you tell? I had a number of climaxes when we were making love. It's wonderful."

Sure she did, but she's a good actress. I wonder.

The morning expired into noon, noon into afternoon, then to dusk, and finally the automatic clocks turned on the streetlights.

"I'm ready for pizza." *Good lord. We've been at this since eleven this morning.*

"Oh. You mean it's pizza rather than me, you rascal?" she giggled. "I think I hear Alex and Tom back. Maybe Tom and you could go out and get some pizza for all of us?"

"Let's put it this way: pizza, then you." He wasn't sure he should have said that.

"Great."

"Tell me something. Are you or are you not happy you waited until marriage?"

"Absolutely, yes. Before you order the pizza, I have a little copycat poem I wrote when you were sleeping. It's from Elizabeth Browning's Sonnets:

> *How do I love thee? Let me count the ways.*
> *I love thee purely, as they turn from Praise.*
> *I love thee with the passion put to use.*

Smiles, tears, of all my life! -- and if God choose,
I shall love thee better after death."

Harry and Tom walked out of the front door on their pizza expedition after both of them held their wives and kissed them deeply.

EIGHT

Harry sat reflecting in Alex's clinic and remembered how much he had struggled with during the last year and a half of high school as a result of the loss of his parents.

There had been just too many reminders of his family in his English Lit textbooks. He had immersed himself in business school and track, perhaps obsessively. In college, when he didn't place first, second, or third in a track meet, he'd imprison himself in his room and sob for hours. He'd taken the most demanding math courses and his compulsion had helped him qualify for Phi Beta Kappa.

He'd won a regional 1500-meter race and qualified to compete in a national NCAA competition. In that meet, he'd finished third by one one-hundredth of a second. His mom and dad would have been so thrilled to see him on the podium wearing his medal.

Harry had resented his mother for dying and leaving him alone. He was angry with her, and he craved attention from women. As a tall, slender track star appearing younger than his years, blessed with good looks and a seductive baritone voice, he found that co-eds eagerly sought his company. He'd discovered, by surrounding himself with women, the loss of his mother became temporarily ameliorated.

His sexual appetite had grown exponentially. On some weekends he'd made love to more than one woman, sometimes even at the same time. But he'd refrained from getting serious with anyone for fear of losing her, opting instead to remain promiscuous. For a while, Tom Campbell stopped double dating with Harry.

Harry's college psychologist had explained that Harry had never forgiven his mom and dad for dying relatively young and leaving him alone in the world. He took this as explanation for his sexual appetite and binge drinking.

Harry wondered: Do *I really resent my parents for dying so young?*

He sat alone and effetely in Alex's barren exam room. For the first time in his life, he realized his death was inevitable. *But, did he want to know when it would be?*

Do you really live if you know you're going to die on a certain date?

No, we can't come over for dinner because I will die the day before.

To son Tim: *No, son, I can't make it to your graduation because I may be dead by then.*

To daughter, Tess: *Why don't you get married sooner? I may be dead on the date you've set.*

Hell, the good news is he wouldn't have to worry about long-term care insurance, Harry thought. Come to think of it, he had better get a fair chunk of life insurance. And a will. The cost of life insurance depends upon life expectancy and health considerations. He wondered, *do I tell the life insurance agent the Seattle Research Institute says I'll probably die on date X?*

Do we have two Last Suppers? One for the family and one for our friends?

We all know about birth announcements, but what about death announcements?

Can you get an obit published before you die? Like, "Harry Adkins, who will die next Tuesday...?" Or, "You are cordially invited to the pre-wake of Harry Adkins, which will be held on...?" Then, do you hold a wake or a "post-wake"?

Do many people meet their undertaker before they die? Probably not. But, is that something to be considered? Harry tried to imagine the conversation.

"So nice to meet you, Mr. Adkins. You must be the family member or close friend for whom you are making final arrangements."

"Well, he's really neither a family member nor a close friend." By this time, the funeral guy would be confused.

"All right, Mr. Adkins, what is his last name?"

"Adkins."

The undertaker would appear forlorn. *"All right, Mr. Adkins, what is the first name?"*

"Harry."

"But, I thought you said your first name was Harry."

"I did."

"A son or father, sir?"

"No, it's me."

Are there any precedents for a date certain for death? Like, how a murderer is convicted and the state will execute him, they set a day for the execution? Is this study like having a date to be executed?

Harry rose and viewed the abbreviated world that could be seen through Alex's window. He couldn't help but think of it as a view from a prison cell, without bars.

To look out at the great world from a prison cell and know there is a date that you won't see it anymore -- the day after your execution, which is comparable to the day after a deadly sudden cardiac arrest.

As he engineered the comparability between death by execution and death by a heart attack, the resulting deaths, the ultimate results -- the shutting down of a human life -- are the same. Of course, the executed criminal is disgraced and men like Harry are likely to be acclaimed. But, dead is dead.

When Harry served as a juror, he sentenced a man to death for a case involving the raping and killing of six boys. And then the judge set a date for Allegro to die. *Allegro knew when he was to die. If the son-of-a-bitch isn't dead yet, he knows when he's going to die. Even though he was a monster, he was a man, wondering about what's it's like to die.*

On the day you're supposed to die, what do you do? Should you drive? Schedule a golf date? Make a visit to the Children's Hospital for your bereavement work? Get a haircut? See the dentist?

Harry glanced at his wristwatch. He'd been in the room for over three hours -- thinking for about two. He realized there were no answers...only questions. At that moment he knew what he should do about the study.

He'd join the study and learn the predicted date.

Well, maybe. He'd at least get back in shape, get rid of his potbelly...even the love handles. But, he wouldn't tell anybody -- well, except for Dr. Dunne and Izzy -- and he'd let Alex know he got a predicted date for his death, but not Carol. Sure, she'd be pissed if she found out he'd known but hadn't told her the Death Date. No, the Alleged Date of Death. A.D.D. He liked the sound of A.D.D. better.

And, damn it, he'd beat the $H^2 L^2$ prediction. That should take care of all of his reservations about the date. And, no, he would not go meet with the undertaker, even though it would be a gas. And he would wait to tell Carol until right after he beat it. Harry smiled. He would triumph.

The perfect answer. The Holy Grail. In this very small and sterile room, he knew he had changed course 180 degrees for himself and his family. *God, this may turn out to be the best thing in my life.* It was like the exaltation he had felt after a 1500-meter race in high school.

Hold on, Harry thought, *I'll do the study, but think over what to do with the information. And it would be good to tell Alex about the plan and see what she says,* he admitted to himself.

In his mind, he heard the theme from *Chariots of Fire.* He had always found strength, triumph, and joy in that melody. Harry stood and looked through the examining room's small window and saw the sun's departing rays on the nearby park's running track and envisioned the film's main character racing past the other runners. Their feet were flying around the oval track, caught in slow motion, and while he imagined it, he could hear the music from that very scene.

Harry closed his dark, intense eyes and collected himself for a moment. Re-opening them, he glanced straight down toward his shoes, but his potbelly still hid them. *I haven't always been this way,* he thought.

Again, he peered out the little window. A team of boys in their mid-teens, clad in shorts and singlets, sprinted down the track. One of them, about sixteen, taller and leaner than the rest, with prominent cheekbones, wearing blue shorts and a white singlet, passed the two leaders. The finish line lay just yards away. As the boy crossed it, he raised his fists in unpracticed joy and kept them skyward on his victory lap.

At the end of the lap, a well-dressed man and a woman, both slender and fit, jogged toward the winner. The stands were exploding in cheers and applause. The boy met them at the finish line and folded his arms over the man and woman, embracing them.

Harry thought, *hey, it's me at sixteen.* His parents, Pat and Jack Adkins, were there when Harry had won the state track Boys' 1500 Meter event, his first track victory ever.

Then his school's band had played *Tequila,* and an entire section of the bleachers had emptied as the band went to the track and marched behind Harry and his parents. With Pat and Art at his side the three of them had jogged another victory lap. Everybody in the stands had stood, clapped in rhythm, and sung *For He's a Jolly Good Fellow* as his schoolmates ran down to the track and followed the band.

Harry checked his watch. It was after six and growing dark

outside. He heard a knock on the door, "Harry, are you still in there?" It was Alex's husky, sexy, alto voice.

"I sure am, Doctor Cool." He opened the door and let her in.

"Do you know what time it is, Mr. Adkins?"

"I do, but I don't believe it. Do you always work this late?"

"I try to get home by six for Little Harry and Tony, but I'm late today. Damn it. But, lately Tom's been real good about getting supper started."

"I've a made a huge shift in my life today. Could we have a short one at Jonah's and talk about it?"

"Not there. I'll call Tom. How about if I let him know we need to talk alone in my den for awhile?"

Tom greeted Harry at the front door with a cheeky smile and an iceless Rob Roy. Harry closed the heavy, dark oak door and tipped the Waterford stemmed glass toward his nose, sniffing it. He took a small taste. "Tantalizing," he observed.

"Glad you like it." Tom's smile faded. "Naomi called from our Tokyo office on my private line today. She couldn't reach you and she was really pissed."

"You know, I forgot she was going to call, and I had my portable phone turned off. I spent most of the day at Alex's office, getting the goddamned prostate exam. I was pricked, prodded, and probed, and a lot of health issues came up. Has she told you about the study at the SRI?" Harry added, trying to change the subject. "She thinks I should sign up for it."

Tom didn't fall for it. "Okay. Anyway, Naomi sounded really anxious to talk with you. Something about a new business possibility. She wants you to call her at 0700 Pacific Time tomorrow. But, I was puzzled because she gave me the impression she's got the hots for you."

"Really? Hmm. That's strange. You said 0700 tomorrow, right?"

"Right. But for God's sake, buddy, don't forget this time. I don't need an anxious Naomi again. I'm not going to begin to fall for her emotional crap. I don't want to know. I assume nothing's going on with you two."

Harry put his free arm around Tom. "Don't worry," he said,

trying to calm himself more than Tom.

"Alex got here a little bit before you did. She's talking with Little Harry and Tony and should be with you in a few ticks. Go ahead and unwind in her den. See you, buddy."

Harry did as he was told.

The frame of the house was Arts and Crafts, as was its wood furniture. The upholstery was regal purple. A dusty mauve color covered the walls. Alex's computer monitor and keyboard occupied the surface of a venerable white marble-top commode with carved feet. Many art works hung on the walls, by Morisot, Monet, Degas, Renoir, and Manet. In the very center of the room had once hung Munch's *The Scream,* but now and for the next six months it would hang in the Adkins Galleries, thought Harry.

He and Carol and Alex and Tom had traveled to Europe years ago, before children. The four of them had brought back sixteen different reproductions. Since they were of the opinion that one's art collection tends to sink into the paint or wallpaper, they thought they would split the cost of the purchases. Half of the paintings would remain with one family, and every six months the paintings would be rotated. His mind focused on *The Scream* and he found himself wondering when his and Carol's turn would come again to take if off the wall; he was in a hurry to get the creepy painting back to the Campbells.

The four of them had found an interesting art gallery in Paris. Alex, Tom, and Harry had walked some distance ahead of Carol, who had been staring for some time at *The Scream.* She finally yelled, "Hello, up there! Take another peek at this Munch reproduction. This is so great."

Harry recalled he'd studied the work carefully and stepped closer to it, staring at the two bowed figures, who walked…stalked?…in back of the man in the foreground with the skull-like head. One of those figures - - a female? -- had a long neck, just like Carol's.

"What's so great about it, dear? I think it's kind of grotesque."

"It is grotesque, but in an epic way. Look at the sheer terror in this quasi-human living figure on a pier, both hands close to, but not touching, the side of its head. It's hardly even a head, more of a skull."

"I think I can live without it."

"But, sweetheart! The colors -- blood red, a dead yellow. Again, the sky reflected in the water...I love the menacing figures approaching in back of the screaming skull figure. It's so enigmatic. Please?"

"Alex, Tom? Okay?"

"Sure."

Carol smiled. "Oh, Alex, you are such a love..."

Not far from the Munch painting, was a photograph of the four of them taken at the U.S. Tokyo Embassy. *See Tom,* he thought. *Still looking preppy and fit.* A caricaturist could dwell on his bird-of-prey nose. Now, most of them appeared only modestly worn since back then, except Harry. He saw himself in a full-length mirror on the far wall. The Harry in the mirror mocked the trim, slim, athletic Harry in the photo. While he wore contacts now, back then he'd worn eyeglasses that seemed as thick as the bottom of soda bottles. In contrast, the words: *slovenly, obese,* and *old* characterized the Harry in the mirror. As he studied the image, he mentally lectured himself, *you're a fat, old, sloppy son-of-a-bitch.*

Moving on, Harry strolled around Alex's den from one artist's work to another. He heard the arcane lyrics of *The Windmills of Your Mind* pouring from Alex's and Tom's sophisticated sound system:

> *Like the circles that you find,*
> *In the windmills of your mind.*

Harry's mind followed those tunnels into a dark cavern, and he hoped for a torch that would light the way to a firm decisions to make a firm decision about the option offered by the study.

And what was he going to tell Carol about $H^2 L^2$? When the subject of death came up, Carol would withdraw for a few days. Harry had learned always to make an effort to skirt the issue of a person's demise. Thinking of Carol's feelings about death compared to his own started to make things clearer to him. *Yes.* He would go into the $H^2 L^2$ Study and accept the option to know the date of his death, and then he would beat the date. *That's it, I'll show the bastards.* He would outlive the doctors' predictions. It would be the best revenge. He would be a centenarian. But he couldn't tell Carol he knew the predicted date.

Harry had always been competitive, while Carol played games for fun. Harry despised people who laughed when they lost. He loved golf and played it well. But after some matches, he shunned the "Nineteenth Hole" if he had lost and drove to some empty park, sat in his car and wept -- just like in college.

As he considered these traits, he heard an authoritative knock on the door and saw the brass handle turn. He opened the door, bowing to her. Alex strolled in, smiling and carrying an empty glass in one hand and a bottle of red wine in the other. She gestured to Harry to shut the door behind her and stood close to him.

Harry complied, moved closer to her, placed his hand on hers on the bottle and read, "Leonetti Cellar's cab. Where did you get it?"

"From Henri. Get a bottle, you'll love it. Or, shall we freshen your Rob Roy?"

"No. I think one should be enough," he said, as he placed a mostly-finished Rob Roy on a table next to him and noticed a larger wine glass within his reach.

"Would you *por favor?*"

"You and your little jokes," Alex giggled as she filled his wine goblet. "Good thinking, Harry. Frankly, I figured you'd want another Rob Roy."

"A short stride toward change, huh?" he quizzed.

Alex stood nearby, sipping her wine and looking at the paintings with him.

"I've always had a lot of fun in this room during your parties," he continued. "Never had a serious talk here though, until today. I've mainly just talked about golf with Tom. You know, sometimes even golf's serious with me."

Alex smiled softly and moved a little closer to him.

Harry basked in her warmth.

There was no sense in beating around the bush. "You know, I think I'll join the $H^2 L^2$ study. But, first I need to talk with one of the doctors in the study. Can you get me the name and phone number of the doc in charge? I can't say deep down I'm excited to know the date of my death. But I wonder what it would be like? I want to know someone's guess a hell of a lot more than not. You know, I want to defy death. I'll look the bastard in the eye and walk away. But, damn it, Carol can't know."

Alex nodded. "The head guy is Dr. Jonathan Dunne out at the Seattle Research Institute. I'll call you with his phone number when I'm in my office. But telling Carol is your call. Don't tell me if you decide to know, just get a copy of the $H^2 L^2$ letter, which predicts the date of your death, seal it in an envelope, and leave it in my office. I won't open it unless it's some kind of an emergency involving you. Carol's a patient of mine, too. I don't want to be compromised."

"It's just something I'm thinking about. Well, no promises about keeping my appointments, but I'll try," Harry said with a grin. "You know, you may be seeing a change in this son-of-a-bitch. I'm going to get a personal trainer at the gym. That's a good first step, isn't it? And I'll eat dinner with Carol and the kids tonight and make it a regular thing instead of eating at the office."

"I'm glad you'll be in the study and I'm glad you're taking it seriously." Alex stepped near to Harry and clinked her glass against his. Harry perceived she had, at that moment, shown him the same seductive come-on as she had used the first time they had met at the U.S. Embassy in Tokyo. There, she also had stood close to him in the same feminine way, close enough so he'd felt a breast brush against his sleeve. He thought wistfully, *maybe she's flirting with me again.* He stared at her for some recognition, some confirmation. A coy smile perhaps, an acknowledgment by her that she was ready to move their relationship to another level. He glanced hopefully at her. No, Alex's eyes betrayed no emotion.

The clock struck seven.

Still pleasantly surprised from what he thought was a move by Alex on him, he stammered, "Ah…well, I'll say hello to my godson and Tony, and then I'm out of here. Will you call Carol and tell her I'm leaving, and I'll see her in about fifteen, twenty minutes?"

Alex smiled and nodded, turning to walk him out. "Forgiven me for the prostate exam yet?"

"Never. Thanks for telling me about the study. It could change my family's life for the better, I think."

He darted his head around. "Where are Little Harry and Tony?"

"Probably shooting hoops with Tom."

"I'll head for your basketball court."

"Oh, sorry, Harry, I was distracted and forgot to tell you about a call I got a few minutes ago from my mom. She and Dad thought they'd have an immediate-family celebration back home for their forty-fifth anniversary on Christmas Eve. We'll be going, so Tom and I thought you guys could use our Sun Valley condo during Christmas week."

"Sounds fantastic, thank you. All that athleticism I'm going to get into during the study could start with skiing in Sun Valley. I'll talk with Carol and the kids and get back to you. In fact, why don't you call Carol about Sun Valley while your guys and me play a little ball? Tell her we can use it as a surprise to Tim and Tess? See you, Alex…Dr. Cool," he said playfully.

Alex gave him a little push on the shoulder and smiled. "Get out of here."

"I'm on my way!" Harry dashed out of the den and headed to the Campbells' basketball court.

Finding the floodlit basketball pad, he dropped his camel hair jacket on a patio chair. Tom held the ball and looked as if he were going to loft it.

"Little Harry! Tony! Playin' horse? Hey, Tom," he greeted them.

The boys rushed pell mell toward him. Little Harry, age ten, and Tony, eight, each grabbed one of Harry's tree trunk thighs. Both children joyously shouted, "Harry! Harry!" *Lordy, lordy,* he reflected, *these guys really think I'm something else.*

Harry reached down, hugging both boys. The kids released his legs and embraced his torso. Little Harry yelled, "You and I'll stand Dad and Tony!"

"Great! Tony and Tom, are you ready to lose?"

"Never. We'll beat your behinds. Since I'm the youngest, Dad and me get to start first," Tony demanded, and Tom humored him, handing over the ball.

Alex appeared just off the basketball pad with a phone, which she held to her ear and mouth.

"Carol, it looks like the State Horse Finals are about to start," said Alex into the receiver, then paused, listening. "Harry, Carol says your family and you are eating dinner together tonight. Be home at seven forty-five. She also sends her love over here." Back into the phone, she said, "Love you too, lady." She handed the phone off to Harry.

"Carol. You still there?"

"Yes, I wanted to make sure you knew tomorrow is my turn to take the kids to swim team in the morning before school."

"What time?"

"Five-thirty, and then I'm going to the other lap pool at the club. I have a master's meet on Friday. I need some laps. Anyway, just wanted you to know. See you home no later than eight."

"Love you, dear. Bye! Here's your phone back, Alex."

"Let the games begin," Harry shouted as Tony stood on the free-throw line preparing for the first shot.

Alex took the phone from Harry.

"It's too damn cold outside. That chilly November wind's driving me inside." Alex strode through the door, walked to the living room, and settled on a sofa. She said to Carol, "You knew this was Harry's annual check-up day."

"I did, any particular problem?"

"Not really, except our Harry badly needs to get into shape."

"Yes, I know about his parents, and they were both in good shape."

"I told him about a new medical study -- $H^2 L^2$ -- offered by Seattle Research Institute and recommended that he participate. He said he'd fill you in and find out more about it."

"Harry and I will discuss it."

"We talked about his depression, Nick Nelson, and all of that. The exam was a wrap, and I was exiting. Then, out of the blue, I found myself asking Harry, 'What's your greatest fear?'"

Carol broke in, "I bet he said, 'Johnnie Allegro.' Mine, too. I'm sure Harry told you about the threat at the end of the trial years ago, and the threatening letter not long after the trial...Seems like it was yesterday.

"Judge Standish and we reported everything to the prosecutor, but nothing more happened," Carol continued. "Sure, I was apprehensive, but, 'out of sight, out of mind.' I guess we tried to put the Allegro thing in the waste can...I don't think I need mental health treatment or anything like that.

"But now that mental health came up, you know that I've been inhibited over a lot of things…sex was high on my list."

"Yeah, girl, I remember your honeymoon at our place. Harry and Tom went out for pizza and you came to me with tears rolling down your cheeks. You were crying because you had problems with sexual inhibition. You just couldn't climax."

"Hush, Alex. But I lied to Harry, I told him that both on the Wellesley campus and the first, second, and third times we had sex I had climaxed. I faked it. In truth and in fact, I began to have orgasms only after a few years of trying."

Alex added, "Also, Harry made an appointment with Izzy Cantor to discuss $H^2 L^2$. Harry said earlier today he didn't mind you talking with me about mental health issues. But, please call my office and make an appointment."

Carol said, "I sure will."

"Well, I better get on with dinner. Oh, yes! One more thing. Tom and I would like to join your gun club, and get Harry interested, too. We should even get gun permits."

"Oh Carol. I forgot something. I told Harry we're going back East for Christmas so you guys can use our Sun Valley condo. Harry really sounded excited about it."

"Oh, perfect! Harry and I talked about going to some ski resort over Christmas. Thanks for thinking of us. The twins will be so excited. Bye. Love you."

"Love yuh."

NINE

Harry noticed as he drove home from Tom and Alex's place, that there seemed to be hordes of other cars on the road, and each driver appeared angry and impatient. In the glare of his headlights some drivers seemed scary, and Harry observed their boiling rage ready to burst.

Through the rain-spattered front windshield, headlights from the vehicles in opposing lanes seemed like wet diamonds, constantly appearing and disappearing with the wipe-wup, wipe-wup, wipe-wup of the wipers. From the front windshield, ruby-colored tail lights continually flashed to the rhythm of the flat music of car horns.

Harry felt compelled to pull out of the motorcade melee to think and reflect on the same thing he'd been reflecting about all day: the $H^2 L^2$ study. As soon as he saw a gas station on his right with parking space, he hit the brakes and pulled out of the *ad hoc* motorcade. He needed to think about his discovery of his soul. Yes, even the prostate probe, as awful as it was, caused him to suddenly realize that he, too, had something central, spiritual, and fundamental, like the widely-discussed and preached-about *soul*.

The prostate, an integral part of a man's urinary tract, offers a recordable impression to a finger and scientific device. The elusive and intangible soul, he thought, lacks credibility because no apostle claimed to have seen a soul, much less measured it.

He felt this day had been a momentous one in his life.

He had gotten a wake-up call from Dr. Alex. Exercise, regular exercise, she had told him. He'd say *goodbye, potbelly*. And from now on, he would get home more often for dinner with his family, and help raise those kids as a peer with Carol.

At the thought of Carol, he felt a rush of joy. He had felt ecstasy when he stood in his morning coat at St. Paul's Catholic Church in Wellesley. He held Carol as they were presented by the priest to their families and friends at the close of their formal wedding ceremony.

And then there were those fantastic kids, Tim and Tess. Another rush of joy consumed him when he thought of them, the same ecstasy he'd known in the delivery room, when the obstetrician who had just taken the babies from Carol, said, "Carol and Harry, here are your twins.

They sure look healthy to me."

Now those twin babies neared their tenth birthday.

Harry, he said to himself, *you are going to change big time. My mom and dad would be so proud...* But, honestly, they had only known him when he was a goody, goody two-shoes, not the licentious lad of his late teens and his early twenties. *God, why did they have to die so young?* Anger invaded him. He had to do something to relieve himself from that feeling. He smashed his right fist into the steering wheel stinging and bruising his hand.

Harry glanced at his Rolex. *Got to get going. Got to get to my family.*

He re-started his engine, turned on the headlights, vroomed into lessening traffic, and turned on the car radio to hear the top-of-the-hour news.

"We have breaking news. The King County Sheriff's office says Johnnie Allegro, who was convicted of the murder and rape of teenage boys here five years ago, is at large after escaping from the county jail. The sheriff's office tells us Allegro was brought to the courthouse from the penitentiary to testify in a case involving an inside prison drug distribution ring. Today, the sheriff alleges Allegro has killed a guard, has taken the deputy's service revolver, and has stolen a white van. Allegro is armed and very dangerous. We'll break for sports as we wait for more news on this important story."

Harry gripped the wheel hard and said out loud, "Oh, my God. Johnnie Allegro."

He stared, transfixed through his Porsche's front windshield.

He drove toward home; with Allegro at large, Harry quaked with dread. He saw his hands shaking.

Frantic, Harry picked up his two-way radio and tried to call home. The display didn't light up. *Son of a bitch.* He had forgotten to charge the damned thing.

He pushed the accelerator to the floor. Agony seized his rationality. He was scared to death, he was confused. Too many red lights through the windshield, too many headlights in the mirrors. Was he too late already?

The graphic testimony of the medical examiner describing the torture of each of the boys flashed into his mind. He heard the disgusting details, he saw the horrific pictures all over again. Allegro had also snapped color photos of his handiwork as sick keepsakes, many of which were introduced in court as evidence. The prosecutors passed the photographs to the jurors; some glanced at them and then swiftly passed them on, and some didn't even take a glimpse at those awful pictures. Judge Standish excused two jurors who quickly left for the jury bathrooms holding handkerchiefs to their mouths.

Harry felt sick as he considered Allegro doing the same things to his family that he had done to the boys in the pictures. He barely had a chance to pull over before the very pit of him warned him he was going to throw up. Swerving around the cars and semis in his neighboring lanes, he nearly hit the curb. He threw open his driver door and barfed over the side of the road with echoes of angry honks swirling around him.

After a few agonizing moments, Harry slammed his door again and slumped back in his seat, his eyes closed, exhausted. A few minutes passed as sweat poured from every gland in his body and soaked every garment he wore.

Edging back into traffic, he turned down a few more streets before reaching the county road, which led to his circular graveled driveway. The rear of his car skidded and gravel churned beneath his tires.

A white van was parked, with the front hood up, about a hundred feet from the house.

Harry screamed, "Oh, my God!" The white van. Tears furled from Harry's eyes and his now-empty stomach lurched again as he imagined what the monster could be doing in his home. He skidded so fast into his own driveway that he nearly hit his garage door. Gravel sprayed in all directions

He pushed open the car door and nearly collapsed on the stones. The lower and upper floors of their house were dark.

As he ran inside, Harry tried to think of the many reasons why the lights could be out. *It's after eight in the evening. November. A school night, kids in bed early…please. Let them be safe.*

Hurriedly, he opened the door leading to the garage and flicked on the light. His kindling hatchet was hanging in its place on the pegboard with his other tools. He grabbed it and rushed in the house.

Hatchet ready, he quietly opened the entry door to the kitchen. It was dark, save for the dim light from the kitchen TV set; he heard a toned-down car commercial. The dreaded sound of the silent house rang around him. He couldn't see or hear his family.

Harry's stomach boiled with fear, more hot sweat soaked his clothes. He was breathing hard and his chest heaved up and down. It occurred to him that if Allegro was in his house he would no doubt hear his hollow breaths. His footsteps weren't quiet either. He removed his shoes and crept through the kitchen. He would save his family no matter what it took. Or he would die trying; life was not worth living without Carol and the kids.

As he neared the dining room, Harry gripped the hatchet. He prepared for the worst.

He heard a woman's voice from the kitchen TV, glanced back, and saw the image of a blonde female newscaster. Harry looked up to the TV. She said, "We have more breaking news about the Johnnie Allegro escape. The authorities say Allegro has just been apprehended and is on his way to maximum security."

Harry collapsed against the dining room wall and put down the hatchet. Sweat and tears rolled down his face to his chin and to his collar. He held his hands as if to pray.

If he had been an opera singer -- he felt he had the physicality of one with his protruding belly -- he would belt out the "Ode To Joy" from Beethoven's Ninth.

He spoke to himself, "Oh, God. Thank you, God. But where's my family?"

Out of the dark, the *76 Trombones* music from *The Music Man* suddenly and loudly gripped his eardrums. Almost simultaneously, lights all over the first floor flashed on, and Harry saw marching toward him in single file, high-stepping to the music, first Tess, then Tim, who carried a long homemade sun-yellow banner, which must have been put together in a big hurry. On the banner, in the kids' handwriting, was *Daddy's Coming to Dinner Tonight*. Carol followed beating both sides of a toy drum. The marchers waved and smiled at Harry, turned right, and circled the dining room table. Torvil, their Norwegian elkhound, raced around and around the marchers, headed to the kitchen, barked, and skidded noisily when his claws hit the perimeter of the kitchen tile floor. Torvil, still running, made it back to the dining room where he leaped up and licked Harry's face like a cow licks a block of salt.

Carol, who carried a whistle in her mouth, took a deep breath and blew, resulting in a sudden shrill, trilling sound.

"Marchers, halt." All marchers (except Torvil) lined up together in the dining room, trying to appear stiff and military, but instead they giggled, wiggled, and laughed. Torvil, not to be outdone, sat down next to Tess and looked up to Carol as if for the next order.

All surrounded Harry who had tears flowing unabated and unabashed down his cheeks. It seemed his deep anxiety had disappeared quickly like an opened box of Girl Scout cookies. Harry was so overcome with guilt in being too busy with his business and with his desires that he couldn't even respond to say he was not worthy of his family that had just honored him.

The twins temporarily suspended their marching duties and briefly hugged Harry. Tim first, then Tess, who whispered, "Dad, you need a shower!"

Carol blew the black whistle again. "Marchers, present the banner."

Tess and Tim stood behind their father and draped him with the banner, running it from his left shoulder to his right hip. They then squeezed and again hugged him hard, laughing, nearly in chorus, "Daddy, Daddy, Daddy, we love you, love you, love you!"

Harry dropped any thought of saying he was unworthy. Though he may have been smelly, he had plenty of time for contrition. He hugged and kissed those kids with his teary wet face and body like he never had kissed and hugged them before.

The *Music Man* CD still played.

Tess spoke to her father. "Before you run out of hugs and kisses, you better give some to Mom."

The kids led him, each holding a hand, to Carol.

Carol wore a clinging, wool, evergreen-colored dress, which Harry had given her for their twelfth anniversary. Carol and Harry, holding both of the other's hands, smiled at each other for some time, seemingly oblivious to their surroundings.

Carol led him into the living room. Torvil sat next to them.

"Children, Daddy and I need to talk alone in the den. Will you set the table with our nice dinner company stuff? When you've finished, please knock on the den door."

Both children glanced at each other and giggled. Tess walked close to Carol.

"Mom, can we use the dark blue napkins and put on Grandma Madden's light-blue place mats?"

"Sure. And, use the gold candelabra." Tim and Tess chortled again.

Harry and Carol waved at the kids, walked away slowly, and threw kisses toward them.

Torvil sat with his pink tongue lying almost eighty degrees to his gums, ears pointed up, looking at Harry; apparently he expected to be invited into the den. Harry knelt on the floor next to Torvil, petted him and said, "Torvil, you can't come in the den. Help Tess and Tim. Good dog." Torvil, obviously feeling rejection, lay down, and his ears no longer pointed straight up.

Carol and Harry entered the den and closed the door behind them.

Carol stood before the dark-oak seven-foot-high Howard Miller grandfather clock as its Big Ben chimes struck 8:45. Harry removed his left hand from hers and gestured that she should rest on the love seat. She raised her right hand, as if to bolt the door, but instead turned and faced Harry. He sensed what she wanted, and he told her, "Carol, I love you."

As Carol looked at Harry her blue eyes sparkled. She pursed her lips and said, "I love you, too, sweetheart."

"A great favor. Tess, of course, suggested I could use a shower."

"By all means. Take your time. Even though it's late."

"I'll be back in ten minutes."

"Make it eleven."

Eleven minutes later, Harry reappeared attired in his p.j.'s and deep-blue bathrobe.

"Is the sun over the yardarm yet?" He consulted his watch. "You know, it is. Great little fire you set."

Carol smiled and plopped into the loveseat, facing the fireplace, which was bursting with flames, bathing their faces with its radiance.

Harry inserted the Glenn Miller CD and set it to play *In the Mood*.

"Sweetheart! Our music. First song, we ever danced to. I'll never forget the way we tripped the light fantastic, and all those people at the Embassy who applauded us when it was over," Carol said excitedly.

"You know, we did boogie, didn't we? I'd just love it if we could go to the dance hall, just the two of us."

"Sounds good to me. Speaking of the yardarm, what wine are you serving us?"

Harry playfully reached for a white napkin from the wet bar and draped it over his arm, speaking in a mangled French accent, "Madam, zee *vine de jour est L' Ecole No. 41 Semillon, sil vous plait."*

"Oui. Sil vous plait."

"When Tom and I hosted a business lunch for our Japanese customers at the Des Moines Crossings a few months ago, Henri selected it for us as a thank you. He thought it would be perfect for some romantic time for you and me. I brought it up from our cellar a few months ago.

"Tonight it needed to be opened."

As he moved back to the bar, he saw Carol looking toward the many library shelves featuring three centuries of English and American literature. Many of the twentieth century works had retained their dust jackets, while a substantial trove of them hinted they'd originated as college literature texts.

"Lately, I have been reminiscing about how much you read the first five years after we got married," she commented. "You were so thoughtful, so relaxed back then."

"You know, I sure was. I think I was making up for what I didn't read after my parents died."

He handed a cut-glass wine goblet to her and poured some *Semillon* for her, then for himself. He set his glass on the adjoining coffee table then sat close to her on the loveseat.

"That's something else I want to get back to -- reading," he continued. "How's the wine?"

She sipped, swished the liquid, savoring it before swallowing.

"Great. I like it better than chardonnay." He refilled her glass.

She raised her glass to shoulder level. "To today, sweetheart." They clinked their goblets.

Harry glanced around the room and spotted a photo of his parents and himself taken not long before their deaths. He remembered his three-person family had often read, debated, and discussed novels, sometimes passionately. He recalled many fond memories of literary discussions with his parents in front of their crackling fire, often with winter's snow falling.

After losing himself in his thoughts for a few moments, Harry noticed Carol had been staring at Munch's *The Scream*.

"I still think *The Scream* is kind of weird," he said.

"I sort of like the creepiness of the whole piece. It gives me a little…tremble. I like to be a bit scared, to have the hair on the back of my neck stand up." Sipping her wine, she turned to him. In all their years of marriage, Harry had never heard her admit that before. He didn't know what to think.

"Why were you so sweaty and excited when we surprised you in the kitchen?"

"You know, partly from playing Horse with Tom and Little Harry and Tony. And, then…Did you have the TV or radio on?"

"We weren't watching it."

"Alex called and said you'd be a little late and told me about the medical study, something like a heart study, and something else -- anyway, she wants you to be in it. Before that I was reading in here and the twins were doing their homework. When we heard you'd be home for dinner, we decided to make a banner and welcome you to dinner in style."

"Oh, my God, Carol. I was so scared. As I was driving home from Tom and Alex's, I flipped on the news radio station and this girl --"

"Woman."

"Yes, dear. Woman," he said, with some humility. "Anyway, this announcer came on with some breaking news that Johnnie Allegro had escaped and was on the loose. I tried to call you, but my radio battery lost its juice. I really panicked, I thought Allegro might be heading here like he threatened to do in court. I drove like a mad man." He laid his glass on the table and squeezed his hands together. He felt sick again just talking about Allegro.

Carol studied him silently. But she said nothing.

"I saw a white van about a hundred feet from the house parked on the grass," he continued. "The news report said Allegro had stolen a white van."

She cradled his head in her hands. "Oh. You poor sweetheart. I had to call the electrician this morning. He was doing some wiring above the garage in your den and his truck broke down, so he decided to leave it here for the night. Oh, you sweetheart." She placed her hand on the inside of his thigh and gave him a long slow kiss on his lips.

"I saw our house dark as a tomb -- no lights. I've never been so scared in my life." Harry found his fear diminishing. He wiped his wet brow with a white linen handkerchief. "I saw terrible visions of what Allegro had done to you and the kids. It was the worst nightmare ever. By the time I got in the kitchen, my shirt and trousers were one big sweat rag."

The phone rang once before Harry reached over to pick it up. "Harry Adkins here." He paused and said, "Deputy Notting, I'm gonna put Carol and me on our speaker." He tapped a phone button.

"Still there, Deputy?"

"Yes, Mr. Adkins. I'm calling you to make sure that you heard the good news about capturing Allegro."

"Sure did."

"The news reports didn't pick it up, sir, but he was driving in the direction of your house." Harry and Carol looked at each other. She grabbed Harry's hand.

"How'd the arrest go?" asked Harry.

"We T-boned him and our third car rammed him from the rear. While we were subduing the big bastard, we found out he had a knife, and he got Deputy Faris in the thigh. Faris will be OK. I got two shots in Allegro's right shoulder. He's in Harborview critical care at the taxpayers' expense. He'll live. As evidence, I got the paper with your address. Want a copy, sir? Funny though -- he's illiterate."

"Thanks for the call. I sure am grateful that you caught the bastard."

Harry caught the nuance -- there's some friend of Allegro out of the hoosegow.

"Please send us a copy. Bye."

Harry felt tears in his eyes and saw great compassion in Carol's expression. For a few moments they hugged, kissed, and cried. Harry was overcome with relief.

Harry gently took Carol's hands in his, glancing toward the door. "You know, you're raising two great kids. I'm really grateful to you for that. When I was sitting in Alex's clinic for a couple of hours after my check-up was over, I realized that I need to be more involved."

"Yes, sweetheart, I could sure use some assistance." Carol said, with a bite in her tone.

"You know, I thought I could do some homework stuff with them tonight after dinner while you do the dishes."

"Fine with me. But if you start this, you have to be consistent," she warned.

"That's part of the plan to change my life."

She softened. They moved closer, thigh to thigh. There was a new desire in Carol's eyes, which were now sultry, almost pleading.

Carol slowly brought her hand up and rested it on the fly of his unbuttoned p.j.'s. Once more, they kissed, each time lingering longer than the last. They breathed heavily, on the threshold of panting. Harry felt closer to her than ever before.

They interlocked their right arms and hands and emptied their glasses quickly. Carol's hand had remained in the same area and was inching up and down, down and up. They looked warmly at each other, then broke into soft smiles. Their lips touched and touched again and again.

The tip of Carol's tongue glided back and forth across Harry's lips. He opened his mouth and felt her thrust slowly in and out, in and out of his mouth. Gradually, their breathing became heavier and more staccato, with deeper and shorter breaths.

Carol slowly moved her second hand inside his fly. Harry felt a deep passion surging within him.

She softly held him with both hands. He grew stiffer by the moment.

He said, "Oh, Lord I want you so badly. It's like it was at Wellesley and the first day we were married."

Their breathing became more gasping, grunting, deeper, and frequent.

Carol breathed deeply and her body sank to the floor. She slid off her shoes, then took him with both hands and brought him to her lips.

"Carol, Carol, Carol." Harry moaned feeling an animal lust. As their breathing grew in intensity, it echoed with passion and want.

Harry bent down and saw the top of Carol's head. He felt her mouth and tongue. She murmured and groaned as if she had lost touch with the world. She too was breathless, gasping with desire. "Oh, God, I'm so turned on."

"With you doing that, I don't know if I can last."

"Not yet. Just hold on. Hold on…just a moment," Carol gasped.

"I'm almost there."

He braced himself, on the brink. He didn't think he could hold it.

Two small fists pounded urgently on the other side of the den door.

"Mommy and Daddy! We want to eat real soon. We're hungry."

Carol whispered, "Mercy, mercy. Did I lock the door?" She abruptly released him and choked, "I don't remember." She paused, still kneeling on the floor. They stared at each other, distraught.

"Just a minute, kids," Harry called.

"Well, hurry up, Mommy."

Carol got back in her shoes, rose to her feet quickly but looked disheveled.

Harry stared intently at the door.

He turned his back to the door, and as he stuffed everything back into his p.j.'s, the door burst open. Tim and Tess stood in the doorway. Harry turned to face the children, chagrined, with his face red like it was sunburned. He felt the heat.

"What's Daddy doing? Well, anyway, Tim and I are hungry. Were you exercising? How come you're breathing so loud?" Tess demanded.

"We were talking and laughing about how funny Torvil was tonight."

"Huh? Why's Daddy's face red?"

"Daddy's just really happy tonight," Carol stammered, as her breath returned to nearly normal and she recovered a bit of her usual aplomb.

Tess, folded her arms and spoke to Tim. "All I can say, Tim, is adults sure are funny sometimes."

Carol and Harry followed the children out the door on the way to the dining room, escorted by Torvil. As the children turned down the hallway, Carol whispered to Harry, seductively sucking on her forefinger, "Once again, *coitus interruptus*. Take a rain check?"

"You bet."

Moments later, the four of them sat at the dinner table.

"Please," asked Tim, "may I say grace tonight?"

"Of course."

"Thanks, Mom."

"Tim and I had a meeting. From now on, we'll be calling you 'Mom' and 'Dad,' no more 'mommy' and 'daddy' words. We're getting too old," Tess announced. Carol and Harry both raised their eyebrows, surprised though not disapproving. Harry grinned. *You know, these are great kids.*

"Yes, Mom and Dad, I very much agree with Tess," Tim piped up.

Tim then folded his hands and cast his head down, "I'll go ahead with grace: Thank you, God, Mom and Dad are eating dinner with us. But, God, let them know we want to eat a whole lot earlier than this. Bless our food. Amen."

They nodded as they began to chew. All continued quietly eating macaroni.

Tess spoke up once more. "Mom and Dad, Tim's right. We very much need to eat a lot earlier."

Carol nodded.

"Daddy -- oops -- *Dad* and I talked about that very subject earlier today. In fact, Dad has agreed to eat early dinners when he's not traveling, and he's going to start helping with your homework. Tonight."

Harry looked at Tess. He saw a lot of his mother in her, especially her lips, fair hair, dark blue eyes, and creamy complexion. Her smart exuberance and big mouth could also be traced back to her mother. Harry also assessed Tim. Tim was not nearly as brassy as Tess, but he was just as smart. They both were in the top of their class. He was a good-looking boy, with a square jaw, blonde hair, and long eyelashes from Carol that girls and women would die for.

What a couple of terrific kids, he couldn't help thinking to himself again.

While the kids were wolfing down their dinner, he peered at Carol who once more seductively sucked her finger and peered at him ravenously.

Momentarily, Harry remembered that he was supposed to call Naomi in Tokyo tomorrow, seven a.m., Pacific time. There was no doubt in his mind that she wanted phone sex. *Could Naomi fit in with his changed life?*

"Harry, sweetheart, where are you?"

"Huh? You know, I just remembered Naomi wants me to call tomorrow morning about seven our time."

After dessert the children sat with Harry and showed him their current homework. The three of them discussed geography, math, and spelling while Carol tended to the kitchen. Out of the corner of his eye, Harry saw her peek at them from the doorway. He knew she was pleased.

Too soon, it was the kids' bedtime. All four -- not counting Torvil, who was present -- kneeled between the twin beds, one with a blue and the other with a pink comforter. They'd shared a room since birth, and neither Harry nor Carol saw a need to separate them yet.

Both kids and parents solemnly intoned on their knees:
Now I lay me down to sleep.
I pray the Lord my soul to keep.
If I should die before I wake,
I pray the Lord my soul to take.

They tucked the kids in their twin beds and kissed them goodnight. Torvil, determined to get his share of attention, stood on his hind legs and lathered Tim and Tess with his busy tongue.

Tess murmured sleepily, "Thank you for coming home tonight,

Dad. Oh, when will you tell us what a rain check is?"

"It's too late tonight, Tess." said Carol.

The parents turned out the light in the twins' room. Carol's eyes welled as she smiled at Harry whose eyes glistened back.

As he left the room, the prayer repeated itself again and again in his head.

He heaved a great sigh. He thought perhaps, the night before he dies, he will say:

> *Now I lay me down to sleep.*
> *I know the Lord my soul won't keep.*
> *As I may die before I wake,*
> *I pray the Lord my soul to take.*

Harry watched as long, lean Carol slid next to him into the king size bed. One of the two lights on the nightstands was dimly lit, and in its glow he could see that her bright blue eyes projected happiness.

Shadows and lights filled her high cheekbones and bathed her creamy, smooth cheeks. She wore a nearly-sheer, long-sleeved, peach silk nightgown with a revealing neckline, which showed her sternum to just below her navel. Harry had brought the piece of feminine fluff home from Japan.

"Let me take off the top of your pajamas, sweetheart."

He complied.

"You've had a big day, Harry Adkins. You need some more TLC. I'll rub your back."

Harry rolled over, and Carol sat on the back of his thighs, spreading her knees on each side of his body.

Her strong hands gently, but firmly, kneaded his steel-like shoulder muscles.

"How did your physical go with Alex? The PSA?"

"Both went all right...I had a real low PSA score -- a test to rule out prostatic cancer," Harry murmured.

"Good news, sweetheart. Now, let me guess what she said. How about, 'You're about forty pounds overweight. Riding in a golf-cart in between holes is not exercise. You've got to cut down on your drinking.' "

"Well, yes, to all of the above. Ouch! Your thumb stirred some gravelly stuff in my left shoulder muscle, but it hurts good."

Carol ignored his pain. "I want to hear a little more about the study. She tell you anything else?"

"She's recommending me for a limited-lifetime health study, by the Seattle Research Institute -- but no free surgeries or medications. You know, they may provide all kinds of medical machines that can be linked to your home computer that will send data to the Seattle Research Institute."

"Why did she ask you to do it?"

"Well, as a part-time medical investigator at the Seattle Research Institute, she's part of the study faculty. I guess they're looking for some guys who are out of shape and overweight and have a poor family heart history, and I sure qualify for all that.

"The research medical group studies the men cardiac-wise for a year and requires them to regularly participate in at least moderate cardiovascular activities, regular physical exams, and to complete daily forms of what they've eaten. There'll be lots of testing, for example, cholesterol levels and so forth. It's all for free.

"At the end of the year, the men get a health evaluation and a committee predicts the date each man will die."

"What's the catch?"

"You have the option to learn the date or not learn it."

"It's interesting. It's fine with me if you do it, except for one thing, and this is a demand, not a request. Do not find out when you are going to die." Her eyes narrowed and her tone shifted abruptly. He watched his loving, passionate wife transform herself to become the Wicked Witch of the West.

"The study is trying to see if the date of a person's death can be medically predicted. It's called $H^2 L^2$. I bet you don't know what that means."

"I'll take the bet. If I get it, you give me a massage and vice-versa."

Still lying on his stomach, Harry grunted, "Yeah."

"Ah…let me see, sweetheart. Let me see. It's about the heart. So, what kind of heart should we want? I'm thinking. Hmm."

Am I going to be able to stump her?

"I have part of it. We want a healthy heart? H^2!" Carol applauded herself.

"Keep going there," he urged.

"And what do we want to do with our Healthy Heart? Let me think. What does that healthy heart want to do? Live!"

Harry knew she was on the verge of solving the mental puzzle.

Carol leaned on Harry's back with her elbows.

"Ouch," he groaned.

"H^2 equals Healthy Heart…L^2? First word is Live; another L word is after Live. Oh. Yes, as Professor Higgins observed, 'She's got it. I think she's got it,' meaning *me;* It's Healthy Hearts Live Longer! I win a massage from you." He felt a hard slap on the right side of his buttocks as if Carol were celebrating.

"Smarty pants, Mrs. Adkins."

Carol took her elbows from Harry's back and resumed sitting on his hind end. Beginning to laugh, she rolled over on the bed. Harry rolled over facing her.

Carol began to tickle him and he her.

You know, I'm so happy that I married this beautiful woman who loves me. Harry found himself and Carol giggling, which kept going for several minutes. Tears rolled sideways down Carol's cheeks. Harry wiped her tears with a corner of the silk sheets. They continued to chortle.

Slowly, the frivolity began to subside.

"My dearest Harry, I haven't been lost in this kind of fervor for years, if ever."

"Whatever started all this?"

"The tickling? I don't know. I do know this night will be one of the most special nights of my life."

"Mine, too."

Harry moved his body to hers and embraced her. "Who's on top?" And brought his tongue to her lips.

"Don't tempt me now. Later. Turn over on your stomach."

"Yes, Ma'am."

Carol resumed her position over Harry's hips. "You were telling me about H^2 L^2, and you said you had the option to actually know the predicted date or not…Harry Adkins." Carol's voice suddenly changed from a seductress to a boot camp sergeant, biting every word she spoke. She grabbed his right arm and twisted it over his shoulder to the point where it hurt. "Don't get the date, god damn it. I could kill you if you do!"

Carol shocked Harry. He felt his body quiver. She rarely swore, and she had never twisted his arm like that. It was as if a stranger had moved into Carol's body. Silence reigned for several minutes. She finally released his arm and the pain fell away. She snuggled against his backside as if nothing had ever happened. After a few moments she turned him on his side.

As good as her touch felt, he was still distracted.

"You know, it would be hell for the family. But, why did you twist -- literally -- my arm? That hurt like hell and I can still feel it."

"I'm sorry I hurt you, sweetheart. I'll tell you why I think I'm kind of bothered with medical predictions like that. You remember me talking about my Grandmother Madden?"

"Yes. Didn't she die when you were relatively young?"

"She did. Her name was Carolyn."

"I know -- the grandma you were named after."

"Good memory, for some things, sweetheart. My maternal grandmother and grandfather...you know that they were both cultural anthropologists...and they traveled a lot, and I mean for two, three months at a time. When they returned from their expeditions, they took care of us kids. I was her pet. She bought me clothes that were a little bit better than the other kids' and she'd slip more money to me than to my siblings. She read to me more than the other kids. You get the idea."

"Sure. Grandma's pet."

"Exactly. I'll tell you something I have never told anybody before. Of course you know that Grandma Madden lived her life fully. Like, she played tennis into her seventies. I remember how she would play with us kids for a couple of hours, break a sweat, and run down balls. I had to be about ten or eleven then. But, as she grew older, it seemed like she was always going to the doctor and then Grandpa would sit with us.

"Before she got sick, Grandma owned most of the vigor between them.

"Then, her face turned pasty. And her voice, which before could have come from a woman in her forties, sounded as if she were in her nineties. She seemed to get weaker. And this is what I never told anybody before -- there was the night she came to read to me alone in my bedroom at her house.

"I heard a feeble knock, where before she would pound at my door so hard I thought she would bust her fist through it. I ran to open it and Grandma held the doorjamb with a free hand; her other hand carried a cane for support. I helped her in. I hardly recognized her. Seemed like she became decrepit overnight. She needed assistance in getting into a rocking chair. I sat in her lap.

"I asked her, 'Grandma, are you okay?' "

"She said, 'No, child, I'm not. This is a secret; nobody else knows this except your Grandfather Charles and my doctor, and now you. I have what they call a virulent cancer. That is, the cancer is fast-acting.' "

"I said, 'Grandma, what does this mean?' "

" 'It means I'm going to die,' she said. 'But, I want you to be brave. You know, you're my favorite grandchild. And the toughest, too. Like when you fall down on the tennis court, skin your knee, and then get up and play your little heart out. Today, my doctor told me I have, at most, four months to live.' "

"Well, I threw my arms around her, and Grandma wrapped her arms around me. I said...and I remember crying so hard...'I love you, but right now I don't feel very brave.' "

"Each day after that night was a torture for me. I counted them all and I was miserable. I told myself I'd never again want to learn when somebody was going to die. Grandma died four months later to the day, just as the doctor had said she would.

"Later, at the cemetery, just before they started to lower her casket into the ground, I ran to it, and grabbed the handles with both hands and screamed, 'Grandma, come alive again! Please!' "

Waves of empathy immersed Harry.

"My father, a fat slob, as you know, but strong nonetheless, told me later he struggled to pry my fingers off the casket handles. I screamed and screamed, and couldn't stop."

"So, after a while, you stopped crying, right?" Harry asked.

"It didn't happen that way, it wasn't that easy. You see, my father was obsessed with social correctness. You know that. And in this case, their daughter had embarrassed him and her mother. She must be punished. They didn't know how much I loved Grandma...I mean, it was like something deep down in me died.

"So my father got a whore psychologist to say I was clinically depressed and that explained why I reacted so badly. Something was wrong with me, and not him.

"So they put me in a hospital for observation. Fortunately, the chief of staff examined me and recommended my discharge immediately. I've never forgiven my father. The whole scene comes back to me time and time again."

"I understand. You never told me that before."

Carol took a deep breath and exhaled sharply. "To change the subject slightly, Alex told me she found you were still in the exam room when she was closing up."

"Yeah...you know, Carol, this was the first time since college that I'd actually sat down and thought something out."

"She told me that. That's good news to me. Did you see how excited the kids and I were to see you tonight?"

"I did. God, it was great. Well, you know, I plan to be home early lots more. The family seems to be taking third place, and that's got to change. But no overnight miracles, okay?"

"Who's in second place?" Carol tickled him.

Harry laughed. "Stop it."

"No, who's in first place? Oh, stop it, Bud Abbott," she giggled, "you're too much -- wise guy!"

Carol looked at the alarm clock. "Oh my God. It's one in the morning. The kids and I have to leave for swimming at five. Before we get to the pending denouement, I have to tell you something which also bears on me twisting your poor arm."

"Oh yeah? It still hurts."

"I'm so sorry. Long before what I call our long days journey into sex just after we were married, I feared giving you oral sex. I was inhibited. One of my inhibitions. Now, I really want to do it. Also, I was inhibited about drinking wine at lunch with friends, which I now do on a regular basis, even though they don't drink. Twisting your arm. I never even thought of doing that. But, I did it to hurt you…that's terrible."

"Dearest, I'm sure there's nothing serious."

"Okay. You're probably right. But right now I want you unequivocally."

Without warning, Carol suddenly pulled down his pajama bottoms. "Turn on your backside, sweetheart," she commanded, and he obeyed.

"Oh, God! I'm going to finish what I set out to do in the den. I'm cashing in my rain check. You hear that, boy?"

In the dark, the alarm clock's red numerals told him the time was 3:36 when he got up to relieve himself. He noticed he was more engorged than he could remember being, and he happily observed the night's love-making had surpassed any other he'd ever had or dreamed of having. He quickly dismissed Carol's aggressive warnings about learning the study's predicted date of death as an aberration and her inhibitions.

As he returned to bed, he saw Carol's naked back and buttocks. Tenderly and slowly, he pulled the sheets and comforter over her. She seemed as if she were held by a spell. Harry slid under the covers, nested on Carol's backside, and soon he too was under a spell.

Toward dawn, with the first perception of the morning, a dreamy image of his Tokyo lover, Naomi, drifted into Harry's mind. He saw himself in her bed, with her on top of him, rising up and down on him like a bronco rider.

In the deep recesses of his consciousness Harry wondered why after Carol's passionate lovemaking, did he look for other women?

The Last Temptations of Harry.

Does he have the guts to change his life?

Should he promise not to learn the date of his death and not keep the promise?

Harry had no answers. He closed his eyes, rolled over, and snored like a wart hog.

TEN

When Harry awoke the next morning, his eyes focused first on the darkened chandelier and later swept around the room and through the windows.

He saw the sunlight-strewn white lace window curtains blowing lightly in the breeze. He heard a chorus of songbirds chirping their unconducted songs. Feeling free from his worries he arose, naked, and walked to the window.

As he stood his arms extended to form an accidental cross. He turned back to see the sun behind him had cast his sharp, but rumpled shadow on the bed.

Autumn leaves, from spring's and summer's syntheses, spiraled from the tree branches on which they had nested to the waiting ground below.

Carol had left the room already. Harry always looked forward to seeing her and the kids. He'd eat a modest breakfast and then get on the treadmill as a part of his physical resurrection.

He paused to sit and see the lightly waving Douglas fir branches dropping their needles. By gosh, except for the dreadful Johnnie Allegro scare, Harry thought, last evening could not have been better. He thanked God for Carol and the kids. His shoulder was a little sore from Carol's twisting it, but he persuaded himself, a bit reluctantly, to dismiss the incident as irrelevant, perhaps related to shedding her inhibitions.

Things were good. But were they too good? He often asked himself that question. A lingering black cloud occluded the windows of his mind, and a subtle sense of uneasiness pervaded him.

Again, he tried to remember what he had to do that morning...he had something important to do, but could not pull up this task. His mind was a black TV screen.

Sleep-filled, he strode, still nude, to the black-and-white marbled master bathroom. He glanced at the nearly sheer nightgown hanging in the bathroom and concluded that Carol and the kids had already risen for their respective swim workouts.

Smells of coffee, breakfast cooking, and the music of Carol, Tim and Tess's voices wafted up to the master bathroom.

Harry soon stood, soaping his body, under the hot shower behind the slightly opaque glass panels. He chuckled as he remembered Carol's and Tess's challenge last night that he needed a bath "badly."

After the shower, he dressed in black and yellow sweats. Leaving their second-floor bedroom he glanced toward the den. The treadmill he was going to mount that day resided there. He was looking forward to his workout; he was going to have a beautiful day to glance at through the window.

Harry reached the winding, carpet-covered staircase, walked down to the entry hall, and passed by the front door on his way to the kitchen.

"Hey, Adkinses. Anybody get the paper this morning?" he greeted his family, pausing near the entryway.

"Hey, Dad. We're late for school. Better go get it yourself," called a voice from the kitchen.

"Who was your servant last year, Tess?"

"You were."

Harry opened the front door, noting his daughter had a way of getting whatever she wanted done for her.

He found the morning paper had landed in the bed of winter violets. He picked it up, scanning the front-page story about the escape and capture of Johnnie Allegro.

He entered the brilliant white kitchen. "Hi, Dad," chorused Tim and Tess, who sat at the table with Carol. They were eating breakfast cereal at a rapid rate. Torvil rendered a short "ruff."

Harry walked over to the radio and turned it on.

Carol looked a little startled and said, "I know you aren't here most weekday mornings, but we made a rule that neither the TV nor the radio are turned on before nine."

"Sorry about that," Harry said as he switched off the radio.

Tess took a big sniff as Harry sat down next to her, still clutching the newspaper. "Thanks for taking a shower."

He smiled and nodded affirmatively, giving her a shoulder hug. "You know, Tess, you sure tell it like it is." Carol winked at Harry, reached across the table, took his right hand, and squeezed it, seemingly, with great approbation. He squeezed her hand back and was at peace at the sunlit white-linen-dressed table. With his free hand Harry opened the morning paper to the front page.

A moment later, he said, "My God, Carol! We're in the paper."

"What's that?"

"Here, see this article." Harry passed the newspaper to Carol, with his finger pointing to the text, *Deputy Sheriff Notting found a note on the stolen white van's front passenger seat. The note, according to Notting, contained the street addresses of both Judge Standish, who presided over Allegro's trial, and of Harry Adkins, who served as jury foreman.*

Harry felt nauseated.

"Sweetheart, you look white..."

"I'll be okay. Close call. Gawd, I wonder how I would feel right now if the cops hadn't called last night."

"Let me read it, Dad."

"Let me finish the article first."

Torvil rested on his haunches at high alert as if he hoped little hands would surreptitiously get bits of food to him. They did.

"Looks like you're almost ready to go with Mom to school," Harry said.

He read his watch again and again with the sense that there was something he had to do.

"Okay, kids. Please finish your breakfast. Brush your teeth for one minute minimum and then we're leaving. Harry, since we're behind will you take care of the rest of the dishes?"

"Sure thing, but there's a price to pay."

"What's that?"

"A kiss for Harry."

Carol carried some of the breakfast dishes toward the sink, and as she neared him, she leaned down to him and they kissed, long enough to instill two tongue thrusts. Harry quickly patted Carol's left buttock.

"Nice, sweetheart," she whispered.

"Anytime. Nice smacks," he said back.

As he finished the article about Allegro, he thought, *what was it I was supposed to do? Call somebody? Did I have an appointment?*

As Harry heard the garage door coming down and saw the red Volvo station wagon leaving on their circular driveway, the phone rang.

"Hello, Harry Adkins here."

"It's Sally, Harry."

Oh, God. It's got to be Naomi. Forgot to call her. For which there will be hell to pay.

"What's up?"

"I've got Naomi on the other line from Tokyo. She's home. She sounds upset and, frankly, a little drunk. According to Naomi, Tom promised to tell you she expected a call from you at seven o'clock this morning, our time."

"Oh, my God. Tom did tell me. I forgot. Son of a bitch."

"What should I tell her? She's not real rational right now."

"Tell her I'll call her in ten minutes."

Harry breathed a sigh of relief that Carol wasn't here. What a break. He waited for several minutes, feeling moisture under both armpits and on his forehead. He glanced at his watch several times.

Sally's voice finally came back on the line. "Harry. Naomi said something like, 'Tell the bastard this needs to be restored; he'd better call in ten minutes or there'll be hell to pay' -- or words to that effect."

"Thanks. I'll call her in ten minutes."

"Please do." He thought Sally's tone was urgent and awkward.

Harry cradled the phone and looked across the kitchen. Hanging over the wall above the kitchen fireplace was Munch's *Scream*. That explained why Carol got up early: to move the picture from the den. But why did she move it? In the kitchen, the kids would be seeing the ghoulish thing; he'd try to talk Carol into moving it back to the den. But that would come later. For now, he thought he'd better hightail it to his home office over the garage.

He walked swiftly from the kitchen to his office on the second floor of the detached garage, his head and neck hung over his chest. He noted that for the first time he wasn't excited about having phone sex with Naomi; for once there was a sense it was wrong.

He gasped for breath after climbing the stairs to his office; he dreaded making the call. Could he possibly get out of talking with her? He sighed. Took a deep breath. Harry dialed her number and listened to her phone ring.

"Harry, is that you?" Naomi's voice.

With some fear, Harry spoke, "You know it's me. What's up?" Harry thought being a little cute might lighten the mood.

"My husband called me on his car phone, he's a few miles away," she sobbed. "If you'd called when you were supposed to, you would have had a good time. I'm all warm, wet, and naked, lying on my back, imagining you're on top of me. Oh, my God. I hear the garage door opening. He's here. I must go. Call me tomorrow. Goodbye for now. I love you."

"Where and what time shall I call?" *I should have said, I'm calling it off.*

"Call me at my home phone. Seven a.m. your time. My husband will be away."

Harry heard the phone click and uttered a big sigh. Sally had been right, Naomi was soused.

He heard the garage door under him opening. Carol was back from dropping the kids off. He noted his watch. *Maybe she'll make another pot of coffee for us?*

Harry dashed down the steps to the garage below. Carol sat behind the wheel and greeted him through the windshield with her great smile. He paused at the driver's door, smiling, before he opened it for her. As she emerged from the car, he bowed and widely swung his arm in the manner of a chauffeur. She played the sophisticated woman and affected a grand haughtiness.

Harry couldn't ignore the flickering image of Naomi lingering in his mind. *What should I do with that woman?*

Carol tugged on his sleeve. "Are you okay, sweetheart? You kind of zoned out on me."

"For some reason I drifted away."

"For a bright guy you're a little spacey sometimes. You were assisting me in getting out of my car."

"I remember. May I kiss Madame's hand?"

She drew herself nearer to Harry and looked into his eyes. "Of course, but Madame has many more interesting places to kiss than her hand."

They wrapped their arms around each other. They embraced closely.

"Since the kids aren't coming back anytime soon, let's have a roll in the hay," he said.

"*Monsieur…Oui!*" she squealed. Carol broke from the embrace and with delight on her face said, "Last one undressed and in bed is a party pooper." With that, Carol, with her dark, wine-colored leather purse flying on her arm, bolted toward the house and took the front porch two steps at a time. A plodding Harry followed behind.

She entered their front door first, headed for their bedroom, ascended three stairs, and suddenly grabbed her head. And held it with the palms of both hands. She sat down on the carpeted stair and screeched, "God, it hurts." Harry put his haunches on the carpet next to her and planted his right hand on her left shoulder.

"What's wrong?" he asked.

"God, I felt like some body builder just grabbed my head and squeezed it with both hands. This terrible pain hit me…No warning." She gasped. "It made childbirth -- even with twins -- a walk in the park. But…it's gone now." She lifted her hands from above her forehead and placed them on each side of her jaw with her fingers covering her ears.

"You're so white…not just pale…maybe you better lie down and have a cup of fresh coffee. And we'll go from there."

"I got kind of scared, sweetheart, with all that pain. But, oh, our garage hug really turned me on," she tweeted, wearing an embarrassed redness on her face now. "You know what, I'm still wet down there. Before the head pain hit, I felt like a bitch in heat. Yes. Let's go from there. Coffee sounds good. You do the coffee."

"Where are you on $H^2 L^2$, sweetheart?"

"You know, I have an appointment with a Dr. Dunne, the head honcho with the study, this afternoon…at two, I think."

"Oh. I'll be anxious to hear about it."

Harry fussed with the coffee preparation, as Carol rested at the breakfast table. He brought two large white mugs from the cabinet. Each cup featured a bright, round, yellow sun with a smiley face.

Harry poured boiling water over the recently ground coffee resting on the bottom of the French press and stirred the brew with a wooden spoon. He looked at his watch after he had placed the metal cap with the plunger on the circular brim of the press.

He glanced at his watch. "It's been four minutes," he said as he punched the plunger to the bottom of the press.

Carol said, "I just love the smell of coffee."

"Me too -- will you pour, Madame?"

"Of course, your highness." Carol filled both cups.

Harry glanced around the table. *Where's the cream? Oh no! No more cream. Wimpy skim milk instead?*

He reached into the fridge and seized the skim milk, and said, "Ta-da!" exhibiting it to Carol, and ostentatiously poured some into his cup, took a few sips, and exclaimed, "Gawd, that's good. Great. I'll never go back to cream. A small step to a healthier way of living."

"Sweetheart, I'm so pleased. Is this a signal you're committed to the study?"

They lifted and clashed their mugs and made contact with solid sounds that clinked through the kitchen.

Carol nodded and looked at her watch. "The twins won't be here for a couple of hours. My headache's gone. Is your recent offer for a roll in the hay still open?" She peeled off her red sweatshirt.

He grinned. "Yes. I'll take care of the answering machine."

ELEVEN

Harry rested on a straight chair in the reception area of Dr. Jonathan Dunne.

Always go to the top level of any organization, he reminded himself. He'd prospered by getting to the decision makers at the bank and the CPAs and the CEOs of companies that he wanted to make deals with. He didn't think this situation should be any different. After all, $H^2 L^2$ was a matter related to his life and death.

He viewed the reception room. It was about as sparse as Alex's. And, like hers, Dunne's decor was a bore, to make a bad poem he chuckled. He found himself happy about being in the study.

Harry held a pamphlet named "Beginner's Guide to Fitness," and had marked its pages with a bright yellow highlighter. He enjoyed its first line: "This book tells the neophyte how to get off his or her ass and begin a successful physical exercise regime."

Ah-ha! The guide included many frontal photos of voluptuous blonde women with generous cleavages mounted on stair-climber machines. *Damn, what I've been missing.*

The freshly lacquered door with a brass plate proclaiming Jonathan Dunne, M.D., Director of Studies, opened. A solidly built man, about five-foot-ten inches of great presence and bearing, stepped to where Harry sat.

So that's him, Harry thought. *Looks like a real character.*

Dr. Dunne wore a white cotton jacket that hung below his knees, signaling his high medical caste. Harry felt the warmth of Dunne's smile and noticed his dark, flashing eyes framed by curly hair that was mixed like coal and silver. Harry took note that Dr. Dunne wore a monocle, unusual for a twentieth century man. He resolved to ask Dr. Dunne why he wore one.

Dr. Dunne's eyes locked like radar on Harry's eyes. The world, according to Harry, demanded that eye contact and jarring handshakes be exchanged before any business began. *I'm going to like this guy.*

"Mr. Adkins, sir?"

With his hand extended and his million-dollar grin spread across his face he answered, "The one and only Harry Adkins, sir."

"Hello, I'm the one and only Dr. Jonathan Dunne out here, but inside my office it's Jonathan."

Harry smiled back. "And, I, sir, am known as Harry." Harry estimated Dunne's age to be sixty.

Dr. Dunne nodded at Harry. "Please come into my office." Harry accepted the doctor's proffered hand and felt as if his own hand had been caught in a grape press.

Dr. Dunne took Harry's upper arm gently at the elbow and led him into his office. Closing the door, he motioned for Harry to sit in a tastefully upholstered maroon chair; the doctor eased himself into a nearby maroon swivel seat.

"Dr. Dunne. Oops. Jonathan." Harry saw a glance of approbation from him. "Pardon me, but I'm an inquisitive person and I'm fascinated that you wear a monocle."

"Yes. Yes. You're not the only one who's asked. Listen to this: 'Into the jaws of death, into the mouth of Hell.' "

"Of course, it's Tennyson. 'Charge of the Light Brigade'...but what does that have to do with your wearing a monocle?" Harry saw a playful smile across the desk. He thought he might be taking a chance, but decided it was a good risk:. "You like to be enigmatic, don't you?"

"That's what my confessor tells me."

This guy likes fun. "Why a monocle? That is the question...Tennyson's your clue. I give up."

"Since you gave up, I will tell you. Alfred Lord Tennyson is a shirttail relative and he wore a monocle. I love his poetry. Besides, I like to think I'm a dandy."

"You *are* enigmatic."

"I plead guilty to the charge. I received a call from your family physician, and a close friend and colleague of mine, Alex Quick-Campbell. She said you expressed some insightful queries about the $H^2 L^2$ Study."

"You know, I did. First, sadly, as you probably have deduced, I'm overweight and out of shape -- to make a poor poem -- and my parents died at about age fifty of cardio-vascular diseases." Harry felt like he was being evaluated.

The doctor nodded. "Yes, yes. It sounds like you will probably qualify for the study. Did you walk up by the stairs to this second-floor office?"

"No. By elevator." *This guy has already sold me.*

"That's the sort of change you'll want to start making. No more elevators. It's legend that Dr. Paul Dudley White, President Eisenhower's heart man, always walked up at least six flights of a building's staircase. I attended a lecture from Dr. White when I was in pre-med. Yes. Yes. Quite a guy."

"Good point." Harry raised his eyebrows, *a la* Jack Nicholson, in awe of such an engaging man as Dr. Dunne.

"Yes. Alex said you wanted to hear the story of how and why we designed the study in the first place."

"You bet. I see my participation in your study could be the most important activity I've ever done. Believe me, Jonathan, I never go gently into any good journey."

"Yes. About five or so years ago, my secretary told me about an appointment I had with an Arnold and Mary Payne, farmers who had large land holdings in Redmond."

"I live on the Eastside, too. One of my biggest mistakes was not buying enough farm land," Harry added.

"The Paynes wanted to fund a grant to the SRI. My secretary told me one of our young staff physicians, Dr. Sophie Pillai -- she's from Bombay -- lived in a rental house owned by the Paynes. At that time, I knew Dr. Pillai only slightly. Apparently, the Paynes had talked with her about funding a study, and she referred them to me.

"Somehow, everything fit together and about six months later, the Seattle Research Institute, Dr. Pillai, and the Paynes reached an agreement. Yes. And six months after that, we had put this program together. Yes. Yes. I really admire Mary and Arnold. They never got much beyond the eighth grade. They're intelligent people but they're sure not grammarians.

"By happenstance, Mary Payne called me to see how the study was going. Among other things, I told her you wanted to find out everything about the program. Then Mary said, 'Do you think this Mr. Adkins would like to talk with me and Arnold and Dr. P and his own doctor, Dr. Alex?' "

Harry responded, "I understand you talked with Alex last night. She called me and asked if it would be okay with me if she talked with the Paynes. Of course, I said yes."

"Indeed, my friend. Alex teaches a class in the Seattle Research Institute, but she came in early to talk with the Paynes. The three of them couldn't have gotten along better. In fact, Mary said, 'You know, Dr. Alex, you and me were grafted from the same tree. I see a lot in you that's me.' "

Harry bet his own excitement showed on his face.

"Right now they're all in the conference room over there."

Dunne pointed to a set of double doors and glanced at his wristwatch.

"Oops. I think Alex had to leave for her class."

"Jonathan, I'd just love to talk with them."

Harry began to feel better and better about getting in the study, and, yes, about possibly taking the biggest gamble of all -- learning the actual predicted date of his death.

Dr. Dunne picked up a file with Harry's name on it.

"First, we have to deal with our bureaucracy. Please sign this consent to permit Alex to divulge your personal information to the Paynes and to us."

"How many attorneys were involved in the paper work? You needn't answer, but let me read the legalese."

Harry addressed Dr. Dunne. "I read it all. I've signed it. I'll take a copy of this."

"Of course. Let's go to our meeting."

Both Harry and the doctor arose. Dr. Dunne knocked, reached for the door handle, and pulled the door back. He stood aside to let Harry walk in first.

The room doesn't seem like anything special, Harry said to himself. It was just another dull conference room with a table with nearly two dozen wheeled chairs. The only unique quality was they were covered with gold cloth.

Brief introductions and handshakes were made all around.

Dr. Pillai held Harry's hand warmly. Her dark features contrasted with the white medical jacket she wore. She possessed grace and beauty. He noticed she wore lots of tasteful silver jewelry and that her engagement ring bore a large diamond.

Both Mary and Arnold looked into Harry's eyes, held their glances, and gave solid handshakes. He noticed that both of the Paynes were of average height and had calluses on their palms.

"You folks do much hands-on farming?"

"You bet we do. Did you say your name is Harry?" asked Mary.

"That's right," Harry affirmed.

"Well, I just knew you were an okay guy because my favorite uncle was named Harry. He was always slippin' a bunch of change to me on the side. He was always sayin', 'Mary, don't tell nobody 'bout it.'"

"What do you folks raise on your farm?"

"We've been growin' organic vegetables, potatoes, onions, lettuce, spinach, peas, kale, and God knows what else for years. We also raise sheep, chickens, and an occasional pig...and have a cow or two for milk and cheese. It's a way of life for us."

Harry closed his eyes when Mary was speaking and didn't hear any age-related cackling.

"You know, I had an Uncle Harry, too."

"You got to be kiddin'," Mary insisted.

"My Uncle Harry...his father -- my grandfather -- had worked with farm animals and vegetables for years. I spent two summers on the farm with him before I was ten. He wasn't much into organic, but I helped him a lot doing everything you do to raise and sell produce." Both Paynes seemed really pleased and gave Harry the feeling that he was all right with them.

Harry gauged the Paynes to be in their middle eighties. Arnold was kind of bent over, but Mary's spine was as straight as a hoe handle. Neither wore eyeglasses and both were attired in clean, but awfully old, clothes. Harry took heart when he peeked and saw Arnold and Mary holding hands below the table rim.

"Harry here is about to make a commitment to join the program," Dunne announced.

"But first, I'd like to ask some questions, if that's all right," Harry chimed in. His new acquaintances nodded. "Mary and Arnold, how did you come around to make your very large contribution to fund a study about the heart?"

"Why did me and Arnold want to make a grant to SRI? Like Arnold always says, 'we have a nickel or two to keep us going,' and there's plenty of other money and land out near Redmond which goes to our two kids who'll still be alive when me and Arnold go."

"But, our youngest, Skip, died in his early forties from a heart attack. Yup. He was a wonderful man, a provider and father and husband to our daughter-in-law and his children, but he was a Type A personality with the worst damn health habits ever. He drank too much, smoked cigarettes, chewed the filthy stuff too, was obese, had high blood pressure, ate all the bad food, rarely exercised, and God knows what else. Both me and Arnold had fathers and grandfathers who'd died real young of heart troubles. Skip kind of followed the same trail his grandparents and great grandparents did. Yup. They died early from bad stuff like heart attacks and strokes. To be honest -- Arnold always says I'm way too honest -- but I must tell you, you remind me a lot of Skip. Kind of in a hurry. Hard to sit still. I bet you're…what is the word? Impetuous? "Pretty overweight…Do you spend enough time with your kids?"

"You know, you got me pegged pretty good."

"Me and Arnold met Dr. Alex. She's kind of frank, tough, saucy, but sweet and pretty."

"Just like you used to be, Mary," offered a smiling Arnold.

"What do you mean 'used to'?"

Arnold sang, in good voice and in tune, "The old gray mare, she ain't what she used to be."

"Well, you ain't either, boy," Mary quipped, her tightly coiled white hair bouncing. Harry liked them.

At the mention of Alex, he recalled his recent emotions that sparked when he'd felt her brushing a breast on his arm.

Harry probed further. "How does that background affect what you had in mind for the study?"

"Our money would be used to study fellas like our son and grandfathers. And you too, Mr. Harry. We said that SRI would say what their estimated date of death was and help the men to change their lives and follow each one during his lifetime."

Harry challenged Mary and Arnold. "Why do you want these men to know what date they're going to die? Didn't you figure that's a kind of thing we humans shouldn't know?"

" 'Cuz me and Arnold figured if these fellas could know their date of death, they might work harder to change their lives so they could live longer than what they've been told by the Seattle Research Institute."

Good point, and my logic exactly. Harry turned. "Dr. Pillai, could you talk about the process of predicting the actual date?"

"Certainly. When I was in medical school in Bombay, I obtained a job in a longevity study where we predicted dates of death of large numbers of obese Indian men."

Harry saw Dr. Dunne was taking notes furiously, constantly shifting his array of pens and pencils. As Dunne briefly glanced up, he clearly showed pleasure at the way the conversations were going.

"...Mortality tables, like you use in this country but adjusted for our India," Dr. Pillai was saying. "And we used a risk analysis based upon genetic factors and all those departures from good health that Mary mentioned. Every man in the study who died of cardiovascular disease was followed, and the predicted dates of death were compared with their actual dates of death."

"Yes. Sounds very interesting. What role did you play?"

"I was one of those who made the final prediction. In all immodesty, some people claim I had some kind of clairvoyance about such things. I'm pleased to have been lucky or something because my predictions and the actual dates of demise had quite a high degree of correlation. The Indian Commission that did the study awarded me a commendation and allowed me to take the data to America."

"Yes." Dunne spoke up. "Harry, that's it in a nutshell. The Paynes gave us a million dollars for the study. We were convinced we might be able to make a significant contribution toward the enhancement of the lives of men. And we're hoping to answer this question: If the lifestyles are significantly changed for the better, will the men in the study group actually live beyond what we predicted? That's what we're going to study."

"You know...do you think many guys will exercise the option to learn the date you predict? Right now, I'm a little skeptical about learning the date," Harry asked.

"That's hard to say. Frankly, giving the patient an option to learn the date of his death has caused quite a ruckus here. But the Paynes were pretty adamant about offering it, and they insisted their vision for this study include the choice. As collaborators, we decided to let their idea stand, despite the heat we're receiving." Dr. Dunne play-acted as if he were wiping off his forehead.

"Who'll make the final prediction?"

"Probably Dr. Pillai."

"Doctor Pillai, you could have my life in your hands."

"Oh, come on now, Harry." She playfully slapped him on his hand. Harry interpreted this move as a come-on.

Harry felt something rapturous that came from his core. He had to talk privately with Dr. Dunne.

He had a hard time subduing the ear-to-ear smile he knew he projected. Sitting forward, and resting his forearms on the table he looked deeply into the eyes of the Paynes and Dr. Pillai.

"Thank you all for taking the time to meet with me; you've helped me make my decision about the study. Now, I think I need to talk privately with Dr. Dunne."

Dr. Pillai said, "Of course. It's getting late, anyway." After the soft touch of Pillai's hand, Harry now found himself thinking about a roll in the hay with her, and scolded himself.

"Oh, good, I was just gonna say, me and Arnold need to be headin' home pretty soon," Mary commented.

Arnold turned on a mischievous smile and said, "It's a good thing I married you, 'cause otherwise I'd have to make my own decisions. I haven't done that in years."

"Oh, come on now, Arnold. You make plenty of decisions."

"The only decision I make for myself is, well, when I'm going to pee."

The two of them laughed together as they strolled out of the room holding hands, followed by Dr. Pillai.

Harry and Dr. Dunne returned to the doctor's office.

"Harry. This morning I received good news that will help $H^2 L^2$. A few days ago, Sprint Communications Company announced it's working on a service which may make possible transferring medical images over phone lines from one computer to another. For instance, blood pressure kits at home might be able to transmit data by computers to the Seattle Research Institute."

"Kind of revolutionary. I always like to be on the proverbial ground floor!" Harry exclaimed.

"As you can tell, we're pleased."

"To abruptly change the subject, Jonathan, this is confidential -- really, really confidential -- but I'm going to go in the study and I'll find out what you've predicted as the date of my death."

Then Harry stood and closed his fist and pounded it into the palm of his other hand. "And, you know what?" he shouted, his voice growing louder and more passionate. "I'm going to get in shape -- I mean in great shape -- and change my lifestyle and beat your god dammed prediction! I'm going to defy death." Harry stood with his hands on his hips -- stridently.

"Harry, I admire you. My guess is that not many men have the guts to learn when they might die. I don't think it's something I'd want to know, nor would my wife."

"Thanks. What's the first step for all of this?"

"Complete an application." The doctor rose and walked to a file cabinet, reached in a gray file drawer, and pulled out a manila envelope. Returning to his desk, he handed the envelope to Harry.

"Yes. The application's in here."

Harry folded the envelope's metal clasps upright and pulled out a shaft of papers. He pulled his black horn-rimmed reading glasses out of his pocket and slid them over his nose.

Centered on the first page in large block letters was the title Healthy Hearts Live Longer ($H^2 L^2$).

"Just curious, Jonathan -- who thought up the name of the study?"

With a twinkle Dr. Dunne touched his chest with his finger and said, "Moi."

Later that dark December day, Harry worked on the $H^2 L^2$ Study Application, and finally reached the signing pages 19 and 20. The wind and rain pounded the windows with such force that the glass seemed to nearly bend, and he noted that the small boats tied up at the docks pitched and heaved, making their lines taut.

Page 18 read: *Upon completion of the H² L² Study, subject to the terms of the H² L² Application, we shall predict the date of your death based upon our evaluation of your medical condition.*

You shall have the option to learn of the predicted date of death or not to learn the predicted date of death.

After you have read the preceding pages carefully, please read and complete page 19. Please sign and date the application and consent form on page 20.

We ask you to consider registering for the "Willed Body Program" of the University of Washington Medical School. If you choose to do so, you will receive a letter from the University's Department of Biological Structure enclosing an identification card.

Harry buried his face in his hands. Again, he was at a brink. This choice may turn out to be the most important, the most fateful decision of his life. Most people don't know how long they will live. He had a choice to know or not to know. There was a certain power to making this choice, a kind of God-like omnipotence.

Warm sweat from his face, chest, and forehead flowed like a soft, summer shower. Why did he hesitate? Were the rigors of the study too intense? No, he had no trouble with that.

But, my God, he thought, what would it be like to know that the respected Seattle Research Institute had concluded I was going to die on a specific date? Isn't that overwhelming? What would the average Joe do if faced with knowing the date of his death?

In everybody's life, notices of death occur on any given day, like the obituary page in the newspaper, the media's fascination with death -- by accident, disease or intent.

What's the strategy? he asked himself. *All right. The strategy. Sign the "I DO WISH" box on page nineteen and circle it. Give Alex a copy of the application from the study in a sealed envelope for her file and place a copy in my bank safety deposit box.*

Good idea. He thought that if he decided not to tell Carol his choice and if she found a copy of the agreement at home or at his office she would know he had lied.

So his bank's safety deposit box it was. Only he had access to it and he, not Carol, paid the annual bill. There was enough room for Naomi's steamy letters in there, too. It shouldn't be a problem, he figured The box wasn't the most convenient spot for him to peek at it, even though he knew he didn't have the world's best memory for dates, who could forget the predicted date of his death! Even a turkey like Johnnie Allegro, who had a definite date for his death, would get more and more upset as time went by. Most people don't have a clue when they're going to go, except maybe those who are ill and have been given an *estimate* by their doctors but not a definite date. *You know, like Carol's grandma.*

Suddenly, Harry remembered his divinely brilliant idea: He would tell Carol the day *after* the predicted date of death when he would still be alive! Somehow, he would get another copy of the application. *Well,* he concluded, *I'm going to live long beyond that date.* He was going to get serious about diet and exercise.

He took his hands away from his face, inhaled a deep breath, and slowly blew it out. He had stopped sweating.

Harry got on his feet and walked from the desk he was using to the receptionist's desk. Looking at the placard "Sheri Ismus" he said, "Hi, Sheri. May I sit down next to your desk?"

A tall, early-thirties, peroxide blonde had big lashes that framed green eyes, and she wore a white nurse's jacket over a St. Patrick's Day green blouse with shiny gray buttons, the upper three unbuttoned.

"Of course, Mr. Adkins." As he stood next to her, looking down, a lot of her chest was on display. He looked around the reception area and said, "It's okay with me to call me Harry."

"I'll try. What can I do for you?"

"Well, you know, I just can't make up my mind about the $H^2 L^2$ form. I need to get a latte and a sweet and go outside on the patio and think about it. A pretty big decision, huh?"

Sheri dimpled her cheeks. "Yes. A big one." he reached to hold his hand.

He reconnoitered around the foyer again. Harry moved a little closer. She didn't move away. "I'd really like to have several copies of page 19…front and back. -- make it five -- and five envelopes. That way, I can practice on one or two, and see how I feel about it."

"I'll get 'em. Be back in a moment." She squeezed his hand. He responded.

Sheri scooted toward a filing cabinet and soon returned with the applications and five envelopes. He took the applications and envelopes from her.

Harry filed the papers in his briefcase and headed for the door. "I thank you…for everything…and I'll be back before five." The wall clock read three-thirty.

"Oh, thank you. You're such a nice man."

Harry responded by making a fist, punching his left hand into the air and saying, "Ta-da!"

Oddly relaxed for him, he strolled consciously, not hurrying at all, to the Seattle Research Institute cafeteria.

At the espresso stand, he ordered, "A grande, skinny mocha in a ceramic cup, no whip." He was proud of himself for not taking the whipped cream. *Harry, you're showing restraint already yet.*

Harry pulled out his money clip and watched the male barista's fingers and hands flying in and around the snorting, steaming, espresso machine.

Moments later, he took possession of his drink and paid for it, tossing a dollar bill in the tip pot.

Ah-ha! The sun's out now. Harry ambled out the door and spotted a picnic table a few feet away, which he quickly occupied. He took out the $H^2 L^2$ applications and the envelopes.

Harry smiled and got out his pen. The power to make his choice came from his soul. He circled "**I DO WISH**" to learn the predicted date of my death on page 19, and with a flourish he signed his name in the box beside it. He turned to the last page, signed his name again, and dated the form. *Damn good decision,* he thought to himself.

He stuffed the original application in one of the envelopes, which was addressed to SRI. He conformed two copies of the original, one of which he placed in an envelope and wrote Dr. Alex Quick-Campbell and Personal and Confidential on it and sealed it.

He signed and marked a copy of the document **I DO <u>NOT</u> WISH** learn the predicted date of my death. He would make a couple of other copies, one copy of which would go to Carol.

He thought of Sir Walter Scott's *What a tangled web we weave, when first we practice to deceive!* He entered the date to pick up the envelope from the study, on the first business day of January one year from now. Mentally patting himself on his back, he aimed to be there first thing Monday morning next year to learn the date. *That's one appointment I won't miss.* He would not tell Carol about the first business day in January; only he and Dr. Dunne would know that he would be picking up the prediction of his death date.

Harry turned in the original application to Dr. Dunne's receptionist.

He took out his notebook and wrote a list of things to do:

1. Consult a nutritionist.

2. Find a personal trainer.

3. Call Joe Kennedy at our law firm for an estate attorney.

4. Check life insurance quotes.

5. Check with Carol about school conference dates.

6. Read a book a month. Start with Mario Puzo's "Fools Die."

7. Talk with a minister?

8. Figure out how to cut off Naomi.

9. Get Willed Body Program info from UW Med School.

Lastly he wrote, *When get date of death prediction, code it and enter it in the extended calendar and on the computer, and also write "bullshit…pure bullshit."*

TWELVE

After Harry left the Seattle Research Institute, he spent the rest of the afternoon visiting the gym mentioned by Alex and picking up brochures and membership forms. He also decided, as a part of his change, he would not stop by the office for a few hours. Instead, he would drive directly home even though the time was 4:15 in the afternoon. He couldn't remember when he had ever left for home so early. Rolling down the driver's window as his car sat at a stoplight, he inhaled deeply; excited about the first steps he'd taken.

As always, a wave of self-doubt swarmed over him like the shimmering heat in a desert. He shouted, "Why the shit do I want to find out the day I'll die?"

Harry heard a voice coming from the passenger side of the adjoining car: "You talking to me, buddy?"

The man sneered at Harry and then turned to the driver of his car and pointed to Harry, saying, in a loudspeaker voice, "All sorts of Looney Toons out there, Mac."

A moment of road rage hit Harry until he started to roll again. *Let's see,* he reckoned, *there's a bottle of good champagne cooling in the cellar, so I won't have to make a stop.* Signing up for the $H^2 L^2$ study was something to celebrate. As he drove up the gravel driveway he honked three times and pressed the garage door opener. As he pulled in, Tim and Tess ran outside and waved with exuberance. Torvil barked and circled his family, and Carol stood behind.

Tess and Tim each grabbed one of Harry's hands, saying, "See all the A's we got on our papers at school!" and pulled Harry into the house, followed by the still-barking Torvil. Strolling behind her husband and kids, Carol appeared as if she couldn't be happier.

When they all arrived in the kitchen, Tess said, "Mom and Dad, please stay with Tim and me and don't go into the den until after dinner, please, please." Carol and Harry winked to each other on the sly and Carol said, "Agreed."

"Why don't you go into the family room and show Dad your school papers? Before you know it dinner will be on the table."

Taking Tim and Tess by the hands, Harry said, "Sounds good to me. But first, kids, we need to go to the wine cellar and get some champagne for Mom and Dad and some sparkling cider for you guys, you know?"

"Dad, you should say 'yes' instead of 'you know,' " instructed Tess. As bossy as she could be Harry was proud of her boldness. He thought it would be okay for her to grow into a strong woman. "I'll work on that. I promise." Grinning at Carol, he said, "A facet of Harry's Reformation." He caught a pleased look from Carol.

"What's Harry's Reformation?"

"I'll tell you at dinner, Goldilocks."

"My name is Tess, not Goldilocks, and you know that."

"Come on, gang, let's go to the wine cellar."

The champagne and sparkling cider procurement crew soon returned and placed the bottles on the dining room table. The table was dressed with a muted white linen tablecloth, matching napkins, flickering candles, and full table settings of Carol's best silver.

"Come to dinner, please."

Harry perked up from the couch he'd been relaxing on in the den. Next to him, Tim and Tess had been playing a word game with one another.

"Tim and I'll take your hand and take you into the dining room, and please let us seat you."

"Who's going to seat your mom?"

"Tess and I will seat Mom, too," Tim piped up.

"Thanks, Tim."

"You're welcome."

As Harry poured the bubbly, he felt a tropical glow on his cheeks and face as they all reached across the table and clinked glasses. He winked at Carol and she winked back, undetected by the kids. Harry recognized another moment of growth. It passed through his mind that had he not signed on with $H^2 L^2$, he no doubt would be in his office at *Nippon/USA* and maybe even pre-occupied with phone sex with Naomi instead of at dinner with his family. A twinge pinched the inside of his stomach. Parting with Naomi frightened him because he felt she obsessively fixated on him. Soon, except for Harry, the family had been seated.

"Dad, are you okay?" asked Tim.

Harry realized he alone still stood next to his usual place at the table. "Sweetheart, come back from wherever you are and be with us."

"You know…Oh! Oh! A piece of our business came out of sync today. Had to repair a small fracture in a relationship at the Hitachi Company today. I was reflecting on that. Sorry."

Harry sat down and announced, "I'd like to say grace tonight, despite my relative inexperience."

"Sure," said Carol, "I'm pleased our family is making some powerful changes."

Harry bowed his head and folded his hands. "We thank you for our wonderful family, our situation in life, and this delicious meal we are about to eat. We also give thanks for Tess and Tim and their good grades." Harry realized he was choked up and struggled to regain his composure. His eyes moistened, and he could not brake the joyful tear that rolled down his cheek. Tim picked up his napkin and extended it to his dad. Taking the napkin, Harry daubed his cheek and patted Tim's shoulder.

"Thank you." All the Adkinses seemed to be caught in the moment, as if they all recognized that something profound had just happened to Harry. No one spoke; for a couple of minutes they were engaged in some serious passing of overflowing food dishes up and down the table. Even Torvil appeared subdued, not that he wasn't ready to pounce on table droppings. Harry slowly took in the smell of the food, especially the fragrance of garlic.

Within minutes, Naomi had almost fully occupied Harry's mind again. There was something about the silence that made her creep back into his mind. Harry thanked God that no device could transmit the images and thoughts he'd been having to Carol or the kids. Harry thought. *Is such a device foreseeable?*

"*Mademoiselle* Tess, would you care to enjoy another round of the kid bubbly?"

"*Oui, monsieur,*" she said gleefully, and Harry poured the sparkling cider.

With similar procedure, he again poured kid bubbly into Tim's glass. "Dad, we asked you to explain Harry's Reformation," he piped up.

"Oops. Yes. Harry's Reformation. Ah. Yes. Alex had me sign up at the Seattle Research Institute for a study to see if middle-aged guys like me, who aren't in the best shape, could change their lifestyle." The kids listened attentively, Carol skeptically.

"The object is to see if the men could improve their health so that they might be able to live longer."

He went on. "Harry's Reformation means I'll be devoting myself to regular exercise, eating properly, and cutting down on my drinking."

"You know, I've got a good smeller; so if you do drink alcohol, I would know."

"Er...uh...Yes. Tess. You know, I've got an idea. For each time you catch me drinking, except during Christmas, and my birthday, and on weekends, I'll put a dollar in a piggybank for vacations. But on the other days, when I'm good, I want you guys to put a gold star on the calendar. Agree?"

"Agree!" shouted both kids.

"Daddy and...I mean *Dad* and I have a Christmas surprise."

Tim and Tess brightened. "What is it?" Tim asked. Harry reveled in the excitement in his kids' eyes.

"During Christmas week, Little Harry, Tony, Alex, and Tom will be in Boston celebrating Alex's parents' forty-fifth wedding anniversary. So, they're going to let us use their Sun Valley condo."

"Does it mean we get skis and ski stuff?" asked Tim excitedly.

"We must take Torvil!" announced Tess.

"If it's okay with Mom," Harry said to both of them.

"Please, Mom?" They both said in unison, turning to Carol.

"If -- and this is a big if -- you are careful, then you may ski. And if you two will be Torvil's principal caregivers, then he goes to Sun Valley. Understood?"

"Oh, sure, Mom! Torvil, you get to go to Sun Valley!" Tess shouted. Perking up his ears, Torvil got up from under the table and sat between the children. He did his usual routine of serious tail waving and face-kissing, as the children reached down and hugged him around his head and shoulders.

Harry awakened from a short nap and noted a lovely blue-sky-framed photograph of Bald Mountain in Sun Valley, Idaho, after a fresh snowstorm. It hung over the fireplace mantle of Alex and Tom's condominium.

He stood up, stretching his arms and shoulders. Carol had curled up in a large stuffed chair with a Hemingway short story collection on her lap. Harry noted the story title was "The Short Happy Life of Francis Macomber." Tim and Tess played checkers on the coffee table near Harry.

He strode in a gimpy fashion -- he guessed from today's ski lesson -- to a window and peeked outside to see the night's darkness settling on the snow. An abundance of outdoor green and red holiday and porch lights appeared on the nearby apartment doors.

He pointed to the window and said, with glee, "Sun Valley is getting blessed by a snowstorm."

Tess and Tim quickly abandoned their checkers game and sped to the front door, said something to each other, which Harry missed, and sprinted to their mother's chair.

Torvil suddenly awakened and bolted for the entry hall.

The twins grabbed one of Carol's arms. As Tim was jumping up and down, he earnestly proposed, "We want to make a huge snowman."

"Yes, yes," Tess joined in. "Mom, would you guys help?"

Harry and Carol stared at each other and brought up both arms, as if to ask, what else could they do? *Doggone it. I'm really beat up from the ski lesson. But, going out in the bitter cold and deep snow with the family is part of Harry's Reformation.*

Carol gave orders that all participants, except Torvil, get on their after-ski boots, hats, and gloves. "Everybody pretend you're in the Army and I'm your leader."

Carol, who was taking her duties seriously, lined up the Snowman Crew including Torvil for inspection in the entry hall.

She walked by each family member and carefully examined them. "Tim and Tess, I declare you are qualified Snowman Crew Members."

Carol paused, and added, "Torvil, you qualify, too," and gave him a good pat on the head, which produced a good deal of tail wagging.

"Mr. Adkins."

"Ma'am." He saluted and stood at attention.

He saw Carol's eyes. Her effort at keeping the thing serious was getting out of hand and he could tell she was about to explode in laughter. "In order to pass inspection, you must substitute your ski gloves for your leather ones."

"Hut. Excuse me while I get in compliance, Ma'am," Harry responded.

"You are excused -- momentarily."

Harry grabbed his ski gloves, displayed them, and then placed them on his hands.

Carol ordered, "Forward, March!" They left the entry and stepped into the deep, dry snow.

Harry called, "I'm getting Tom's snow shovel in the condo. Go ahead."

The snow shovel and Harry soon appeared. The Crew had moved massive amounts of snow, but it was apparent that the snow was so cold that neither a Snowman, nor, for that matter, more critical, a Snowwoman, could be sculpted.

The adult part of the disappointed Crew moved slowly, single file, through the waist deep snow, which translated to chest-deep for the kids, and somehow Torvil found a way to get to the porch.

After a struggle, all but Torvil hung their outside garments into what Carol captioned the "snow room."

"Oh, my. I'm really glad we're eating in tonight." Carol held a piece of a pizza in her hands. Harry decided, *you know, all in all, things are pretty great.*

They again populated the living room while Carol nuked the previously uneaten pizza.

"Sweetheart, will you please pass the claret? I need it to finish off my pizza." The wine was passed. Carol filled her glass about half full.

"Did you kids like the pizza?"

"Mom, this is even better than Pietro's Pick-Up Pizza at home."

"Yes," agreed Tim.

Tess leaned close to Harry and sniffed.

"Darn."

"Huh?"

"You don't have to pay five dollars because you haven't

been drinking."

"Thank God for small favors."

Still standing next to Harry, Tess said, "Where did your ski instructor take you to ski today?" Harry heard a saucy tone in Tess's voice.

"My darling daughter, you do not intend to embarrass your old dad, do you?"

"Oh, no, I would never want to embarrass my darling father."

"How can you say that, darling daughter, when you show your mischievous eyes?"

"Who? Me?" Tess was being her in-your-face self Harry realized.

"Yes."

"Dad, how come your class isn't skiing on Baldy?"

"Because a few of us aren't ready to ski Baldy."

"Are you?"

"Well, no. You know. I'm just a beginner. And besides, I'm not in very good shape. Out of breath. I'm slowly getting used to being at six thousand feet here on the Valley floor."

"Tim, Mom, and me are beginners too, but we ski Baldy. You ski Dollar."

"I'll ski Baldy before we leave or die trying."

Suddenly, Harry again remembered the study would predict his death. It struck him more occasions would arise -- *God knows how many* -- when casual hackneyed sayings referring to death like, To die for, Died and went to heaven, and the like, would come up. How would he handle such offhand references? Best to ignore them. Not call attention to it.

"Ha-ha. Tess, it's two games of checkers for me to zero for you," boasted Tim.

"Did somebody call me?" Harry asked. Torvil lay on his side, asleep, adjacent to the brick fireplace. He noticed Torvil's feet were moving as if he had been running, but Torvil was dreaming. Just like himself.

"No, sweetheart, Tim just announced he was ahead in checkers two games to zero."

Harry felt that just getting up from the overstuffed leather maroon chair was getting to be a work in slow progress. "My God, am I ever stiff after only two days of skiing." He struggled to straighten his body to get more or less perpendicular to the floor.

He noticed the fire's orange and yellow tongues still lapped far off the grate. The family's ski boots, no longer active, rested on the wool carpeting near the hearth.

"You asked me," Carol said, "when we were driving near Boise if we should think about getting our own condo here."

"You know, you were kind of cool to the idea. I wasn't proposing anything, just thinking out loud."

"Well, it was cloudy and cold and blowing. Then we were near...um...Fairfield...And you had to pull off the road because we simply couldn't see. But, after we had been skiing a couple of days and the sun came out...Well, I'm exercising my prerogative."

"Oh, yes...the divine right of a woman." Harry saw gleeful sparkles in Carol's eyes.

"Precisely. But...why does 'pig' come to mind?"

Harry cradled his head in his hands and reacted to Carol's smile, grinning, and said, "You're not definitely labeling me an M.C.P?"

"Not definitely."

"You're in a rare mood tonight, my dear."

"I'm really, really happy to be here. I've fallen in love with Sun Valley." Carol glanced toward the children, looked back at Harry, placed her right forefinger in her mouth, and moved her finger slowly in and out seductively. Without taking her eyes off Harry, she placed the bookmark in her book and rested it on a nearby table. Harry saw her eyes dancing as she crossed the few feet between them and sat down on the well-upholstered arm of Harry's chair.

She shot a glance at the children who were immersed in their checkers game, sat with her back to them, and dexterously moved her right hand on his interior thigh.

As she got up from the arm of the chair, she whispered in his ear, "Time for all of us to bed down," and blew a little puff into his ear before walking slowly to the checkers game.

"It's getting late, kids, time for bed. You too, Torvil."

"Oh, Mom. Come on. I think I have a move that would win the game for me."

"Just leave all the checkers as they are and finish tomorrow."

"Oh, Mom."

"Scoot. Both of you to bed." Carol gave the children an endearing hug. Harry thought Carol sure had been a great mother to their kids.

Both Tess and Tim headed off for the loft, threw kisses, and said, "Good night, Mom and Dad."

Later, Harry rested in bed on his side and read a paperback. Then, Carol climbed under the covers and aligned the front of her bare body along his backside, and draped her arm over his shoulder. He said softly, "Oh, boy."

She removed his novel from his hands and placed it on his nightstand, turning out the light.

"Carol. How's your headache?"

"Pretty much submerged since we've been here. I have a great idea, sweetheart."

"What's that?"

"Let's meet in Ketchum tomorrow. In the Pioneer Saloon bar. I'll check my skis for an overnight tune-up at Warm Springs and take KART from Warm Springs. We could have a drink and then drop in one of the realtor's offices to shop for condos."

"You know, that sounds like an idea. What time?"

"How's five?"

"You know, there should be plenty of time for me to go to the condo and leave my boots. Then take the KART bus to Ketchum."

"Also, we need some adult time away from the kids. Sometimes too much togetherness is a little smothering...for all of us. Now roll over on your back."

Several hours later, Harry awakened. He wore no clothes. He heard Carol crying softly.

He moved close to her and placed his arm over her. "Are you okay?"

"I don't know...I got up an hour or so ago with a terrible headache, the likes of which I've never had before. I took some aspirin, which helped a little bit. I was kind of scared."

"Oh, my gosh. I do remember you hurting awhile ago when you

were running upstairs."

"I really never had one like it. Oh, my. We're necked as jaybirds." Her tone brightened a tad. "We'd better get our 'jamas on and snuggle up close together." They both donned their pajamas and cuddled.

"Thanks for the wonderful lovemaking."

"You're welcome. And thank you. How's your headache now?"

"Marginally better. It will be better soon. I know."

Soon, Harry heard Carol lightly snoring.

After they had returned from Sun Valley, Harry congratulated himself on cutting down on the booze and fatty food intake. He and Carol now walked together every day and she had not complained about headaches since the big one in Sun Valley. He assumed they were both feeling good after their trip.

The Seattle Research Institute study held its orientation session in early January. The program included about forty fat guys of his vintage. So far, he'd lost fifteen pounds from working out at the club every other day. He didn't stay late at the office much. All in all, he thought things were going well.

Carol and Harry had bought a Sun Valley condo, in the same complex but in a different building than Alex and Tom's. They decided to remodel their unit and enjoyed weekly planning sessions at Des Moines Crossings, still blessed with Henri's French cuisine.

One particular night in mid-February the two decided to have a dinner meeting. Harry was happy to spot Henri Eiffel as soon as they were seated, and he beckoned to him.

Henri came over, attired in his customary black tuxedo complete with a red cummerbund. He stood six-foot plus and wore a perpetual smile, except at those rare times when a real or imagined culinary disaster intervened. Henri constantly carried a white linen cloth napkin over his sleeve. A black Salvador Dali mustache curled under his aquiline nose. He claimed to have been born, unexpectedly, on the top level of the Eiffel Tower, which accounted for his parents giving him the middle name of Eiffel, but Henri had changed it to his surname.

Bowing, Henri said, *"Bonjour, Madame, Monsignor.* May I serve you on this Valentine's Day?"

"Henri, so we can study the menu longer we'd like the usual champagne."

"Oui, Monsignor. In a moment, sil vous plait."

Carol moved her chair toward Harry's, and soon he felt her thigh against his. Their table's flickering candle cast images on Carol's clear complexion. She laid her hands on his hands.

"Happy Valentine's Day, sweetheart."

"Happy Valentine's Day," he replied. For a few minutes, they studied the menu and each other, occasionally squeezing hands. *"Pardon, Madame and Monsignor."*

"Huh? Oh. Henri, we got distracted."

"Monsignor, one of the distractions of being in love." He stood holding two champagne glasses and a bottle, teeming with its cold sweat.

"May I pour?"

"Oui, sil vous plait, Henri," Carol answered graciously.

"Oui, Madame."

"Give us just a few more minutes to order."

"Oui, Madame."

Harry and Carol each picked up a glass, intertwined their right arms and held their wine ready. Henri poured to an inch under the rim and retreated from their table. They said "Happy Valentine's Day" again, chimed each other's goblet, and sipped the golden "adult bubbly."

"I bought a book for us to read and practice with. Go ahead and open it," Carol said, slipping out a gaily-wrapped loud-red package tied with loud-pink ribbons from under the table.

"Thank you," he said, beholding Carol's sparkling eyes as he fumbled with the wrapping paper. He saw delight and pleasure in those eyes. "Oh, my gosh. *The New Joy of Sex"* he exclaimed, holding up his copy.

"Yes. Alex's parents gave her the original *Joy of Sex* when she was sixteen. And Alex loaned it to us on our first time in bed, remember?

"And then Tom and Alex gave us our own copy of the original at our Marriage License Celebration." She held his hand tightly. He felt no one had ever been as intense with him before, not even Naomi, who went beyond intensive to obsessive. *Oh, God, why does Naomi come into my consciousness at a time like this?*

"Remember that afternoon we were engaged?" she asked softly.

"How could I ever forget it?"

"You don't know how hard it was for me to…place my hand on your fly, et cetera. I really was embarrassed when you told me you could see my breasts, when I leaned over to pick up your boater…"

As it had been back then, a small froth of perspiration lay on her forehead.

Breathlessly, she continued, "You see, I was raised with admonitions from my mother that I should never be sexy with a man until I was married. And I should never, never be aggressive, even after being married. Tell me the truth, sweetheart. What were your feelings about my sexuality, beginning with the first days after our Seattle wedding?"

It was clear to Harry it was hard for her to ask him such a question, even after all their years of marriage. He took a deep breath and said honestly, "I was a little concerned. You seemed pretty shy about it. But, of course, the moments before the lightning strike…Ooh la. But, remember, after my parents' deaths, as I told you, I was pretty promiscuous and had done all sorts of kinky sex with women."

"*Ménage a trois?*"

"*Oui.*"

"I have to tell you I have some friends who have had their husbands cheat on them." Carol lowered her voice and appeared as serious as he had ever seen her.

"Now, I'm not asking any questions, but I know you come from a different background, and I've noticed some changes in you in recent years that make me think. I want to be your exclusive lover *par excellence* and know you would never cheat on me, and I can't say that I feel that way right now. My father did that.

"There was another occasion I never told you about besides the time my brother and I saw him with the floozy. My mother had left town to go to a funeral, and my father had the temerity to take *another* lover to the guest cottage on our property. I was about thirteen. That enraged me. I got up in the middle of the night and took my dad's thirty-eight caliber out of his den and was on my way to the guest cottage when Chad came back home and saw me carrying the gun.

"He took the gun from me after chewing my butt. But he had me help him slash the tires on our dad's girlfriend's car. That woman never came back to our place. I hate the idea of cheating, and I despise the thought of you doing it too. I had to tell you that has been on my mind lately."

"Were you really going to shoot your dad?"

"Honestly, I don't know if cartridges were even in the chamber."

The conversation left Harry a little perplexed.

THIRTEEN

"Harry, do you like it here?" Naomi blew smoke from her nostrils.

A few hundred miles south of Bangkok, Harry saw the well-lighted beachfront and heard the waves from the Gulf of Thailand lap on the sand of Cha-Am. They had eaten dinner on a beachfront table and now watched the palm trees waltzing in the late-night wind.

"You know, this is about as good as it gets. We're close enough to Bangkok but far enough away to relax. Light up one for me."

"Waiter," beckoned Naomi, "bring us another champagne bottle."

"Yes, *Mademoiselle.*"

"Before we make love tonight let's do a joint. Oh, let's toast the big business deal we put together in Bangkok. We deserve to take a few days off down here." He noticed she slurred her words more than she had at dinner. Her wine was clearly catching up with her.

She added, "Tom will be proud of us--a real coup."

The waiter brought the champagne and poured two tall and slender ice-cold glasses. Naomi emptied half of hers in one gulp then snubbed her cigarette in the ashtray. Pulling a fresh one from the pack, she said, "Please give me a light, darling."

"Thank you, my darling lover," she whispered. With every pet name, he wondered how he could get out of this relationship.

"I've been thinking: it's been several years since I've been in Seattle and I need to renew my acquaintances with our customers. Don't you think so?"

"Whatever you think," he said passively.

"I wonder if I could be more effective if you could get another manager for here and I could be assigned to Seattle?" She batted her eyes at him. One look at her face showed her request was far from business-related.

Harry thought he'd better field this one carefully. "Have you discussed this with Tom? He's the head of Human Resources, you know."

"I have, and he said it's your decision, darling." Naomi sounded as if she had been confronted. *Thanks a lot, Tom. Don't do me any more favors like that, partner.*

"Why don't you send a memo to Tom and me and then the three of us could discuss it?"

"I'll do it. Do you think that Tom suspects we're lovers?"

"Frankly, when you called in November and were angry you couldn't reach me, I think he could have suspected something. I would appreciate it if you would keep your cool about our relationship."

"Does Carol suspect anything?"

"I don't know. But, I really don't want you calling me at home."

Harry knew he had spoken harshly, but he was sore. It was about time he finally brought it up.

"What would happen if Carol did find out? Would she divorce you?" Naomi leaned in close, her voice in a hush.

"I just don't know if I want to answer your question."

"But, darling, you told me you didn't think she would."

"The last time she talked about her possible actions if she learned of any infidelity, she told me about the time she took her father's gun out and was thinking of shooting him because he'd screwed his lover on the family estate. You take it from there." He glared at her.

"The talk has become too serious. Let's think about making love tonight. God. I'm hot for you. Let's go to my room before I start humping you here -- in the sand." She giggled as she rose unsteadily. There was no doubt she was drunk and obsessively passionate. He held her up with one hand and carried the champagne bottle with the other. On the way to her room the two of them nearly finished the full bottle.

As they left the elevator, Naomi took off her clothes, a garment at a time, and dropped each item on the hallway floor, leaving them for Harry to pick up. Each time she removed an item she paused to lean heavily on the wall or sit on the floor. The walk down the hall took nearly ten minutes. By the time they got to their room she had shed all her clothes except for her panties. She never wore a bra.

Harry inserted the room key into the lock. He was so drunk it took him several tries to open the door.

As he struggled, Naomi rubbed her body against his, holding on to him for stability. She slurred filthy language as they stood outside the door. He missed her words but received her frantic message.

Finally, he opened the door. As she staggered through the doorway, he could barely make out her mumbles to the effect she was slipping into "something more comfortable" and would be ready for him in a few moments. Harry obediently moved to the bed and decided not to take off his tropical shirt and short pants, which he knew would infuriate Naomi.

Through the haze of smoke and drunkenness, it came to him. He wanted to be with Carol. But, maybe Carol when she learned of his lecherous life with Naomi wouldn't want him. Harry snuck a glance at his watch. It was two on Sunday morning here and noon on Saturday at home. He visualized Carol sitting at lunch with Tim and Tess. Of course, Torvil sat on his hind legs at full alert for food droppings.

Naomi, totally nude, returned from the bathroom smoking a joint. Harry turned his back to her as she crawled into bed.

"Here, darling, take a big draw." Her words were just barely intelligible. She delicately placed the joint in his mouth. "Why are you wearing clothes? Let your lover take them off." Harry took a big draw on the joint.

Naomi leaned over and began to unbutton his shirt. Harry ripped the joint from his mouth and snubbed it on the ashtray.

"Darling," she asked as she continued to sloppily unbutton his shirt, "Why did you do that?"

As he sat up, Naomi made a clumsy effort to straddle him.

He made a quick move and rolled off the bed. Looking down at her, he glared at her through blurred vision. He was unsteady on his feet, reeling from too much booze and too many joints, but his anger was clear.

She screamed, louder than anyone Harry had ever heard, "God, I want to devour you."

"I just can't continue our relationship. I'm going to tell Carol, come what may," he said calmly.

Naomi became hysterical. Great sobs erupted from her. As if in a nightmare, her soprano screams of "No, no, no! I must have you!. I'll kill myself!" pierced the darkness.

Tumbling off the bed, she crawled to his legs. She got on her knees, wasted. She continued to cry as she wrapped one arm around his legs and reached for his fly with the other.

He broke away, leaving her a lump on the floor. "Keep away from me," he demanded.

"Please drop your shorts and we can make up -- yes. I'll come over and take you right there. It's better when we make love after a fight," she breathed, her voice dripping with desperation. Naomi started to waddle over to him with her arms outstretched and tears running down her face.

Harry eyed her skinny neck and throat and suddenly was compelled to shut her up. He moved toward her with both hands out, his anger engulfing him.

Still on her knees, she half-cried and half-smiled in an attempt to seduce him. He felt he did not want to be with her. Her hands went to his fly again and she started to pull his zipper down. Opening her mouth wide, she was frantic, shouting, "Let me have you, let me have you!"

Harry lost control of himself. He had no power over his hands. He wrapped them around her slender throat and slowly tightened his grasp. She responded first obsessively, then quizzically, then fearfully. He touched the front of her neck and began to push it in.

She coughed.

Her scream evolved to a retch.

Harry heard a frantic knocking on the door of the room. "Open door! Security."

His power returned to his hands and he released Naomi's neck. She looked up at him and felt her throat. With her face on the floor, she coughed and gagged. He offered his hand and pulled Naomi to her feet.

"Come with me to the front door," he ordered. "Lean on me. We need to talk with the hotel people." Naomi complied.

In a loud voice, Harry bellowed, "Just a moment, we'll be right there!" He pulled a white bathrobe off of the bed and placed it over Naomi's slender frame.

Finally, he opened the front door with Naomi holding his arm. In the hall stood two Cha-Am male hotel employees.

Harry smiled and bowed to them. It was Charlie One, the wily reception guy, and Charlie Two, the inscrutable security guy.

"Good morning, my friends. I know why you're here. We were making too much noise. We're both actors and we were practicing a scene. I think we, as they say, got into the play too truly, madly, deeply. Isn't that right, Naomi?"

"Yes, that's what happened." Naomi had been covering the front part of her throat with her sleeve, and then she dropped her arm and her throat appeared red.

Harry felt his eyes narrow as he guessed her ploy was to let the two men know something had happened to her.

Harry noticed that Charlie Two scrutinized Naomi's neck under her ears. It seemed to Harry there was some kind of an abrasion under her left ear where his left hand had been. He'd better seize power once more.

"Charlie One, we're very sorry if we disturbed your other guests and you. Please tell those people how this disturbance came about, express our apologies, and give anyone who complained about us a bottle of champagne and put it on my room bill." He reached into a pocket in his dress shorts and handed a roll of bahts to each man.

The reception man said, "Thank you, Mr. Adkins." But Harry suspected Charlie Two wanted more. He scowled at Harry, and eyed Naomi's neck before whispering to Charlie One who, luckily for Harry, just shrugged off Charlie Two.

"Good night," said Charlie One. They all bowed and Harry and Naomi went behind the closed door.

Naomi pressed her body into Harry's. He felt her pelvis poking through the robe. She presented a dismissive smirk, and he noticed her looking at her reflection in the room's mirrored closet door. "Are you grateful, Mr. Adkins?"

He wondered *what's she up to?*

"Grateful for what?"

"If I hadn't played your game and had told them the truth that you were trying to choke me to death, we wouldn't be having this conversation. You might be in a Thai jail."

Harry was stunned.

"Darling, you were out of control, maybe it was the booze,

maybe it was the joints. But, man, you went crazy. I think I'd be dead if those hotel people hadn't knocked on the door. I can say I was seeing the first fringes of death. My throat is still sore. See the red marks?" She threw the white robe on the sofa and placed both hands on her throat, as he had done to her.

"That's absurd," he spat back. *What was Naomi up to? Harry got the drift and didn't like it.*

"In fact, I'm still a little afraid of you. But, knowing this resort has now posted a security person close to my door I'm not as scared. And darling, we can keep what happened just between us." Harry knew that Naomi had cut the cards just right. *Oh, shit.* Would he ever get this woman out of his life? He looked toward the door.

"You want to check it out, darling?"

"No."

"We both need a shower. Let's save Thai resources and bathe together."

She came over to Harry and finished unbuttoning his shirt. She took off his outer and under shorts and led him to the bathroom. Harry knew he had lost the first round in severing his ties with Naomi. In fact, the ties that bind may have tightened. Things were bad enough with having to tell Carol about Naomi, but Gawd, now the choking incident, too?

Damn. Suddenly, he succumbed to an overpowering lust for Naomi as they embraced under the drenching warm shower.

At about six in the morning he left Naomi's room feeling dreadful, with a pulsating headache and a booze, joint, and sex hangover. Before closing the door, he went back and stood next to the bed. He stared at her slender, almost boyish hips. He may have had affection for her at one time, but now his only emotion as he stood there was pity, laced with anger for her manipulation and his own lack of contrition for cheating on his wife. Harry said out loud, "Harry, you're a no-good bastard."

She stirred, but didn't open her eyes. "Naomi," he said in a conversational tone. She still gave no response. "It's over, Naomi. All over. Forever." She rolled over and snored loudly. He closed her door to the hallway.

Charlie Two stood at "Parade Rest" opposite Naomi's door.

"Good morning, Charlie Two," Harry offered. In response, Charlie Two held out his hand and said, "Please to pay for the rest of the night, Mr. Adkins." Harry thought he was being held up -- again. Once more, he reached into his dress shorts and pulled out a fistful of bahts.

Knowing that Charlie Two knew little Japanese, Harry smiled as he pressed the bahts in Charlie Two's open palm, smiled, and said the Japanese equivalent of "fuck you, you bastard," which was acknowledged by Two with a smile and a "Thank you, Mr. Adkins."

He walked about fifty feet to his own room. With a sigh he unlocked the door and kicked off his shoes. His room phone's message light flashed red. Curious, he dialed the message desk number.

Harry recognized Charlie One's voice: "Hello, Mr. Adkins. I got a call for you earlier tonight."

"Yes?"

"Yes, sir. I took the message about two-thirty in the morning, just after we visited Ms. Naomi's room. It was from Mrs. Adkins. She said it was noon Seattle time. She was worried because you did not answer your phone. I told her that I thought you had gone for a walk because you told me you could not sleep."

"Thank you, Charlie. How soon could I get to Bangkok? Just me, Charlie One."

"Without Ms. Naomi?"

"Yes."

"I get you on the way to Bangkok in less than thirty minutes."

"Great. I'll check out and be at the front desk in twenty minutes."

"I will call Charlie Two and have him keep an extra eye on Ms. Naomi until you leave."

"I'll bring more bahts for you to thank you for all your help, specifically with Mrs. Adkins."

"Thank you, sir. And I will do my best to prevent any problems from Ms. Naomi."

PART II

ONE YEAR SINCE HARRY ENROLLED IN $H^2 L^2$.
HE LEARNS PREDICTED DEATH DATE

TG: "Are you afraid of death?"
Carol Shields: "No, I'm not afraid of death. I think it's just one instant away from being alive. I don't think it's far away at all, and I'm not afraid of it at all or anything involved with it."

"Excerpted from '*All I Did Was Ask: Conversations With Writers, Actors, Musicians, & Artists,*' by Terry Gross."

FOURTEEN

A year passed. Christmas came again, as well as the New Year, both of which were spent in the Adkinses' Sun Valley condominium. The entire family had arrived late Sunday night at their Eastside home after driving all day in a snowstorm that went from Boise to a little past Issaquah.

Carol, Tim, and Tess sat at the kitchen table on this Tuesday morning, nearly finished with their breakfasts, when Harry joined them. Spreading out the morning paper, he sipped on a cup of coffee.

Carol glanced at her watch and announced, "The Adkins School Express leaves in three and one-half minutes."

Harry leaned over Carol and gave her a kiss on her lips.

"Thank you," Carol said distractedly.

Harry turned on his radar as he pushed the accelerator too far down, heading for *Nippon/USA*. Luckily, he got there without a traffic ticket.

He unlocked the front door and turned on the lights. No one else had arrived. As he walked through the reception area, he heard his office phone ringing and echoing throughout the office.

He picked up his pace and jogged to his desk. He grabbed for his phone.

He smiled into the receiver. "Hi. It's Harry."

"It's Naomi. I'm on my office couch, nude, and my door is locked. Remember all the wonderful lovemaking we did on my couch? I'm all ready for you again. I haven't heard from you since Cha-Am. Is everything all right between us?"

Harry took a breath and sat down. "Naomi, I told you it was over. Just before I left your room in Cha-Am I stood next to your bed and I said, 'It's over...all over...forever.' But you were out of it."

"You can't mean it, darling."

"I do mean it. That morning I realized that I never loved you. I only lusted for your body. My only emotions about us since have been pity for you and anger for me that I'd betrayed Carol."

"Lover, let's have a little phone sex, which I really need...badly.

Then think it over. Now, unzip your trousers, please!" He heard her panting hard.

Harry shouted into the phone. "It's over! Didn't you hear me?"

"Carol and Tom will not like it when I tell them what has gone on," she hissed. "You always said that you were afraid of Carol divorcing you."

"Naomi, I'm disappointed. Now you're blackmailing me? You know that can't possibly work."

Naomi began to cry. Her rage escalated; she screamed, railed, and shouted epithets. In between her spurts, Harry heard her say, gaspingly, "I will kill myself, Harry. My blood will be on your hands, you bastard."

With as much calm as he could muster he placed the phone in its cradle.

Harry waited for a few minutes to be sure that he was more or less rational, turned to his keyboard, and typed a fax to Naomi.

Harry spell-checked his note and printed it. He read it thoroughly, walked to the fax machine, placed it in the outgoing bin, and dialed the fax number of their Tokyo office. He put a copy of the fax in his pocket, and laid the original note, upside down, on Tom's chair. He wasn't expecting him to come in until that afternoon.

As he walked away from his desk, he heard his phone ring. He knew it was Naomi.

On his way out, he strode to the reception desk. He was glad to see their receptionist had arrived. She greeted him politely, and he responded by leaning on her desk and looking her in the eye.

"I'm leaving for the rest of the day. Carol and I'll be eating lunch at The Crossings. Please let Tom know right away, but nobody else. Please do not talk to Naomi, no matter what she says or threatens. Bye."

As he turned and walked away, he knew if the Naomi story wasn't around the office already, it would be soon. *I mean it: mea culpa, mea culpa, and mea maximus culpa.*

As Harry neared the Seattle Research Institute, he concluded that he better reach deep inside himself and divulge ninety-nine percent of everything that he had hidden from Carol. Before he left, he had checked her calendar and noticed that it contained no commitments from noontime 'til three today. He would invite her to lunch.

He pulled into the Seattle Research Institute parking lot, turned off the car, and inhaled deeply. Without wasting time, he hustled to the $H^2 L^2$ office.

As he opened the door, Dr. Dunne loomed before him, looking not a little hurried, and two briefcases burdened each arm. Dr. Dunne backed up into his office.

"Dr. Dunne, I presume," Harry said mischievously. Dunne smiled at Harry. His face seemed a bit more ruddy than usual.

Dunne gave Harry a wry smile. "Yes, yes, Mr. Adkins. A good new year, sir. Did you come to see us yesterday and pick up your envelope?"

"No, I forgot."

"Yes, yes, yes, very interesting. Are you a bit anxious, Harry?"

"Sure."

"I would be too, especially if I were you. I could be in error, but I think you're the only patient who has chosen to learn the date we've predicted. You may withdraw your option. It's not too late."

Harry paused and took in the offer Dr. Dunne had just made. For a moment he considered its appeal. He watched the many fish darting about in the office's tank. His eye caught a dead fish floating on top of the water. Harry brought the elbow of his right arm to rest on the fist of his left arm.

Dr. Dunne may have seen the expression on Harry's face change, because the good doctor glanced in the direction Harry was looking. "Do you think that the dead fish might mean something?"

"You know, funny you asked."

"Great minds run in the same channel, huh?" Dr. Dunne smiled.

"Of course. And also, I could see that some fiction writer threw the dead fish in, perhaps to puzzle his reader?"

"Yes, sort of a cheap writing trick." Dr. Dunne read his watch, the rosy hue of his face deepening every minute. "I'm late. Do you want to opt out?"

"My sensible side wants to, but my adventurous side doesn't. I won't opt out."

Dr. Dunne patted Harry on the shoulder. "Good luck, Harry. Bye."

Harry watched Dr. Dunne as he trotted out the door and down the hall. He was portly, but fast afoot, dodging herds of patients, visitors, and medical men and women garbed in white and green, capped and uncapped with their surgical masks at half-mast.

Harry again studied the fish tank and walked closer to it. *Maybe there's a message for me in the tank.*

For a few moments he simply stood watching the fish bobbing. He slowly walked to the counter and said to the attendant, "I'd like to use your phone."

"Sure, Mr. Adkins." She pulled out a phone and handed it to him. "Dial nine and then your number."

He followed her directions and soon heard the other phone ringing. He knew he had to brace himself for the onslaught Carol would probably bring upon him when his revelations came forth. He considered whether or not his belongings would be on the front lawn the next time he returned home. He should have thought about doing a little packing before he left for the office that morning, but it was too late now.

"Hello?" she said, in her sweet voice.

"Hi, Carol. It's me."

"Harry? Calling at noon?"

"Oh, you know."

"You've never called me around lunch time. What's up?" Carol was the most ingenuous person he had known. A lot of women would throw in some sarcasm, but she seemed genuinely bowled over that he had called her at lunchtime.

"Let's do lunch today."

"You're kidding," she said with genuine surprise.

"No. I'm not kidding. I need to talk to you. It's important."

"Well, okay. Lunch sounds nice. When?"

"One o'clock?" he asked.

"Sure, where? Des Moines Crossings?"

"Perfect. I'll see you then." He replaced the receiver in its cradle and slowly rocked in the office chair. Arguably, today might turn out to be the most pivotal day of his life.

It was The Day Harry Cut Naomi Out Of His Life. He considered a list of "Fifty Ways To Leave Your Lover" before one of his favorite dialogue lines of all time from *"A Thousand Clowns"* slowly crept into his mind. As he remembered it, the Murray character said, "If most things aren't funny, Arn, then they're exactly what they are; then it's one long dental appointment interrupted occasionally by something exciting, like waiting or falling asleep. What's the point if I leave everything exactly the way I find it? Then I'm just adding to the noise, then I'm taking up some more room on the subway."

Will I, Harry Adkins, leave everything exactly the way I find it?

The Day I Am to Know the Date of My Death. The common wisdom is that human beings should not know that date. What will be the consequences that will follow?

The Day I Told My Wife That I Had A Lover. What will be the consequences that will follow? It's time, as they said in the military, "to move out smartly."

Harry stood up and headed for a stairway. Will he react when he reads the letter? He didn't know.

Okay, Harry. Get upstairs.

He was pleased that he was not short of breath after climbing one floor above the main floor of the medical center -- not exactly heroic, but Harry saw it as a precursor to maybe even climbing Mount Rainier someday. He paused and took a big, big breath and opened the door to Medical Center Room 535E and strode in.

All the while, he still considered the same questions that had been plaguing his mind for the past year. *Do I really, really want to know the future? Heck,* he said to himself, *gives me a lot of time to plan my funeral, which is going to be a wake -- at my golf club and not in a church or funeral parlor thing -- put that in my will.*

"What may I do for you, sir?" a husky female voice asked. He awakened from his reverie and saw a tall, smiling, slender woman in her mid-twenties with flirtatious hazel eyes framed by jumbo eyelashes and coarse straight red hair just touching her shoulders. A different receptionist. She wore a white silk blouse, its cloth buttons tugging at their buttonholes at the weight of her more than ample bosom. She sat in a rolling chair at a clean and uncluttered standard issue gunmetal desk. The cloth of her black skirt terminated at mid thigh. She wore a rock on her third finger left hand. *Hmmm,* he said to himself. *Play it straight, Harry Adkins, play it straight.*

He finally answered, "Hi, honey. I'm Harry Adkins. I came to pick up my envelope." *No more "honeys," Harry, you jerk, you've got to get over that.*

"Come sit down," she beckoned. "Oh, Mr. Adkins – "

"Harry, please. Ms…?"

"Dorothy, like in the Wizard of Oz."

"I forgot to pick up my envelope yesterday."

Harry observed Dorothy as she glanced through a file. "You know, I just plain forgot about it. I kind of have a bad time keeping dates straight. I thought for sure today was Monday. Can I still pick up my envelope?" She smiled and placed her hand, with her fingers spread, over his arm. "Of course, Mr. -- I mean -- Harry."

"Whew, I was scared for a moment I wouldn't get the envelope," he fibbed, flashing a smile at her.

Rising, Dorothy said, "Excuse me, I'll get it out of the safe."

She was gone for only a few minutes.

"Here's your sealed envelope, and here, please sign this receipt." Harry accepted the envelope, and complied. He clutched the envelope with both hands and hoisted it toward the fluorescent light above her desk. Harry noticed that his name had been handwritten on the envelope in a calligraphy typescript.

"You know," he said as he pointed to it. "Did everybody in the study get an envelope with their name in a fancy script?"

"No. Just you." A few moments of silence passed. Harry felt his feet literally had turned cold. Another fragment of self-doubt hit him right between his eyes.

"Dorothy, I'm kind of scared to know the day I'm gonna die," he finally admitted.

"I guess I would be too, but you decided to know that." She put her hand on his arm again. "But, nobody's going to force you to take it."

He agreed. His braggadocio had melted to vulnerability. "Will you make a copy for Dr. Alex?"

"Sorry, I can't open the envelope, but you can. Use that copier over there and make a copy for Dr. Alex."

Dorothy handed Harry a letter opener. He slit the envelope, took out the letter, and held it as he would an angry copperhead, far from his body, and walked to the copy machine. He placed the letter on the machine's glass surface and punched the green "copy" button. Seconds later, he retrieved the original and two copies from the output tray, still without looking. He returned to Dorothy's desk and sat in a vintage office chair.

"Here are two envelopes for you," she offered.

"Thanks. Oops, I really mangled the envelope you gave me. Would you be so kind as to write my name on a fresh one?"

"I sure will." Flattered by the attention he was giving her, Dorothy pulled out a light leather briefcase, took an ink pen out, and within a minute or so presented the envelope to him. "Don't smear the ink," she warned.

Harry held the envelope. "Thanks. You have a real talent." He inserted the original $H^2 L^2$ letter in it but did not seal the envelope.

"Oh, Dorothy," he added, as if it had just occurred to him, "could you give me a blank sheet of typing paper?"

Silently, she passed a single sheet to him. He placed the original $H^2 L^2$ letter in the envelope he had slit open a few minutes before. It had the Seattle Research Institute logo and return address already printed in the left corner, preceded by "$H^2 L^2$" in green and yellow.

"Hey, I'm a little nervous about reading the letter. Would it be okay if we get some coffee in the cafeteria? I'll buy."

Again putting her arm on Harry's, she said, "I'd love to, but I just can't leave the office. Tell you what though, here's my business card. Call me if you get psyched out."

"Good luck, Harry." She flashed him a smile. "You know how to reach me. I'll be thinking of you."

"Thanks for everything." He held back a wink.

She must have sensed it; she winked at him. He did not reciprocate and felt good about it, though he couldn't help saying, "If you can get loose, I'll be having a mocha at the cafeteria." Tucking his hands into his pockets and the envelopes under his arm, he strolled out the door.

Harry wandered to the Seattle Research Institute cafeteria and heard the cacophony of the silverware, dishes, trays, and shouts from the cooks, cashiers, and students. He smelled the competing odors of fries, hamburgers, soups, and the coffee from the espresso stand. He stopped and asked the bored male barista for a "grande mocha, skinny, skip the whipped cream, in a ceramic cup, please."

After the sounds of coffee grinding and steamy sounds of espresso brewing he was handed his drink in a paper cup.

"I guess you didn't hear me. I said 'ceramic cup.' " The barista poured the mocha from the paper cup to a mug. Harry accepted it.

It was déjà vu.

He sat at a table, alone, and stared at the white envelope containing the original letter -- the $H^2 L^2$ letter. His eyes seemed to blur. Glancing up, he contemplated the gray and wet Seattle sky. As his gaze danced around the room, he caught sight of a clock. Only forty-five minutes until lunch with Carol.

Harry opened the original letter, rested his black half-framed eye glasses on his nose and silently read:

Dear Mr. Adkins:

You had agreed in writing to learn of the predicted date of your death in connection with the $H^2 L^2$ Study Team (Study).

Subject to future unknown events outside the parameters of our Study, which cannot be anticipated, we predict, under the terms of the contract you signed, that your death might occur on July 18th, 10 years from the date of this letter. However, we cannot rule out your death prior to 10 years, or later from the date of this letter.

Dr. Jonathan Dunne has been assigned to you as your Primary Study Physician and your personal care physician, Dr. Quick-Campbell, has been assigned as the alternative. Dr. Quick-Campbell will not be told the predicted date of your death, unless she becomes the Primary Study Physician under the circumstances stated in our written contract.

Thank you for your community service in participating in this Study.

The letter was signed, but he didn't bother to take in the name of the author. *Ten years, huh? You know, that's not too bad. The bad news is that I'm going to die on July 18th, ten years from now. The good news, I'm saying, despite the legalese, is that it's not likely that I will die earlier, and, it might be later. But, I'll be damned if I'll tell Carol or the kids. I don't want them to carry that burden. They'll only know the date after I beat it.*

As he walked toward his car, his right hand touched the envelopes that he had received from Dorothy. He said to himself, *now that Naomi's gone, I damned better cut out gettin' it with other women, including Dorothy.*

Harry sat in his car in the hospital parking lot for a few moments. First, he would give Alex's secretary one sealed envelope containing a copy of the prediction letter, then place the original letter in the envelope he'd slit open a few minutes ago in the secret safety deposit box where he stored Naomi's steamy letters, and then meet Carol. He placed the blank piece of paper in the new envelope on which Dorothy had written his name a few minutes ago.

The drive to Alex's office only took him a few minutes. As he arrived, Kathy, her medical assistant, a waddling, dull woman, whose jowls reminded Harry of a venerable Miss Piggy, stood guard in back of the receptionist. He handed the envelope to Kathy, instructing her to deliver it to Dr. Quick-Campbell unopened, and strode out of the building. It was simple enough.

His next stop was the bank. He signed in at the safety deposit office, and the robotic, apparently sexless, woman bank attendant escorted him to his box. He removed it and took it to a private room. The box, in his name alone, was larger than most. It held a ten-inch-wide rubber-banded batch of Naomi's steamy letters to him.

Harry took out the original $H^2 L^2$ prediction letter and placed it in the box and laid the ripped envelope next to it. He pulled off the rubber band circling the Naomi letters and picked up one of her letters, dated March 3rd 1987.

Dear Harry,

We have just finished talking on the phone. I'm in bed, still nude. I want to come again. I take my finger and insert it in my vagina and the -- you know what I'd do...

He put it down again before going further. Feeling intensely aroused, he consulted his watch. There was not much time to get to his lunch with Carol. He knew what he would do if he read any more of the prediction letter, and he couldn't be late. Hurriedly, he stuffed about half of Naomi's erotic correspondence in his soft brief case and decided the original prediction letter, plus the rest of Naomi's letters, would be the only documents in his safety deposit box. He would read each of Naomi's letters once more and then destroy them all in the small stove in his office over the garage. Then he'd come back and pick up the rest of Naomi's letters and do the same.

Destroying Naomi's letters, he decided, would be a symbolic confirmation of his retreat from his long-standing unfaithfulness.

FIFTEEN

Harry turned off the Porsche's radar as he cruised into the Des Moines Crossings Restaurant parking lot. Patting it affectionately, he said, "Nice job." A few minutes earlier, the machine had screamed at him when he'd been driving pretty close to seventy miles per hour in a thirty-five zone. It was on his $H^2 L^2$ to-do list to quit collecting so many traffic tickets.

Thank God. Carol's Volvo was not in the parking lot. Harry heaved a relieved sigh, glad that he had gotten there first. It was another part of the changes he wanted to make, for the simple reason that he had overheard Carol joking at parties that whenever she was supposed to meet Harry, she would always take *War and Peace* along.

The wind revived and dark clouds hovered near the ground. The rain returned with a frenzy, hitting the ground and splattering, so that the parking lot tarmac ran with rivulets of water. *Damn,* he thought. *Come out sun, don't fail me.* He thought the sun might help Carol's mood, and make his confession easier to take.

Harry opened one of the restaurant's two white pine doors decorated with stained-glass windows. He stood on the rich Oriental rug covering much of the well-polished pinewood floor. It was the first time he'd taken Carol to lunch in years. Before that day, they'd been at the Crossings only for dinner.

He reached in his brief case and turned off his portable phone. The great room hummed with patrons' voices, the tinkle of ice in glasses, and the shoving of chairs to meet tables of a popular restaurant during the lunch hour.

Henri Eiffel greeted him, wearing his long, thin mustache that looked as if he painted it on every day.

"*Monsieur. Bonjour.* Delighted you will join us. How many?"

"Two," Harry said as the two men shook hands effusively. He leaned close to Henri, placed a twenty-dollar bill in his coat pocket, and whispered, "Carol and I need privacy and a long lunch."

"Ah, *merci, Monsieur.* The next floor up we have a very private table with a view of the water and my very rained-on parking lot. No others will be seated up there."

"Merci, Henri." Harry started to move away from him.

"Monsieur," Henri took his arm, pulling him back. "This weather makes our patrons guarded. Look at them, a bit glum, yes?"

Harry said, "You're right."

"A great favor, *Monsieur. Madame* and you do a few tango steps, yes? I will turn on *Hernando's Hideaway,* okay?"

Harry smiled. "Sounds good."

Behind Harry, a familiar perfume wafted to his nostrils. Her long fingers covered his eyes and her long body snuggled his backside.

"Guess who?" Carol purred.

"My sainted mother down from heaven?" *At least I have an exuberant wife at this moment.*

"Nope," She pressed her breasts to his back. *Ooh!*

"My holy aunt Esmerelda?"

"No." She firmly pushed herself further against him.

"My lustful wife?"

"Oui."

Harry turned around. Carol threw her arms around him, encased in a damp raincoat. The couple locked in a frontal embrace. He whispered into Carol's ear, "Henri needs us to do a few tango steps."

"Whatever you say, Fred." She grinned.

Henri had deftly removed the couple's raincoats from their backs and handed them to the waiting staff members.

The first notes of *Hernando's Hideaway* streamed into the room. Harry saw the sexual excitement in Carol as they took their first steps. He swept away his bad feelings and transformed them into the joy of the tango.

It took only moments before the noontime crowd assembled behind them with mild smiles growing into joyous faces.

"You would think it's France," observed Henri.

Harry and Carol faced each other dancing, and their mutual intense stare was broken only once as she bent her back toward the floor, supported by his arm. The audience roared *"Ole!"*

"Applause, *sil vous plait,* for *Monsieur* and *Madame* Adkins, Americans who are acting very French." Henri led the applause, and the lunch crowd laughed and clapped heartily.

Out of the corner of his eye, Harry spotted a tall, muscular guy. He had a crew cut and was a Swedish-type blonde dude standing with a slim young knockout of a woman at least a foot shorter than he. Her most striking feature was her white-blonde hair that cascaded to her waist. Both wore fresh gold wedding rings and appeared as if they were about to view an embalmed body in an open casket.

As he and Carol danced, Harry couldn't help twisting his head to watch the couple. The girl was weepy-eyed, and there was no conversation. *Uh-oh,* Harry thought, *it's their last lunch.*

Carol and he tangoed up the stairs and waved to their audience.

Once they were upstairs, the music stopped suddenly. Their dance was over. Harry swept her into the kind of a dramatic finishing pose found in ice-skating performances. With a flourish, Carol's back was arched and her hair nearly graced the floor while he supported her. He brought her to standing. Their lips slowly united in a buss and then into a deeply passionate kiss.

They released each other, still holding hands, and bowed to the audience below. Their fellow restaurant patrons exploded into cheers. They turned and threw kisses with both hands to the applauding crowd. At the bottom of the stairs, Henri roared with laughter.

Finally, the entire crowd roared, *"Ole, Ole, Ole!,"* with the exception of the tall blonde man and the short woman.

A series of silent *"Oh, boys"* came into Harry's head. *What a great way to start this lunch!* A lot was at stake. From what he could tell from Carol as they followed Henri, hand in hand, to their table, lunch could begin with a romantic tone, that would allow him to slowly ease into the other stuff.

As soon as Carol was seated and Harry had taken his place, Henri handed them menus, and then artfully opened a bottle of Veuvey Cliquot Yellow Label NV and poured a taste into Carol and Harry's glasses. The couple nodded approvingly after their sips, and Henri filled their glasses, despite their protests.

"Henri. I really didn't order it."

"Monsieur, Madame. It is on the house. Listen to the hum of my customers and their laughter." He extended his hand toward the main floor. "You two started all of that. It is good for business."

Beyond my wildest dreams.

As one, Harry and Carol said, *"Merci."* Henri grinned, silently excusing himself from their table.

Harry lifted his glass, caught Carol's attention, and said, "Here's to us."

She raised her eyebrows and touched her glass to Harry's, which resulted in a small chime. "I'll drink to that."

"Your dress looks gorgeous. It's the same color as your eyes."

"Too much cleavage, Harry?" she teased.

"Heavens, no, my lover. It's a feast for my eyes and imagination."

"I bought this dress awhile ago and thought it didn't belong on a hanger anymore. Today is my maiden lunch day at the Crossings."

He thought, *has that been an issue with her? Was I supposed to take her to lunch before this?*

"I guess that's true, my love. Here's to many more." *Why did she bring that up?*

Again, their glasses chimed.

As he took a sip, Harry considered what his strategy should be. *Start out by telling her how you have and will continue to change,* he told himself.

"Honey, you know, do you think I've made changes in my life since the study started?"

Carol frowned contemplatively. "A few. You drink less. You seem like you're eating less. You've lost weight. You work out a lot. You still spend too much time on company affairs and not family ones. I want you at home more."

Disappointed, Harry kept silent as Carol rummaged in her purse. "I went to target practice this morning and have to show you how I did. Oh gosh. I must have left them in my car. I made these shots from about forty feet, and every shot was right on the money."

"Please don't mistake me for a burglar, dear," Harry joked.

"The private lessons from Steve Rindal are starting to pay off."

During a moment of silence, Harry and Carol peered through the rain-drenched window. An intense storm had gathered over Vashon Island. The wind, tide, and current heaved the cold, green waves and transformed their tops into frothy white caps. The power, cable, and telephone lines were getting whipped in all directions. *Gawd,* thought

Harry, *why this crappy storm? It sure fits the mood that could hit this table.*

The wind wrenched fragile branches from the trees, and the detached limbs floated, tossed, and turned until they fell to the ground. In the parking lot visible from their table, people struggled with car doors and fought to keep hats and umbrellas.

Harry peered over the railing to the main floor and spotted the young couple, who had looked so stressed a few minutes ago. They each were now wearing a glimmer of a smile.

"Carol, did you notice that young couple, a tall guy and a short woman?"

"The gloomy ones? Yes, I did. Why do you ask?"

"Take a look at them now."

Carol glanced at the couple's table. "Sweetheart, I think something positive may be going on."

"Yeah. Me too." He grinned.

The two of them fell silent, sipping their champagne and reading the menu. How could he best confess the Naomi thing? To end the affair with Naomi and to tell Carol about it would be consistent with his desire to change his life. *Has Alex told her already? Would she cry? Would she get a nasty lawyer and get him kicked out of the house? All of the above?*

Suddenly, she placed her spoon down firmly and challenged Harry's eyes. With a bit of urgency, she demanded, "Did you get the letter from the $H^2 L^2$ study that said when you would die?"

Harry was startled. Carol just took the initiative. *Damn it.* He must lie to her. "No, I didn't. We talked about it," he said, glancing out the window. "It's too much to have us know when we'll die."

"What's the difference," she continued, confrontationally, "between the letters of those who choose to know and those who don't?"

Harry chose his words carefully. "When a guy signs up for the study there's one page, page 19, I think, that says something like, 'mark only one of the options -- I do wish, I do not wish -- to learn the predicted date of my death.' "

He continued. "You turn in your choice to the study office and get a copy of that page. At the end of the first year of the study everybody gets an envelope containing a copy of that same page and a medical analysis of his health. Only those who have chosen to learn the predicted date get another letter-sized paper actually stating the date."

Carol, looking skeptical, with her arms folded on her chest, said, "I want to see your envelope."

Harry reached into his inside jacket pocket and pulled out a sealed envelope and handed it to her. He inwardly struggled with his lie and his subterfuge, but he convinced himself that it would be best for his family not to carry the burden of knowing for ten years his exact date of death.

Carol removed a knife from the table setting, slit the envelope, and pulled out the blank sheet of paper.

She stared at the envelope's contents. "Oh, thank God. I worried so much that you would know the date. It's kept me awake at night."

Carol seemed at ease, and she smiled at him. Harry reached out and took her hands in his. Taking a deep breath, he started to tell her that he loved her.

"Je vous demande pardon," Henri placed their usual onion soup before them with a flourish. "Good champagne, eh?"

Carol and Harry said, almost simultaneously, *"Merci."*

Once again, Henri bowed deeply and pirouetted toward the stairs.

Before getting the Naomi deal out on the table, Harry wanted to reassure Carol that he loved her and her alone. He wanted to dispel any notions that he had romantic feelings for Alex.

"Carol, dear, do you think I may have a romantic interest in Alex?"

She sat back, clearly surprised by his question. Glancing around the room, she considered her response. Finally, she said, "Yes, I've had that impression. Alex is my best friend. Frankly, I was jealous that you two have danced so up close and personal all of these years. I've had bad dreams about you making love to Alex in our bed. This has been a thorn in my side for awhile now." She looked him in the eye, "I need reassurance."

"Carol, I give you that reassurance. I admit that I've had thoughts about Alex in the past, but never would I compromise your friendship with Alex."

"For God's sake! I'm glad you're telling me, Harry, but that doesn't make it okay. Why are you bringing this up?"

"Carol, you're my only romantic love," he said, clutching her hands across the table in desperation.

Carol avoided his eyes and looked toward the Sound. She was a flash frozen sculpture while she spoke, "I feel better now. Thank you."

Better get the Naomi thing out. Right now.

Dense, dark clouds covered the sky. Torrents of rain dropped and splashed on the skylights, broadsided the windows, and turned the parking lot into a shallow, raging river. Thunder drummed, and the lights flickered.

Carol stared out the window. "I haven't seen Naomi in the last five years," she said slowly. "How's she doing?"

Oh, shit. What possessed her to bring up Naomi? This is not going like I had planned.

"Why don't you answer my question? How's Naomi?"

"I know my answer will hurt you. I do love you."

She grimly stared at him, remaining silent.

"Naomi and I have been having an affair."

Carol's hands left her tableware and seemed poised to take action.

"You don't mean that. You're lying, you're making it up!"

He continued, "About five years ago, I went to Japan to solve a big technical problem. We drank a few sakes…quite a few. We took a cab to my hotel. That's how it began." Harry began to regret his confession. His forehead grew damp; his palms felt clammy.

"Behind my back?" She looked as if she had touched a high voltage wire brought down by a storm sparking in the street.

Harry nodded. "Behind your back. It was in-person and over the phone."

"You bastard." Carol suddenly stood, raised back her fist and before Harry could react, her knuckles landed on his right cheek. Nobody had ever hit him as hard.

Harry held his hand to his right cheek and felt warm, thick liquid oozing from his wound. Harry dipped a cloth napkin into his water glass and held it to his right cheek. Carol paced next to the table, clutching her face with both hands.

Henri stepped onto the floor, carrying the entrées. The aura upstairs was as cold and quiet as deep space. As he picked up the soup bowls and delivered the entrees without saying a word, he acted as if he couldn't get out of there quickly enough.

Harry reached out to hold her, but she jerked away. "Don't touch me, Harry. I despise you."

The hair on his back froze as if a grizzly had cornered him.

"Why did you tell me today? Why not last week, a year ago, five years ago? Why now? It had a lot to do with a threat, didn't it?" she spat out at him, as hostile as a hyena tearing flesh out of a dead wildebeest.

"Do you want me to be honest?"

"I don't know what to say." Her anger waxed.

"Yes, that had something to do with it. I've been trying to get the bad shit out of my life. Cutting down on drinking and eating healthier, you know this. And Naomi? She's out of my life, Carol, I swear she is." Harry realized he must have sounded as if he were pleading for his life

"Bullshit. Did you enjoy your little chat room sex, you son-of-a-bitch? I know she went with you to Cha-Am. When I called your room at one in the morning and talked with Charlie One, he lied to me that you had gone for a walk alone. I bet you were in your room or her room, screwing the shit out of each other."

He almost said that it was not in his room, but thought better of it. Harry felt as though he had been kicked in the balls. Carol shook her head and trembled.

He reached into his briefcase and pulled out a paper. His hands were shaking.

"I sent her this fax this morning." He handed it to Carol, who snatched it out of his hands.

Carol read the page in a half-whisper, with anger and in despair.

"*Naomi: It is best for you and me to end our relationship. I shall ask Tom to take over as liaison with our Tokyo office. I never want to see you or talk with you. Never contact me again. You knew all along about the Seattle Research Institute study. I am changing my life, and our relationship has no place in it now. I'm ashamed to have betrayed Carol. Harry*"

She supported herself with her other arm as she slipped slowly in the chair, and read the fax again, silently, and began to sob, angry tears running down both cheeks.

They sat quietly for several minutes. Neither looked at the other. Harry barely heard the hustle and bustle from the first floor of the restaurant.

The dark clouds began to part their curtain, allowing the blue sky and sun to paint the restaurant's rich wool carpeting and the light wood walls. Outside, the sky and sun danced on the fretful waters of Puget Sound. On the Sound, a sailboat smartly laid to starboard sliced and pounded the confused blue-green water.

Harry, still holding the damp napkin against his cheek, reddened and awkwardly pointed to the sailboat. "Our sailor friends would say, 'She carries a bone in her teeth.' Hey, why don't we get a sailboat?"

Carol turned away. Her anger and tears mottled her otherwise unblemished cream-colored face.

"I bet Naomi told you that she'd tell me and Tom if you cut her off, didn't she?"

"Yes."

"Once would be bad enough, but I suppose that you lost track of the many times you fucked her for at least five years. And all that time you were still fucking me. I'm angry, but I'm more disgusted." A shaft of sunlight fell on their table.

"And, I don't know if I feel more hurt or more anger. To be honest, I also can't say I don't love you, but I sure don't like you. I feel like I married my father. Mother lived with knowledge of my father's infidelity, but never took any action. I'm not my mother. Harry, you're right; you did betray me. And I'm not going to sit back like my mother; I'll get a lawyer and I'll kick you out of the house."

Harry sat immobile. For the first time, the enormity of what he had done to Carol came to him.

"Please tell me, truthfully, who else did you fuck during our marriage? God, that's such an ugly word, but what you did to me is so ugly."

"Nobody."

Carol and Harry did not fight for nearly ten minutes. Harry ached, and he hated not knowing what Carol was going to do.

"What else should I know, Harry?" she finally asked.

"Charlie One tacked three hundred dollars onto my bill as the price of him not sending a video to you."

"Am I having a nightmare, or is this all too real?"

Harry felt within himself a sorrow that he could liken to the death of his parents. The grief that he realized he must have caused Carol. Harry ached in the back of his throat, and he could not contain the tears that flowed from his eyes.

Although the ambient inside weather surrounding Harry and Carol's table at The Crossings appeared to be cloudy at best, the outside weather began to sparkle. Harry considered that, year in and year out, he was a "cockeyed optimist." Something good will come soon, somehow. He looked across the table to Carol who cast her vision toward the window, daubing her eyes with a linen napkin.

Suddenly, the young couple, with the sunlight at their backs so that their shadows fell on Carol and Harry, appeared at the top of the stairs.

Harry saw the eagerness and hopefulness coming from the young woman; her eyebrows were raised, saying without sound that they wanted to talk. Harry raised his brows and glanced at Carol for approbation. She was still red-eyed and exhausted, but shook her head and said, "I don't care." Skepticism and hatred permeated her face.

Harry nodded at them, and the young couple approached hesitantly, holding hands.

"The *maitre'd* asked us not to disturb you, but we told him we wanted to thank you both for helping us. I'm Trish Gallagher and this is Pete Pickens, my husband." Pete smiled and gestured hello.

Trish and Pete stood close to the table. "Thank you for letting us talk to you. You both look very serious, so we won't be long," explained Trish.

"We've been married for nine months. And just last week, we got into a big fight over something, I can't remember what now, and we didn't think we could work it out. In a fit of anger, Pete slapped me so hard I fell on the floor and he walked out in a huff."

Trish glanced at her husband, then continued. "To strike back, I cheated on Pete with an old boyfriend. I told Pete about what I did yesterday. He was pretty pissed off, excuse me, mad about it. We came here to have our last lunch together and settle our affairs and split. We arrived here when you guys were giving big hugs like you meant it. You know, you seem kind of old to us, but you could still be romantic. Especially when, at the foot of the stairs, you gave each other such close hugs, stomach to stomach, and kissing and laughing like teenagers."

Harry noted that Trish, except for a few fond glances at Pete, fixed her gaze on Carol and himself and never looked at any of her surroundings, like the sharp shadows that the sun projected through the skylights, or the rich blue, white cloud dotted sky overhead and the sailboats on Puget Sound.

"Well, Pete and I began talking about you at lunch. You're two older people, married for a long time, who still seem to love each other a lot. The more we talked the more it seemed right for us to stay together, get some counseling, and stay married. And we talked about forgiveness, too. Thanks for your inspiration of what it's like to be in love."

Trish took a step toward their table and gently grasped first Carol's forearm and then Harry's and said, "I mean it. Thank you."

It was the most heartfelt thanks Harry had ever heard.

It looked like Carol had brushed her skepticism away. She stared at Trish as if transfixed, then rigidly shifted her attention to Harry. At least for that moment, she seemed less angry. Addressing Trish, Carol reflected, "We're having some trouble, too. Harry just told me about him being unfaithful for five years, and I lost it. I've never bloodied Harry, or anybody, before." Harry still held a white linen napkin on his cheek.

"You know, I had all of these threats running through my head, getting a lawyer, booting him out...But it's not that simple. We have kids, we have to think of them, too. And I do love him. But, I sure don't like him much right now."

Harry had never heard Carol shed her coat of armor before a complete stranger, but this young woman seemed to have the leadership qualities of a modern day Joan d' Arc.

Pete blushed and looked down at Trish and she turned her attention to him.

Pete addressed Carol. "You know, I'm kind of like you, ma'am. I love Trish a lot, but I don't like her very much now. Before we came up here, I told Trish that she had better tell you guys about what she did to me. But, we got a lot going for us, kind of like what you older folks seem to have had for a long time. So Trish and me are going to get counseling. And, maybe sometime soon, or in five or ten years, we'll see you folks here again." Tearfully, Carol got up and hugged Trish and then Pete. Harry had never seen Carol embrace a stranger. He fantasized for a moment that Trish was an angel who had been just sent down from heaven.

"Trish and Pete," said Harry, pulling his notebook from his briefcase, "Will you write your names and numbers on this page?"

"Here's my business card from my last job," said Trish, "I'll write down our home address and phone on the back of it."

Harry took the card and stared at it for a few seconds. "You're a CPA with your MBA?" It suddenly struck Harry that an audit of the Tokyo office might be needed.

She laughed, "I know, but I don't sound like one, do I? I'm between jobs right now, actually."

"Truthfully, no," Harry said, handing her his own business card.

With a winsome smile, Trish said, "I was raised in hillbilly country, so when I'm off the job, I revert to my roots."

"You do much auditing?"

"Yup, more auditing than tax stuff. Actually, I just completed a big audit as manager in charge in a big bankruptcy case involving fraud."

"Pete and Trish, thank you. You've given me lots to think about," said Carol.

The foursome said goodbyes and exchanged good luck wishes. Trish and Pete disappeared downstairs.

"Do you think they're going to make it?"

"Right now, Harry, I don't know if you and I will make it. I don't even want to think about anyone else." Harry was dismayed, but not shocked. He refrained from speaking, or even looking at Carol, but did note that she refilled her glass of champagne and downed it in a gulp.

"Nobody has done anything as bad to me as your complete betrayal of me."

Henri poked his head out from the top of the staircase, holding a phone with a long extension cord.

"I am sorry to again disturb you, but Mr. Tom is on the line. He says it is very important."

Harry looked at Carol, who nodded, with her head turned away, that he should take the call. Henri passed the phone to Harry and scampered away.

Carol watched as Harry took the call.

"That's okay, Tom. Carol and I are having a 'heart to heart.' I told her about my relationship with Naomi...finally." He remained silent as he held the phone to his ear. His expression slowly hardened.

"Tom...tell Carol what you just told me. Please. Hold on."

He passed the phone to Carol. She glared at him for a moment and then angrily snatched the phone from him.

"Hi, Tom. It's my duty to warn you that I'm angry with Harry." Carol paused, and appeared to listen. "How am I? Shattered. A little relaxed now, but a lot shattered. Do you know any good lawyers?" Harry took a proverbial virtual bullet in the gut at close range.

Carol listened attentively, moved her gaze beyond Harry, and looked to the emerging sun and sky brightening Puget Sound.

Carol said nothing, but her blue eyes opened wide in apparent disbelief, and she clenched her free fist so hard that her knuckles were white.

"Oh, no, Tom. Where did they find her? She asked for my *forgiveness*? Oh my God. She must've bled to death." Harry saw horror in Carol's eyes. Carol, appearing shaken, passed the phone back to Harry, who tried to listen acutely.

"Harry here. Let me get this straight. Naomi sent another fax to you, asking me to forgive her? She explained that she was deeply in love with me, could not live anymore without me, and that by the time you got this last fax she would be dead? The office person could not get into Naomi's office, so they called the police? The police came...broke down the door...and found Naomi dead on the floor with a large knife in her stomach?"

Across the table, Carol watched with wide eyes as he talked to Tom.

Finally hanging up, he looked at her, shaking his head. "It might be a while before we get our questions answered."

Carol nodded.

"You know. I'm still reeling from your punch. I deserved it though."

Carol turned slightly to Harry. "How do you feel?"

"About all of this? I don't know yet. The impact on me of what I have done to you is still a greater sorrow than anything else that has happened."

"I'm glad you said that," she offered.

Nothing more was said.

The skylight poured sunshine over them. *What could he do to help the situation. Maybe he should see a psychiatrist? Hey, what about including this in my existing appointment with Izzy Cantor?*

"What do you think about me going to see Izzy for awhile?"

"I think you should," she said without hesitation. "I really don't know Izzy Cantor very well, but the girls at the Club think he's really good. God knows I could use a shrink. We should get another psychiatrist for the two of us."

Carol suddenly held both hands to her head and slumped to her chair, as if in agony. "More and more I get these headaches. I feel like my head is being squeezed in a giant press. Just like my dad used to complain about." She sighed.

"What?" Harry asked. He didn't think he had heard her right. "Your dad? Is that what you said?"

"Don't ask me now. I feel sick to my stomach. Everything's spinning. Help me to the car."

"The doctor's or the emergency room?"

"Just drive me home."

He got her to his Porsche in a heartbeat after making arrangements with Henri about her Volvo. The drive home seemed to last longer than a decade.

Harry pulled into the driveway and stopped next to the porch. "How's your headache?" he said, turning to face her.

Carol looked straight ahead and said, "It's gone from vicious to just awful. Thanks for asking." She looked at her watch. "You have one hour from now to move your stuff to your office over the garage."

"Okay." He looked at his watch. He felt a sharp pain in his

stomach. *Harry, you've been a real jerk.*

Harry marched to his study in the garage and surveyed the space. Until he got a real bed his camping cot would have to do.

Hey! I'd better call Tom about Trish. He dialed Tom's direct phone.

"Hi, this is Harry."

"Oh, hi. I've been worried about you."

"Carol's kicked me out of our bedroom. I'm pretty depressed and have a lot of guilt when it comes to you and Carol…But, the reason for calling. Carol and I met a young woman named Trish Gallagher, and her husband, at Henri's place. What happened is another story. But we exchanged business cards. Turns out Trish is a CPA, with an MBA. She just left a job at a CPA firm where she was a supervisor of an audit in a fraud case."

"Good idea, you figure we need an auditor in Tokyo, and…What's her name again?"

"Trish Gallagher. I'll ask her to call you."

When Harry came back into the main house, Carol was sitting on the leather couch with Tim and Tess.

"I have a bad headache. Please get ready for bed and I'll say goodnight to you. Harry, please say goodnight to the children."

Harry smiled and started to walk toward his children for hugs, but neither said anything, only ran up the stairs. *I guess I'm getting my just desserts.*

Harry followed them as if nothing happened. "Hey kids, get ready for bed and I'll come in to kiss you goodnight."

He headed for what had been Carol's and his bedroom. Harry ventured into their spare bedroom to get a suitcase so he could begin loading his stuff.

He was flying around picking up things to take to the garage when he heard Tess shouting, "Okay, Dad, we're ready." He ventured into the children's bedroom and they gave them perfunctory hugs and kisses. He turned off the light and closed the door. *Harry, you're a selfish bastard.*

Harry went to the kitchen and rested on a chair near the phone. He held Trish's business card and dialed her phone.

"Hello. Trish here."

"Hi Trish, it's Harry. I called my business partner, Tom

Campbell. My conduct also has caused all sorts of hell in our Tokyo branch office and the business in general. This is an emergency for us. The business card I gave you at the Crossings includes his home number. Will you call him tonight?"

Harry paused and said, "You'll call Tom? Thank you. I'd better hang up."

Carol returned from bedding down the twins and walked into the master bedroom. Harry had filled two large suitcases and was in the process of closing and zipping them.

"How's the headache, Carol?"

"About the same. I want to tell you I'm not happy with myself letting you stay here in your office. Trish had a lot to do with you still being here." She admonished him. *Another sting.* Carol looked at her watch. "You don't have much time left to move out…I'd say you're out of here in ten minutes."

"For the next couple of nights, before I buy a twin bed, I'll sleep on that cot that's been in the attic of the garage. May I have the bedding tonight in the guest room, and I'll buy some new bedding?"

"Yeah." She sneered as she bustled by him to go to the den and didn't look back.

This is the worst day of my life.

SIXTEEN

Harry arrived at Dr. Isidore Cantor's Mercer Island office a little before nine. and was warmly received by Rebecca, medical assistant and receptionist, who opened the door to Cantor's personal office.

He heard the door close behind him. "Good morning, Izzy, love your office already. It's so well-lit...so many skylights, artificial light, living plants, and small trees, I feel as though I'm outside."

Harry loved to shake hands with Izzy because he gripped Harry's hand strongly and Harry gave it back. He looked into Izzy's eyes and found warmth and support.

Immediately after Harry sat down, they gabbed a while about golf, tee times, and that kind of thing.

"Does it work for you to live and maintain your office on Mercer Island?"

"Oh, yes. My home is twelve minutes away. I do a lot of forensic work in the King County Court House...I walk about ten minutes from my office to get the bus to Seattle. Lots of buses available both ways. Love it here."

Izzy's speakerphone carried Rebecca's uneven voice into the room. "Dr. Cantor, It's an urgent call from...Mr. P."

"Harry, I think I may have an emergency. Would you be so kind as to walk out through those glass doors and close them behind you?"

"Sure, Doc." Harry arose and turned to leave. Suffering from an acute attack of impatience syndrome as he watched Dr. Cantor shift behind his dark oak desk and stare at the phone, Harry said, softly, "Izzy, please tell me if you've stashed a collection of Penthouse magazines and where can I find them?"

Trying not to laugh, Izzy pointed to him, and whispered, "Get out of here, you scoundrel." Harry closed the two glass doors behind him, hanging onto the new Penthouse magazine he had just bought for Izzy.

While standing outside the office, Harry stuck his hands in his pockets and looked at the numerous certificates and degrees that hung on Izzy's lobby wall, serving as a miniature indoor advertising billboard.

Izzy had dark, perpetual-bad-hair-day hair and the build and stature of Woody Allen. Like Allen, he spoke as fast as an auctioneer, always gesturing and glancing, with his oversized, owl-like pupils and soda-bottle-bottom eyeglasses skidding like a sled down his nose.

Harry focused on a framed certificate that declared Izzy was a Board Certified Psychiatrist. Through the glass doors, Harry saw that Izzy had placed the phone receiver to his ear, attached by a very long coiled cord that stretched across his office. Izzy walked back and forth, seeming frantic. Then, he seized the moment and began to speak into the mouthpiece. This went on for a number of minutes, and then he stopped talking suddenly, slammed the receiver in its cradle, and sat down in his chair, exhausted. Harry tried not to stare at him as the doctor caught his breath, then finally beckoned Harry back into his office.

Harry plopped into the chair he had previously occupied. "Looked like you had a big crisis. What happened?"

Izzy shook his head. "You'll have to excuse me, I'm shaking a little. Naturally, I can't identify my patient, but his wife had just pulled a gun on him and then he locked himself in their bathroom and called me. I had Rebecca call the police and his wife's psychiatrist. They do this about once a year, but it's still worrisome."

Harry raised his eyebrows, "You know, sounds like a big problem. I suppose you guys get of lot of loonies."

"Harry, I'm tempted to make you my straight man."

"Don't succumb. Nice duds, man. Dr. Cantor, the Suave Shrink." Harry smiled.

"*Touché*, patient." Cantor shot back, and both men laughed heartily. "Thank you for the extensive written presentation in a three-ring binder that I call your 'history' and that you call a summary of why you consulted me. Also, Alex faxed a complete history based on what you told her in her office. Plus, I called Tom about his observations about you, *vis-à-vis* your company.

"Further," Izzy went on, "we're dealing with the implications related to your anxieties about the study. The issue of the study is separate from the Allegro matter. And, I've spoken with Dr. Dunne -- a true gentleman and medical scholar.

"First, I see you've been living in your home office over the garage for a couple of weeks now, and my colleague Dr. Mary Beth Barto has contacted me about her visit with Carol. Dr. Barto will be seeing Carol twice a week for four weeks and go from there. After that, If Carol and you both consent, Dr. Barto and I will exchange information about Allegro and the study from Carol."

"Sure, I consent," said Harry. "Stepping away from this, it almost sounds like a TV soap."

Izzy smiled. "Of the pending matters, which do you wish to discuss first?"

"A Hobson's choice?"

"Well, yes. But which one comes first?"

"Oh, God. I guess I'll talk about Allegro first. He's my greatest fear, which really got to me...both the courtroom threat and the more recent one when he got caught on the way to our home."

"My friend, were you aware you shivered? And your usual bravado disappeared?"

"Yeah, that happens, come to think of it. My persona includes lots of swagger and smiley face, I guess."

"Yes, I talked with Tom about that. He told me that his strength lies in financial structures and that you're the rainmaker. He joked that you're one of those guys who can pass through a busy airport anyplace in the world and come out with three new clients."

"That sounds about right," said Harry.

"Let's talk about the courtroom incident. After that episode, how successful were you in bringing in new business?"

"Well, hell, nobody had ever done that kind of thing to me before. I mean, threatening to torture and kill my wife, my kids, and me. I took that threat seriously and visualized it...I mean, at the trial they showed some pretty gory stuff that big bastard did. I thought about it during the day...And at night I had trouble sleeping -- very bad dreams -- sure to put the damper on smiley face and swagger, I'll tell ya. Time after time, I fell asleep during the day. Like one time I fell asleep when I was making a pitch to a potential new client. This mental thing also affected our old clients. The onset of these things was shortly after the trial."

"And how long did the disturbances last?"

"After the trial, two to three months.

"Forgot to tell you, for several months after the trial, I had an uptick of my blood pressure."

Harry paused awhile and stood marveling over Izzy's sun-drenched office, the light pouring through the rectangular and circular skylights.

"Well, you remember I was pretty frantic when I heard the news item about Allegro's escape when I was heading for our home. All the images of torture and shit I had seen in the courtroom before surged back right when I heard the radio broadcast in my car, and then I saw the white van in my driveway and thought Allegro might be in my house.

"Hmmm. You know," Harry continued, "the situation was about the same as what happened after the courtroom outbreak, like nightmares and lack of sleep and lack of concentration. But, I think the effect on me after Allegro escaped also lasted longer. The blood pressure also escalated."

Izzy pointed his pen upward and said, "Chronologically, your history records your contacts with Allegro. I want to get that clear. You served as the presiding juror for the trial on guilt or innocence and also for the penalty phase."

"Yes."

"You kicked him in the balls, no doubt causing him excruciating pain?"

"I sure did!"

"Allegro threatened you and the judge with bodily harm just after the verdict."

"Correct."

"After the trial, but before he went to prison, a threatening letter came in your mail?"

"It did. It frightened us."

"After opening the envelope, what did you see?"

"Basically, it was the same diatribe he shouted to us in the courtroom, except in the courtroom, he had a firearm which he aimed at the judge…"

"And you interceded?"

"Of course…I did what every citizen like me would do. Also, I want to point out that Allegro signed 'Johnnie Allegro' cursively, but somebody else printed the actual death threat in neat, block letters.

Obviously, somebody else was in on the message because a deputy sheriff told me Allegro was illiterate."

"What happened next?"

"The bastard went to prison.

"Allegro came to Seattle from prison to testify in some criminal case. He escaped, killed a guard, got hold of a white van, and headed to the judge's house and ours, but was intercepted, and will be tried for that."

"Tom also told me he went back in the books after both incidents and your company income for those two periods substantially diminished," Izzy remarked.

"Oh, yeah! I forgot to mention that I was grumpy during those periods, and my golf went to hell for awhile."

"Let me know from your golf records if you can document changes."

"Sure. If we get another threat?"

"Both Carol and you should get a short appointment with me. We'll be able to explore the way things are going."

"Are you going to make a diagnosis?"

"Yes, but let's hear about the rest of the problems. I think we should defer making any diagnosis until the whole picture is drawn. Let's take a five-minute break." Izzy buzzed Rebecca.

"How's Mr. P?"

"Things have pretty much calmed down. The police came and Mr. P was able to leave the bathroom."

"Thanks. Anything else brewing?"

"Nothing in particular."

Izzy said, "I'm heading for the little boy's room."

Harry and Izzy again were settled in their respective chairs.

"My friend, let's explore Carol's personality. First, give me some adjectives that describe Carol."

Harry sat back in his chair. "Try loving, caring, devoted, soft-spoken, bright, a great mom...I feel she's mentally stable if that's where you're going."

At the mention of stability, Carol's recent headaches popped up in Harry's head, but he dismissed them, deeming them irrelevant. He merely nodded, confirming that by saying, "I believe that Carol and I love each other very much."

Izzy consulted his notes.

Good idea to write a comprehensive history.

"Harry, you mean to tell me that Carol actually said to you, 'I'll kill you', and that doesn't concern you?"

"Listen, Izzy, I can't tell you how many times Carol has said, 'If you don't do such-and-such, I'll kill you.' This started years ago. She's been doing it for years; it's just a figure of speech she uses. To illustrate this--you know that I'm pretty bad about not remembering appointments."

"I've heard her say it. To be brutally frank, it's one of the big jokes around the Club."

"Oh, shut up," Harry joked. "She called me at midnight the night before our wedding and at six a.m. on the day of, and both times she said, 'Harry, if you forget 'I'll kill you.' "

"I get the point." Izzy was scribbling notes. "Do you know if there's any mental illness in Carol's family?" Izzy said, without skipping a beat.

"Nope."

Studying him, Izzy said, "Excuse me while I look at my notes."

Harry rose and wandered around Izzy's office, stopping to admire the teak bookshelves. While roaming, he spoke to Izzy without looking at him.

"Well, if I learn something, I'll get back to you." *Talk about mountains and molehills. Go on to something else. At a hundred and eighty bucks per hour!*

Harry noticed the pen moving furiously across Cantor's page.

Izzy ignored him and kept his eyes on his notes. He finally looked up to ask, "Are you prepared to discuss Naomi?"

I'm going to dread this. I guess I can't take the Fifth.

"Ready as I'll ever be."

Izzy held Harry's history, placed his forefinger on a page and asked "You say you throttled Naomi?"

"Yes." *He visualized Charlie Two's smirk in the hallway.*

"Were you drunk?"

"Tipsy, but not falling-down-drunk." *What did I say in the write-up for Izzy? I forgot.*

"Remember that you wrote a history, which included an account of what happened in Thailand," Izzy remarked.

"Yeah."

"Didn't you write that you were so drunk it took you a long time to get the key in the lock to get back in Naomi's room?"

"I guess I did say I was drunk, Mr. Prosecutor." Harry realized he had been a smart-ass. "I'm sorry, Izzy. I didn't mean to come off like that."

"If there is anything I'm concerned about, it's your choking of Naomi. If the hotel people had not knocked on the door in response to Naomi's scream, was it possible you could have killed her?"

"Yeah, I guess so. I did lose it. I guess I was in a rage. I can't say, 'I know I wouldn't have killed her.' " *I'm in big trouble.*

"Had you ever been in such a rage before?"

"No. Never."

"Since?"

"No."

"How do you feel about Naomi's suicide?"

"Other than John Donne's poetic observation that 'any man's death diminishes me,' I felt no sorrow at her death."

"Are you saying, in effect, her death was fortuitous for you?"

"Yes. I guess so. I never loved Naomi, and never represented I did. I lusted for her body. Izzy?"

"Yes."

"Do I come across as being crass about Naomi's death?"

"You do. *En Espanol, si? No simpatico.* Which is completely contrary to who you are. I'll make a note that we should review this in our forthcoming psychotherapy." Izzy scribbled a number of phrases in his notebook.

"Another Naomi question, Izzy: I noted to you that Naomi strongly supported me when we were confronted by the two Charlies. Isn't that kind of bizarre?"

"No. In the literature of domestic abuse -- "

"Excuse me. But are you classifying what I did to Naomi as *domestic abuse?*"

"Harry, domestic abuse includes your choking Naomi. You don't have to be married."

"Then Carol's punch is an instance of domestic abuse?"

"Technically, it is, but we won't go there now."

"After you married Carol, except for Naomi, did you have any other liaisons?"

"No."

"You wouldn't be surprised if there's under-the-table talk at the golf club about Alex and you."

"Those rumors have no foundation in fact. The most I can say is I love Alex in a special way, but we have never had any sexual relationship."

Izzy read his notes for several minutes. He came up for air saying, "Why are you so defensive?"

"I am?" *Where in hell is he going?*

"Yes. Tell me what happened when you told Carol about Naomi."

Harry pointed to his cheek where Carol had smashed it with her hand and ring.

"Exhibit One. She was pretty upset. Like, in nano-seconds. Izzy, you forget, suddenly this woman learned that the man of her dreams, me, had been fucking his company employee for years."

"Carol punched you in the face?"

"Hard, Izzy, hard. She gave me a hell of a punch."

Izzy nodded. "I don't blame her. But she calmed down after that, right?"

"Yes! A glass of water, please?"

"Sure. Cool water in that Waterford pitcher on the table back of you." Harry rolled his chair to the water supply station, poured himself a glass, and gulped the water down like a thirsty camel on a scorching day in the desert.

Izzy studied his writing pad again, and then said casually, "I just have a couple of questions for you and then an opinion to offer."

"Your opinion, Doctor." *Harry hoped that Izzy would take his side.*

"My friend, my opinion is that from what you've told me, both orally and in writing, at this time, Carol does not pose a threat to you. Nor does it appear from your history relating to Carol's family, without further research, that mental illness runs in her family."

Harry nodded approvingly. "That's good news, I guess."

Izzy made his hands into a tent again. "Seriously, a competent psychiatrist is compelled to take a history because he has heard what could be construed to be threats to you and I had to rule them out."

"I thought that's where you would come out. I agree."

"Except for a discussion concerning the loss of your parents, have we covered all the points you're concerned about?"

"We have." Harry asked himself if he should tell Izzy about regretting joining the study. Decided not to talk about it.

Harry moved back to his chair and pointed to the walls. "You know, you have quite a professional pedigree up there."

"Well, thank you." Izzy didn't miss a beat. "I've read my notes and re-read your history where you say that you lost both your parents when you were sixteen. What issue relating to that shall we discuss first?"

Harry slouched back in the chair and pulled some tissues out of a box. He dabbed his eyes and cheeks and felt clogged by his emotions.

When Harry finally spoke, he asked softly, "Something I've always wondered is whether or not there is any connection between their deaths and my shift from celibacy to promiscuity and from a guy who had rarely sipped a brew to a guy with a budding drinking problem."

"It's quite possible."

Looking out the window, Harry whispered, "Izzy, this is what happened to my dad that day. It had been really hot out. Dad had been running ahead of me. He was so competitive that if I had run ahead of him...well, it doesn't matter. Dad tried to pass me up that day, just like any other. He didn't care how hot it was. He turned his head back to me, and he was so excited, he said, 'Let's ratchet it up.' And he did.

"In the next moment, he fell to the pavement like a limp scarecrow. I placed my mouth on his and blew my ass off -- repeatedly -- but I knew at the moment he hit the pavement my father had died."

Harry had brought himself back to that day. And couldn't come back from the past. He touched the fingers of his right hand to the palm of his left. "Izzy. I just gotta bawl a little." He grabbed several tissues out of the large decorative box on Izzy's desk and brought them to his eyes. "I'm sorry."

"Take some time out, Harry, take all the time you want."

"At a hundred and eighty bucks an hour. I better not want very much time," said Harry with a laugh. His emotions were mixed as he sat there half-chuckling and half-weeping. He took some deep breaths and rested his hands on his knees. "It seemed a short eternity, but soon a 911 team relieved me from CPR. A medic turned to me and said, 'He was your dad?' and I couldn't talk; I just nodded yes."

"He said, 'Your dad didn't stand a chance. I bet he must have died from sudden cardiac arrest before he hit the ground. We see that too often. Was your dad a runner?'

"I said, 'He ran five days a week. Five-K's to marathons.' "

Izzy interrupted, "How are you doing? Want another break?"

"Naw, let's sweep all the shit off the shelf. I think I still need some counseling about Mom and Dad."

"Sure, it's on my agenda if it's on yours. What about your mom?"

"Well," Harry answered. "Mom and I were both pretty devastated over Dad's death. And that's when I began thinking that I was drinking too much. But, I didn't do anything about it. I was just sixteen. I'll tell you that lots of weepin' went on for quite a few months. Neither of us slept very much. We did a lot of late-night book reading."

Harry's lip continued to tremble as he stared out the window, avoiding eye contact with Izzy.

"Tell me about your mom's death," the doctor pressed.

"We had just come back from a rousing Christmas Eve dinner party at Uncle Harry's. Oh, you know…that's why I'm a Harry. In truth, I never liked Harry as my name. But I hung on to it out of respect for Uncle Harry.

"Anyway, it was the first Christmas without Dad there at the party. For me, it was a huge chill compared to when Dad was alive. Dad was a pretty funny guy and could tell a joke better than Bob Hope. I kept looking around for him to be there. I found myself looking around a corner in the kitchen at his gang of guys. Oh. I didn't tell you he went by Jack. And no one would talk about how weird it was that Jack wasn't there until finally, at the end of the night, Uncle Harry, my father's brother, lifted his glass and said, 'Here's to Jack, a fine man and an un-paralleled joke-teller. I can see it right this moment -- Jack just told a joke to God and God's laughing.' My dad's gang busted their guts on that one."

Izzy smiled warmly as Harry relayed the memory.

"Except me. I went to the open bar and poured a hearty glass of Irish whiskey and guzzled it in a couple of frenzied gulps. I kept it all down, but got pretty tipsy. I was supposed to be the designated driver since no one thought a seventeen-year-old would drink, but I proved them all wrong. So Uncle Harry, who'd only had two healthy glasses, gave Mom and me a ride home.

"Once we were there, I said, 'Mom, would you like a sip of Irish whiskey?' and she said yes, so I got a couple of glasses. Mom said, as she put her arms around me, a little bit choked up, 'One year ago tonight, you, Dad, and I came home from your Uncle Harry's Christmas Eve celebration. Dad served drinks for the three of us, for you the first time -- you were sixteen -- then the three of us sang *Silent Night.*'

"And I said, 'You know, Mom, I can remember since I was six or so, we all sang *Silent Night* at Harry's and then back at home. I kept looking for Dad tonight, not believing he wasn't there.'

" 'I feel the same way,' she said to me.

"Mom and I still clung to each other. I told her, 'Mom, I couldn't handle myself if something happened to you.'

" 'Nothing's going to happen to me,' my mom said. 'I can just imagine that I'm holding one grandchild while the other grandkids are trying to get in my lap, too. Now, I'm getting a thirst for our drinks. So hustle, Harry.'

"I asked Mom if she'd put on the *Silent Night* album we all liked while I poured our drinks.

" 'Sure, hon,' she said, and then from the kitchen I heard Bing Crosby singing *Silent Night.* I recall my immediate family sang lots of Christmas carols together. I heard my mother started singing. It only took me a couple of minutes to mix the drinks, so the same song was still playing when I went to take her glass to her, and I was even singing along by then. But when I got to the hall, I suddenly discovered that I was singing alone.

"I stopped singing…I panicked and froze. I had to force myself to go into the living room. I swallowed, still not shifting my gaze from the window.

"I came into the living room and saw my mother -- she was just slumped inertly in my father's rocker, next to the Christmas tree, while *Silent Night* spilled from the record player. I called 911, and I tried to give her CPR, but it didn't work. Nothing worked. I lifted my mother's body to the floor as carefully as I could and gave her more CPR until the medics came, despite the fact that she showed no pulse and didn't breathe.

"The ambulance crew told me my mother suffered a stroke and had died almost immediately.

"One of the medics said to me, 'You're Harry, right? We met a few months ago when your dad went down on the sidewalk. You remember I was on duty? I'm Ivan. You look pretty young. There are three of us in the truck. I'd be happy to stay with you. If I were you, I don't think I could handle this alone.' "

Izzy commented, "That was nice of him."

Harry nodded absently. "I said 'That's okay, I'll call my uncle.'

"Ivan said, 'Punch in his number and I'll talk with your uncle.'

"I punched in his number, heard Uncle Harry's voice, and said to Ivan, 'Talk with Uncle Harry. I can't handle this.'

"Ivan said, 'I'm Ivan Borkovich, Medic One. I have really bad news about your sister, Mrs. Adkins. She died of a sudden stroke. Young Harry can't stay here alone. I think he's in shock. How long would it take you to get here? Ten minutes? We'll wait for you. Thank you, sir.' And they waited with me until Uncle Harry got there, but I don't remember any of it."

Harry slowly turned away from the window and back to Izzy. He looked in the mirror behind Izzy's desk and saw his own image, his eyes red and cheeks damp.

"You know, that's me. Sorry. The images of my mother's and father's last minutes rushed over me like a rogue wave. Can't stop crying."

"You okay, Harry? That was a pretty tough story."

Harry absently shook his head, not addressing Izzy's question.

"A few minutes off, my friend? We can indulge ourselves for awhile and use my office putting green."

Harry mopped his eyes and face again. Somehow, he felt a wee bit better. "You know, it's tempting." He forced a smile. "Let's putt. I might add, on your nickel." Harry noticed he had to work to get a smile out of himself. Again, Harry looked at his image in Izzy's mirror and saw the Teflon smile.

Izzy handed Harry a golf club. "In retrospect, I've never seen you as vulnerable as you are now. It's not a bad thing. A harbinger of change. Let it flow."

"Back to Trish Gallagher for just a moment. Carol and I both think she's charismatic. Is that in the realm of psychology?"

"It is. There's a particular focus on charismatic leadership. A guy named Max Weber wrote about a person who has exceptional powers and qualities. I think both Carol and you could easily find someone like Trish, as you have portrayed her, charismatic. From your history, I gathered she provided leadership during her audit in Tokyo and when she joined your firm as Chief Financial Officer."

"Okay, Izzy, let's putt a few."

"Damn," Izzy said as his ball failed to fall in the cup. He tried again and sunk it.

Harry smirked and said, "Too bad, Doctor, get your money out. My first's going in."

Harry took a small swing with his putter, clicked on the golf ball, and watched it roll right into the cup. Standing close to Izzy, he held his hand palm up, near Izzy's waistline.

"Dammit. It looks like I owe you five bucks. We'll settle at the end of the day."

"You know, just credit me five bucks. We'd better get back to business."

Harry looked at his watch. It was getting to wrap time.

Harry took his seat in the same chair.

"What do you want to talk about? I think we're about at the end," Izzy asked, propping his feet up on his desk.

"Izzy, in my multi-list of things that I wrote to you as my history you know that I'm working out most of the time at the gym, and how when I'm on business, I eat more healthily, and steaks only come to me on my birthday. On the day after Christmas I knew I was in better shape than anybody else in the whole shitty study."

"You also told me about cutting way down on booze and spending meals with Carol and the kids," the psychiatrist chimed in.

Harry stood and laid the palms of his hands on the desktop. He noticed the mirror image of himself from the glass top. His usual happy-face countenance was reduced to a slight smile.

"Look me right in the eyes. Check me out to see if I really mean what I say, or if I'm a first-class phony. Tell me like you would testify in court under oath." Harry took a big gulp from his water glass as a preface to an observation and stared at Izzy with piercing eyes. He grabbed a tissue with his right hand and dabbed at his forehead to swab a fine layer of sweat. He wondered if Izzy grasped his message.

"You want me to tell the truth and I want to do that, too."

"Now, let's change course for a moment, Iz. I need to tell you that although I enjoy the sight and smell of a woman, I'm working not to flirt with one, even if she gives me a come-on, which has not been infrequent."

Izzy gave Harry the up-and-down. "I'm comfortable enough to admit that you're looking better and better. In all honesty, you're a good-looking guy."

"Thanks. Flattery will get you everywhere," he joked. Taking another sip of water, he shook his head. "It would be a terrible thing if Tim and Tess, and Carol knew that the Seattle Research Institute predicts that I have only ten short years to live." He pounded his fist on Izzy's desk to punctuate his point. Harry's almost-empty glass of water had begun to turn on its side before he caught it with his other hand.

"That's not a lot of time, is it, my friend?"

Ten years is not reasonable. Harry saw that Izzy's poker face had been transformed into a mask of sorrow. His friend's voice broke.

"I'm so sorry. But I happen to believe that only God allows us to live and die, and it's not a good thing to have any one of us know when that will be. I've told you, my friend, you shouldn't have learned the predicted end of your days."

Yes, Harry thought. *He's probably right; I shouldn't have learned. Did I make a Faustian bargain? How do I pay?* He shuddered at his whimsy. "What can I say? I shouldn't have learned it. But, now that I have it, I want you to know that it's not the final word. I'm going to live long beyond the ten years. I have much to change. I need to wake up." Then Harry pounded out each word with his fist on Izzy's desktop: "I -- can't -- die -- before -- I -- wake."

Izzy made his finger tent. His ten digits seemed to go up regularly as a preface to a comment or an opinion.

"What are you getting to?" Harry agonized.

"That means I'm contemplating. Scientifically, I'm skeptical that any study could generate the wisdom to predict accurately a human's death."

Harry sprawled his arms out over Izzy's desk. "I have so much of me to change. Look what I did to Carol. I'm sleeping in my office over the garage. This is confidential, real top secret, but I have a collection of steamy letters from Naomi stored in my secret safe deposit box." *I shouldn't have said that.*

Izzy shook his head. "Oh, God. First, in the write-up you gave me, you never mentioned those steamy letters. I'm disappointed in you for holding back on those. If Carol gets a lawyer those could get sniffed out. I know lawyers who would claim they'd be relevant in a child custody case. Why don't you burn them?"

"You're kidding," Harry said incredulously. "You think I might not get custody of the kids because of those letters?"

"Well, just raising that as a possibility."

"Shit."

"I was talking about changing," Harry said. "I don't even want to think about child custody. All I know is that I wanted to keep those letters and I like thinking about what they say."

"We're going to need to talk about them. You really do need this therapy. Those letters are a kind of sexual fetish."

Harry felt both distressed and angry with Izzy. He buried his face in his hands; he sobbed and shouted, then rose up again, and in one stride brought his body to Izzy's right side. Harry proclaimed in heated terms, with his face reddening, "I thought psychiatrists were supposed to help, or at least do no harm. Has it ever occurred to you that by telling my family the date, you would be a party in harming them?"

"Quit the study. Tell Carol," demanded Izzy, folding his arms and looking defiantly at Harry.

Harry pulled Izzy out of his chair and used both hands to grab the lapels of Dr. Cantor's blue blazer. Pulling Izzy to his chest, he saw no fear in Izzy's eyes.

"Look me in the eye, you pompous bastard. I'm no quitter. I agreed to see the study through. Besides, I already know the goddamn date! Come on, give me some advice, other than that I shouldn't have learned the date!"

Harry released Izzy's clothing and returned to his chair, still upset. Giving the information about his death to Carol would be as explosive as telling Carol about his relationship with Naomi.

Izzy tried to straighten the disarray caused by Harry's manhandling. Patting at his clothes, he said, "Okay. Calm down. Keep your blood pressure down. Your face is red. Calm down, friend. And you need to apologize to me and promise me this will not happen again. To be brutal, I'm thinking about Naomi's throat."

"Izzy. Oh, God. I just lost it. I'm sorry, and this will not happen again."

Izzy studied Harry, then sat back down. "You passed the point of no return. You truly regret that you've taken yourself to the brink. I see a lot of guilt in you about your unfortunate decision. We can work on that, too. Stay on your course to change your life. Continue your doggedness in refusing to accept the ten years. You asked me a few minutes ago, to probe if you really mean what you say. I must admit I see my share of charlatans in my practice."

What will he say?

Izzy looked Harry squarely in the eyes and said, "Harry, I believe you're telling me what you believe. But, you told me you made a promise to Carol that you would not learn the study's predicted date of your death. You didn't keep that promise. In fact, you lied to Carol."

"Yes, but I'll tell her the day *after* the predicted date when I'll still be alive, and she will forgive me!"

Izzy shook his head. "I have to go to the little boy's room."

Izzy returned quickly, "I want you to see Rebecca before you leave and make six appointments, one appointment per week for the next six weeks. What disturbs me is that I don't know what the popular culture would call 'the end game' here. Good luck, my friend."

"What is the 'end game' here? The day I die? But, I'll do counseling, Izzy. There's a lot I didn't like about the old Harry, but I think...maybe, just maybe...I'm beginning to like the emerging Harry. Thank you, Izzy. Sorry about your jacket." Harry slouched in his chair and shook his head. "I've got to tell you something else."

"What are you talking about?"

"I may have omitted a key thought."

Izzy looked startled.

"Izzy, I can't tell you how hard it's been to know I may be dead on a specific day in ten years."

"My friend, there's no fee today."

"Oh. No, I'm paying your fee -- less, of course, my five dollars worth of putting profits. I insist." Harry showed his brightest grin.

"All right, my friend, let's compromise. When you get my bill, less the five bucks, will you pay it to the development fund for my synagogue in my name?"

"You know, I'd love to do that," Harry responded.

"Thank you for what you did, my gosh, about ten or fifteen years ago in getting my family and me into the Golf Club. The first African-American family. You showed a lot of courage, my friend. I know you took a lot of shit." That kind of language was rare for Izzy. Harry knew he meant it.

"It was the right thing to do. By the way, Izzy, how did you get the name of Isidore Cantor?"

"Oh, that. My grandfather embraced Judaism in the last century and felt he should change his name from Canbrook to Cantor. My father stayed with the faith and thought Isidore would be a cool Jewish name for his eldest son."

"What's tee time tomorrow?" Harry looked at his watch and

found both the time and some anxiety, realizing he was late for another appointment.

"Your favorite time," Izzy joked, "Seven a.m., bright and early."

Harry smiled broadly, at the same time mocking the early hour, by uttering a pretend-offended, "Ugh. Hey, Izzy, big favor -- could you have Rebecca call my secretary? I'm late for my next appointment. Have my secretary call me on my mobile car phone."

Izzy nodded.

"Oh! And I almost forgot something which might be important."

"What's that? About golf?"

"Hell, no. The study and Allegro."

"I told you, they're separate."

"Not true. I wrote a note on the $H^2 L^2$ application under 'Other.' My words were to the effect that I made an appointment with a psychiatrist because a number of years ago I received a death threat in the courtroom from Johnny Allegro, the killer of six boys, when I was a juror in his trial. After that, Allegro escaped from custody and got caught by the police on his way to do my family and me in."

"Anybody from the study contact you about Allegro's letter?"

"No. the reason I wrote that down is I thought my lack of concentration might affect my participation."

"Frankly, I didn't notice any serious problem with your concentration this morning. But, today, I did not hear your *modus operandi* of quick quips. If you do stay with the study, and find concentration a problem, let Dr. Dunne know about it."

"I will." He shook Izzy's hand, and they made their way out of the office. As they approached his car, Harry could tell that Izzy was going to have a little fun.

"Ah, Harry, why am I thinking about that saying, 'not being late to a wedding or a funeral?' "

The two shook and grasped each others forearms.

"You've done a lot for me here...I'm grateful."

"You're a great guy and a credit to your community, but I wouldn't sign up to learn when I'm going to die."

Harry got into his car and had started the engine when he heard Izzy shouting something.

"Harry! Stop! At least tell me where you hid that damned *Penthouse!*"

"Try the ladies' room!" Harry burned rubber as he exploded out of Izzy's parking lot.

His mobile car phone rang, startling him. Must be Sally.

In his rearview mirror he spotted Izzy shouting something and waving his arms. He replied by repeatedly tooting his -- *ah-ooga!* -- horn. He reached for his radio and said, "Hey, Sally. I've got a whole slew of appointments with Izzy. Can you take 'em down now? Good. Do something spectacular to remind me."

SEVENTEEN

Harry remained at his desk in his den, his running log open in front of him. He had thrown down a couple of cold orange juices trying to refuel his body.

His phone rang. He pushed on the speaker button.

Last January, Harry had received an inquiry from his company's oldest and best customer, Kurosawa. It was the biggest Japanese computer conglomerate out there. His old drinking and carousing buddy, Takano, KIL's CEO, had written to him expressing interest in purchasing the stock of Harry and Tom's company. Harry was pleased; for years he had been telling Tom that they should consider selling *Nippon/USA* if the right offer came along.

Harry had not revealed to Tom that he had been glancing over his shoulder at the dark shadows of the $H^2 L^2$ prediction study. He wanted to travel, play golf at his whim, and not be imprisoned by the business. If the damned prediction had any validity, he wanted to get a lot of money up front so he could do what he wanted to do. *Self interest? You bet.*

At first, Tom had stoutly resisted a sale. He told Harry that he could see himself working well into his seventies. The two of them had never been able to reach an accord on the terms of a buy/sell agreement. That stalemate also could present a problem if one or the other wanted to buy his partner's interest.

All of these changes were producing sharper conflict between them. But it was nothing compared to the underlying clash between the two men over the women in their lives. From time to time, Tom reminded Harry that he held Harry partly responsible for Naomi's death, and he was also not afraid to demand that Harry stop "chasing Alex's ass."

Then, unexpectedly, KIL had made a first offer about two months ago.

Tom admitted that he was pleasantly surprised that it was better than he ever had expected. However, he still wanted to up the ante, so negotiations intensified.

Tom agreed KIL's Masura Takano, Ry Hayami, and Shuji

Muramoto should visit Seattle to "do a deal" since the trio comprised Tom and Harry's first introduction to KIL.

Masura Takano, the most formidable negotiator of the KIL group, was a sleek man, inscrutable, taciturn, and smart. He was also a womanizer, just as Harry had been before embracing $H^2 L^2$. Harry could never understand why Takano seemed indifferent to his niece's suicide.

The Kurosawa men arrived at SeaTac at about four in the afternoon. They were met at the gate by Harry and Tom, who drove them back to Harry's home for dinner.

After they deposited their luggage in the new *Nippon/USA* white van, Tom suggested they should drive by their five-year-old Woodinville Headquarters. Other *Nippon/USA* employees had made their way to and from the Woodinville offices, but no executives had yet visited the site.

Tom and Harry had hired award-winning architects to design the several-story building. *Nippon/USA* occupied the first floor and leased the other three reserving the space for future expansion.

As the van circled the building, Tom made the point that their lawyers and CPAs had arranged the ownership of the building to allow tax advantages to Tom, Alex, Harry, and Carol. *Nippon/USA* was a tenant.

At Harry's house, Trish, Pete, Tom, Alex, Carol and the reigning elkhound greeted Harry and the KIL contingent as they left the van.

As they were all mingling over hors d'oeurves and alcoholic beverages, Ry said to Harry, "Mr. Harry, you have broad shoulders; were you in swim races?"

"No. I was a platform diver in high school and punted for the football team, and I ran in track in high school and college. I work out fairly often now. What about you?"

"I swam in what you call high school and college and then after in seniors' -- is that a good word to use? -- I do seniors' now."

Harry feigned interest in Ry as he strained to listen to a conversation between Alex and Carol that was taking place behind him.

"How are your headaches these days?" Alex was asking.

"Oh, probably worse. I would have said that five years ago they were a two on a scale of one to ten…now they're more like four or five."

"That's interesting. I saw Dr. Snyder's report and all the tests came out clean --no pathology. Have you thought any more about seeing a psychiatrist like we talked about?"

"I don't think I'm there yet."

"Well, I think you should keep it in mind."

"I will. Excuse me." She turned to her guests. "Will you all freshen your drinks and follow me to the gazebo?"

Several minutes passed. Carol beckoned to Harry. "Please notice the stone bench." With his other hand, Harry flipped a switch and lighted the bench with dozens of small white bulbs to the guests' oohs and aahs.

"We copied the original bench near Lake Waban on the Wellesley campus. We became engaged while sitting on it. We celebrate with an anniversary toast on this bench."

Moments later, Carol rang the dinner bell.

Ry stood next to a chair at the dinning room table. "We now sit down to dinner, Mrs. Harry?"

"Yes," Carol replied with a big smile. "We would be honored if you would not sit all together so we could get to know you better."

"Oh, of course, Mrs. Carol," replied Ry.

"I would be pleased if you called me just plain Carol," she smiled.

"Of course, ah, Carol."

Throughout dinner, Harry worried that the rapport between the Japanese and the Americans seemed a little flat. Something was needed to get the negotiators to loosen up.

From the kitchen, Carol brought out what looked like a decadent dessert and placed it on a side table.

Ry, reverting to his American accent, commented, "It looks familiar. When we lived in the U.S., my mom cooked that dessert. I bet it's a Queen of Sheba chocolate almond torte."

"Absolutely, Ry, it's a Queen of Sheba chocolate and almond torte."

"What's in it exactly?"

"It's rich," Carol warned cheerfully. "Brandy, bittersweet chocolate, butter, eggs, sugar, flour."

"If you're ready for something to do justice to the torte, Carol and I will be serving a rare brandy." Harry reached into his liquor cabinet and brought out an ornate teardrop-shaped bottle with an elegant base, defined by a serigraph that portrayed a fanciful mermaid in a blue sea. She was carried by curvaceous, red-and-white-tinged waves.

Carol placed a delicate brandy glasses at each place.

"Hey, Harry. What's in that bottle you're uncorking?" Trish piped up.

"You're looking at a bottle from the Courvoisier Collection, specifically the container is Bottle Number Five...and pardon the mispronunciation, but -- here goes nothing -- *Degustation,* French for *tasting.*"

"Where did you get it?" shouted Ry over the din.

"Well, some of you know I'm a volunteer at the Eastside Children's Hospital. We went to their auction during my serious drinking days, and I got snockered and wound up being the successful bidder for the Courvoisier."

"I drove home," added Carol, coldly.

As Harry was opening the bottle he noted, "We wanted to open the bottle for the first time in honor of our friends from Japan."

Ry rose. "A toast to our hostess and host with the mostest on the ball. Let's all touch each other's glasses." Harry heard the resulting chimes produce a kind of impromptu melody.

After desert was served, Shuji remarked, "Delicious. May I ask...how it is made...Ah, what is the word?"

"Recipe? I'll e-mail it to your office," Carol offered.

"Yes, thank you. I am honored."

They washed the Queen of Sheba production down with brandy and dark espresso coffee. Harry felt that openness was slowly overtaking rectitude.

Ry said, "Mr. Harry, Takano has told us about your garage doors. May we see them operate?"

It was not long before all of them ventured outside and Harry turned on the searchlights, lighting the three garage doors. He loved this exhibition of his whimsy.

Ry raised his hand. "Mr. Harry, I don't believe it. You have one garage door, with a very big picture of a Japan Air Lines 747. It is as big as three garage doors. It looks like the Boeing is just leaving the runway...what do they call it? Nose up. Thank you for the Christmas card with your garage door on it," he laughed.

Ry held up his two camera cases. "I have the still camera. I have the video camera. I would like to take pictures." Dozens of pictures, still photos and hundreds of feet of film were shot, with everyone posing and overacting, using the remote to open and close the garage door. Harry also dragged Tess and Tim from their computers to get them into the shots and to take some photos. Turning to Takano, he remarked, "Just like little kids with a new toy." Between the Queen of Sheba production, the brandy, and the 747 doors, the ice had melted. It had been quite an evening. As they were going back inside, Ry asked Carol, "I like your home, Mrs. Harry. Is there any torte left?"

Carol displayed her smile. "Of course."

Despite their congenial evening, all of the men, plus Trish Gallagher, shared two days of hard bargaining at *Nippon/USA's* Woodinville office.

The next morning session had not produced an agreement -- just the considerable exhaustion of most participants.

Also, the damp and dismal weather seemed to pervade the room.

Harry, slouching in the wheeled dark leather chair at the head of the table, decided to change the venue of the negotiations.

He spotted Trish standing next to the large window on the other side of the conference room, explaining an enlarged profit and loss statement for *Nippon/USA* to Takano, Muramoto, Ry, and Tom. Tom was doing his best to stay awake.

Harry raised his voice: "Excuse me, Trish, gentlemen, come on over and sit down here."

They sauntered to the table and rested in their chairs. Tom yawned.

"Takano, when does your plane take off tomorrow?"

Takano reached inside his jacket and pulled out what looked to be his itinerary. "Two hours after lunch time."

"Then we have time to work toward agreeing on a deal. You know, another business group is interested in buying us. I told them I'd get back by the first of next month, which is very soon. Tom and I think we can make a deal. Okay. This is my suggestion, since we're getting nowhere out here...let's get closer to Sea-Tac Airport. We'll drive our van to the Bellevue Hotel where you can check out and then we'll drive to the Crossings, which is pretty close to Sea-Tac. Okay?" Harry looked hard at Takano.

Takano returned Harry's hard look. "Okay."

Muramoto said, "You did not say we would have hotel rooms near Sea-Tac."

Takano murmured. "We would not have time to sleep. We will sleep on the plane."

Muramoto appeared disappointed.

Takano chuckled, turning to Muramoto, "As Harry is thinking, 'tough shit.' "

Everybody laughed, including Muramoto, and Harry punched the phone's key pad that lay on the conference table and spoke into the speaker phone, "Sally, call the Bellevue Hotel and tell them that our Japanese friends will be checking out within the hour. Get Henri on the phone."

About three minutes later the phone carried Sally's voice into the room.

"Harry, Bellevue Hotel expects our friends, and here's Henri."

Harry touched the dial pad. "Henri. How are you?"

"Good, *Monsieur* Harry. How may we serve you?"

"Our Japanese friends, Tom, Trish, and I need a conference room at The Crossings for six people and a small one for three -- plus availability of food and drink into tomorrow. We're trying to get a deal sealed, so we'll work all night, if need be. Oh." He gestured toward Trish. "And do you have an easel we could borrow?"

"*Oui!*"

Trish pointed two thumbs up.

"*Merci*, Henri."

"*Monsieur* Harry. We do all of that. How soon?"

Harry creased his face with a smile. "See you in about an hour. We're in a van."

"We stand ready to take luggage and brief cases, and park your van when you arrive."

Once settled in their conference room, Trish stood and placed her hands on the table. "You guys and this girl are grouchy."

Harry noticed that indeed everybody, including him, looked grouchy -- confirmed by a mirror in the men's room.

Trish went to the telephone near Harry and pushed a button.

Henri's voice resounded. *"Oui."*

"Henri, this is Trish. I got a lot of grouchy old farts with me. Bring us menus and a couple bottles of white Bordeaux."

Harry noticed that each man suddenly wore a smile, some bigger than others.

"Oui, Mademoiselle Trish -- er, pardon, you look so young -- *Madame."*

"Flattery will get you everywhere."

"Eh? Madame. I come *rapide."*

One half-hour later, everyone at the table was munching on sandwiches and sipping white Bordeaux, smiling and joking. And Harry observed, nobody seemed grumpy. Thanks to Trish and Henri. Harry turned to Tom and Takano. "Here. I'll pour a little sip or two of wine in our glasses and let's step outside in the hallway."

"Good idea."

The three men left the conference room, closed the door, and walked down the hallway to a window.

Harry observed. "Oh, hey. I think we'll get a little break in the weather." *Like a few years ago, the sun came out of hiding and changed everything.*

"Takano -- we're running out of time."

"We are."

"One thing I need to know that we haven't talked about...if I were to ask if you had authority to make a deal without getting permission from your Board of Directors, what would be your answer?"

"I do not have to consult with them."

"Should that give Tom and me comfort?" Harry relaxed for a moment and privately felt ecstatic.

"Not necessary."

"You mean, not necessarily."

"Oh, yes."

Harry became concerned. And Takano probably sensed that he guessed.

"Please. I explain. I get authority to a certain amount -- no more after that without consulting Board of Directors and asking more money, which I will not do."

"Oh." *Shit.* "Well, should we continue?" *Should we worry?*

"Yes."

Tom and Harry raised their not quite empty glasses, as did Takano. The three men touched glasses. Harry spoke. "To a settlement."

"Yes. To a settlement. Tell Ry and Muramoto to join me in the Vashon Room."

"I will. Take your glass?"

"No, I have not finished." Takano placed his hand on Harry's shoulder.

Harry stepped into the conference room and passed on Takano's message. Ry and Muramoto left the room and Harry shut the door.

Harry pondered why KIL, Tom, Trish, and he hadn't made any progress the last two days. In his mind, he replayed all of their meetings, their breakfast, and their lunch.

"Hmm," Tom said approvingly. "What's your read on Muramoto?"

"He reminds me of a Sumo wrestler. But here, he's Takano's grunt, the designated black hat. I knew I'd never have him on my side."

"And Ry?"

"A nervous Nelly. He wants us to make a deal so he can go home. But he's a good guy."

"Come in, Henri." Harry beckoned. Henri walked in and stood next to Harry.

"I came to check on you. What do you need?"

"Merci beaucoup, Henri."

"Monsieur. With all respect. I can tell that you have not practiced your French since you and *mademoiselle* last dined here."

"Oui?"

"Oui. How may I serve you?"

"We're done with these dishes. Would you clear them, please? And we'll need fresh ones and fresh pots of coffee, leaded and unleaded. Oh, and please get oatmeal raisin cookies. Our guests are conferring in the Vashon room. We expect them back here soon. If Trish, Tom, or I call you and say 'Brut,' please personally bring us a magnum of your best champagne and six glasses."

"*Monsieur,* seven?"

"Seven, excuse me. And a Queen of Sheba torte."

"*Oui. Oui.* I clear the table myself now."

If I succeed here, Harry thought, *Carol and I and the kids will rent a house, maybe buy one, in Provence. Near a golf course.*

Harry stood beside Tom and watched him staring at the newly golden landscape, colored as if it had been caught on fire by the setting sun; the white contrail of a high flying jet over them for a while carried the sun's retreating fire. Then Tom started to pace before finally retreating from the window and going back to his seat.

Harry took a deep breath of relief. Putting his arm over Tom's sloping shoulders, he said, "You know, look, Tom, I'm telling you. We can get some more dough-ray-me. I know we can. *Hang on, Sloopy, Sloopy, hang on,"* he sang, finally getting his friend to crack a smile.

Hours had passed since the sun disappeared over Puget Sound and the western evergreen forests. Scattered lights from houses and streetlights twinkled like stars.

The KIL guys had all reconvened and had made themselves comfortable again in the conference room. Their jackets were off, their neckties loosened. They all had been silent for a while. Henri and a portly waitress quietly and unobtrusively swept away the dinner dishes, cleaned the table and carefully placed urns of fresh coffee, cups, saucers, and an abundant supply of oatmeal raisin cookies on the conference table before them.

A sense came to Harry that dawn was creeping toward them. They had better get to Sea-Tac by noon. *It's time to make a move.* He got up abruptly and stood in back of the trio.

A grin spread all over Takano's face. "Ah, Harry. As you Americans say, you are quite a guy. I said we will pay eight million dollars."

Tom said, "Harry and I are not talking about selling the

Nippon/USA building. We gave you a copy of the lease."

Harry sat huddling with Trish and Tom. Trish walked to the erase board and wrote in block letters: "Offer for *Nippon/USA:* Nine Million U.S. Dollars."

Takano approached the board. With a gruff smile on his lips, he wrote on the board: "Counteroffer: Eight and one-half million U.S. Dollars. Firm."

Tom, Trish, and Harry excused themselves and stepped outside the conference room.

"Okay," Harry said, "It's eight million, seven hundred fifty thousand U.S. Dollars, plus two bottles from the Courvoisier Collection. *Degustation.* Firm."

Both Tom and Trish laughed.

They returned to the room. Trish marched to the eraser board and wrote under Takano's offer: "Eight million seven hundred fifty thousand U.S. Dollars plus two bottles from the Courvoisier Collection. Degustation, FIRM."

Takano went to the board and wrote under what Trish had offered: "Eight million, six hundred twenty five thousand US, and one bottle from the Courvoisier Collection, FIRM." He circled the "one" and "FIRM."

Tom, Trish, and Harry conferred, Trish walked to the board, circled Takano's last offer, and wrote within the circle, "Accepted."

All shook hands.

Tom walked to the phone and pressed a button. "Brut."

Harry smiled, doing everything in his power to contain his excitement. "Yes."

Looking into Takano's eyes, Harry spoke quietly, and seriously, "I take it Tom and I are not selling the local *Nippon/USA* building."

Takano's Adam's apple seemed to have gone up and down, as if he had forgotten the building.

For a minute, Takano was silent, and then he spoke, "No, you keep the building."

Harry looked like a schoolboy who just won the agate in a marbles shoot.

As the men stood shaking hands, Henri walked in with a rolling cart carrying a magnum of *Moet & Chandon Brut Imperial,* its container sweaty and cold, champagne glasses, and a Queen of Sheba torte, supported with forks and dishes.

With a grand flourish, he popped the cork and poured the bubbling light-amber liquid into their crystal goblets. Harry took the magnum and poured the seventh glass and passed it back to Henri.

Takano and Tom, who stood next to each other, said in unison, "A toast."

Tom continued, "A toast to Harry and Takano. This very fair agreement could not have been reached without them."

Harry let the fizzle and sweetness linger on his tongue and raised his glass. "One more toast. To the Rising Sun." All smiled and chorused with him, "To the Rising Sun."

The men and woman, of two cultures, hoisted and sipped their glasses as the sun hinted at its ascendancy over Puget Sound.

After a few minutes, Harry interrupted, "I don't want to spoil your fun, but we need to sign a memorandum of understanding before you leave, and the plane takes off in just a few hours. Takano, we'll work off Tom's computer at the airport."

The men nodded, their mouths full of the Queen of Sheba torte.

Harry stepped away from the group, hoping for a few moments of peace. He looked out the large window, and saw himself again jogging around the track, hand and hand with his parents, followed by his fellow students and high school band, playing *For He's a Jolly Good Fellow.*

He was sure that his determination to successfully conclude the sale of *Nippon/USA* had something to do with his parents.

He realized he had, in these moments, this day, arrived close to the place where he could finally forgive his father and mother for dying too soon and leaving him alone in the world. Silently, he lifted his glass, toasted his parents, and sipped the golden champagne.

Harry floated in time and space back to Tokyo to his first date with Carol. They too had drunk golden champagne that night. Silently, he toasted Carol. *My spouse. My children. My best friend. Each comes back to intersect during one's life. Magical.*

That's why I'm going to live after July seventeenth.

PART III

HARRY RETIRES FROM *NIPPON/USA*

"Dying is no big deal. The least of us can manage that. Living is the trick."

- Red Smith

EIGHTEEN

Harry loafed in his den on a dreary November day. The clouds seemed grayer than usual. Even the Douglas firs appeared to be more gray than green.

He wanted to look away and be someplace else, like in his new home in Provence. He reached for a DVD of photos from his personal library and inserted one in his player. "A two-story white mansion, overlooking the Mediterranean with Cannes a few miles down the road…this is as good as it gets," he remembered Tess saying.

They had bought a home in Provence about a year ago. The photos were taken when Tess and Tim had visited them. One photo depicted Carol talking with the kids. *The white two-story villa in the background looked like what you see in travel ads.*

A series of pictures showed Harry, Carol, Tess, and Tim eating lunch, accompanied by bottles of red and white wine and goblets, on the north side of a half-moon-shaped gleaming white table, sitting in the shadow of a dark green parasol. All wore scanty, pastel-colored clothes, and sunglasses masked their eyes. Their tanned skin glistened with freshly applied sun-tan lotion. Several pictures had been taken of the Mediterranean from the area between the villa and the luncheon spot.

He recalled Tess had asked if he'd been keeping up with running and weight lifting, and when he confirmed that he had, Tess had said, "Dad, you're a hunk." He checked out his stomach, now, sitting in this den: yes, his tummy was as flat as the bottom of a frying pan.

Frankly, he was upset that Carol had frequently made calls to Steve Rindal's gun store from Provence. She'd shipped her Beretta to France and regularly practiced with paper targets. And then there was the strange behavior.

The tenth year will be here shortly. Carol's headaches seem to be getting worse, Harry noted to himself. Looking around, he couldn't help assessing his current situation as he'd been doing more and more frequently as the year approached.

They'd left Provence to come back home so Carol could get a second opinion from another neurologist. He couldn't understand why she refused to take the Minnesota Multiphasic Personality Inventory, which according to Izzy, was a comprehensive psychological test that had been used for years on millions of people with a high level of validity. He was perplexed and didn't know where to go with his Carol problem.

Also, she would not subject herself to the scrutiny of a brain scan.

Carol's issues aside, Harry was in much better health and in better condition than when the prediction had been made ten years ago. As he sat in his den after breakfast, listening to *White Christmas,* it suddenly occurred to him he wanted badly to be present in the next Christmas and the ones after. This Christmas, he had, for the first time, purchased gifts some time in advance because Carol and he were going to Sun Valley to spend Christmas with Tim and Tess.

He paced around his den, holding his hands behind his back. *Dr. Dunne may be able to shed some light on the accuracy of the predicted day of death.* Maybe, Harry reasoned, in light of all the healthy changes he had made in his lifestyle, he really *would* live longer than July seventeenth -- only a few months away. *That's it, call Dr. Dunne for an appointment.*

Dr. Dunne's receptionist -- Sheri this time -- beckoned Harry to sit down. "Dr. Dunne will see you in a few minutes," she informed him. Moments later, Dr. Dunne opened his private-office door and greeted Harry.

"I haven't seen you in awhile."

"It's been about ten years since we last met each other, no?" Harry asked.

Dr. Dunne consulted his clipboard. "You're right." The two men shook hands and Dr. Dunne stood by his door and gestured Harry into his office, then shut it behind him.

Harry ambled to the large windows and saw an eight-oared women's crew on an early morning sun-struck Portage Bay. "Great view. Look at that crew row, look at their arms and shoulders."

Dr. Dunne stood next to Harry, looking him up and down. "Speaking of physicality, you hardly look like the Harry Adkins I met about ten years ago. And, I must say, when I saw you on television last night, I didn't recognize you at first."

"Sometimes I hardly recognize myself," Harry admitted.

"That was quite an award you got. Wasn't it recognition of your years of service at Eastside Children's Hospital?"

Growing modest, Harry responded, "You know, I usually don't talk about my work out there because working with dying kids upsets me. And I don't like to clash my own cymbals about what I do there, either."

"I understand," Dr. Dunne said, nodding. "You seem drained. Everything good?"

"You know, mostly. But I just came from volunteering, and I'm kinda upset."

"Yes?"

"Well, it's strange, but...I actually came from *One Hundred and One Flavors.*"

"The ice cream place that's on the way here from near eastside Children's?"

"Yeah, I was with the family of Kirsten, one of my kids I visit. I was in Kirsten's room with her and her siblings and parents. Kirsten's about eight, and just wild about life. She's a towhead; she wears a long ponytail with all sorts of flamboyant colored pieces of yarn holding it all together. She's got these vibrant light-blue eyes and eyelashes that are so long you swear they had been bought in a store. There's an imp dwelling behind those eyes. And she's got a smile that keeps smiling even when she sleeps. Her leukemia was diagnosed at an early age. They aggressively treated her to try to save her, but she suffered a lot from it."

Harry felt he had started to choke up, but he didn't fight it. He continued, letting the tears roll. "Tissue please, Doctor."

Dr. Dunne pulled two out of the box and passed one to Harry, keeping one for himself. Harry saw that the ebullience Dunne always exhibited had diminished.

"In kindergarten, she tested way up in the genius stratosphere. Kirsten loved to play chess. She took me to the cleaners when she was six. One day, she challenged Dr. Peter Hinckley and me to a game. She worked on two chessboards and skunked both of us. She played several musical instruments. And, man, her art with a brush won all sorts of awards." Harry had daubed his eyes frequently with his tissue and signaled to Dunne he needed two more. Quietly, Dunne obeyed.

"Thanks. The docs told me today that Kirsten had run out of

days. I got her family to come. Kirsten knew that she was going to go. She had her family and me surround her bed and make a chain of hands. She kept her parents and siblings at her sides.

"She said, 'I love you all. It's time for me to go. Please smile at me and please don't cry. On the way home, stop at *One Hundred and One Flavors.*' Kirsten, wearing her constant smile, looked at each of us with those magical eyes and said good-bye.

"She closed her eyes and soon her breathing stopped. We kept holding hands until her nurse, who had joined us holding hands at the end, said, 'It's time to head for Kirsten's favorite ice cream store just like she wanted.'"

Harry sighed, and swallowed back more sobs. "Thank you. I know that I don't look like the Harry of ten years ago. I think I've changed. The free exam last week by your staff shows I'm in good shape. But back then the study predicted I would die this year in July. I want to discuss that."

Dr. Dunne walked over to his desk and pulled a second chair over. "Sit next to my computer with me. I got here early today and studied your file through the years, right up to last week. On the left side of the screen you see our recommendation of ten years ago." Harry studied the large screen.

Displayed on the screen was: *Harry Adkins - Summary: When Mr. Adkins first presented himself in January of the first year of the Study, his family heart history, his hypertension, his adverse BMI (Body Mass Index), his excessive use of alcohol, high cholesterol, his unhealthy diet and generally poor physical condition, we note that his decade of inattention to his health may have compromised his future physicality. Once he settled into his routine, he stood out and became an exemplary patient in the Study in all respects. We recommend that the Select Committee forecast a Year of Predicted Death 10 years from the date of this letter, and specifically the month and day he will die.*

Harry kept his eyes on the screen long after he finished reading.

"Now, Mr. Adkins -- " Dr. Dunne began.

"It's Harry."

"Yes. Okay." He paused. "You know you can call me Jonathan, right?" Harry nodded, still distracted by the screen.

Dr. Dunne still wore his monocle.

Finally, Harry spoke. "At the beginning, after I started the regime, I missed a number of appointments, and came late to a number of them. The very thing Alex warned me not to do. I've never been real good about remembering appointments."

"That's true enough, but let's move down screen. I detect a distinct, albeit slow, improvement in keeping appointments. And look at the right side of the split screen, which is a conclusion from your exam last week."

The text on the monitor read: *Harry Adkins, Summary: Except for his currently unalterable genetic history and his age, Mr. Adkins's blood pressure, his low body fat, and his good physical condition, all combine to conclude that his presently Predicted Year of Death should be extended.*

Harry was elated. "Then shouldn't I get a new predicted date?"

"Yes. But, our work in the study exhausted the grant we'd received with respect to altering the prediction. That's why we said in our literature that we could not modify the forecasted date of death no matter how much we wanted to. We just don't have the means to officially recalculate."

"Oh, shit. I guess I remember that now."

"I don't have access to the exact predicted date of death. Just the number of years. Setting the specific date was the job of the Select Committee. That can't change," Dunne explained, watching Harry's reaction closely.

"I see."

"Yes. Yes. But, speaking frankly, I think the years would be substantially enlarged if we were able to sit down and figure it all out."

"Jonathan, I've been sweating this out for a long time. Like, I've been worried sick about what I should be doing the last night I'm supposed to be alive. I mean, should I go to bed, just like it wasn't going to happen?"

Dunne stroked his chin thoughtfully. "I've studied a great deal of psychology…I've got a PhD in it." He paused and glanced at Harry. "You read, don't you? Didn't you and your parents read together when you were younger? I remember reading that in your Study Autobiography."

"Yes, and I studied a lot of English Lit in college. And I've subscribed to and read *Ploughshares* and *The Atlantic Monthly* for years."

"Then I know that you would heed the words of Dylan Thomas and *'Go not gentle into that good night.'* And, Harry, don't forget… *'Rage, rage against the dying of the light.'* Yes, don't think that you will die that night. Defy death. I'm not saying lightning won't strike someday, but I don't think it will happen on whatever day we predicted."

Harry got up and looked out on Portage Bay, turning his back on Dr. Dunne. Those were the words he'd been waiting years to hear. "Are you saying that some of my former health risks might have faded?"

Dunne nodded affirmatively.

"Which means it's now less likely I'll die this July?" Harry continued.

"It should." Dr. Dunne extended his hands warmly, and Harry gripped both of Dr. Dunne's arms excitedly. *God, that's good to hear!*

"Thank you, Jonathan!" He felt liberated.

Dunne laughed. "You look like Atlas must have looked when he put the world down and went off to lead the Titans to fight the gods."

Carol and Harry invited their children to fly over to Seattle for Thanksgiving, paying the kids' round-trip airfare.

Harry picked them up at Sea-Tac and drove them home.

Carol, Harry, Tim, and Tess sat in the den where the fireplace was roaring and the sunset bronze flames danced through and over the wood.

Harry said, "Tell Mom and me what's going on with your life there."

Extending his hand, Tim gestured to Tess. "Tell 'em, Sis. You have the biggest news."

"Well, Mom and Dad, has there ever been a firefighter in the family?"

I would never have expected that from her. But, you know, she's beefed up a little. Been working on weights I bet.

Carol looked askance and suddenly she coughed. "My cabernet went down wrong. What did you say you were?"

Tess, smiling broadly, spoke softly, and said, "I'm a firefighter and medic with the City of Ketchum. I competed against both male and female candidates."

With deep furrows in her forehead, Carol said, "I thought after pre-med you were going to go to practice with Alex."

I really think that's great for her to be a fireman, but I don't want to quarrel with Carol.

"Mom, you know that both Tim and I spent our last two summers working in Ketchum, and we just loved it there. Right, Tim?"

Tim raised his glass and said, "Here's to Ketchum. And to our parents for letting us live in the Lodge Apartment."

All, except Carol, raised their glasses.

"Look, Mom, not to be disrespectful, but it's my life."

She's still feisty. That's my girl. From where he sat, he was able to wink at Tess without interception from Carol. Tess winked back.

"It would take so many years for me to get my medical license. I love the outdoors. You know, Mother, I don't know how many years I have left on this earth, but I want to direct my own life rather than have my patients run it."

Yeah. Tess, state what you believe in. But, if you believe the study, I'm out of this earth come next July.

Carol rose, scowling at Tess, and carried her wine glass together with her Wally Lamb book to the bar. She poured herself a full glass and left the room, muttering, "Totally disrespectful to me."

Tim looked at Harry. "Is Mom like this all the time?"

"Not all the time, but some of the time. I'm worried."

"Shouldn't she see a mental health specialist?"

"There's ongoing medical care, including psychiatric observation and studies by neurologists. Mom won't do a brain scan. Even when the docs advise it."

Tess intervened. "Dad, and Tim…I don't want to be here. I want to go back home tomorrow…to Ketchum. I know the return tickets will be expensive, but I'll pay you back for the difference."

"That's not necessary. What is necessary is to get a better idea of what you're doing at your job. Also, bring me up to date about your job, Tim. Let's pour another glass of vino and when we've finished we'll go online and get the tickets."

"Sounds good to me. You know, we left our car in Boise."

Tim and Tess exacted a promise from Harry that Carol and he would drive to Idaho from Woodinville around the fifteenth of December.

Also, Tom and Alex would drive to Sun Valley in their separate cars, but in tandem with Harry and Carol.

After a workout at the gym, Harry drove home around noon during a short burst of Seattle-like cold rain, the kind of weather that Sun Valleyites pray to move across the mountain ranges and dump on Baldy.

He saw the U.S. Postal truck coming down his road after delivering their mail. Gabriel, the postal driver, usually brought the mail at noontime. Both drivers waved as they passed each other.

When he got home, Harry often launched all three of the 747 graphics doors because of the boyish thrill that he always got, and he noticed that Carol's car space was empty as usual.

After parking his car and lowering the garage doors, Harry trudged up to the mailbox and opened the box with the key. He pulled out the mail and locked the box. Harry usually didn't look at what was delivered until he had a chance to sit down in the kitchen and begin a cup of coffee.

The mail pile revealed a black envelope, addressed to him in red. No return address. *Shit. Allegro. Probably a threatening letter.* Harry found himself spontaneously sweating on a cool day. He ripped open the envelope. Inside were about a dozen colored photos similar to those entered into evidence at the trial. He glanced quickly at one shot that depicted a boy bound to a cot. Allegro held a knife in his hand close to the boy's penis...the boy was obviously terrified. Harry could look no more as he ran to a bathroom and up-chucked as he knelt over the toilet. He dropped all the photos next to the toilet.

Harry remained motionless. He struggled to move to his cot, and finally made it.

After a while, he placed a call to Izzy and heard Rebecca's voice.

"Hello, you've reached Dr. Cantor's office. Dr. Cantor and his family are vacationing in Florida. If this is an emergency, hang up and call 911. Otherwise, please leave a message when you hear the beep, giving your home and cell phone numbers."

Harry recorded the requested information.

He fetched the Allegro letter and its enclosures, turning away so he would not see the photos, and dropped them in a paper bag.

He then turned his attention to the letter. First, no date appeared on the black paper letter, and had been hand-written in some kind of red ink. From prior experience, he knew that the Post Office's marking on the envelope's upper right corner would give no clues. Harry quietly read:

"Judge Standish and your family, Harry Adkins and your family.

"Mr. Johnnie Allegro will, some day kill you and your family members using a small sharp knife -- over many hours for each person."

Harry recalled that Allegro was illiterate. Allegro used somebody on the outside, without a doubt. *Who in the hell is his surrogate?*

He would not tell Carol. *She'd probably go bonkers anyway. Ah ha. It's a police matter. So I'll wrap up the letter and envelope and call Deputy Wayne and have a squad car pick up the envelope. I'll tell him how to get hold of me in Sun Valley and here.*

He sent an e-mail message to Judge Standish.

NINETEEN

That Christmas, Carol and Harry visited Sun Valley, with Torvil Two, and were pleased their adult children lived there. On Christmas Eve, they planned to eat out at Warm Springs.

Carol and Harry invited Tess's boyfriend, Jason, and Tim's girlfriend, Odessa, to their condo for a pre-dinner glass of wine.

While everybody was bantering, Tess spoke. "Mom and Dad, there's something very important that Jason would like to talk with you about."

Harry and Carol exchanged curious looks. Harry nodded to Jason.

The young man fidgeted nervously. "Well, I've never done this before. But...I want your daughter to marry me, and I would like your blessing."

"Jason, you know, I thought, only the father is asked," Harry slapped him on the shoulder. "But, I think it's a great idea to involve both parents. Carol, what do you say?"

"I say, 'Yes.' What do you say, Harry?"

"It's unanimous." He grinned at his little girl, and extended his arms to hug her. Carol and Harry shook hands with Jason, and they all lifted their glasses in the air.

Odessa walked over with a glass of wine in one hand, and with Tim's hand in the other.

"Guess what?" Tim asked playfully.

Harry responded, unsuccessfully trying to look stern. Turning to Carol, "I suspect that we have another request."

Odessa handed her wine glass to Tim and knelt before his parents. "Prithee, (with a clipped British accent) Count and Countess Adkins, I humbly solicit your favorable response to my request to marry your second-born."

Harry chimed in, "Wouldst thou knowest, he has not been known to clean up his own room, or the bathroom?" They all laughed.

"I knowest that first-hand, me Lord and Lady."

"Countess Carol?"

"It shall be done."

"I concur."

Jason and Tim each had brought a small Christmas-wrapped package from under the tree and handed it to his respective lady. Clearly, the two men had been plotting for quite a while. Tess and Odessa opened their gifts and held up simple, narrow, white-gold engagement rings. Both men slipped the rings on their fiancées, and each couple kissed like they meant it.

A round of hugs by the multitude ensued, and Harry charged to the small refrigerator to withdraw a bottle of Alexia Sparkling Brut. Six glasses were poured, clinked, and sipped, with Harry delivering his standard toast. With tears streaming down his cheeks, he managed to choke out, "Here's to the brides, here's to the grooms; may their lives be two, long, happy honeymoons."

When Carol came to him and touched her glass to his, he felt a moment of love and tenderness, contrasted to her general indifference of the past couple of years. Looking longingly at his wife, he remembered when he had gotten engaged to her on the Wellesley campus.

The Adkins family and their two recent additions and Alex and Tom agreed their Christmas could not have been more joyful and to come back next year. They all pledged to get Little Harry and Tony to the Valley next Christmas.

TWENTY

Months later, back in their Lodge Apartment, Harry groggily reached toward the nightstand as he lay in bed. He consulted his watch. It was 6:25 a.m. Clad in dark blue pajamas, he swung his legs off the bed to the light-tan carpet. Sitting there, looking through the windows, he saw the soft June morning sun gently touching the manicured grass and blooming trees surrounding the Lodge.

He walked to one of the several windows, opened it, and saw the cloudless light-blue sky. He gazed downstream between stands of tall, dark-green trees. The air seemed fresh, for the Lodge stood about six-thousand feet above sea level.

He reflected that the twins really picked a great place to live. *Maybe they would never earn as much dough here as in the big cities,* Harry thought, *but awakening every morning in paradise surely made it all worth it.* Last winter, when Carol and Harry came here for Christmas and the New Year, they had seen the ski runs as rivers of snow.

Harry looked through the window and gazed on Bald Mountain. The peak is affectionately called Baldy by the locals and the ski world. After buying the Lodge Apartment, they'd remodeled it to allow for an extended stay for themselves and for their guests now that Harry had retired.

He rose from the bed, stretched for a while, and after getting dressed and finishing his morning routine, he wondered where in the hell Carol had gone. He was upset and felt abandoned by her. Carol the Predictable had left the building.

He checked the closet and noticed that her hiking boots were gone as well as her blue-green sweats. Harry donned his red, white, and blue sweats and his blue cap.

They had planned to walk the mile or so to Ketchum, to eat breakfast with Tess and Tim and their soon-to-be daughter-in-law and son-in-law. The double wedding was the day after tomorrow. Harry looked every possible place in the Sun Valley Lodge. No Carol. He picked up his cell phone, rang her cell, and left a message on her cell service.

At home, during the earlier part of June, she had more frequently risen long before Harry, and would come back between nine and nine-thirty. Sometimes when she returned, she was lovey-dovey and other times, as distant as a star in Orion's Belt. His watch said 7:35. Just enough time to hoof it to the Eatery for breakfast by eight-fifteen.

He walked the path to town, looking at his feet and fretting about Carol's absence, instead of enjoying sprawling, deep-green Bald Mountain ahead of him.

When he got closer to town, Harry paused to admire the Episcopal Church where the double wedding would take place. The kids had told him that the church's remodeling had just been completed. He crossed the road to get a close up. One lone car passed him before the road was clear. A brilliant morning sun reflected from a refurbished, yellow, mid-fifties Ford pick-up truck. Harry chuckled as he read the bumper sticker of the old pick-up: "Ketchum? Hell, I can't even find 'em."

Once at the church, he peered through some windows and found the view to be none other than the majestic Bald Mountain.

Harry pressed on, and had worked up quite an appetite when he finally arrived at his destination. Harry opened the Eatery' s front door, walked in, and smelled freshly brewed coffee, eggs, sausages, and pastries. The restaurant motif looked like Harry imagined one would have seen in Ketchum fifty years ago: tasteful mid-southern Idaho art hung on the rough and darkened cedar walls. He heard the bustle of waitresses -- there were no waiters in the Eatery that day, though Harry wasn't entirely sure why -- the jingle of silverware, the clatter of glasses, and the cacophony of conversations arising from about twenty-five filled tables. The ceramic likeness of a mustached, blue-jean-wearing cowhand, complete with a flannel shirt, a ten-gallon hat, and calf-high boots, sat in a chair near the entrance. The statue was the quiet tablemate of three more animated and articulate locals.

A few tables away from him, Tim and Tess rose from their table and called to him, "Dad!" The picture of the two of them with their fiancées struck a chord in Harry, and he realized that the twins were forming their own families and existing apart from him and Carol. A burst of pride, coupled with joy, welled up from his chest, dulled by a moment of long-range loneliness, complete with tears spilling down his face.

Tess, now willowy, tall, and athletic like Carol, her face coated with a layer of white sunscreen, reached out her arms as Harry moved toward them. Tim, a taller, huskier version of Harry followed. *Wow -- what biceps and shoulder muscles!* The biggest difference between the two was that, unlike Harry, Tim was well on his way to completing his inadvertent journey to baldness.

Tess wrapped her arms around Harry and kissed him on his cheek.

"Move aside, Sis, it's my turn."

Harry turned to Tim and they squeezed their arms around each other.

"You know, Tim. That was no bear hug. It was a grizzly hug."

"Hi, Mr. Adkins," Jason greeted him. Jason's hair was abundant, coal-black, and coarse, with tight curls -- like Alex, Harry thought.

"Jason, two things. First, this is the last time you're ever gonna call me Mr. Adkins."

"Yes, Harry, sir."

"And the last time you're ever gonna call me 'sir.' Second, remind me never to arm wrestle you."

"Yes..." Harry could see Jason was still struggling to avoid the names Harry had declared off-limits. "...Yes, Harry." He awkwardly added, as a smile spilled slowly from his lips.

Odessa looked at Harry's eyes and folded her arms around him. "Harry, you've raised two great kids."

"You know, thanks. But, until the teen years, Carol did almost all of the work with the kids. I was pretty into my work back then," he admitted. All the kids and their intendeds were well tanned, and reminded him of Muscle Beach.

Tess handed a menu to Harry. "Dad, order. We're hungry."

"Yes, ma'am."

"Is Mom on her way?" Tim asked from over the top of his menu.

"She should be," Harry predicted. They shrugged off her absence and all ordered, assuming that Carol would be joining them any moment.

Everybody in this soon-to-be family sat and bantered as fast as an auctioneer -- except Harry. He was looking at his kids and kids-in-law-to-be as an outsider. Right now, he was the happiest man in the world, he was so proud of the adults the twins were becoming. Had he been up walking, he would have clicked his heels. He kind of wished that he were wearing suspenders, so he could pull each strap with his thumbs as far as he could reach.

He felt his smile, which was so broad that it made his eyebrows almost conceal his eyes, dim, but only for a moment, when he thought of the $H^2 L^2$ prediction. *Next month. Bullshit to that.*

The redheaded model waitress brought five large, steaming breakfasts to them. The food delivery briefly muted the buzz of the five garrulous diners, but only momentarily. It soon resumed its prior peak. Harry listened to the repartee while he spread strawberry preserves over his wheat toast with a shiny silver knife.

"Daddy, where's Mom?" Tess's question seemed to catch everyone's attention.

He shrugged. "You know, we planned to walk here from our apartment. I noticed her hiking shoes and sweats were gone this morning. I left a message for her in our room on her cell and at the front desk. She'll probably be here any minute," Harry mused. A few years ago, Carol had been Mrs. Reliable, but that had changed, yes, changed so much. When they got home, he'd push hard for the brain scan.

Tess leaned in close to Harry. In a "for your ears only" tone, she said, "Does Mom do this sort of thing at home?" Harry placed his full fork back on the plate. He didn't know what to say, especially because Carol and Tess got along so well. Tess knew something had gone on with Naomi. He put his hands on the sides of his face.

"Mom!" Tess exclaimed. Carol had just walked into the Eatery.

Carol approached the table and another round of kissing and hugging ensued. Harry was pleased that Carol gave him a smile and a kiss on the lips. "Hello, sweetheart," she greeted him. He felt momentarily cherished, something that didn't happen too often anymore.

Tim signaled to the waitress. He pointed to Carol, and said in a loud voice, "Angie, will you bring a cup of decaf and a menu to Mom?"

"Right away, Tim. Hi, Mom." The waitress grinned.

Tess squeezed her mom's shoulder. "Where were you, Mom? We

were getting worried."

Angie handed Carol a menu and a mug of decaf. Carol calmly held her coffee cup in both hands. "Well, I got up at the crack of dawn. I didn't want to rouse Harry. He was sawing a big cord of wood," she said, drawing some chuckles 'round the table.

Harry was miffed that Carol had taken off without him, but he didn't want any kind of showdown. No gunfights at the OK Corral today. He reached across the table, smiled, and placed his hand over Carol's. "As your adoring spouse, dear, you can wake me up any time you want."

Everyone but Carol snickered. She reacted like a stone sphinx. Out of the corner of his eye, Harry glanced at Jason and Odessa, and interpreted their silent, quizzical look to mean, *what's going on with Carol?*

"Anyway, I saw the sun rise over Baldy as I walked up the hill toward Elkhorn. When I reached the top of the hill, I thought I could walk through Elkhorn to Ketchum. I was way too early to get here, so I sipped a latte at The Cheery Kitchen, where I met an Austrian man -- I'm not very good with names -- who was a ski and tennis instructor here for years until he retired. He looked kind of familiar."

"Mom, did the man you saw today have a scar on his right cheek?" asked Tess, wearing a puzzled expression on her face.

"Yes, I think he did. He said he knows you kids. He had a lot of charm. He had a deep tan and white hair, and he seemed really interested in letting me know all about Sun Valley. I just lost track of time." Carol was hardly apologetic. Harry found her matter-of-fact and dismissive, scanning her menu.

Harry didn't like all the time Carol had been spending with other men lately. She never showed any romantic interest in them, especially in the last few years since the headaches started, but he still hated all the attention she gave them. His jealousy was sparked when Carol would flirt with a guy at a party. Whenever that happened, he found himself squeezing his hands so hard they hurt, to quiet the rage that he felt coming up from his core like lava. He suddenly realized he was doing the same thing now, under the breakfast table. He let the rage go and relaxed his hands.

Recently, she had begun talking a lot about Steve Rindal, the gun freak, who was married and a good friend through the Golf Club. Something wasn't right there; Harry always got a twinge in his stomach whenever she mentioned Steve, just like the twinge he got now at the mention of the Austrian man.

"That would have to be Hans Flammer. Mom, look at me. Was he the same guy who came over to our table at the Sun Valley Grill last Christmas?" Tess seemed almost like she was cross-examining Carol. The other kids were watching incredulously.

"Yes, the same fellow. A scar," Carol said blankly.

Tess grabbed Harry's hand hard and whispered in his ear. "Dad. We've got to talk alone."

Harry whispered back, "The first chance we get."

Why in the hell does she want to talk alone?

Carol had finished her meal and was chatting, and savoring coffee, when she looked at her watch. "Oh, my god. We have family landing at the Hailey airport in about fifteen minutes. Who's giving us a ride to the airport?"

Harry watched as his daughter got up and whispered to Jason. Then, in a no-nonsense voice, she said, "Dad and I'll go alone to the airport. We have to talk about some financial stuff. Mom, will you take care of the bill? Go ahead and ride with Jason. See you at the airport."

Tess seized Harry's hand hard, and pulled him up from his chair with ease.

Tess's white Explorer was parked in front of The Eatery. It seemed only seconds before Tess and he were sitting in the front seat, seat belts fastened, and turning left out of the lot. The green left turn arrow had turned red against Tess's white Ford Explorer at Sun Valley Road and Main.

"Why do you want to talk with me, Tess? Why were all you kids looking at each other so funny?"

"First, Dad. I have to get some stuff straight about you and Mom. Okay? Then, we'll get into that. I'm still pissed at Mom over Thanksgiving."

Harry didn't argue, he only waited for her to continue. The traffic light's green arrow pointed to the left and the Explorer headed south for Hailey and the airport.

"Okay. Did you and Naomi have a sexual relationship?" Tess said, gripping the wheel.

"You already know the answer to that, Tess."

"That's what I thought. For a long time?"

"Five-plus years. I think she was obsessed with me. She had a husband too."

"And did Mom know about your affair?"

"I don't think she knew for sure until I told her, many years ago. But I always felt that she knew something was going on."

"Why did it stop?"

"Do you remember when I signed up for the H^2 L^2 Longevity Study? The one Alex got me in?"

"Okay, I think so."

"Anyway. The study got me thinking about my life, especially my health and my family. I began thinking that I had to straighten up my life. Early on in the study, I began working out, I really cut down on the booze and I've kept it up.

"We learned Naomi stuck a knife in her belly and bled to death in her office. She said she wanted me." Harry tried to stifle a sob, but it didn't work. Tess reached over and squeezed his left hand.

He looked at Tess. "I was secretly glad that Naomi killed herself. I told Izzy about my feelings and we spent a number of appointments discussing my cavalier assessment of Naomi. He finally brought me along to grieve about her death."

"Okay. Gee, I remember Naomi committing suicide, but I never heard why." She said, staring straight through the windshield. "Dad…did you and Alex ever have any kind of affair? Lately, when Mom and I talk, she talks about the affair you and Alex have going on now."

Harry was startled. "Not now, not ever. Not because of me, though. When I was younger, I was kind of hot to trot, as they say, but Alex wouldn't have anything to do with it."

"Okay. It bothers me, though, that Mom gets those thoughts in her head." Harry wondered if this had anything to do with Steve Rindal.

"Tess, Izzy…You know, the shrink…has explained to me it's his theory we're dealing with a brain tumor that may be squeezing on Mom's brain which accounts for Mom's craziness. Izzy wants a neurologist to do a brain scan."

"You're kidding Dad."

"Not at all."

"Does Mom object to the brain scan?" asked Tess.

"Yes. I suppose her objection could be laid to the pressure on the brain by a tumor…When you and Tim were in middle school, or younger, Mom had her first bad headache. The day I told her about Naomi, she had another splitting headache. Then they got worse. The neurologist could find no physical cause; we're still trying to see people and get it figured out. We have an appointment with a shrink on the eighteenth."

"Dad, do you still have romantic thoughts about Alex?" Tess interrupted. Harry paused. *Should I tell my daughter the truth?*

"Yes." He said, before he could stop himself. He suddenly realized the burden he must have laid on Alex all these years. As if Tess respected his long silence, she said nothing.

"Any further cross-examination, Ms. Adkins?"

"No, your honor." Tess looked at Harry, smiled, and placed her right arm around his shoulders, drawing him closer. "Okay. Thanks for telling me the truth and being there for me during those years when I decided to be a rebellious teenager."

"It's all right to tell Tim, too," Harry admitted. "The fewer secrets we all have, the better. We're all adults here. Now, what were you going to tell me about Hans Flammer?"

"Dad. I'm really worried about Mom. I'm glad you guys are seeing a psychiatrist."

"Why are you worried?"

Tess pulled into the Hailey airport parking spot and killed the engine. "Okay. For a lot of scary reasons. But the biggest one is that just after you guys left the Valley on New Year's Day, Hans Flammer died of a heart attack. If Mom is losing touch with reality, that's not good news."

Harry didn't move a muscle. He felt confounded by the implications of what was swirling around him.

"Dad, I don't want you to think I'm holding out on you. But, after we introduced Hans to Mom and you last Christmas, I saw Mom talking with him at the Wood River Gallery. The bottom line is that she was flirting with him pretty heavily. I was shocked, and pissed at her. The number of Austrians left in the area is not large, so for her to say that she was talking to someone like him, she must have been having flashbacks or visions or *something*. I don't know, but it's scaring me."

"It scares me, too." He paused.

"It's okay that you didn't tell me back then, but I'm glad you did now. One more thing about Mom."

"Yeah?"

"Are you ever concerned that Mom always brings her Beretta over here and does target practice?"

"Why should I be concerned?"

"A long time ago, when I was a kid, I overheard Mom one night, say that she was going to kill you."

"It was more than once. Look, I discussed the threats with Izzy and he gave them no concern. She just says that. It's a saying."

Harry felt Tess's arm around his shoulder, and she said, as they looked into each other's eyes, "Yuh know Dad, when a child like me is growing up, it's a full-time job for the kid to do the growing up, and I confess I was too interested in myself to pay attention to what was goin' on with Mom and you, so thanks for being straight with me."

"You said 'a child like me.' Long ago, Mom looked it up and found a reference to a 'spirited child.' I, too, missed what my parents were about, but I never had the opportunity in their later lives to learn who they were."

"A great talk, Dad, but some of our guests are in their 'final descent.' We'd better scramble. Look who just pulled up in the Green Dodge Caravan next to us!"

Tim, Carol, Odessa, and Jason walked with Tess and Harry into the Hailey International arrival area. All the greeters stood together anxiously. A thunderstorm pelted the area and the worrywarts thought that the airport was a little too close to the mountains on each side of the runway. When Alex, Tom, and their sons, Tony and Little Harry -- now in their early twenties -- Joan Madden (illness prevented O.W. from attending the wedding), Trish, and Pete disembarked from their plane, great big hugs erupted everywhere, and the room seemed overwhelmed by shouts, squeaks, squeals, kisses, hugs, and hearty handshakes galore.

Harry was approaching the group, when, suddenly, from behind him, a short female placed her hands over his eyes. He smelled Alex's perfume, and a male voice behind him said, "Guess who? It's us!"

Harry offered: "Let's see…It's three men from Venus and a woman named Alex from Mars." The hands lifted, and Harry turned and saw a grown Little Harry, now called L.H., and was immediately smothered with embraces from Alex, Tom, Tony, and L.H. Then, Alex stepped up and took his face in her hands and delivered a big peck on his lips. For the first time, Harry felt that it must be like being kissed by a sister.

Tony stood back and looked at Harry. "L.H., remember when we were just high enough to hug his formerly fat thighs? Now, look at him. A trim dude, isn't he?"

Trish and husband Pete joined the vivacious throng a few minutes later after rescuing their luggage from going back to Seattle and held it a tad tighter than one would expect.

All of them, each talking at close to the speed of sound, went arm and arm to collect their luggage.

After the bags were sorted out and loaded into the waiting vehicles with the wedding goers, Tom poured glasses of champagne before they headed north to Sun Valley.

Later, Harry returned to the airport with Tim, Tess, and Carol to pick up Odessa's and Jason's parents and all who were awaiting Alex's parents who were flying their single-engine plane from Boston.

Finally, the bad weather abated and Sun Valley's sun predominated, greeting the arrival of Felix and Emmy Hungar, Tim's in-laws-to-be, and Jim and Jayne Johnson, Tess's in-laws-to-be.

While waiting at the airport for one last flight, the senior Hungars and Johnsons related that the four of them had graduated from different colleges, separately met as Sun Valley ski instructors, married, and each couple had one kid, who was raised in the Valley area. The Hungars and the Johnsons had formed a successful real estate firm, acquiring property that turned out to be valuable, enabling both couples to enjoy homes in Hawaii and Sun Valley.

Also expected was the private jet that would bring two of the three other members of the Board of Directors of *Nippon/USA,* Masaru

Takano and Ry Hayami, to the Hailey Airport, to be guests at the wedding. Tom and Harry, under the *Nippon/USA* Purchase Agreement, had remained on the board for five more years. Harry and Carol had become closer to Ry and his wife when they attended the Tokyo wedding of the Hayamis' oldest child. Muramoto was deterred by a last-minute emergency, and wouldn't make it to the Valley.

Carol, Alex, Tom, and Harry agreed that Tom and Alex should personally pick up the other directors. After the wedding, the *Nippon/USA* directors had scheduled a formal meeting.

Harry privately fretted that Carol might embarrass him by saying the wrong thing, which she had done a lot lately, a problem that could be related to a brain tumor.

By coincidence, the private jet that would bring the other members of the Board of Directors of *Nippon/USA* and the plane that the Quicks were on would land within ten minutes of each other.

TWENTY-ONE

Harry thought the rehearsal at the Episcopal church later the same evening went off well, given the fact that it was a double wedding. But it did kind of throw off Father Oxford that Tim was Jason's best man and Jason was Tim's. To say nothing of Tess being Odessa's maid of honor and Odessa being Tess's.

Father Oxford would not go along with simultaneous vows. "Too complicated," he ruled. So, the couples flipped a silver dollar to see who would have the choice to be married first or second. Tim and Odessa won the toss and elected to be married second. Each of the grooms carried the ring of the other. Tess and Odessa temporarily wore the rings for Tim and Jason as this was to be a double-ring ceremony.

Harry pointed out that the couple who was married second would have a matron of honor, whereas the first couple married would have a maid of honor. The coin toss and the maid-and-matron-of-Honor thing seemed to perplex Father Oxford. But, after extended debate, Father reluctantly concluded that he could see no serious theological problem about that, so he would not be forced to consult the reigning bishop. Harry thought Father was a crushing bore.

The wedding rehearsal adjourned while the daylight was still at large and that evening the rehearsal dinner was held at Warm Springs. Harry served as master of ceremonies at the request of his children and their fiancés and spotted Alex's parents standing next to the bar. After an extended cocktail hour, he introduced Father Oxford and asked him "to lead us in prayer." Father Oxford responded with a long, insignificant, and insipid message about marriage.

Harry asked the two couples to stand.

With the four kids on their feet, Harry reached in his pocket and pulled out a paper. "With apologies to Tennyson," he announced, "I have a short poem for this occasion:

> For I dipt into the future, far as human eye could see.
> Saw the Vision of the world and all the wonder that would be.
> Heard Sun Valley fill with the voices of babies born and
> there were quite a few,

From Jason and Tess and Tim and Odessa to make the
Vision of the world anew.
Forward, forward let us range,
Let the great world spin forever down the ringing grooves of change.

"Will you stand with me and toast Jason and Tess and Tim and Odessa?" Harry asked, then paused, took his handkerchief out and dabbed at his eyes. His voice trembling, he continued, "This is hard for me. I think of the loss of our two children, but I'm joyous at gaining two more children." As Harry faltered again, Carol, in her pale-yellow silk dress, rushed to stand next to him and hold his hand.

She smiled nervously. "Everyone, please raise your glasses. Tess and Jason and Tim and Odessa, here's to a life of peace, health, prosperity, and fidelity."

At the last word, Carol and Harry exchanged eye contact. Dozens of glasses made music around them, including their own. Still holding his hand, Carol led him back to their table. He saw the same melancholy as he had first noticed in Tokyo at the U.S. Embassy. Although he may have deserved it, he felt anger toward her for publicly using the word "fidelity" in her toast. In his mind, it could have implied to some that he had been unfaithful. Her word choice aside, he was pleased that Carol came to rescue him and save the day.

He put the incident on his mental list to discuss with the shrink on the eighteenth, that is July 18.

The next day, the weddings began at four in the afternoon. Harry remembered taking Tess down the aisle and later saying, "Her mother and I" in response to Father Oxford's question, but aside from that, the ceremony was quite a blur.

He stared at Baldy standing outside, green and sun-brushed, as if it were another witness, a mile or so away from the church's glass-ceiling window. He imagined himself and Carol holding hands with little grandchildren, all on skis, at the bottom of Baldy at Warm Springs, on Christmas, on a blue Sun Valley day.

Moments later, he found himself with Carol, and Odessa's and Jason's parents, standing on the right of the brides and grooms in the reception line. Harry thought he must have greeted most of the people who lived in the expanded area of the Valley.

When the wedding dinner concluded, Tim and Tess and children-in-law went back to their accommodations, delivered to their homes by a limousine hired by Carol and Harry. He had offered to put them up at the Lodge, and the couples had graciously accepted, promising to return early in the morning for their rafting trip the following day.

In the morning, silently, at first light, Tess, Jason, Odessa, and Tim walked out of the Sun Valley Lodge, carrying their personal gear. They walked over to the Lodge parking lot and boarded Odessa and Tim's green Dodge Caravan.

The plan was to have the others board the yellow school bus in the Lodge parking lot between nine-thirty and ten in the morning, and then to breakfast at the Eatery. Ben Bottomly, just nineteen, who they learned was a want-to-be U.S. Ski Team racer, would drive the bus to Stanley after breakfast.

A good deal of the river rafting gear had been placed in the Caravan, and the balance was loaded by Ben Bottomly onto the bus, which also had been parked near the Lodge parking lot. Both vehicles were equipped with burglar alarms, just in case, and Ben had cat-napped in the bus and van, which were parked near each other the night before.

After breakfast, Ben stood by and assisted the eager would-be rafters as they climbed aboard the waiting bus parked near the Eatery. Ben spoke to each guest by her or his first name and added a personal note to each, making it clear, Harry thought, that red-haired Ben possessed some valuable people assets. He was not overly tall, but he hadn't bulked up yet. Ben wore his red ponytail so that it lay on his back, a bit below his shoulders.

Ben shut the bus door and started the engine, and Harry rose as the bus turned left onto Sun Valley Road, and then north on Highway 75.

"You've all met Ben at the wedding. Some of you know he's a downhill racer, but he'll be a cautious driver on this trip. Won't you, Ben?"

"Whatever you say, boss." Harry observed: *A resonant Boston accent.*

The brides and grooms, Harry speculated, had driven north out of Ketchum on Highway Seventy-Five in the black Expedition the evening before, as the night's last star was about to go out. The brides' white, floor-sweeping gowns and the grooms' penguin-like attire probably had been exchanged for short pants and light-colored tops to fit the roles of rafting guides.

Harry thought it was a little strange that the newlyweds did not escape from their parents by car, train, airplane, or -- for heavens' sake -- a motorcycle, but were on their honeymoon *with* their parents and well-wishers accompanying them on a couple of nights' rafting trip. Harry smiled to himself as he thought of the closeness of their family and the generosity of their kids and their new partners. He was springing not only for the breakfast, but for his own birthday bash today at Mormon Bend, located a few miles downstream from Stanley.

He fell asleep on the bus soon after they left Ketchum. However, it wasn't long before the din of raucous rafters finally reached his consciousness. He awakened after a short catnap, still sitting next to Carol. He saw that the members of the Kurosawa confederacy all held bottles of sake, which they poured freely into the glasses of the other rafters.

Takano shouted over the tumult, "Harry, here, I pour you some sake."

"I'll have some during lunch, promise."

"Harry, you're a party pooper." Carol held up her hand. "Takano, Takano, please bring a glass to me."

Carol elbowed Harry mischievously, unsuccessfully egging him on to drink. After she received her glass from Takano, and gave up elbowing Harry, Carol settled back to read Wally Lamb's *I Know This Much Is True*. He ignored Carol's light jab.

Harry was startled because he'd never known Carol to drink in the morning. Also, he was taken aback by Carol's book choice for a vacation: a novel narrated by the brother of a paranoid-schizophrenic protagonist. *Maybe the fact that Carol's reading that book should be discussed with Izzy.*

Izzy had been unable to come on the river trip because of his son's bar mitzvah. *Damn!* Also, Dr. Dunne had come down with an inner ear infection that affected his balance, so he was regretfully absent from the trip as well.

The bus stopped. He looked at his watch, which read eleven o'clock in the morning. The near-noon sun shone brilliantly, and unlike in the big city, no pollutants obscured the horizon.

He gazed at a roadside sign that announced that they had arrived at Galena Summit -- elevation 8701 feet. Stanley, a tiny town (summer population one hundred), was near their launch site.

The bus's headlights tipped downward as it slowly descended toward the town. Harry pulled out his map and located the Sawtooth Wilderness and lakes like Yellow Belly, Grand Mogul, and Hell Roaring, plus more lakes and more peaks. Harry thought to himself that he would love to take on the challenge of hiking to all those places, and more.

Looking at his map, Harry found the drainage basin that feeds the Salmon River. Dozens of summits and lakes. The clear blue sky and the green valley floor framed the Smokey Mountains to the southwest, the Sawtooth Mountains to the west, the Boulder Mountains to the east and the White Clouds Peaks to the northeast. The tops of these mountains had exploded to the ten-to-eleven-thousand foot range eons before humans found fire. Harry reveled in the blue, dark green, and golden sun-struck panorama that surrounded him. He wanted to be smothered by what stretched before him for years to come. Like, what would the landscape look like on a blue-sky day after a fresh snowfall? Would it be unthinkable for him to ski down from Galena Summit? And he saw the evergreens bedazzled by the brilliance of the falling and felled leaves of autumn. Thinking of Carol's book, he knew that this much was true: *next month's prediction is dead wrong.*

They descended downward through a few switchbacks, some mental *gee-whizzes,* and hopes that the flex beam could contain the bus if something went awry. The two-lane road became more or less level and straight to Stanley, passing by the Salmon River flowing east.

The bus lumbered left to Highway 21 in Stanley to stop near a small café.

Harry arose and walked to the front of the bus. "Hi, gals and guys. First, before I begin, Takano." Takano looked up. Harry closed his left hand to make a kind of cup and used his right thumb as if to pour something in his left hand.

Takano, with a smile that made his face crinkle, dutifully grabbed a nearly empty bottle of sake and a plastic glass, strode to Harry, poured the sake into the glass, and handed it to him.

Harry bowed. "Thanks, Takano."

As Takano made his way back to his seat, he raised the bottle. "More?" On his way to the rear of the bus, he poured sake into the empty cups held up by their owners.

While Takano was dispensing, Harry said, "We'll be here for about forty-five minutes. We'll put in at the Salmon River, heading east, at a place called Mormon Bend." He noticed that Carol was reading her book and had never looked at him. Harry was miffed and disappointed.

Holding up his satellite phone, he said, "I'll get in touch with our guides at our put-in and let you know. So," looking at his watch, "be back here in forty-five minutes."

Harry took a look at Carol as he passed by her on his way out of the bus. *Guess what? Still reading.* He continued to the door, turned to his left, and saw that Carol appeared to be devouring Lamb's bestseller. *No wave, no kiss blown, no nothing from Carol. If this was in a story, it would be a story of unrequited love.*

Harry returned to the bus after jogging a bit, give or take twenty minutes or so, and found himself sweating, which had permeated his clothes. *Wow! Did that feel good.* He also stretched outside the bus. He regularly attended the Yoga classes offered by the Golf Club. *Yes, all in all, I've found a tranquility after the sale of Nippon/USA that I haven't experienced since my parents were alive.*

As he leaned against the bus, he watched the river rafters returning to the bus, carrying all sorts of newly bought paper cups of lemonade and espresso, plus new supplies of sun-tan lotion, despite the low cloud cover.

Once the rafters plopped into their seats, Ben started the bus, turned left at Highway 75, passed through Lower Stanley, and headed for their launch site, Mormon Bend, just a few miles away.

Now at the campground, Ben Bottomly slowed down, turned right, and parked. The passengers arose and lined up to get off the bus. Ben opened the doors. Ry, first off, carried the camera equipment, followed closely by Takano. Ry walked away and stood on a felled tree. The rest of the passengers streamed off the bus.

Tess yelled, "We're all going to have to get ready for dinner. Fortunately, we have lots of soap, and we brought along enough towels. I think our Stanley buds will be able to help us out." She looked at her watch. "Your chefs will start working on our evening meal. Be back here in two hours for dinner."

After enjoying good steaks, baked potatoes, a giant-sized salad, and more beer, the time was ripe to serve dessert -- Harry's birthday cake. By the time it was served, coffee, and beer by some, were being consumed.

Darkness finally ruled, but a campfire lit the immediate surroundings, all covered by the darkened sky tattooed with glistening stars. The only sounds came from the rhythmic rushing river, from frogs, maybe even coyotes and cougars. And of course, the other sound was of the many Happy Birthday choruses in Harry's honor.

Slowly but surely, the rafters excused themselves, some stretching both arms while showing wide yawns, wishing Harry yet another "Happy Birthday," shivering a bit, and apologizing for calling it a night.

Carol, Alex, Harry, Tom, Ry, and Takano huddled together in their warm clothing, for they were now inhabiting a place near Stanley where the elevation stands higher than six-thousand feet.

Takano stood before the fire and said, "Carol, Alex, and gentlemen, I need to get present for Harry."

"Oh, come on -- you were asked not to get a birthday present for me," Harry mildly protested.

Takano arose, zipping his parka. "Return soon."

When Takano was taken by the darkness, Alex said, "We're sure lucky to have him as a friend and a business partner."

Harry moved a little closer to the fire. He shouldn't be saying this, but it had to be said. "Bygones be bygones, please, all, but I've always wondered if Takano felt guilty that he brought Naomi to us."

Carol, covered by a bright red Pendleton blanket, walked off in the direction of their tent and soon disappeared into the night.

Silence resonated among the five of them. Harry got to his feet and tossed a few pieces of wood into the dwindling fire.

It was not long before Takano came, carrying a backpack.

He paused to look at each person. "Where did Carol go?"

"She said she wanted to go to bed."

Takano kneeled and sat on the back of his legs. He reached into his backpack and pulled out an elaborately wrapped birthday package. He counted, "One, two, three, four, five," as he took five short Waterford glasses from his sack and placed them in front of each person. He handed the package to Harry, and said, "Happy Birthday to Harry."

Harry looked at Takano and the others and was close enough to see the reflection of the fire in their eyes. "I'll open it," he said, as he placed both hands over the top of the package, and moved them over the sides to form the shape of a bottle.

He slowly removed the wrapping, placing the paper in his backpack.

"Takano, you shouldn't have done this. My God."

Harry held the bottle for all to see the legend, "L'Espirit de Courvoisier."

Everybody talked at the same time and was visibly moved about Takano's gift.

Harry said, "I'll pass this 'Nectar of the Gods' for your own pour."

Alex, who sat next to him, poured a healthy slug into her glass, and passed it to the others to do likewise.

When all glasses were filled, Takano raised his and said, along with the others, "Happy Birthday," and the clinking tones of a toast made a new sound in the night. All took a swig or two, and sat back silently.

"Did you get authority from KIL?" Harry couldn't believe the Board of Directors would approve.

"No."

"Why?" Harry frowned.

Takano crossed his arms, with one hand holding his glass. "Why? Because I pay for it by my own checking account."

Harry perceived that he must be as awed as the rest because that's exactly how they all looked, eyes wide with disbelief.

Harry shuffled over to Takano, and said, "Nobody has ever done anything like that for me before. I don't want to cross your customs, but I'd like to give you a hug."

Takano nodded and smiled as if to say, "Yes. Okay." And the two men stood with one arm over the other, each with one hand holding his "Nectar of the Gods." The two of them sat down and then all five linked hands as if the moment joined them all.

Alex extended the glass she had been using to Takano, who waved it away and said to all, "Please keep your glass. It is my gift."

Takano reached in his backpack, brought out another Waterford glass and said, "Harry here is one for Carol. You have been my family for many years. My wife died a long time ago; I have no children."

No more toasts were added to the sounds, but Harry observed that each of the five cried softly, but happily. A moment forever remembered -- *huh* -- even by him.

Thinking of his predicted date of death, Harry wondered whether another gathering, just like this one, would occur again. As if to find an answer, he found himself looking at the stars. *Perhaps the answer will be there tomorrow.*

All rose hand-in-hand. Still grasping their empty glasses, they strolled to their tents, under the sky, by the river, and listened to the now-hushed tones of the night.

Ben approached the group, coming from a chair that he had been sitting in out of sight from the campfire.

Harry broke off from his friends as they exchanged good wishes all around.

Ben said to Harry, "You want me to douse the campfire that you all were enjoying?"

"Yes, please."

"Happy Birthday, Mr. Harry. When I grow up, I hope I have friends like yours."

"Thanks, Ben."

TWENTY-TWO

Harry opened his eyes. He heard water flowing -- fast. For a moment, he didn't know where he was. He was in a green tent. He sat up in his sleeping bag, saw and heard Carol, as she snored vigorously...*Of course, you fool -- it's six-thirty in the morning., and you're a few feet away from the Upper Main Salmon River. Today, we float east on the river on an adventure. Yes, must not forget to use the satellite phone to call my attorney, Joe Kennedy.*

He put on his float clothing and shoes, grabbed his shaving kit, and was out of there leaving Carol still snoring. Just in case of rain, he draped a light parka over himself before he crawled out of the tent.

Somebody had turned off the stars, and the clear sky was covered with gray clouds. He wondered if there is a God, if he, or she, does that kind of work up there, or where he or she hangs out. Harry looked to the sky.

He found no answer to his question of last night.

Harry dialed Joe Kennedy's office number on his satellite phone.

Harry heard, "Hi, it's Joe Kennedy. I'm away from my office, or with a client, so leave your message and number when you hear the beep. I'll get back to you ASAP."

"Joe, it's Harry calling from the shores of the Salmon River near Stanley, Idaho. It's about six-fifty on Saturday morning. Hey, big guy, I need an appointment. I'm thinking about changing my will -- I'm not talking about Carol's and she won't know anything about it. Send me an e-mail as to the time and day. I should be back by a week from today. Thanks, Joe. Call my office and have somebody put the appointment on my calendar. Goodbye."

Harry decided not to shave, so he attended to his morning ablutions quickly.

Jason, Odessa, Tim, Ben, and Tess were working in the kitchen shelter, and already the morning meal smells, including coffee, wafted toward the tents.

Ben came to Harry, carrying a bugle.

Harry thought he'd tease Ben. "You look like you're going to ask me if it's okay to play *Reveille?*"

"Jeez, how'd you guess that?"

"You figure it out."

Ben paused. "Yeah. Kind of obvious."

"Time?"

"Seven-thirty?"

"Blow it, boy," Harry said as he patted Ben on the shoulder.

As Ben walked to the middle of the sleeping area, a few people had already crawled out of their tents.

At precisely seven-thirty, the familiar notes soared throughout the campground and beyond. After finishing his bugling, Ben walked by the tents, shouting frequently, "Breakfast is over in one hour!" A large exodus ensued from the tents. Ben busily rolled up the tents that were empty.

Harry had first heard those notes when Tom and he began ROTC summer sessions.

He saw Tom and Alex coming toward him.

Tom said, "How will we ever forget our first *Reveilles?* Good morning -- and another Happy Birthday."

Alex and Harry met in the chow line and they exchanged the inevitable kiss on the lips. *Great birthday.* "How will we ever forget last night -- the four of us sipping that ambrosia, the conversation, and warming ourselves before the campfire? We won't." Alex looked around. "I don't see Carol. How's she doing? Worried?" Alex took Harry's hand.

Harry looked at Alex and shook his head.

"Your eyes are telling me things are not going well."

"Right, not very often."

Alex headed back to the tent area.

At about ten in the morning, the tents, sleeping bags, cooking utensils, most of the food, and extra clothing were loaded in the bus that was to be parked at Mormon Bend and secured by an off-duty sheriff who would drive the bus to Torrey's Hole Take-Out.

Most of the other gear, except the rafts, and everything relating strictly to the rafting, such as the paddles, a defibrillator and an oxygen canister, all in a red waterproof bag would be carried down in the rescue boat. The rafters' individual safety equipment -- helmets, lifejackets, and wetsuits -- would be handed to them before the put-in.

The guides had arranged for several red rubber rafts with paddles. Each guide -- Tess, Tim, Jason, and Odessa -- carried a clipboard holding the guests' names. They assigned the rafters to specific rafts. A guide interviewed each passenger.

Tess strode to Harry. "Mom and you are going to ride with me in the safety boat."

"I thought we'd be in Odessa's boat."

"We were unanimous that it'd be the safety boat."

Harry hunched up his shoulders, arms, and hands.

The other passengers milled, mingled, gabbed, fiddled with cameras, snacked, laughed, read maps, drank copious gulps of water from plastic bottles, fiddled with their helmets, life vests, and wetsuits, applied sunscreen to themselves and to others, fitted life jackets, stuffed their small items of personal gear in waterproof duffel bags, all while Harry secretly imagined what would happen if they fell out of their rafts.

Harry noticed that Ry, wearing a black wetsuit, stood ankle-deep on the shore. Then, he lofted his body toward the other side of the river, landed smack on his stomach and thighs, and began swimming powerfully.

Odessa came running to the shore, shouting at Ry to get out of the water because it was too cold. She watched anxiously. Ry was doing a strong crawl and arrived at the middle of the river. Odessa placed her lips on her whistle, then hesitated as she watched him race toward the other side and disappear under the water. He surfaced then swam back to where he had first plunged in.

Seconds later, he stood next to Odessa, his hands on his hips, smiling.

She marveled. "You didn't happen to be on a Japanese Olympic swim team?"

"I did." He bowed.

"How did you do?"

"When I practiced the day before my event, I tore my Achilles tendon somehow. I never competed."

"Oh, that's terrible," said Odessa, placing her arm around his shoulder.

"As a Westerner may say, you lose some and win some. No big deal."

She politely nodded, then jumped to stand on a log. Waving her hands, Odessa blew the whistle. "Hey, you guys! Pay attention to Tess." Harry swelled with a parent's pride. Shifting his weight from foot to foot, he was anxious to begin.

"Thanks, Odessa. It looks like you all have the right clothes to run the river and we saw you all dousing yourselves with sunscreen. That's great! Since it's still early, for safety's sake, while our crew is loading the safety boat, we'd like you to take a bus trip to scout the big rapids where, later, we'll take a rest stop and pull out after we finish running this section of the river.

"That's about it before we board the bus. We're passing out maps, take one from Ben as you get on."

In a few minutes, the passengers were loaded on the bus, which Tess drove east on Highway Seventy-five.

Tess picked up the bus's microphone. "Folks. I want to assure you that nobody's ever been seriously injured rafting with us. Having said that, Jason, Tim, Odessa, and I need your utmost cooperation. Nobody's freelancing. The most important rule is to do what you're told. We also depend on you to stay in the boat. Do not jump out to save somebody. Let us save them.

"If you take a drink – river talk for going overboard -- aim your feet downriver, and we'll get you out. We use this throw bag. It contains a long line." She held up a canvas contraption for the group to see.

Harry asked himself, *Why is my talented, articulate daughter wasting her life to be a fireman in a small town, albeit a tennis and ski instructor, rafting guide, mountain climber, and all of that? Because my children are not my children, except for a short period of time.*

"The safety boat is for your protection. Our safety boat goes through each of the four rapids, pauses after each of the rapids, makes sure all the paddle boats make it through with all the passengers, and then heads downriver, passing the paddle boats. My safety raft goes down river first. After my boat gets through the rapids, we turn around to support the other rafts.

Tess spoke again. "The Official Rapid Rating System says something like this: Class Four rapids are 'very difficult, long rapids; powerful, irregular waves, dangerous rocks; boiling eddies; difficult passages to scout. Scouting and precise maneuvering required. Demands expert boaters.' Class Three is listed as only 'Difficult.' I emphasize: Stay in your boat. I believe that the stream flow has gone down so that gives us a better margin of safety. Again, if you do leave the boat, point your body and feet downriver and grab the throw bag.

Tess paused. "Anybody want to bail out? So to speak."

A friendly chorus of boos rang out.

As they bounced along the rocky road Harry felt the bus start to slow. The river and the road were located in a narrow canyon, featuring steep embankments on both sides of the river.

"We'll stop here. Let's get out and look -- we call it scouting. We're looking at 'Shotgun.' Remember this is a Class Four. This route has already been scouted today, but it's still important that we see it as well." Tess pointed to a long section of the Salmon. Harry followed her gaze, and saw wild, white water, green water, and huge boulders edging up out of the rapids.

"Your guide steers the boat from the rear and knows the best course to take. Any questions? No? Let's keep driving down river and we'll scout the Sunbeam Dam."

Again, the group re-loaded the bus, which Tess drove into a woodsy parking lot overlooking the rushing water. When the rafters were off the bus, they were led upriver along the road to a promontory about one hundred feet above the river.

"First, I'd like you to look upriver from the remains of the Sunbeam Dam. What do you notice about what's upriver above the dam?" Tess addressed the group.

Harry spoke up, "You know, it looks kind of peaceful to me right up to the remains of the concrete."

"I agree with you, Dad. As an aside, after the Sunbeam Dam was built, legend has it that an early conservationist, maybe just a fisherman, or a pioneer terrorist, was annoyed that the dam interfered with the fish run and the guy destroyed part of the dam, which had extended to the cliff on the other side. What else do you see, Dad?"

"Just an observation, but the end of the dam that sits in the river kind of looks like the prow of a ship. It must be about sixty feet high. From here it seems that the guide has to steer the raft to the right and be sure to head straight through the dam side and the other side...both shore sides of the river look like cliffs."

A murmur erupted from the group standing behind Harry.

Harry turned, with his hands on both hips. "I'm not trying to scare anybody. After all, this is recreation so it should be fun. But I'm giving you a heads up to be aware of the fact that there seems to be a steep drop in the river right where the dam is, and the cliffs make the river channel really narrow. There's white water being thrown up. Wouldn't that make it hard to steer?"

Tess pointed downriver. "It's hard to steer and see ahead. With the rock faces on each side there's no shore, no place even to clutch with your fingernails if you got tossed out of the boat. And there are plenty of boulders near the surface that could give you a bad rap on the old noggin."

Harry added, "What Tess didn't say was that if you were tossed out, you would be madly driven, twisting and turning, through the narrow passageway, down the steep drop, by torrents of rolling white water. And the Class Three rapids, not far downriver from the Dam, are not exactly a picnic either."

Harry noticed Ry frantically taking all sorts of still and rolling-film shots.

As Harry watched the river on the drive back to the rafts he felt a sudden wave of fear wash over him, despite the fact that he knew he was in good hands. He shuddered. Somehow, he calmed himself, and let his mind wander to something other than the rapids.

For a few moments he drifted back to the prediction of the study. *Few creatures know the day and the year that they will die.* Despite all the H^2 L^2 contract drafter's obfuscations, Harry felt assured that he would not die before the date next month. He felt slightly reassured that there was more life for him, and he knew today wasn't his day.

Going down this wild river journey would be one of his great life experiences, like summiting Mount Rainier for the first time. *Doing is part of the living.*

The bus returned from the rafters' scouting of the Shotgun and Sunbeam Dam rapids. No rain, but dark clouds appeared over them. The rafters kept up their general jubilation. All the rafts lay on the shore of the Salmon laden with gear and ready to launch. Slowly, rafters positioned themselves and their paddles in their assigned boat.

A few steps away from the group, Carol and Tim stood together arguing. Tim was scolding her. "Mom, you should've gone scouting the river instead of reading that book."

"Thank you for your advice, Son," Carol said bitingly.

"I think that's a huge mistake," Tim muttered as Carol walked away, stowing her book in the watertight bag.

A few minutes later, Tess's safety raft pulled away first from Mormon Bend to be followed by the other rafts. All aboard wore red life jackets, black wetsuits, red helmets, and short pants of mixed hues, plus so much sun screen that their faces looked like those of mimes. The rafters had received brilliant yellow "Sun Valley" tees from their guides.

Tess steered her safety raft from her stern position.

In the safety raft Harry heard Tim's voice and turned around to see him. With a megaphone, he was shouting, "Mom and Dad, you got your helmets and wetsuits on, fine, but you forgot your life vests. Dammit, put them on."

Harry noticed that Carol did wear her life jacket over her shoulders, but did not attach the vest straps in front. *Well, monkey see, monkey do, my dear.* Carol smiled at Harry. Somehow, her smile came off to him as "gotcha!"

As they became waterborne, black clouds darkened the river. Tim, using his megaphone, yelled, "Don't worry about the weather! Happens a lot on the river." Tim continued steering from the stern, calmly holding his paddle with both hands.

Over the river's roar, Tess shouted, "Remember what I told you all about using your paddles, go right side, left side, both sides…"

Tess's safety boat entered the hell-broth called Shotgun. "Right side!" She commanded. Those on the right pulled deep and hard, and the boat swung rapidly to the left. A wave washed over the crew. "Fantastic, right-siders! Left side!" The raft swung rapidly to the right. "Great job, left side!"

For a moment, the raft and its rowers seemed airborne, but then splashed down with a smack on the river. Tess's strong, competent voice rose over the sound of the Shotgun. "Both sides!" The raft pitched to the right. "Left side!" she screamed. The rocks in the river and the river's velocity combined to make it seem as if giant turbines were churning the water.

In the safety raft, Harry trembled as he glanced over the side of the raft at the ferocious water.

"Right side!" The right-side paddlers grimaced as they stroked into a wall of water, depositing gallons of it into their raft. Harry began to panic, wondering if too much water got in his raft whether they could still navigate with all that extra weight, but his thoughts were quickly interrupted.

While steering aft, Tess shouted over the rush of the water, "If you feel you're going out of the boat, grab the lines!"

Harry thought that all the rafters dug deep inside themselves to continue paddling, and Tess shouted, "Left side, right side, both sides…Great, guys!" And with grunts, screams of half-joy and half-fear, she and her crew rocked and rolled through the boiling white water of Shotgun.

Under the gray and black clouds, claps of thunder rumbled in the canyon. They ignited fear in Harry's heart and aggravated his already deep apprehension.

As the safety raft conquered a nasty drop going through Shotgun, Takano excitedly shouted, "Tora! Tora! Tora!" He touched Harry's shoulder in laughter. His jaw chattering, Harry shouted a cautious, "Yippee!"

"You guys are awesome!" yelled Tess to her crew. "I've never seen anybody get through Shotgun better, especially in fairly high water!"

Tess and her safety-boat rafters shouted and screamed with delight as Tim's craft completed its wobbly roller coaster ride and drifted near the safety raft and quietly bobbed in the now slow river current of the Salmon.

Harry sat on the left side of the safety raft, Carol on the right. He looked over at her. She had laughed, screamed with joy, had even sworn a few times, uncharacteristic for her. Moments earlier while the rapids had run tumultuously and had threatened to spill the crew, she caught Harry's eye and winked at him with a good-times smile just after she had caught her breath from shouting a lingering "holeeeeeeey shit."

It was relieving for him to see her express such passionate feelings, something she hadn't been doing recently. She had not complained about headaches since they arrived at Sun Valley, yet she complained about them at home constantly. Then, there was the Hans Flammer thing at the Kitchen, Steve Rindal -- *could it be an affair?* -- and the stuff at the Eatery. Something just wasn't adding up.

But, at this moment and in this place, he still felt better about Carol than he had for ages. Maybe it was the juvenile-like happiness he had just seen on her face, her tan, her wet, blonde, pigtailed hair, and those blue eyes without any sign of melancholy.

They drifted downriver, following Tess's craft. Explosions of rolling thunder, followed by lightning, shook Harry down to his gut. When the Salmon turned right toward Sunbeam Dam, rain came straight down in billions of drops as big as elephant eyes. Tim's raft was a hundred yards away from going through the cauldron of white water that shot above the river's surface before plunging down in a near-vertical drop.

Tess, her crew, and her raft moved into the witches' brew of white water of the Sunbeam Dam rapids and disappeared over the brink.

Harry remembered that the hell of Sunbeam did not begin until they were well into the narrow passage. Fear paralyzed him, and nausea captured the pit of his stomach. He felt as weak as a skeleton; his paddle dragged down his arms as if he held an iron anvil.

Tess, looking confident, steered the raft right in the middle of the river's green water as they passed the remainder of the cement wall. Between the edges of the dam on the left and the opposite shore's cliffs on the right, lay the narrow passage that squeezed and disturbed the torrents of water going through it.

The raft's bow suddenly plunged down the steep fall and the rafters' paddles had no water in which to dig. Harry feared they would be thrown overboard if their raft pitchpoled. In a flash, Harry imagined them all tumbling into the rocky water.

An instant later, Carol screamed as Harry saw her drop her paddle and grab for a life line. She failed to snag it before she went over the right side, disappearing into the raging white water. Tess tossed the throw bag with one hand toward where Carol had entered the water.

Harry instantly decided he must help rescue Carol, no matter what. He quickly rolled out of the boat, ignoring that his life jacket had come off.

He spotted her when her head and shoulders burst from the river. She quickly vanished under the waves as fast as she had appeared.

He shivered with fear that Carol might drown in the icy water despite the protection of her wet suit. At that moment, Harry disregarded any danger to his own life.

He swam as hard as he ever had through the torrent of white water. He took a deep breath, dove under the water, and glimpsed Carol's seemingly unconscious body slowly twisting and turning as it sank in the murky depths. As he got nearer, he sensed that she looked at him with one eye. Abruptly, that eyelid shut. He swam to her backside, placed his arms under her armpits, and kicking with his feet he brought her to the surface.

Their chests both heaved with deep breaths as they surfaced. He had his mouth wide open and a wave choked him. His fears, the shock of the cold water, and the water in his gullet sapped his strength and will from him. He no longer held Carol. She had disappeared.

He felt hands grip his knee, pulling him under the water. *What was happening? Whose hands? Not Carol's?*

The raging current seized him, tore him away, and as he grasped at his heart he felt as if a giant had placed both hands over his chest. Blackness arrested him.

TWENTY-THREE

In seconds, Odessa's raft and the others got through Sunbeam Dam's rapids, and Ry pulled his red-framed swim goggles over his eyes. He gestured to Odessa that he would dive to get Harry, and Odessa nodded affirmatively.

Ry stood, bent his knees, and extended his arms and hands together with thumbs touching, arching into the classic position of a skilled swimmer. He dived in the tumult of the frenzied water near the Sunbeam Dam and took strong strokes toward the place in the river where Carol and Harry had last been seen together.

Carol surfaced near Odessa's raft and Ry swam to her within seconds. They appeared to talk briefly, bobbing in the choppy water. She pointed her finger in an easterly direction, as if giving instructions. It was Odessa she was pointing to. He swam in the direction she had pointed as she shakily boarded the raft. Tim maneuvered his raft and followed him.

Everything seemed to happen at once. Ry paused, waved his hand, and pointed his finger down toward the water. He ducked his head under water, followed by his back, then his legs, and finally his toes. Moments later, he surfaced, holding Harry's limp body with one muscular arm.

Odessa and her crew brought their raft to Tim's and made the lines fast between the two.

Tim swiftly brought his raft close enough to allow himself and Masaru to pull Harry over the stern. Alex stood at the stern of the support raft and shouted, "Ry, does it look like he might have hit a rock?"

As he climbed aboard, Ry shouted, "Yes! It looks like he hit the back of his head! I don't think he's breathing. He must have been hit hard on the chin, there's a lot of bleeding from his chin."

Takano jumped in the water. Masaru and Ry floated Harry and brought him parallel with Tim's raft's stern. Tim, L.H., Tom, and Tony reached over the stern together, brought Harry aboard, and laid him on the deck of the support raft.

Alex knelt close to Harry and her finger probed for a pulse on his carotid artery. She frantically cried, "Damn it! Harry's not breathing and I can't find a pulse. He's bleeding from his chin. Tom the AED...the defibrillator...it's in a black bag with a yellow stripe...we picked it up from my office when we left town. I need it now for Harry."

"Here. I put it in the yellow waterproof bag...right here."

Alex said, "Tim take it out of the yellow bag and carrying case and give it to me."

Tim kneeled on one side of Harry, Alex on the other. "Tim, start CPR now!"

Alex shouted again, "Do it. Is he breathing?"

"No." Tim leaned over Harry's head and tilted it back. He pinched his father's nose shut and sealed his lips around Harry's mouth and breathed twice.

"No air's going in. He's obstructed. I'll give him a couple more breaths."

Tim once again breathed into Harry's mouth. "Still obstructed. I'll try some abdominal thrusts."

Tim slid his legs over Harry's legs, faced his chest, and gently turned Harry's head to one side and pushed his hands on Harry's abdomen.

About the fourth time, as he pushed, water and vomit oozed out of Harry's mouth.

Tim said, "No pulse. Not breathing."

Alex said, "Tim, set up the AED now."

Alex dried Harry's chest.

Tim placed two AED pads on Harry's body and ordered, "Stand clear."

He then turned on the AED and pushed the "analyze" button that looks at the heart rhythm.

The AED advised to push the "Shock" button.

The one shock jolted Harry.

Alex again touched Harry's neck, looking for a pulse. She smiled, with tears running down her cheeks. "Thank God. We have a pulse."

Tim again tilted Harry's head back, pinched his nose shut, sealed his mouth, and began two slow breaths.

Harry began to cough and gasp for air. Harry was breathing on his own.

Alex touched Harry's pulse again and did an examination from head to toe. "I think he's going to live, but he needs to get to a hospital right away. Could you call for a chopper? And let's get him on dry land." Tim said, "Yes."

"Tim, see that little blue and yellow duffel bag? Pull out the green bag and give it to me." Alex pulled out a piece of paper. "When I was interning at Harborview Hospital in Seattle, I learned about something called the Glascow Coma Scale. Harry's in a coma. Harry's is, say about, nine or ten. Call it serious. Not critical."

While on their knees, Alex and Tim embraced each other. As he began to work on getting a chopper, she turned to Carol.

Alex folded her arms over her friend. "He's doing okay. Serious, though."

Carol continued sitting and stared straight ahead. In a flat, eerie voice, she said, "I'm really upset and not thinking very clearly. Everything seems whirly. I can't talk. Thank you both for saving Harry's life."

Alex starred at Carol quizzically, as if something about Carol disturbed her. Alex shrugged her shoulders, unzipped her belt pack, and took out sun cream.

They had laid Harry on the sand beach on the highway side of the Sunbeam Dam.

Harry opened his eyes and saw a blur of people standing and kneeling over him, the blue sky above them. He was lying on his back with a blanket over him. He heard the roar of the river.

A rainbow arced over him and then faded to wherever rainbows fade to. Maybe, instead of a pot of gold at the end of it, there was hope. It was all fuzzy...the hope that he would live to an indefinite date, not just months, but years. He felt grateful to be alive. But, something nagged at him, something uncomfortable. He could not bring it up.

Alex kneeled by him. He started to rise. Alex's arm gently pushed him back. "Harry, this is Alex. You have to lie quietly. I suspect you were in cardiac arrest. Your heart stopped beating. Tim gave you CPR. It and the AED saved your life."

Harry felt Alex's hand on his. He looked up to see her and said, with a funny face, "Doctor, don't I get a discount?" Harry managed a feeble smile.

"Hell no, Harry."

"Just thought I'd ask."

They both laughed.

Tim yelled, holding his satellite phone, "The chopper's on its way, getting close. They'll have a stretcher, and they're taking it down here to haul ya up to the road."

Harry closed his eyes and remembered a freshet of water had poured into his mouth when he was in the river with Carol. He recalled the moments when he'd sunk into the murky water, and something started to bother him. It was the same nag he had had a few minutes before. There was some other element in those moments. Something important, but he couldn't draw it up. *Damn.*

He opened his eyes. Someone had her fingers on his neck. It was Alex.

"What in the hell you doin' now, Doctor?"

"Just checkin' the old ticker to see if it's still going, Mr. Adkins."

"Is it?"

"It is."

Although it was kind of hazy, as he was easing in and out of consciousness, he thought he heard the voices of Alex, Carol, Tim, Tess, Odessa, Tom, and Jason. He saw Ry and Masaru standing near his feet.

"Tim, your old man thanks you."

"I love you, Dad." Tim kneeled over Harry and rested his cheek on his dad's chest.

Harry smiled. "You know, during the wedding, I saw what some believers would call a vision at the bottom of Warm Springs. It was Christmas time. Carol and I were standing with one of your kids and one of Tess's. The two grandkids and the grandma and grandpa were all on skis. I want to be there. Thanks, Tim."

"Oh, Dad. I want you to be around when Tess and I have kids, too. It would be pretty awful for me not to have you around."

Harry wondered if it would be hypocritical to ask God to make sure that his vision about Warm Springs would happen. Harry never went to church, but he felt the urge to ask God to extend his life beyond the middle of next month. In that moment, Harry looked straight up and asked God to give him more time.

Harry looked up toward Ry and they spoke in Japanese. Harry said, "Thanks for saving my life. Carol and I owe you at least a Queen of Sheba torte."

"Harry, Masura shot a lot of video and 35 millimeter film. We'll develop them and give you copies." Harry gripped Ry' s hand.

Alex remained on her knees by Harry's side. She smiled warmly at him.

"Thanks, Alex. You know, today's treatment sure beats that damned prostate exam."

Harry saw Carol sitting on a towel nearby; she was reading *This Much I Know Is True.*

The Air St. Luke's chopper dropped down on the parking lot next to the highway above the beach. It looked like Tim and the chopper were in communication as a stretcher was slowly lowered from the aircraft. Tim untied the stretcher, and the line was taken back into the chopper.

"Dad, I got the stretcher," Tim shouted over the noise, "We're going to carry you up to the roadway where Air St. Luke's is waiting to take you to the hospital."

Gently, Harry was loaded on the stretcher and his bearers soon left the level beach and began climbing the fairly steep trail to the road. Harry heard their deep breathing, and he saw sweat rolling down their faces and bodies, soiling their clothing.

Harry soon found himself supine on the deck of the chopper.

Carol appeared at Alex's side. Alex grabbed Carol's upper arm, and moved her closer to the aircraft.

Alex said to the pilot, "I'm Dr. Alex Quick-Campbell, Harry's PCP, and I'd like to go with you to the hospital. His wife Carol wants to go, too. Any problem with that?"

"I'm Chester with Air St Luke's. Okay with me."

Carol lifted herself into the aircraft, and, with no smile, pulled Alex through the door.

"Ready to take off, Doctor?"

"Ready."

Harry lifted his head and said, "Just a darn minute. Tim, Tess, Ry.

I'd be damned disappointed if you didn't celebrate my birthday tonight on the river and finish the trip. Well?"

Tim and Tess looked at each other. Tess nodded and Tim said, "Sure thing, Dad."

"Love you, Dad," they said together.

The crowd cleared the landing site.

The air ambulance cranked up its engine, bowed to the ground, and slowly disappeared from Sunbeam Dam, heading for St. Luke's Hospital.

As the chopper rose, Harry exhaled deeply. He knew that he had been right: Today was not his day to die.

Harry said, "Ladies, why can't I sit up and drink in what must be a beautiful view on our way to the hospital."

Carol, reading her book, pointed to Alex. "It's your show Alex."

"Silly boy, we're almost there. Beside, you have to rest."

"Okay, Dr. Cool."

The skipper of the chopper, said, "I see medics with a gurney near the landing pad. We're cleared for landing."

About one hour later, Harry was processed in St. Luke's, lying in a hospital bed.

"When in hell am I getting out of here. I feel great." Harry groused.

"When, I say so Mr. Adkins," said, a short, chunky, red-haired woman, featuring shoulder-length hair and wearing, it seemed, many pieces of silver jewelry, as she ambled into the room.

She came directly to Harry and shook his hand. "Hi, I'm Dr. Venus Christopher, a heart specialist," she said in a booming voice.

Turning to Alex, Dr. Christopher said, with a wink and an extended hand, which Alex took, "Dr. Quick-Campbell, I presume."

"Call me Alex. May I call you Venus?"

Carol, still holding her book said, "Dr. Christopher, I'm Harry's wife."

"Sure. Alex, I can't thank you enough for all the information you got the Seattle Research Institute to send me about Harry. Okay, Harry?"

"Sure, Venus," replied Harry. "You should know that Alex is my personal doc. I can't tell how many prostrate probes I've suffered through with her."

"Oh, shut up, Harry," decreed Alex.

Venus grinned. "I wouldn't know, being a woman and a heart doc."

The phone next to Harry's bed rang and he picked it up. "It's Tess -- that's my daughter. They're someplace on the Salmon."

Alex came to the phone, punched a button, and said, "Now it's a speaker phone."

Tess's voice reverberated in the room. "Dad, I have my baton, and the Salmon River Singers are ready to sing another 'Happy Birthday.' "

Harry and all heard the song -- *maybe polished by a few beers*. After the song, each person wished him a happy birthday for the second time.

For the next few days, Harry underwent test after test after test, which he passed with not much problem. But, there was some blockage in his heart, which could be helped by statins and some cardiac rehabilitation back in Seattle.

As they prepared to check out from St. Luke's, and head for home, Harry's cell phone rang. Looking around the room, Harry said. "Hey, it's Tess and Jason. You want me to sit down? I guess I could do that." He listened attentively and exploded with joy as he said, "Tess and Jason are pregnant!"

Carol rushed to Harry and seized his cell with the most expansive smile he'd seen from her for years.

The same vision of Harry and Carol with two grandchildren, all on skis at the bottom of Warm Springs, surged through him again.

Tom drove home with Alex, who alternated driving the Adkinses' car.

Carol and Harry took the plane back to Seattle.

TWENTY-FOUR

Seattle Law Offices of Jones & Jones

In the morning, Harry, still tan from the Sun Valley celebration trip, sat in the Law Offices of Jones & Jones. He had finished a review of *The Wall Street Journal,* which he had started at least a half-hour before. His total waiting time to see his attorney and buddy, Joe Kennedy, was -- he looked at his watch -- about forty minutes.

He decided to stand up and look at Jones & Jones's western view of Elliott Bay and Puget Sound from the fiftieth floor of Seattle's newest skyscraper. The law firm occupied two floors, and no buildings blocked the view, which, at least today, featured Mount Rainier and the Olympic Mountains in their full majesty, and blue sky overhead. White and green ferries scurried to and from the Olympic Peninsula and Seattle. Freighters crowded the bay.

The furnishings were a sea green. Unlike the last time that Harry had visited Jones & Jones, when the wooden furniture ran on the darker and conservative side, now the motif featured tempered glass and burnished nickel. Instead of rectangles, curves predominated. A soffit of tempered glass and burnished nickel sprawled under the ceiling.

Harry heard Joe's deep baritone. "Hey, Harry. I bet you thought I'd never show up. Sorry I'm late. But this time I have a real excuse." They shook hands warmly.

"What's today's excuse?"

"Let's go to my office on the next floor up."

Joe and Harry marched up stairs to Joe's personal office, which also had a western view.

"I see you still walk slow. Frankly, Mr. Kennedy, you walk the Golf Club course slower than anyone else -- anyone."

"My advice is to run fast and walk slow."

Joe Kennedy also played at the Golf Club. *Pretty good golfer.* Harry and Joe grew up together, but went to different schools. They both were long-distance runners, and frequently had competed against each other. He admired Joe for keeping his shape into middle age. Both men stood over six feet.

In high school, Joe, like Harry, had been something of a jock. He looked more like an Irishman than anyone else Harry knew. Joe, a lanky guy, had wavy, coarse hair that had just begun to show streaks of gray, but he displayed no baldness. His eyes were, of course, green.

"Today's excuse? Of course. Had a big case. A will contest."

Harry was interested in wills. That's why he was here.

"Tried the case in Kitsap County for...four to five weeks. Can almost see the Court House from here," he exaggerated. "Judge's name -- you wouldn't believe it -- Brian O'Flannery." Harry chuckled.

"Judge was trying another extended case, which had to have a recess. Judge told us he would give us an oral opinion by telephone at nine o'clock this morning about our will contest."

"Joe, did you win?"

"Thought you would never ask. Like Henri would say, *Oui.*"

"Congratulations!"

"That's why I was late. I first got your message when you were on the river near Stanley, Idaho, just before you went rafting. You're here about a will."

"A little history. After we ate breakfast and broke camp, I got in the first raft with Tess and Carol. We went through some pretty husky water. For some reason Carol left the raft, I tried playing rescuer, and I ended up in the water myself. Blacked out."

Joe's face seemed frozen in disbelief. "For God's sake, what happened to you?"

"Of course, I was out of it. They pulled me out of the river and my heart stopped beating. Tim brought me back to life with CPR. A chopper took me to the hospital in Hailey, and here I am."

"Yes.

"My secretary pulled out your wills -- Carol's and yours. They looked fine. Both of you leave everything to the other."

"Carol and I have had problems. I should say, I have problems with Carol. I want to change my will to give Carol less than the present will provides."

Joe turned away from Harry, who picked up a sudden diffidence from Joe.

"You hesitate. You don't want me to know something that you

should be telling me."

"Clairvoyance, Harry."

"Right. Tell me, Joe."

"I don't think you want to hear this."

"I said, tell me." *Is he playing a game with me?*

"Damn it! All right. I'm in a book club -- fiction for guys and gals. Since the smoking ban, no more cigars, except for some of us. On a dry day, we might walk outside and puff after lunch. Meet every other Wednesday for lunch at the Golf Club. For about the last year, when I pass by the bar, I'm able to see the backs of people sitting up at the bar." Joe got up and looked out his window.

Speaking to the window now, he continued. "Gawd. I feel like Jimmy Stewart in *Rear Window*."

"I'm all ears."

"Yes, every time I walk by that bar, I see Carol and Steve Rindal."

"They ever see you?"

"I doubt it."

"Why?"

"They're too involved with each other."

Harry felt like somebody had kicked him in the nuts. "Like...Can you give me an example?"

"Oh, shit. I wish I never told you."

"Continue, Joe."

"They sit close to each other and I see hands on legs, on her chest and below, and lingering kisses."

Joe returned to his desk. Neither looked at the other.

Worst news he'd ever had. Nobody talked for about five minutes.

"Maybe you should hire a private detective."

"I'll think about that. But, I do want you to write a will. Basically, I want to leave the least I can to Carol and make a gift to the Golf Club of $100,000 to provide golf scholarships for needy Eastside kids."

"How soon do you want this?"

"I think we talked about the medical study that I was in."

"Oh, yeah. I remember it. I told you at the time that I'd never get in such a study. Did you actually get the date you were supposed to die? Now, Harry, you're giving me the Jack Nicholson look."

"I am. To change the topic for a moment, several years ago, I saw Jack in the Sun Valley Lodge. We were both checking in. He looked over at me and I did the Jack Nicholson face and eyebrows. And he gave me that look back! He patted me on the shoulder, we smiled, and went back to checking in."

Joe laughed.

"Yeah, it was either July seventeen or eighteen. I'm not sure. I saw the study's head honcho a short time ago and he told me the date that they gave me probably wasn't correct. So, I'm betting on living a lot longer."

"Well, you certainly look good. Okay. I'll work on your will after lunch. What's your e-mail address?"

"Harry at K.I.L. dot com."

"I'll e-mail instructions. And I'll add your will as an attachment to my e-mail. Call me with any questions."

"And I'll ask Alex and Tom to be witnesses." Joe nodded yes.

Both men got up, approached each other, and gave big men hugs.

"Good luck, Harry."

"Do you Irishmen get any better breaks than the rest of us?"

"Probably."

Although not obligated to do so by $H^2 L^2$, Dr. Dunne assisted Harry enrolling in the Seattle Research Institute cardiac rehabilitation program.

After the first day in re-hab, Harry visited Dr. Dunne. Yes, he continued to sport his monocle.

"Hello again, Harry," said Dr. Dunne. "What did you think about the program?"

"I was completely satisfied," acknowledged Harry.

"Harry. A *caveat.*"

"Yes?"

"I know you went all out in the year of preparation during $H^2 L^2$. I know you're going to run, which is fine, but don't try to break any -- I said *any* -- prior running record. Tap on the brakes. Okay?"

"Okay," Harry muttered. "Oh. Almost forgot. Anybody in the study die yet?"

"Not yet." He boasted.

"What is your overall evaluation, as a scientist?"

"Perhaps, we lucked out with the present one-hundred percent success rate. We were satisfied in having a large percentage of the men sticking to exercise and better eating habits, along with their wives, to whom we offered free exercise opportunities."

Harry arose with the dawn, threw on his sweats and running shoes, and stood close to the window. The sun's top rim peeked over the next ridge, coating the earth with gold on all that lay before him. He had completed his morning ablutions and strapped on his silver Omega wristwatch. *Oh my gosh,* he thought, as he looked at the watch's face…it was July seventeenth. The day they said he would die. He knew he hadn't ever been real good about dates, to say the least.

*But…*he paused. *Wait a moment. It was the seventeenth.*

Harry wished that he had taken the letter out of the safety deposit box to verify the date. Today was supposed to be his last day on earth. And he was still here!

He pinched himself to make sure. "Ouch." He touched the pulse in his wrist. Slow and rhythmic. Harry grinned. *I ain't dead yet.*

These days, he was never surprised by what Carol would come up with. She had refused his frequent sexual overtures for about a year after the Naomi revelations, and later, their sexual encounters were still only occasional, despite his persistent solicitations. And there was Steve Rindal and that Austrian ski instructor in Sun Valley.

He tied his running shoes and headed for the ascending sun. He was still here. He pinched himself again to make sure and grinned. Not dead yet. He always knew he'd beat the prediction. He could assume now he was like the rest of humanity and really didn't know when he was going to die.

Harry backed into the hallway, and was flooded, once again, with the feeling of his aliveness. He mounted the curved banister and slid down with his arms stretched out for balance, calling, "Yippee," as he landed gracefully on his feet on the carpeted floor.

Outside, he vaulted with one arm over the railing of the porch, landed on the grass, and seconds later he was off the property and on the tarmac.

Harry picked up the pace to about a seven-minute mile. It was time to start planning the rest of his life. Maybe he'd climb mountains, snowboard, and travel more. He'd do a lot of things he hadn't done before.

After one mile of his five kilometer run, he looked at his stopwatch and saw he had run it in less than seven minutes. A chance to get a personal record of doing the 3.1 miles in twenty minutes. He pumped up his pace. His sweatband could no longer collect his sweat, which stung his eyes.

He clicked off his stopwatch as he sprinted through the driveway entry and heard his footsteps crunching on the gravel.

Wow! 19:50:10. His best personal record since college. As he jogged toward the front porch, he punched the air and said loudly, "Did it! Did it!" He held his hands on his waist, and his chest heaved up and down, inhaling and exhaling. His excitement had consumed him. As he walked up the stairs to the porch, he caught a glimpse of his face in a large wide window, flanking the two French doors. The sun's rays had etched the window in gold. He stopped and posed as if a camera was ready to capture his sweaty countenance.

Harry smiled at seeing such a happy man. He cried with happiness; his tears and sweat joined to make a facial deluge; he remembered those moments when, years before, his mom and dad had jogged with him, holding hands, on his high school victory lap.

He reached the inside curved staircase to the second floor and bounded up the stairs. Harry felt short of breath, with some moderate chest pain. He sat on a stair for about three minutes. His breath came back and the chest pain disappeared. *What was that about? Well, it was a pretty fast run. No sweat.*

Harry resumed his stair climb, and at the top of the stairs began to undress for his shower.

Around eleven, Alex and Carol rested in one of many overstuffed two-person mauve couches, reminding Alex of Izzy's office décor, but unlike Izzy's reception area, no skylights ushered in natural light. Carol and Alex stared at empty chairs. No one else waited in the reception area.

Lettering on the double-glass entry doors showed that this was the medical office of Janis Jennings-Jonas, M.D., Neurology.

Carol spoke quietly to Alex. "Thanks for kidnapping me to get aboard the helicopter to St. Luke's.

"You know about my horrendous headaches -- they've changed me and my life."

A few minutes before the time of the scheduled appointment with Dr. Jennings-Jonas, the receptionist from behind the counter said, "Dr. Quick-Campbell, Dr. Jennings-Jonas asked me to give you and your patient a copy of a URL from the National Brain Tumor Foundation that she'd like you to read before your appointment begins."

"Of course," Alex said as she wheeled around to pick up two copies of the document.

Alex and Carol read the two-page statement.

"Yes, that's me. I guess I didn't wake up to any of the shitty stuff I was doing to Harry and myself until I almost killed him when I jumped from the raft, and then you and I talked about the whole big mess for, what was it, four hours, by tape recorder."

"Tell me truthfully, we talked a lot about disinhibition."

"Yes. Sometimes, I just can't stop impulsive behavior, like, well, jumping out of the raft, making sexual overtures to you, to whatever guy I'm with, that I think comes from whatever causes my terrible headaches."

The receptionist said, "The doctor will see you now."

Alex and Carol walked into the doctor's office and shut the door behind them.

"Janis," said Alex, "this is my best friend, Carol Adkins." The two women shook hands and Carol sat down.

Janis and Alex embraced. "Carol, Janis and I met when we were interns at Harborview." Janis stood about an inch or two taller than Carol, and maybe was a little heftier; she had straight red hair that cascaded over her shoulders to mid-waist.

Janis said, "Let's sit down. Alex, thanks so much for the transcript of the four-hour tape, it's a great history. Of all of the interns at Harborview, you were the most thorough and methodical.

"Carol, I believe that your long-standing headaches, coupled with your disinhibitions, leads me to consider the possibility of a -- don't be shocked -- brain tumor. I'm looking at your skull. Here, I'll come 'round my desk and feel your forehead." Janis paused and rummaged around Carol's scalp. "Did you ever have a skull fracture?"

"I did, when I was a fourth grader. You've just scared me spitless."

"I understand. But, I urge you to get a brain scan to rule out a tumor or find out what's going on. You may have a brain tumor that's known as a meningioma. That type of tumor is usually not malignant nor inoperable.

"Carol, how are you feeling about all of this?"

Carol grimaced. "How about numb? With a serving spoon of fear. Please give me twenty-four hours to think it over. How about until noon tomorrow? Is the company that does brain scans close to your office?"

"Yes. Alex and you could walk over to Eastside Imaging to see what kind of equipment they use for the brain scan."

Alex and Carol arose, shook hands with Janis, who said, "Let me know your verdict."

Alex replied, "We will."

In ten minutes, they had arrived at Eastside Imaging and were inspecting the 2007 model of a CT scan. Alex thought *nobody -- nobody -- could possibly be claustrophobic.*

"I don't like those red dashes from the machine all over where my face and head would be…give me until tomorrow."

295

TWENTY-FIVE

He opened his e-mail and saw a message from Alex:
I hope you still have your appointment with the psychiatrist tomorrow, July 18. I'm really concerned about you. Please do come to our place for the night.

Harry had intended to go to bed around ten on this quiet seventeenth of July night, fully expecting to awaken the morning of the eighteenth. Ten years ago, he recalled, when he received the $H^2 L^2$ letter, he had vowed that he was going to beat the date and continue his life. He had renewed his resolve.

*Why not just go to bed as usual and, well...*He hummed to himself, *Que sera, sera, whatever will be will be,*

After all, July 17 so far had been a rather trying day.

Harry's home-office phone rang, interrupting his thoughts. "Harry here."

"Tess and Jason, calling from the shores of the Salmon."

"Gosh, thanks for calling grandpa."

His daughter laughed. "We've pulled a few trout from the river and they're sizzling in the fry pan. Tim's drinking a few White Clouds. Gordon's rafting with us and he just shouted hello."

"Say hello back to him. Best beer in the solar system."

"Dad, before our cell dies, we really called about Mom and you...We're pretty worried about her. She was acting kind of nuts when she was here."

"I know," Harry said. "I'll send you an e-mail about what's been going on between Alex and her...Pretty strange stuff. But, I have some great news for you kids. Remember when I was in that Seattle Research Institute study about ten years ago?"

"Yes, the one about your heart? And that whole date-of-death thing?"

"That's the one. We had the option to learn the date or not. I didn't tell anyone at the time, but I chose to learn the date they said I would die."

"You didn't."

"I did," Harry said triumphantly.

"I just knew you were going to know the date!" she exclaimed.

"The date was today, Tess! The seventeenth of July and I'm still alive." Saying it out loud felt amazing.

"That means you've almost beat the prediction. Oh, thank the Lord. Have you told Mom yet? Oh! Oh! My phone's running out of juice."

"No, I'll tell her tomorrow morning and then you can call me."

"We can't re-charge out here. It'll be a few hours before we can get near a working phone. I'll call the house phone. Dad, that's great and all, but I'm still really, really concerned about --"

"What? What did you say?"

Silence. Her phone had died.

Carol had preceded him to bed and was snoozing soundly like a cat lying on a pillow with a full tummy. Harry tried his best not to wake her as he crawled in next to her.

TWENTY-SIX

Harry awakened the next day in their bedroom and saw darkness inside. No coruscation of dawn outside. He touched his wrist pulse. *Okay.* He rejoiced.

Carol slept next to him, breathing slowly. The red digital clock radio pronounced *04:37*.

Out of the bed, he held the rail as he walked slowly downstairs and, wearing his candy-cane-striped p.j.'s, he sat at the kitchen table. He looked at his wrist to verify the time, but he saw only a circular band of white skin bordered by a modest tan. *Oh.* His watch was upstairs.

Harry thought of yesterday's yet-to-be's. All at once, like when the sun revealed itself, coming from behind a strapping white cloud, soiled with dark patches, he became aware of a question he had never asked himself before.

What shall endure him?

His children and grandchildren and other progeny.

Paraphrasing sportscaster Red Smith, Harry thought, *the least of us can have progenitors.*

Well, what about *Nippon/USA?* Tom and he were worth millions from its sale. But wasn't that just money? *Sure, but the "least of us" could not accomplish that.*

He climbed back up the stairs and crawled into bed.

Harry opened his eyes to see that dawn had begotten the day.

Birds chirped busily, harshly conflicted by the dreadful caw-caws of a squadron of crows. He turned his cheek to his pillow and fell back asleep.

In the distance, he heard the doleful wail of a siren and the inevitable accompaniment from Torvil Two, awakening in the front yard. Harry imagined him turning his chin up to the sky. His howl had always stirred some primeval feeling deeply within him.

Harry lifted his head from the pillow and checked the radio. *07:30.* The warm sun streamed into their bedroom. A light breeze made their white, frothy curtains dance like ballerinas in *Swan Lake.* If he was alive, today was the eighteenth of July. He pinched his thigh. It hurt, gloriously.

As his feet hit the rug, his mind exploded like a rocket to Pluto just off the launch-pad -- he should celebrate his reprieve with a good workout on the treadmill. Harry hitched off his pajamas and pulled his shorts up to his waist. He tried to jump into his sweats, attempting to not put his pants on one leg at a time. So, it was unsuccessful? He'd try some other time.

Harry walked out of their bedroom and looked down on the main floor where his treadmill rested. *Oh, my God.* Carol had gotten that awful painting back from Alex. Munch's *The Scream* now hung on the wall where he would later encounter it head on. The bright lights that hung on the back wall would cast his shadow on the wall ahead.

That didn't matter; what did matter today was that he was alive, when he was supposed to die on the seventeenth of July and today was the eighteenth! He still wasn't positive the seventeenth was right, but he was still alive and kickin' on the day after he was supposed to die.

He pondered for a moment... *Bastille Day is July 13; four days later would be July 17.* So, the study predicted his death to be the seventeenth of July. He had beaten the prediction! As he said he would.

Again, he punctuated his absolute victory over death by punching his fist into his hand. So, he did it yesterday and today. This deserved two celebrations.

He dashed out of the front door to revel in the morning's sun. Harry stood on his well-tended lawn. His arms extended toward Heaven.

Harry looked down at his running shoes. He smiled when he saw them, now not impaired by his potbelly. The pot was replaced, after lots of exercise, by a flat, hard stomach.

Ecstasy radiated from his face. He could think of no finer day in his life. *You know. Even better than yesterday.*

He picked up the morning newspaper in the driveway. Yes, today was the eighteen of July.

Torvil Two, with his bushy thick tail and wiggling hindquarters, charged Harry, in celebration, as if he also understood his master had survived the night. Holding the newspaper under his arm, he bent down to stroke him. As he petted Torvil, the dog's ears flattened and his black, wet nose pointed toward the sky.

For a few moments, Harry snapped his thumb and forefinger

rhythmically. He was drunk with his *joie de vivre*. By gosh, he had not died on the date they said he would. Time for another change in him.

He searched for something that he could do that would maybe serve as a…*What is it? It's…a change in me, of course!* He folded his hands behind him as he strode to the garage with Torvil Two at his side. He looked up at the second floor over the garage where he had his home office.

Yes, I need to burn the rest of Naomi's steamy letters.

He walked to the garage. And then he ran up the stairs to his office. Torvil Two was with him every single step.

Harry sucked in just a little air and, for a moment, felt just a touch of chest pain, which seemed to go away.

He inserted his key in the door at the top of the stairs, opened the door, with Torvil Two scampering into the room; he spun the combination on his home office safe to open it. He reached in the safe and yanked out the Naomi letters, pulled one aside, and stuffed the rest in the black porcelain Waterford wood stove.

He read the surviving letter. Naomi must have been doped up to have written it. It sure was sexy, but he wasn't stirred at all. Harry tossed the last letter in with the others, all to become ash.

To finish the job, Harry doused the letters with lighter fluid, threw in a match, closed the door on the stove and heard the rush and roar of the flames. Did the fire cleanse him?

Does fire exist in Purgatory? Or only a state after death? Could he make amends to Carol now?

He'd intended to torch Naomi's correspondence years ago. But hadn't done it. *Oh, my.* Out of sight, out of mind, he guessed. Maybe he had forgotten.

His cell phone rang. *Alex and Tom?* He picked up the phone. "It's Harry."

"It's Alex."

He felt relieved.

"Our car won't start and our other car's in the shop. A cab's on the way to pick us up. Also, we lost our power so it'll be a good time for Tom and me to leave the house."

Should he offer to go over to Alex's house? Yes.

"Why don't I come over and get you?"

"Just a tick." Harry heard Alex saying, "Tom, Harry wants to come over and pick us up...Harry, Tom says it's up to you, but we wonder if you feel safe being alone with Carol until we get there?"

"You know, I'm just great." *Why would I be afraid of being alone with Carol?*

"Good news, Harry, the taxi's here; we'll be over--"

"In a few ticks, as you'd say, Alex."

"You should never mock your doc, Harry."

"You know, Dr. Cool...Oh -- idea -- I'm going to tramp on the treadmill -- I'll put my cell in my pocket. Call me. Bye. Oops -- one more thing. You still there? I just remembered it."

"Yeah."

"Joe Kennedy sent a will that I'll sign. Will you guys witness it?"

"Ah. We'll take a look at it. We'll see you in a few ticks. Bye!"

"Bye. I'm leaving it on my desk in my study over the garage."

"Okay."

Harry picked up his will and placed it on top of his desk. *I guess it won't hurt if I sign it now. I can tell Alex and Tom that it's my signature, not that they haven't seen it hundreds of times.*

Harry signed the will; he paused and admired his signature.

Without re-locking the door to his office, Torvil Two and he dashed downstairs to the outside. He looked up at the stove's chimney and saw a long, thick, white and blue plume of smoke pulled from the chimney and sent on its way by the wind that had made the white curtains dance.

He would make full amends to Carol, something like, "forsaking all others," and get down on his knees to beg forgiveness.

It wouldn't be easy. Particularly since Carol had not been herself for some time.

Her headaches had become worse. They did have the appointment with Carol's psychiatrist later today.

He looked up at their bedroom window and thought he saw Carol standing at the side of the window in her white nightgown, but it must have been the curtains.

He skipped like a child on the way from his office to the kitchen, but stopped outside the doorway, picked several irises and put them to his nose, sniffed the fragrance, smiled, and felt great pleasure in knowing he had dodged fate.

Torvil Two barked objections when his master walked into the kitchen alone, closing the entry door with him outside.

Carrying the irises he had picked, Harry opened a large pantry door and extracted a tall, pale-blue vase. He placed the irises in the container on the kitchen table. After he scanned the front page of the newspaper, he paused to again verify the date on its masthead. *You know. The wonderful eighteenth of July*. He refolded the newspaper, pivoted one hundred and eighty degrees and his hook shot dropped the newspaper on the kitchen table.

For the first time, as he found himself staring at Georgia O'Keefe's *Cliffs Beyond Abiquiu;* he didn't see cliffs, he saw flesh and muscles flexing and extending. *God! Was Carol's craziness catching?* For a moment, he became disquieted as he stared at the drawing. He pondered, why hadn't he seen the flesh and muscles interacting before? Too enigmatic for him.

Once more, he thought, the seventeenth had passed and he was still alive. He felt rapturous. He pirouetted gaily, like Henri, a few times around the kitchen table. The sun's rays, for a moment, blossomed, but in another instant, were held back by the shadows of the clouds, but again burst forth drawing Harry's dancing body on the white walls.

Time to make peace. And, maybe, make love with Carol. He took the stairs two at a time and floated into their bedroom. He looked in the wall mirrors and caught his Happy Face smile, which he hadn't seen for a while.

Harry sat on the edge of the bed and said quietly, "I'm alive. I'm alive. The study was wrong. I found out the date."

The bedroom's curtains still danced with the wind.

Carol opened her eyes, her head still on her pillow. She held her head in her hands, as if she were suffering a severe headache.

"Carol, I did learn the date of my death. So, I fudged a little about not choosing to get a letter. But I was supposed to die yesterday, and...I'm alive. I know. I'm still living because I changed my lifestyle. I apologize for lying to you, Carol." He approached her with his arms opened, intending to embrace her and to beg for her forgiveness.

Harry grinned. "Do you remember that day on the Wellesley Campus?"

For a moment, Carol's face relaxed into a small, but capricious smile, and she said, "Yes, fondly."

Harry thought this might be a breakthrough and looked at Carol plaintively, with his arms still open.

But for now, he would celebrate the best day of his life; it was like *a…ah…a rebirth?*

He waltzed out of their bedroom and walked downstairs with both fists upraised.

Gosh. Alex and Tom should be here by now.

Harry returned to the white-on-white kitchen.

The windmills of his mind were spinning.

He pulled his cell phone from his pocket and his fingertip dialed Alex's cell phone.

"Alex, this is Harry. I just told Carol that I did learn the alleged date of my death."

"Has she been hostile to you?"

"No. I can't say that. No. To change the subject: I'm kind of hyper today. Haven't been this way for years. This morning I thought of you probing my prostate ten years ago. And you know what? I made a big discovery about myself."

"And what was that?"

"I know now why I had been so goosey about prostrate exams. The rectal probe of another person's finger sought my prostate, my core. I had felt, even if it was only for a moment or two, that I had lost exclusive control of my being…my private domain…to an intruder. Even you, Alex. But it wasn't such a big deal. It was just for a moment. And for a good purpose…a necessary evil in one's life as a male…a medical diagnosis to rule out prostate cancer and if found, fought by medical science."

"I'm pleased that you've finally seen the light."

"When you get here, I want to express my apologies to Tom and you, if it seemed as if I was in hot pursuit of you, Alex. You know what, maybe I was." Suddenly, Harry noticed that his shoulders and neck were pliable. *How about that?*

"Yes, we should discuss, as you called it, your 'hot pursuit,' but it's good news to me that you've had that awakening, also."

"As you very well know, I took the option to learn the so-called date of my death. It was yesterday, the seventeenth. I'm alive. This means that they were wrong. Nobody's predicted any other day."

"Oh, my God...Harry, you left a copy with my office ten years ago. And we just picked it up -- I haven't opened the envelope yet. I'm...so surprised -- shocked! My God, only ten years? Is that all we gave you?"

"Yes. Dr. Dunne said that since the study was completed, there would be no update. I'm in the kitchen now and heading for the treadmill."

Alex said, "See you soon, bye for now."

"Bye."

Harry walked out of the kitchen and into the den and did a complete twirl, landing on the treadmill. His back was turned to the balcony.

Again he noticed he was looking right at *The Scream* reproduction where one of the Monet lily prints had been the day before.

Harry revved up the speed of the treadmill.

The grandfather clock gonged nine.

For some reason, he remembered the last song that Carol had sung at the Fourth of July party. The words:

> *Oh, when the saints go marching in,*
> *Lord, how I want to be in that number,*
> *When the saints go marching in...*

TWENTY-SEVEN

Harry strode on the treadmill. His hands swung forward and backward near his thighs. He had inserted his cell phone in the right pocket of his gray sweat pants.

As Harry moved his hand toward his pocket, he felt a sudden, crushing pain in his left chest. His right hand instinctively began to clutch his chest near his sternum.

Carol lay awake on the bed upstairs that overlooked the back yard; the window was open. A talking head appeared on the bedroom TV screen and said, "We have breaking news. The sheriff's office has just informed us that Johnnie Allegro has escaped from the King County jail. He allegedly stole a police car, drove to the home of Judge Standish, and killed Standish and his wife. The sheriff believes that Allegro may be headed to the home of international businessman, Harry Adkins. The sheriff's office reported Allegro was not accompanied. Like Ted Bundy of the seventies, Allegro has now escaped two times from imprisonment. Hold on. I've just been told that the police car that Allegro stole was found abandoned near the Adkins' home. Stand by for further developments."

Carol's hair on the back of her neck stood up, and she quickly rolled out of bed, still in her nightgown and rushed to open the top drawer of her dresser. She glanced at the photograph of Johnnie Allegro and reached in the drawer and withdrew her Beretta.

Carol heard the elkhound outside barking and growling furiously, unlike anything Torvil Two had ever demonstrated before. She looked out of the window, and *my god, it's Johnnie Allegro*. Torvil Two stood only a few feet from him. Allegro held a service revolver as he advanced closer to the downstairs door to the house.

Allegro turned and aimed the gun at the dog. Carol held her Beretta with both hands. While Allegro's back was turned to her she fired a bullet that hit him in the back of his head. As he fell, she shot another round into his neck. He dropped on the tarmac and lay inert on his back, hemorrhaging from the neck. To be sure, after Allegro hit the ground, Carol aimed and fired to the left side of Allegro's chest. She placed her gun in the drawer and closed it.

She heard the treadmill still rolling. Carol shouted, "Harry."

No response.

She dashed down the stairs and screamed when she saw him lying on the floor. She clicked the treadmill's off switch. She knelt next to him. He wasn't breathing. He must have been thrown off the treadmill to the rug. She held her head with both hands and grimaced as if she were suffering severe pain.

A cab stopped near the front porch. Alex and Tom quickly found themselves in the freshly painted sky-blue front entry. Alex held her cell phone to her ear and said, "Harry must not have turned on his cell."

Torvil Two suddenly appeared next to them.

"Tom, while you were talking with the cab driver, I heard three shots coming from the master bedroom."

"I heard them too…"

"You look around the driveway, and I'll go inside. Keep your phone on."

Alex opened her purse, gripped her gun, and opened the front door. "Anybody home? It's Alex."

Alex walked down the hallway. As she turned left she saw Carol kneeling beside Harry. Torvil Two scampered to Harry, licked his face and lay down next to him.

Alex knelt next to Carol and gasped, "What happened?"

Carol sobbed, "Harry's not breathing. It's the predicted date. Please examine him."

She spoke unevenly, "I killed Allegro."

Alex brought her face close to Harry's nose and mouth. And felt for a pulse.

She said, "No pulse."

Harry was dead.

APPENDICES

On this page, please mark only one of the following alternatives: I DO WISH or I DO NOT WISH to learn the predicted date of my death. (Please circle either "I do wish" or "I do not wish" and sign your name in the box immediately adjacent to your selection) After you make your choice, please sign and date below and return the document to the $H^2 L^2$ office at the Seattle Research Institute.

Circle the option you have chosen:

I DO WISH to learn the predicted date of my death

```
┌─────────────────────────────────────────┐
│                                         │
│                                         │
│                                         │
└─────────────────────────────────────────┘
```

Sign your name in box above

I DO <u>NOT</u> WISH to learn the predicted date of my death

```
┌─────────────────────────────────────────┐
│                                         │
│                                         │
│                                         │
└─────────────────────────────────────────┘
```

Sign your name in box above

If you choose to learn the predicted date of your death, you may pick up a sealed envelope containing a letter setting forth that date from our receptionist in the first floor lobby of the Seattle Research Institute from 9:00 a.m. to 5:00 p.m. on the first business day of January after the conclusion of the Study.

End of page 19; go to page 20

I have read and understood the preceding 19 pages and have received answers to any questions I have about the $H^2 L^2$ Study. I have received a copy of the entire $H^2 L^2$ application and signed consent form (pages 1-20).

I understand that I may withdraw from the study at any time without penalty.

_____   _____

Signed   Date

_____

Print Name

For office use only:

Received by:

_____   _____

$H^2 L^2$ Staff   Date

National Brain Tumor Foundation

A brain tumor or its treatment can cause changes to a person's cognitive (thinking) abilities, behavior, and/or emotions. The extent of changes can vary considerably from person to person and may affect a patient's ability to work or go about his/her daily life.

Some causes of behavioral and personality changes include tumor size, type, and location; side effects of surgery, radiation therapy, and chemotherapy; side effects of medications; and the patient's psychological reaction to the diagnosis of a life-threatening illness.

Cognitive changes can include difficulty speaking, writing, and/or reading; being easily distracted, confused, and disoriented; difficulty doing more than one task at a time; short-term memory loss; slowed thinking; trouble with problem solving; and poor judgment. A combination of medication, modifications in behavior, and simple lifestyle adjustments may help the person dealing with these issues and symptoms. For example, a person who has difficulty with multi-tasking can avoid confusion and frustration by limiting themselves to doing one thing at a time.

Emotional and personality changes may include depression, irritability, anxiety, mood swings, obsessive-compulsive tendencies, disinhibition, and withdrawal. Troublesome symptoms such as lack of sleep, forgetfulness, and chronic pain can play a role in making things worse by causing irritability and frustration. Sharing feelings with family and friends is essential for any person dealing with a life-threatening illness. Psychological counseling, spiritual help, and support groups can help tremendously. Anti-depressant or other medications may be prescribed.

In all cases, it is important to notify your medical team about behavioral changes. Chronic illness of a family member can cause emotional distress to the entire family. Talk with your treatment team, as there may be help and treatment available.

National Brain Tumor Foundation
22 Battery Street
Suite 612
San Francisco, CA 94111-5520

http://www.braintumor.org
email: nbtf@braintumor.org:
Brain Tumor Information Line
1.800.934.CURE (2873)

Donor Registration Forms available at:

http://wbp.biostr.washington.edu/PDF/donor.pdf

or call 206-543-1850

DONOR REGISTRATION FORM

UNIVERSITY OF WASHINGTON
MEDICAL CENTER
UW Medicine

University of Washington School of Medicine
Willed Body Program, Department of Biological Structure
Box 357420, Seattle WA 98195-7420

Telephone: 206-543-1860, *(Alternate number 206-598-3300)*

- I agree that the University may use my body and any of its parts, including body fluids, tissues and organs, for the development of one or more research, diagnostic, or therapeutic product or procedure.

- I agree that the University may loan my body or any of its parts to other institutions for purposes of medical or surgical teaching and research.

- I agree to cremation of my remains as a condition of donation. If I want my available cremated remains returned to my family I must check the box and initial in the space provided for this purpose at the top of the second page of this Donor Registration Form. The available cremated remains exclude any of my body parts retained for continuing teaching or research. If I do not choose to have my cremated remains returned to my family, they will be buried at the University burial site at the Evergreen-Washelli Cemetery in Seattle, Washington during an annual nondenominational burial service. Cremated remains will not be recoverable after burial.

- I agree that the University may keep any of my body parts for continuing teaching or research purposes. Body parts that the University keeps will be cremated after they are used and will be buried at the University burial site at the Evergreen-Washelli Cemetery in Seattle, Washington during an annual nondenominational burial service. These body parts will not be returned to my family.

- I agree that the University may decline to accept my body for any reason.

- I agree to inform my family and physician of my decision to give my body to the University of Washington.

- I have read and understood the Donor Information Letter. I have had the opportunity to ask the Willed Body Program any questions I have, and I have had my questions answered before signing this form.

- I agree that the specific details of how my remains have been used are confidential and will not be disclosed to my family after my death, unless provided for by law.

AUTHORIZATION

I wish to give my body to the University of Washington School of Medicine immediately after death to be preserved and used by the University for medical or surgical teaching and research.

Your signature below implies that you have read and are in agreement with the statements written above. (References to "the University" refer to the University of Washington).

NOTE: If the donor is medically unable to sign his/her own name to this registration form, the legal next of kin should call the Willed Body Program Office prior to mailing in this form. (Call 206-543-1860). (Alternate phone: 206-598-3300.)

Print Full Name	(LAST)	(FIRST)	(MIDDLE)	Last four (4) digits of Social Security No.
Donor Signature (See "NOTE" above)				Date of Birth
			Date	
Complete Address	(STREET)			Apt. #
	(CITY)		(STATE)	(ZIP)
Phone No.	— —	Alternate Phone No.	— —	

UW 1939 3/06

DONOR REGISTRATION FORM continued

It is _required_ that you respond to one of the following two questions. (Check only one box)

Option 1: ☐ Bury my cremated remains in the University Burial site at Evergreen-Washelli

INITIAL HERE

Option 2: ☐ Return my cremated remains to my family or personal representative

INITIAL HERE

WITNESSES

It is _required_ that you provide the signatures of two witnesses. A witness can be a family member or a friend. Each witness should print his/her name, enter the date and then sign name.

Witness 1:

Print Name   Date

Sign Name

Witness 2:

Print Name   Date

Sign Name

ESTATE REPRESENTATIVES

Identify your spouse or other family member(s) and the personal representative of your estate

Representative 1:

Print Name and relationship to you   Date

Address of representative   (STREET)

(CITY)   (STATE)   (ZIP)   Phone No. (include Area Code)

Representative 2:

Print Name and relationship to you   Date

Address of representative   (STREET)

(CITY)   (STATE)   (ZIP)   Phone No. (include Area Code)

IF YOU HAVE QUESTIONS: Please contact Mavis Carpio Montgomery, Program Operations Specialist at 206-543-1860.

Be sure to complete this form entirely. Sign it, date it, and return _the original_ in the enclosed envelope.

University of Washington School of Medicine
Willed Body Program
Department of Biological Structure
Box 357420
Seattle, WA 98195-7420

NOTE: You should also make a copy and keep it with your other important papers such as your will or power of attorney. You may also make additional copies and send them to your attorney, doctor or family members.

American Medical Association
Physicians dedicated to the health of America

PRINCIPLES OF MEDICAL ETHICS
Adopted by the AMA House of Delegates June 17, 2001

Preamble

The medical profession has long subscribed to a body of ethical statements developed primarily for the benefit of the patient. As a member of this profession, a physician must recognize responsibility to patients first and foremost, as well as to society, to other health professionals, and to self. The following Principles adopted by the American Medical Association are not laws, but standards of conduct which define the essentials of honorable behavior for the physician.

I.   A physician shall be dedicated to providing competent medical care, with compassion and respect for human dignity and rights.

II.   A physician shall uphold the standards of professionalism, be honest in all professional interactions, and strive to report physicians deficient in character or competence, or engaging in fraud or deception, to appropriate entities.

III.   A physician shall respect the law and also recognize a responsibility to seek changes in those requirements which are contrary to the best interests of the patient.

IV.   A physician shall respect the rights of patients, colleagues, and other health professionals, and shall safeguard patient confidences and privacy within the constraints of the law.

V.   A physician shall continue to study, apply, and advance scientific knowledge, maintain a commitment to medical education, make relevant information available to patients, colleagues, and the public, obtain consultation, and use the talents of other health professionals when indicated.

VI.   A physician shall, in the provision of appropriate patient care, except in emergencies, be free to choose whom to serve, with whom to associate, and the environment in which to provide medical care.

VII.   A physician shall recognize a responsibility to participate in activities contributing to the improvement of the community and the betterment of public health.

VIII.   A physician shall, while caring for a patient, regard responsibility to the patient as paramount.

IX.   A physician shall support access to medical care for all people.

Sunbeam Dam – Salmon River at Sunbeam, Idaho